Praise for Vicki Pettersson's Celestial Blues Trilogy

"Pettersson impressively deepens and darkens the compelling romance between her complex and irresistibly tormented protagonists. Even minor figures are fascinating, as is the ruthlessly realistic setting."

—Publishers Weekly (starred review) for *The Lost*

"*The Lost* is one exciting follow-up! The romance between Kit and Grif is equal parts passion and doubt, keeping readers hanging on to reach the conclusion. And what a conclusion! . . . This is a wonderful sequel."

—Romantic Times BOOKclub

"Pettersson's amazing new series is off to a rocking start with this compelling read."

—RT Book Reviews (top pick) for *The Taken*

"Exceptional. Mystery, crime-scene drama, and more than enough romance to keep the heart pumping blend seamlessly into an enthralling read that kept me glued to the pages. I can't wait for the sequel."

—Kim Harrison

THE GIVEN

BOOKS BY VICKI PETTERSSON

CELESTIAL BLUES SERIES

The Taken

The Lost

THE SIGN OF THE ZODIAC SERIES

The Scent of Shadows

The Taste of Night

The Touch of Twilight

City of Souls

Cheat the Grace

The Neon Graveyard

THE
GIVEN

CELESTIAL BLUES

Book Three

VICKI PETTERSSON

HARPER Voyager
An Imprint of HarperCollinsPublishers

Harper Voyager and design is a trademark of HCP LLC.

THE GIVEN. Copyright © 2014 by Vicki Pettersson. All rights reserved.
Printed in the United States of America. No part of this book may be used
or reproduced in any manner whatsoever without written permission except
in the case of brief quotations embodied in critical articles and reviews. For
information address HarperCollins Publishers, 10 East 53rd Street, New York,
NY 10022.

HarperCollins books may be purchased for educational, business, or sales
promotional use. For information please e-mail the Special Markets Department at SPsales@harpercollins.com.

FIRST EDITION

Library of Congress Cataloging-in-Publication Data

Pettersson, Vicki.
    The given / Vicki Pettersson. — First edition.
        p.   cm. — (Celestial blues ; book three)
    ISBN 978-0-06-206620-6
    1. Private investigators—Fiction. 2. Paranormal romance stories.
I. Title.
PS3616.E877G58   2014
813'.6—dc23
                                                                    2014007696

14 15 16 17 18   OV/RRD   10 9 8 7 6 5 4 3 2 1

For Virginia Lavish, with love

ACKNOWLEDGMENTS

This book is for my readers—my VPeeps, my friends, my Tribe. Thank you for taking time to reach out to me via my website, for chatting with me on Twitter, and for giving me a home on Facebook, where I am as teased about my cooking as I am encouraged to write. (Just like real life.) Extra thanks to Facebook friends: Justin Allen for allowing me to abuse his good name and Michelle Ritter Pearsall for suggesting the name Eric. Jann McKenzie and Joy Bannister served as beta readers for this final installment in Kit and Grif's journey, so if there's anything amiss in the text, I'm happy to forward along their personal e-mails as places to rant. Finally, to every reader who has opened up his or her mind to meet me on the page, I thank you.

CHAPTER ONE

A rule of thumb for all the aspiring angels out there: it's damned tough to go incognito when you've got a twelve-foot wingspan trailing behind you like a big, feathery flag. That, along with the stardust dripping like celestial sauce from those feathery tips, is a dead giveaway that you're doing more than popping to the Surface for a doughnut and a cup of joe. Sure, the mortals can't see you, even if you're only six feet behind them and closing in fast, but guys like Griffin Shaw—who were both angelic and human—could spot that semitransparent form coming from a galaxy away.

Not that there was anyone else like Griffin Shaw.

Grif's first instinct was to ignore the whole situation. Unfortunately, the angelic herald currently trailing cosmic matter all over downtown Las Vegas had dropped right into Shaw's path on an evening that was both chilly and boring. Defying the cold precisely because of his boredom, Grif was sitting alone on the patio of a wine bar, sipping a doppio espresso just to be contrary, and trying not to let his depression get the best of him. There was nothing sorrier than an angel with a case of the blues.

Of course, there was more than mere boredom gnawing at Grif. He'd been reading the front page of the *Las Vegas Tribune* just before the other angel traipsed into view, brooding over a headline that would've been just as at home atop the page when he'd died in 1960 as it was now: LAS VEGAS WOMAN DIES IN VICIOUS ATTACK.

Grif snorted. People rarely expired from a sweet-natured one. As he read on, even his sarcasm fled.

"Barbara McCoy," he said aloud, "age seventy, was found shot dead by her cleaning service when she neglected to answer the door for her biweekly appointment. No one had seen the victim, who reportedly lived alone on the fifteenth floor of the exclusive Panorama Project high-rise, for two days. McCoy was the widow of the famed and notorious mobster Sal DiMartino and had left Las Vegas after his death fourteen years ago, only to return recently. An anonymous source said the victim had been dead for at least twenty-four hours. There were no witnesses, and no suspects at this time."

There was also no photo to accompany the article.

Grif rarely swore, but he let a good one rip now as he threw the paper down and slumped in his seat. He'd been looking for Barbara McCoy for six whole months, scouring records and deeds and dead-end leads . . . all while obsessing over the words she was supposed to have said about his death fifty years earlier.

Both Shaws got what was coming to them.

What Grif had gotten was a knife in the gut. His memory of the event included little more than a visual snapshot of his wife, Evelyn, falling to the floor and sharing his fate.

Yet Grif had recently learned that Evie *hadn't* died that long-ago day, and McCoy had been his best shot at finding out where she was now. He'd also been looking forward to asking the woman . . . just what the hell did she think it was that Evie and he deserved?

Grif stared at the headline, unblinking, and felt heat boiling, building in his chest. He was back to square one just like that, without even one decent lead into his past. Six months of gumshoeing down the drain. Six months of thinking he was closer to finding out who killed him, and learning what had befallen Evie.

Six months of walking the same earth as Kit Craig, yet living without her by his side.

Grif shook his head to clear his mind, because of all of them it was *that* thought that would undo him. Blowing out a hard breath, he looked up and squinted into the distance . . . and that's when he spotted the Centurion.

The other angel didn't seem to notice him, and neither did her mark, a man with a baseball cap drawn low, hands tucked deep into the pockets of his black leather jacket. His mind was obviously occupied by whatever mischief was going to kill him in the next few minutes, and he didn't even glance Grif's way as he disappeared around the corner of the building adjacent to the wine bar. He didn't look behind him, either, though that didn't mean anything. Most people never did see death coming their way.

As for his celestial shadow, Centurions were angels who'd once been human as well, but had been pressed into duty as heavenly tour guides for newly murdered souls. Most people who died traumatically—murder, suicide, or simply an unexpected accident—had trouble reaching the Everlast on their own. Since Grif was still half Centurion as well as half human, he could recognize a fellow tribe member as far off as the Milky Way.

The curious thing about this sighting, however, was the timing. Centurions usually showed up in the moments just *after* a soul was freed from its earthbound flesh. As far as Grif knew, he was the only one ever forced to witness a Take's death. Assisting the newly dead into their celestial forevers was supposed to be healing for the Centurion, too.

So what was this little chit doing stalking her Take like some haloed feline looking to take down an oversized mouse?

The question fused with Grif's boredom and disappointment to fire his curiosity, so he downed the rest of his espresso, tucked his paper under his arm, and rose to follow. By the time he reached the corner, both the angel and the man she'd been trailing had disappeared. Yet downtown Las Vegas was laid out like a waffle, an easy grid of crisscrossing streets, and this one was also one-way. All he had to do was pick up his pace and head west.

Or was it east?

He sighed. It didn't matter. Orienting himself in this town required little more than a skyward glance at the Stratosphere hotel's spearing tower, though Grif personally preferred the midnight view, when neon scattered the darkened sky. Right now the day had briefly settled into the halfway mark, and in the crawling gray shadows of dusk Grif could easily track the shimmering thread of plasma curling around the corner. The silver tail sparked with undulating light and was another sign of impending death. It wouldn't be long now.

Grif turned into an alley that was more of a narrow afterthought, and was struck by the sight of dirty brick walls pocked with blackened doors and pungent Dumpsters tilted in disarray. Dusk had a harder time stretching in here, and he had to squint from beneath the brim of his fedora to locate the thread of plasma. There, he thought, catching its silvery tail, and he craned his neck upward, following it into the sky.

A jumper, Grif thought, catching sight of the Take just as his pant leg disappeared over the rooftop. The man's Centurion guide was nowhere to be seen, but she'd have been given a case file before hitting the Surface, and it would've included the Take's physical description and the location of his death. She was likely already waiting on the roof.

Grif had to follow more discreetly. He still possessed a degree of celestial strength, and wings that flared defensively against supernatural attack, but donning mortal flesh for a second go-round meant that he could also die again. It wasn't a fate he was anxious to repeat.

As he wrapped his fingers around the ladder's cold rungs, Grif told himself he didn't intend to interfere. This wasn't his Take, and he was fine with that, but there would be a cosmic pause right after the man died, a few slipstream moments that would pass unnoticed by the mortal world as the soul unhinged itself from its terrestrial body. It'd be nice to talk shop with the other Centurion, if only for a few minutes.

Grif had been utterly alone for months.

When Grif finally reached the jutting ledge, he slowly peered over it to scan the flat rooftop. He spotted the angel first, if only because she immediately turned and waved at him, though he hadn't made a sound. One glance at her half-flattened auburn hair and her neo-classic American uniform—blue jeans and a white T—and Grif was startled into speaking.

"It's you."

The man in the leather jacket, who'd been leaning over the opposite ledge and down at the place where Grif had been seated not two minutes earlier, started at the sound of Grif's voice. Turning, he gasped when he saw Grif standing there on the ladder, and took one giant step back. His heel caught the rooftop's ledge, and he came up short against the stunted wall behind him. Before either of them could say another word, the man fell backward, arms pinwheeling, a small yelp escaping his lungs as he disappeared over the building's side.

Grif and the female Centurion looked at each other. A dull thud sounded below.

"Well," she said, blinking at Grif. "That was anticlimactic."

Good news," the Centurion called back to Grif, raising her voice to be heard over the shocked screams that'd begun as soon as the man's body hit pavement. She was leaning over the rooftop edge, studying the ground, her wings instinctively flared for balance. "He didn't land on anyone."

Still shocked by the abruptness of events, Grif didn't move. "Did I . . . did he? I mean, did I cause that?"

The Centurion responded by motioning him onto the roof. "Kinda like the chicken and the egg, right? What came first? Don't think about it too much or it'll mess with your mind . . . and you can just ask him when he gets up here. But he's going to need a minute to untangle his soul from that messy splat he just made all over the sidewalk."

Grif gained the rooftop on rubbery legs and headed over to join the Centurion at the ledge, but she held up a hand, stopping him in his tracks. "I'd stay there if I were you. They can actually see you, remember?"

And from where every other human was standing, it might look as if he'd pushed the guy. Grif froze, then began his own backpedal. "I gotta get out of here."

"Nah, you're all right," the angel said with a dismissive wave, and she would know. Her case file would have also included the amount of time she had to clear out with the man's soul. So, smiling, she took a seat on the ledge where the man had just taken his header. Despite the flat half of her hairdo, her silhouette was pretty in the grays of dusk. "You're looking good, Shaw."

"So are you, Nicole."

Her smile widened. "You remember my name."

"Sure," he said, shoving his hands into his pockets. "I remember the names of all my Takes."

She quirked an eyebrow. "Especially the one who got you busted back to the Surface."

"Especially that one." Yes, Grif was the first and only person ever allowed to claim both angelic and human status, but his dual nature hadn't been intended as a blessing. It was meant as punishment.

Only the most broken souls were pressed into service as a Centurion. Assisting other traumatized souls into the Everlast was supposed to help them move past the pain and guilt of their own violent deaths, allowing them to eventually move on as well. It was a job for the hardest cases . . . and, well, Grif had proven harder than most.

Nicole Rockwell's meter had come due just over a year

earlier. She'd been working undercover in her job as a photojournalist, posing as a prostitute in order to try to elicit information from women she suspected of being forced into the world's oldest profession.

Not women, Grif remembered now, but girls.

Surprisingly, in the immediate aftermath of her death, Nicole's primary concern hadn't been her near-severed head but the clothes she'd died in. She would evermore exist as a soul that seemed to have a soft spot for squeaky latex and cheap lace. How could Grif not feel sorry for that? So he'd gone above and beyond his celestial call of duty, and allowed her spirit to reenter her earthly remains long enough to change into some clothes more fitting for eternity. However, in the short time that his back was turned, she also left a note for her best friend . . . one that would have gotten that woman killed if Grif hadn't stepped in there as well.

He'd interfered, altered fate, and paid for it. Yet he still wasn't sorry. After all, Kit Craig—girl reporter, rockabilly enthusiast, and, yes, Grif's subsequent lover—still lived, and he'd do it all again in a heartbeat . . . even though she now lived her life without him in it.

Nicole shrugged one shoulder. "I'm sorry about that. I didn't mean to get you in trouble. If I'd known it would put Kit's life in danger . . ." She trailed off, and silence swelled between them. Grif wondered how much she knew of what had gone on between Kit and him in the last year. How they'd married his P.I. skills with her investigative journalism and seen an end to that child prostitution ring. How they'd put the drop on two vicious drug cartels.

How they'd fallen in love.

"Don't worry about it, Nic." He tried to keep his voice light, but it was hard. His throat still had a tendency to close up at the thought of Kit. "We got out of it alive." Then he changed the subject. "But what about you? Guess you didn't make it through the Tube?"

That was what Grif called incubation, the divine process of erasing all memory and emotion from a traumatized soul's mind so that it could move on into God's presence. Obviously it didn't always work that way. Grif was still haunted by his death . . . and so what? Why *shouldn't* he be allowed to know who killed him fifty years earlier?

Maybe Nicole felt guilty over putting Kit in danger the day she'd died. Maybe by letting it go now she could finally move on.

Instead, she surprised Grif again. "Nope. Didn't move on. And it's all your fault."

He drew back. "How's that?"

"Well, you shoved me through that door, right? One moment I'm freshly dead, and the next I'm swinging from star to star, traversing universes, sipping from the Milky Way."

"So." Grif shrugged. "That's how it works. You go into incubation, clear your mind, then enter the Pearly Gates as angels pluck harp strings and sing hallelujahs."

"Yeah, but first I had to listen to a lecture by Father Francis about—"

"Who?"

"You know, the angel in charge of our rehabilitation?" She rolled her eyes, and recited his official title. "Saint Francis of the Cherubim tribe. The Pure charged with rehabilitating Centurion souls, blah, blah, blah."

"You mean Frank," Grif said, silently adding "the immortal pain in my ass" to Frank's title. "Father Francis" appeared to each person in the form they most closely identified with authority. For Grif, it was a sergeant in a police bullpen, so he called him Frank, or Sarge. Nicole apparently had Catholic schoolgirl issues. Father Francis it was.

"Anyway," Nicole went on, fluffing and resettling her wings behind her. "I couldn't get what he told me about you out of my mind. How you were just trying to help me. How I used your latent humanity to manipulate your broken emotions and put you in danger." She winced again in apology. "So I decided to pay it forward."

A decision that'd obviously gotten *her* in trouble, otherwise she wouldn't be forced to witness the deaths of her Takes before escorting them Home. "What'd you do?"

Nicole was eager to defend herself. "It was my second-ever Take, right? A murder-suicide, if you can imagine. The file said that a woman was going to shoot the man who was beating her, then turn the gun on herself, and I thought, this is the one."

"Let me guess. You messed with the time-space continuum and stopped her."

"That's what you did," she pointed out, like that made it okay. Grif pinched the bridge of his nose between his thumb and forefinger. "There was a six-month-old baby in the next room," she said defensively.

"So, what, you bound your soul to hers while it was still in her body?" That was how Grif had helped Nicole. There'd been just enough blood pumping through her veins that, with the help of his angelic energy, she had time enough to change her clothes and tidy her hair—or half of it—before totally bleeding out.

Nicole shook her head. "She was alive, and too jumpy for me to make a decent connection. So instead I lined up my chakras with her dead husband's body and animated him. It was gross, too. He was a smoker. There was tar in his veins." Tilting her head, Nicole grimaced. "He also had a big wad of chewing gum for brains."

"He'd just been *shot*," Grif pointed out. "His thoughts were likely a bit scrambled."

Nicole scoffed, which caused her wings to flare behind her in a downy white cloud. Their tips were threaded with silver and sparkled prettily as they settled. "No, *my* thoughts were scrambled when I died. This guy's mind was a book of pornographic mad libs."

By this time, the screaming from below had been replaced with ominous silence. Someone had taken control of the situation. Grif made out the sound of sirens in the distance, though they were too far away for the humans yet to hear.

"Oh, right," Nicole said, picking up the sound with the strength of her celestial hearing. She glanced back over the ledge, but her Take was apparently still trying to work out that he was dead, because she just sighed and crossed her legs. "So I get in his body and I'm sorting through this briar patch of mental bullshit until I finally find a memory that doesn't make me want to puke. It was one of those before-memories. Before . . . before . . ."

"Before whatever happens between two people who love each other that makes them want to kill each other."

"Yeah," Nicole said softly, and frowned. "And it's beautiful, you know? He's not as gross, and she's beautiful, all filled with love and hope, and so I say the words—through his voice box, of course—that are attached to the thought so that his wife can hear them. And maybe not do what she's going to do."

"What did you say?"

"I said, 'Margarite, you are the only good thing in my life that I never ruined.'"

"Cheery."

"Hey, she was shoving a smoking pistol down her throat. It was the best I could do."

"So, lemme guess. She latched on to that good-ish memory, put the gun down, and ran into the other room to hold her baby, thanking God for her life."

Nicole rolled her eyes. "No, she came over, and kicked her husband's corpse in the balls as she screamed that she knew he'd been fucking her twin sister all along. Then she shot him in the skull again."

Grif stared.

"That shit hurts, by the way," Nicole added, rubbing her forehead. "Nothing should ever touch your third eye."

Grif was starting to regret he'd followed Nicole onto the rooftop. "So, this is your punishment for interfering? You gotta watch all your Takes die just like I do?"

Nicole shrugged, and one golden-white feather fell to the rooftop. She was molting. "Father Francis is a stickler for the rules."

Yes. *Frank* was.

Just then, a transparent hand appeared on the ledge next to Nicole. The Take had finally found his way to the rooftop. Instead of offering to assist the dead man up, Nicole shifted to one side and sighed. "I don't really mind. Being back here, I mean. Seeing mortal turmoil and struggle. It's helping me remember."

And that was the problem. Grif frowned. "It's supposed to help you forget."

"Yeah, but I'm remembering the *good* parts," she said, looking up at him, sadness etched in her face. "I remember everything from the first bite of chocolate ice cream on a hot day to laughing until your sides hurt. I recall what it's like to want something that isn't totally unattainable. Of having choice and chance. I remember how it feels to still have hope for the future, your life laid out before you like an unopened gift. You know?"

Grif nodded as the Take threw his leg over the ledge and fell gasping—sans air, of course—onto his back.

"I want more."

Nicole's words were so soft that Grif almost didn't hear them, but when he shifted his gaze back to hers, her eyes were moist with unshed tears.

"That's not really how it works," he grumbled, looking away. He wasn't very good with tears.

"Hey . . . hey, guys!" The newly deceased began waving his arms in the air. Like he was easy to miss.

Ignoring him, Nicole stood and crossed the rooftop to square up on Grif. "But it worked for you. You came back. You get to search for whoever killed you fifty years ago. And you found love again."

So she did know about Kit.

"That's different," he said, shaking his head. "It was a . . ."

He was going to say "mistake," but it wasn't that. The love of a woman like Katherine Craig was nothing short of a miracle.

"Hey!" The dead man began stumbling their way.

"That's all I want," Nicole said, arms out, like Grif could help her. "I died before I could fall hard, you know."

"Maybe your Take could teach you something about that," Grif said, as the man joined them.

"You know what I mean. I died before I knew what it was to

love someone unconditionally . . . and now I never will."

"Hey!" The man reached for Grif, screaming when his hand slid right through him. "What the hell is going on?"

Grif shifted slightly and cocked one eyebrow. "Son, you are not going to get very far in the Everlast with that kind of language." He turned back to Nicole. "Look, maybe you're lucky. Once you know love, you also know loss."

Nicole shook her head as the dead man turned to her. "Don't give me that 'Woe is me' bullshit, Shaw. You got a second chance with a woman worth more than a thousand lifetimes, and then you ruined it all just because you couldn't get over your past."

"Goddamn it! Would somebody listen to me?" The dead man grabbed Nicole's arm—now that they were both transparent, he could do that—and she immediately shifted and reversed grips, yanking so fast he fell forward. She grabbed him and held him down by the scruff of his neck. Even Grif had a hard time seeing the speed of her movement.

"Don't touch a woman unless and until she asks you to," she growled, and stars burned in her eyes. "Got it?"

Grif snorted. "Gee, what a shocker that guys weren't crawling all over you. Oh well. Better luck in the Everlast."

Her eyes narrowed, extinguishing stars. "You know what, Shaw? I'm not just here for a Take. I actually have a little something for you, too."

Grif shoved his hands into the pockets of his baggy suit and lifted one eyebrow. "What?"

"It's a gift from me to you." Nicole smiled coldly. "For breaking my best friend's heart."

And she whirled with the speed of light, rapping Grif's skull with the bony arc of her beautiful left wing. Sunbursts exploded as his eyes rolled back in his head. He could do nothing to stop his fall, but as the rooftop rose to meet his face, he did have time for one fleeting thought.

Thank God I didn't know this broad while she was still alive.

CHAPTER TWO

The nightclub possessed the sultry warmth derived from quickened breaths and writhing bodies, along with the irresistible pulse of a rockabilly beat. Yet chills still shot along Kit's limbs as she walked, keeping to the edges of the dark room while she squinted through stage light and smoke, searching for what she'd lost. There. A glimpse of a broad-shouldered man just before a handful of couples, swinging to surf guitar, obscured her view. Shifting, she spotted him again, wearing a Sinatra suit and a skinny tie, a tilted fedora and beneath that, if she wasn't mistaken, a smile just for her.

Kit's breath caught like it'd been snared. She dodged the sweaty limbs of a couple marrying their actions to Imelda May's bluesy, rasping voice, which soared over the sound system and climbed into their bones. Kit's heart tripped over itself as she took two more steps directly toward the man, almost a run. Then he closed the distance between them.

Kit recoiled. It wasn't him. It wasn't Grif.

She missed him like rain. She was as parched as the cold, unyielding desert outside, longing for his voice or touch or anything to make her feel alive, or at least less desiccated. Hating herself for feeling that way, she turned to find a drink. Maybe one of the greasers would buy her a Pabst. She needed something that would go down easy and quickly.

The hand fell on her arm before she could move. The man in the fedora had caught up with her, and his fingertips trailed her wrist. His gaze was bright and playful in a face too youthful yet to be chiseled. His size was close, though. And a slow song was beginning. She might be able to close her eyes and pretend.

"Would you like to dance?" he asked, as she knew he would.

She gave him a gentle smile and wondered how he'd respond if she said, *What I'd really like is to die.*

Then she shook her head—both an answer and a way to empty her mind of the thought. Kit tried not to think too much these days. She didn't like where her thoughts led. The man took it well, doffing his hat, offering up a rain check with a shrug, and returning to his crew in the club's center. Kit smiled wistfully after him. What a life. Checking out Betties, rocking to Elvis, slamming back brew. Kit was not much older than the guy, only thirty, but she felt ancient.

She was wondering when and how that'd happened when she suddenly felt another pair of eyes on her. Searching the room, she found him. Dennis Carlisle. He stood out because, like her, he was the only other person who wasn't moving. Light rocketed off the planes of his face, and though he otherwise fit in—

dressed like a greaser in a white T and cuffed jeans, hair slicked and sideburns long—his rigid stance still reminded her of a police officer. His frown also reminded her that she'd broken his heart by not returning his calls, his texts.

And that, again, reminded her of Grif.

After another moment, Dennis shook his head and sighed. Then he turned away, and Kit just let him go.

"That's it." Another hand appeared, this one on the opposite arm, and way less gentle than the first. Kit spun like a top and found herself being dragged directly across the dance floor by Fleur Fontaine, her friend's steps quick and light in a mermaid-tail dress that sparkled in the strobes. Kit actually stumbled in her vintage peep-toes, trying to keep up.

"What's going on?" she said, as Fleur pulled her into the side bar. Velvet walls muted the MC's voice from the other room, along with the upright bass that meant the start of a new set. Seated at a high-top table adorned with a flickering red-domed hurricane lamp were three other of Kit's besties. Lil DeVille, Charis Cointreau, and Layla Love—new to their inner circle. All sported stage names, de rigueur in the rockabilly subculture where they lived and thrived. False identities . . . for true friends.

Yet she tilted her head as she looked at them now. Despite their smiles, Kit noted concern in their gazes, and that had nerves jumping in her belly. "What is this?"

"This," Fleur said, depositing Kit dead center, "is an intervention."

Layla slid a drink across the table. Not a Pabst but a gin fizz. It'd do. Kit picked it up. "What are we intervening . . . in?"

"Not we," Fleur corrected, then waggled her finger to exclude Kit. "Us."

Kit set down the drink and rose to leave.

"No." That firm hand again, pushing her back to her red-cushioned seat. "Hear us out. We love you and if we don't tell you this shit, who will?"

She placed her hand on her hip. "What shit?" Though she already knew.

"You're in trouble, Kit-ster," piped in Charis, eyebrows drawn low beneath Betty bangs. A bright yellow poppy pinned back one side of her dark hair. "You've stopped living."

"I haven't—"

"You used to laugh—" started Lil, whose own smile lines fanned out in winking flirtation from eyes that were always alight. Except for now, Kit noted.

"You did. All the time," cut in Fleur, no stranger to fun. None of Kit's girls were. That's why they were . . . well, *Kit's*.

And now she was mute. She lowered her gaze. She already knew all this.

"You used to smile," Charis pressed.

But now Kit cried even before she was awake.

She said nothing. She didn't press back.

That seemed to embolden Fleur. "And you used to *dance*."

But Kit couldn't even imagine that anymore. Sometimes she had trouble just getting to her feet in the morning. Forget the dance floor.

"Talk to us, Kit," said Layla. She was powdered and dyed into Monroe perfection, and Kit found herself thinking, But you'd never understand. You're too perfect. Too whole. You've never been broken like this. "You used to talk to us."

But Kit had run out of things to say. For the first time in her life she felt alone, solo in a world she'd once felt a part of, without even the desire for something, someone, more. She was a reporter who dealt in fact and had once believed that the truth really did set you free. But then she learned that the man she loved had a wife who was still alive, and he left Kit to go find her. It hadn't set her free at all. Instead, it'd set her adrift . . . and now nothing really touched her anymore.

She closed her eyes and lifted her drink. "I know. I'm . . . pitiful. Mooning over a boy. I'm a fucking country song."

"It's okay, honey," Fleur said, voice overly bright now that Kit had said something, *anything*. "We all know the tune."

"Sure," said Layla, edging so close her perfume threatened to clog Kit's pores. "When I was with Joe I thought I was Eartha Kitt, all 'C'est Si Bon.' Then he met someone else and it turned out I was Tammy Wynette. 'Stand by Your Man.'"

She made a gagging motion with her finger, and Kit almost smiled. They were trying so hard.

"Look," Fleur said, folding her hands over Kit's. "Griffin Shaw is just one man. One of millions who are just waiting out there for you to either moon over them or break their hearts. I bet there's some greaser in the other room right now who would be willing to take you for a swing and heal that beautiful heart."

Kit thought of Dennis, how patient he'd been with her, how he'd waited for her to turn her mind from Grif and finally choose him. That patience had eventually snuffed out, along with the expectation that lighted his gaze whenever he looked at Kit. He was right to turn his back on her. He knew that Kit's heart was a seeping wound.

Kit thought about playing along just to end this uncomfortable conversation. She could flash her own dazzling smile— God knew she was good at hiding behind that—but these were her best friends, the girls who knew of her frailty and faults, and loved her anyway. If she didn't share what she was feeling with them, who would ever really know her?

"Look," she said, leaning over the table. The other four women did the same, closing rank in a tight huddle. "I used to think I understood the world at large just because I got paid to report it. I thought I could intuit a person's motives by merely adjusting the focus of my critical lens. Zoom in close enough and any news story will reveal itself. I trusted my gut. I always sought and spoke the truth. And I believed that most people out there were like me, like you." She gestured to them all. "Good people who treated others the way they want to be treated. Who wished strangers well and meant it. Who took joy in the simplest things . . ."

And these girls did. They understood the glory in one blade of grass, a singular sparrow's song . . . a kiss truly meant and felt. If Kit could exist on such simple fuel—and do it after she'd endured the illness and death of one parent and the murder of the other—then other people out there must as well, right?

"And then Nic died."

If someone took a picture of their tight huddle just then, they'd have been mistaken for pin-ups of the past. Sad ones. Every one of the women froze, a stillness Kit broke with the shake of her head. "And I realized that some people victimize others just because they can. They use their power to manipulate the young."

Like Caleb Chambers had, until Grif and she had stopped him.

"Or feed a junkie's addictions just to line their pockets with green."

Like two warring drug lords had . . . until Grif and she had stopped them, too.

Or tear two people who loved each other apart, Kit thought. Just because they could.

She thought of the angel, the Pure, whom they hadn't been able to stop at all.

"I thought that I could stop some of that. That *I* could make a difference."

And perhaps it'd seemed obscene to God, and all His winged monsters in heaven. The so-called Pure. Because what did she get for trying to live her best life daily? For loving a man who suddenly appeared before her, and for wanting love in return?

"I was betrayed. I was abandoned. I was left worse than when He found me."

The girls thought she meant Grif, and all began babbling at once, trying to console her. Kit let them, because there was no explaining what she knew of the Everlast and of the Pure and of Griffin Shaw's true nature. And she *really* didn't know how to state that she'd very simply lost her faith—in the truth, in the world, and in God.

Kit had been holding her drink throughout the telling, but she put it down now, because even though it was wet, she knew it would taste dry. "I'm going home."

"Wait. We're sorry," Fleur said, trying to pull her back to her seat. "We won't talk about Griffin Shaw, or men at all. Just . . . stay."

"Someday," Kit promised, and folded her hands atop Fleur's for a brief moment. She meant it, too. She was still optimistic enough to believe she'd feel better someday. "But not tonight."

She simply didn't feel like dancing.

She didn't look back as she left the side lounge, returning to the main club, where a sole male crooner was singing over the heads of a crowd of couples. You could choke on the pheromones rising in that room, and the hope in it—the life and the joy—had Kit rushing to the front door, which a man dressed like a fifties bellhop held open with a smile. Only when the cold night air finally hit her heated cheeks did she dare take a breath, though she kept up her pace until she'd reached her vintage Duetto and opened the door.

Then a silence closed in around her, a too-heavy blanket that made her ears want to pop. She whirled, searching, sure someone was watching her—from the doorway of the club, from behind the building, from within the cars around her.

Nothing.

She gave the lot one more scan, then huffed, sending a white puff of air into the night before climbing in behind the steering wheel of her car. There was nothing out there, she thought, as the car rumbled to life. At least, not for her.

How's the head, Shaw?"

Stars, the imagined kind, floated and swirled before Grif's eyes in a pattern that made his stomach flip and churn. He bit back bile and groaned in annoyance. He recognized that voice. Tilting his head in the direction from which it'd sounded, Grif caught a burst of bright light between his slitted lids before everything went black and vision again slid away. Blinders.

The voice, Sarge's, tsk-tsked. "The flesh. It's just so weak."

That steeled Grif's resolve, and he managed to sit up straight. "Does God know you're knocking His children around like this?"

"I never touched you, Shaw."

"No, you just sent your pretty little lackey to do your dirty work."

"So sorry to interrupt your life-in-progress. I know how busy you've been trying to find out who killed you."

"Sarcasm is ugly on the Pure."

"How do you know? You can't even see me."

"Because you attacked me, kidnapped me, and then put blinders on me." Grif stood up, because he couldn't just sit and take it, yet his legs swayed.

"I understand you're upset."

Upset? Scowling, Grif folded his arms. He'd ceased taking calls from his celestial superior after the Pure had used Kit's goodness against her. Against *them*. He wasn't upset. He was downright furious.

"Please, sit down," Sarge said, his voice coming from Grif's left this time.

"Or what?" Grif rounded on the voice, on the Pure angel who'd given him a second chance at life, and then went ahead and destroyed that, too. "You'll smite me?"

It was hard to toss off a pointed look when he couldn't see—he couldn't even tell if his eyes were open—but he gave it a decent try. "You're a created being who will never know what it is to be born or die. To live or love. You don't understand a damned thing about how I feel."

"But I do. At least, I do now."

Grif neither knew what that meant, nor cared. He just wanted to figure out where he was so he could get out of there, but that wasn't going to happen until Sarge willed it. So he located the hard surface he'd been propped against when he came to, some sort of giant wooden box, and plopped back down. "Where's your mercenary little angel?"

"Mr. Naumes was starting the Fade, so Ms. Rockwell had to take him for processing before he washed out completely. She asked me to apologize for the shiner."

Grif huffed. "No, she didn't."

"No, she didn't," Sarge admitted. "I didn't realize when I asked for volunteers that she had her own reasons for offering to secure you."

That's because he hadn't asked Grif, who knew firsthand how fiercely Kit and her friends covered for each other. Even, it seemed, in the Everlast.

"She'll be punished."

"Nah, don't do that." He *had* broken Kit Craig's heart, after all, and he'd feel the same way if he were Nicole. "Let's just get this over with. What do you want?"

At that, the blindness tore away, stinging like duct tape being ripped from the skin. Grif rubbed his eyes, blinked, and looked around. Wooden cargo boxes, stamped and stacked in neat piles, lined the sides of an oblong room. Everything from ceiling to floor was made entirely of wood. Planks, Grif realized, tapping his feet. The sound was more hollow than he expected, and he frowned as he spotted the netting strung from the low-hanging beams. Thick hemp ropes coiled along the walls, and along with the swaying, it put him in mind of a . . .

"It's not really a ship," Sarge said from somewhere behind him. "We're still in Vegas. Treasure Island, to be exact. It was Rockwell's idea. We needed someplace central but quiet—though the next pirate show is in an hour, so we should make this quick."

A pirate show. Grif shook his head. "The Rat Pack would be appalled at the—"

But Sarge stepped into view just then, and Grif's words cut off in a sharp gasp.

The angel's once-great arms had shrunken down to a quarter of their former size, and were now spindly, as frail as kindling. His wings were as bald in spots as his head, as if he'd picked and worried those feathers out of place. The remaining plumes had lost their glossy black sheen and lay flat against each other in dull, uneven rows. His skin, once as dark as those onyx wings, was ashy and sagged in all the wrong places, and his frame was more of a reminder of strength than the threat of it.

Sarge's face had altered the most. His sunken eyes resembled craters and his mouth had collapsed in a permanent frown. Even his nose appeared diminished, great furrows etched from the corner of each nostril down to his mouth. The vertical striations repeated along his cheekbones, fleshy landslides carved into his skin from his eyelids all the way to his chin. Like melted wax, these new features had hardened into a grotesque mask. Only his gaze, mist swirling over shining black marbles, remained the same.

"What the hell happened to you?" Grif whispered, as Sarge drew closer. Sarge was a real angel. He was Pure spirit created from the same worldstuff as Paradise itself. Angels couldn't die, because they'd never lived, and they couldn't be injured for the same reason.

So what had happened to Frank?

"Are you even still an angel?" Grif blurted.

"Don't be stupid," Sarge snapped back, which actually calmed Grif a bit. Sarge might look different on the outside, but at least he still had the same haughty demeanor.

"Sorry, it's just that you look . . ." Grif hesitated.

"Say it. I already read it in your mind."

Grif hated that, so he crossed his arms and did say it. "Puny."

Sarge's misshapen jaw clenched, but he leaned against a crate marked EXPLOSIVES and nodded. "I am . . . much diminished."

"I don't get it. What happened?" Grif asked again.

"You happened, Shaw," the new Sarge said, folding his hands in his robe and regarding Grif with that surging gaze. "You and Katherine Craig."

Grif tried not to look as gut-punched as he felt. Six months. That's how long since his own name had been coupled with Kit's. It was also the last time Sarge had appeared on the Surface. Appeared, more important, to Kit, who was sitting vigil over a friend's deathbed. Angels could possess the bodies of those nearer to death than life—the very old or the very young, the sickly and the dying—even those with bodies weakened with drink or drugs.

Angelic possession usually healed or otherwise improved the life of the host body, but Sarge's reasons for appearing in Dennis Carlisle's body hadn't been altruistic. Dennis, a cop, had taken a bullet meant for Kit, and using Dennis's body, Sarge had told Kit that her friend would die if she didn't do exactly what he wanted.

So Kit did. She told Grif—the man she loved, the one she'd saved just as thoroughly as he'd saved her—that Evelyn Shaw was still alive. And Grif—who'd been looking for any sign of his wife for the past fifty years—had left. And Dennis had lived.

"I believed I was doing God's will," Sarge said now, following Grif's thoughts into the past.

"You tricked her." Bitterness sat like ash on Grif's tongue. *This* was really why he hadn't talked to Sarge—or any of the Pure—for the last six months. Not for his sake. He knew how to be an island. He'd do fine alone. But Kit . . .

"You used her emotions and her natural goodness against her. The finest woman I've ever met, one of the people you were created to support and protect, and you manipulated everything that was good in her. You knew she'd do anything to see that Dennis lived."

Including give up Grif.

"Yes," Sarge said simply. "And my actions brought you both pain."

Now Grif opened his eyes. His fists clenched as he stared at the Pure, his biceps twitching. Unfortunately, even in his weakened state, Sarge would see a blow coming. And, of course, he already knew Grif's thoughts. So, instead, Grif said, "And since when do you care about that?"

Because even though Grif had been gutted, whacked over the head, and buried so deep no one had ever found his bones, what Frank had done to him and Kit was even worse. It was the cruelest thing he'd ever known, and looking at the Pure, he had to wonder if God didn't feel the same.

"Since I was punished," Sarge confirmed.

Considering all the ways God doled out punishments—floods and famines, pestilence and disease—Grif almost felt sorry for him.

Almost.

"He do that?" Grif jerked his head at Frank's shorn wings. They'd once soared in beautiful black arches from shoulders that reminded Grif of rocks. Gold-tipped, they'd glinted even in full dark. Now they sprawled in spikes from ashy shoulders that were withered and hunched.

"No. I clipped those myself."

Like a monk who voluntarily lashed himself until his back seeped with blood, clipping one's own wings was significant in a way that Grif would likely never understand. It was the most visible aspect of angelic power, and an obvious lessening of status and strength. More than that, the shearing appeared to have changed something on the inside of Frank. Ghosts moved behind his marbleized gaze. Something heavier than gravity turned his mouth low.

Something vital, Grif thought, something *Pure,* had been lost.

"My job," Sarge began quietly, "has always been to see that the souls in my care, the Centurions, work through the pain of their own deaths, forget their mortal lives and loves and regrets, and move on to the safety and absolution of God's presence. I've always been able to fulfill my duty. Until you."

Grif shifted uncomfortably, but Sarge continued.

"I should have known you were different. Your recollection of your life in the fifties was more acute than those possessed by other Centurions. Most have memories like line drawings, scratched in dull pencil, erased and rubbed over a dozen times. But yours burst like hothouse flowers in full bloom. Still, I thought it would be okay. You remembered that you'd been murdered, but you didn't recall how. I should have told you then that your wife still lived."

"Yes. You should have."

Sarge shrugged one shoulder. "It's not our way to reveal All. We're concerned with moving souls into Paradise, that's it. Forcing you to don flesh again and return to the Surface— making you feel the pain of living and dying all over again— was supposed to be a punishment for assisting Nicole Rockwell."

Grif rubbed the knot on his skull where Nicole had knocked him out. No good deed went unpunished.

"Never did I think that you'd use the free will that comes with being human to try to save those you were only supposed to Take. You should have heard the uproar from the Host when the time for Katherine Craig's death came and went, and she still lived."

Grif could only imagine . . . though he still couldn't bring himself to care. Kit had been alone in her bedroom when two men had broken into her house. Grif had hesitated, he'd watched the plasma swirl about her naked ankles as her attackers closed in, but in the end he couldn't just sit by and watch her die.

Sarge nodded, following his thoughts. "And then you fell in love. We decided that if we couldn't force you from the Surface, we could at least use you to find lost souls. Those who hid from their guides. Those who fell prey to the Fallen."

Grif shuddered. He didn't even want to think about the ghastly, distorted, and truly evil fallen angels.

"You have to understand," Sarge was saying, "nobody had ever possessed both angelic power and free will at the same time. You were the first. An angelic human."

"I was a tool to be used until you didn't need me anymore."

Sarge lowered his swirling gaze. "Like I said, my job is to see that all the souls in my care move on to God's presence."

And he didn't care how that got done.

"I was returning to the Everlast when he struck." Sarge pursed his lips at the memory, his legs loose as he rocked with the ship. "I had just left Dennis Carlisle's body, and I was so pleased with myself, thinking that you'd find your wife easily and quickly now that Ms. Craig was out of the picture. I was so sure that she was the one standing in the way of your progress. He caught me just as I reached the Gates of the South Wind."

"Who? God?"

Sarge huffed, a bitter laugh. "Even I haven't seen His face yet. No, it was Donel. A Seraph."

The highest of the celestial tribes.

"God uses the Seraphim to settle things . . . in-house, if you will."

"I thought the archangels were his heavies?"

Sarge shook his head. "Too unpredictable. They're fanged and untouchable and full of righteousness. Plus, you can't look them directly in the face."

"That would make it hard to have a good heart-to-heart."

Sarge tried to smile, but the grin wobbled on his face. It looked like the action pained him. "Anyway, Donel said he had a message from God. So he grabbed me by my robe and told me to open my mouth."

"Your mouth?" Grif tilted his head. "Why not your ears?"

"Because messages from God are not something you hear. They're something you feel." Sarge swallowed hard, and his Adam's apple moved like a boulder in his throat. "He made me feel it all, Shaw. Everything you're still angry about. The manipulation and the pain. The cruelty in the way I drove you and Kit apart. As Pures, we are not allowed to help mortals—it intrudes upon their free will. But we're not allowed to hurt them for the very same reason."

The thought of it, all that pain and longing and heartache hitting someone all at once, made Grif sag on his feet. And he'd never heard of a Pure feeling true emotion before. After all, they, too, were tools—created for a specific purpose. Life lessons, and the weight of them, were not gifts that God bestowed on mere tools.

Yet not a day went by that Grif, too, didn't feel the pain caused by Frank's actions. Who was he to question how God dealt with His creations? So he crossed his arms.

"You want me to say it, don't you?" Sarge said, and his face contorted in a wry, pained smile.

"Why not?" Grif said. "After all, confession is good for the soul."

Pures didn't have souls, but Sarge confessed anyway.

"I could have told you at any point that your wife was still alive, but I guarded that information and used it against you instead." The words poured from him like they'd been building inside of him all these months. He nearly shouted, as if thrusting the confession at Grif would relieve him of its weight. "I also knew Kit loved you so much that she would insist that you return to that first love. It hurt you both. *I* hurt you both, and I feel your pain even now." He paused, then offered Grif another wry smile. "And yes, I feel that, too."

"What?"

"That." Sarge lifted a hand, finger shaking with palsy as he pointed at Grif. "The agony of not having seen Ms. Craig in six long months."

Grif looked away. There was agony, yes. It was sewn across his heart, stitched there in Kit's initials . . . therefore he rarely bothered anymore about his heart. But the rest of Sarge's statement wasn't quite true. He had seen Kit, though she didn't know it. He'd used his ability to enter and exit buildings undetected to watch her while she slept. He needed to see for himself that she was okay, something that would be easier on them both if she wasn't awake.

Yet there was torment in that as well. He'd only visited her three times, but on the third he'd been compelled to let her know he was there. She should know he was thinking of her, he'd reasoned. That despite their separation, the need for it, he would always be there.

So he plucked a feather from his wing and left it on the pillow next to her, watching her breath stir the individual vanes, remembering the way it'd once felt on his neck and chest and mouth.

Kit must have remembered, too, because the next time he came to watch her sleep, he found that she'd left him something as well.

The note read:

This isn't Twilight, *and I'm not your Bella. If I catch you stalking me again I'll pray so hard that your boss in the Everlast will have no choice but to listen. God knows that feathered beast owes me.*

Funny how the dearest memories could evoke the exact opposite reaction in people.

"I didn't know," Sarge said softly, reading the memory.

No, how could he? He was a created being, not a birthed one. He had the power and intelligence and expanse of the Universe at his disposal, but he was also soulless.

Sometimes, like six months ago, that made him a monster.

"I didn't know," Sarge repeated, voice cracking this time, "that love in the heart was as indispensable as breath in the chest."

"I don't want to talk about it," Grif muttered, feeling his own chest seize up, the stitches coming undone.

"I didn't know," Sarge said again, "that I was digging out that poor woman's heart with a dull knife."

"Stop talking!" Grif's voice bounced off the hollowed planks overhead and thundered along the ones at his feet. Sarge actually cringed; he truly believed Kit's pain was his own fault, yet even after all he'd done, Grif knew better. He was the one who'd returned to the Surface, broken the rules, and fallen in love with one woman while still searching for another. With one foot in the present and the other stuck firmly in the past, it was Grif who had broken Kit Craig's heart.

And true agony was in having to live with that.

I want to die," Kit said, only two months earlier.

"No," Grif whispered, but his hiding place swallowed the word, smothering it in shadows. Despite her written warning to stop stalking her, to go away, he still followed. He'd always follow. And now, despite his aversion to tears, he was crying, too.

She was folded up in the fetal position, her good friend Fleur curled around her as if she was all that was holding her together. Kit's entire covey of girlfriends was unabashed in their friendship, clinging to each other in a way that men never did, and these two alternated their tears, though only Kit sobbed. Grif had followed her to Fleur's home, because she hadn't been spending much time at her own mid-century ranch home. There were, he knew, too many memories of the two of them there together.

"Forget Griffin Shaw," Fleur told Kit, smoothing Kit's hair from her face, the flaming dice of her shoulder tattoo flaring with the motion.

"I don't want to forget him."

"Why?" Fleur and Grif whispered at the same time.

Kit stilled and looked up at her friend. Her face, usually powdered perfection, was naked today, almost translucent, and it only added to her air of vulnerability. Her eyes, swollen like storm clouds, were rimmed in angry red and swimming with tears. "Because if I forget that I loved him then it would be like it never happened. And that would mean that it didn't really matter or that I never really lived it. And it did. I did."

"You torture yourself."

"No . . . I just don't know how to get over him."

"That's because there's no getting over a love like that." Fleur cupped Kit's face between lacquered fingers, and bent down until they were touching foreheads. "You just move on anyway."

"But I can barely lift my head." Kit's voice cracked, and Grif's heart went with it. "I know it makes me needy and really stupid to hold on to a man who doesn't want me, but I can't stop thinking of him. I close my eyes and he's there. I wake and it's worse. There's no name for this . . . for this heartache."

"Sure there is," Fleur answered, her smile bittersweet as they both fell still. "It's called life."

Kit didn't answer, making Grif wonder if that meant that she agreed or she didn't. Finally, Fleur shifted. "Come on, we can't hole up here forever. Let's get dolled up and go out. We'll call up some greasers with a hot rod. Go drink rum from a tiki mug. We'll raise some hell and get tattoos."

"A tattoo?" Kit sniffled, then tilted her head. "Yeah. Maybe."

"Something to mark the occasion," Fleur declared. "Kit Craig's return to the real world!"

Grif could have kissed the woman for that.

But Kit shook her head. "No. Not that. But something to mark that I'm different. That I've changed not in spite of Griffin Shaw, but because he was here."

"Oh, come on, Kit. You can do better than that."

Suddenly Grif no longer wanted to kiss her.

"Get some ink as a badge of honor. You survived Griffin Shaw and now you're ready to start a new life. One without him in it."

Was she? Staring at Kit, not blinking, Grif realized he was holding his breath.

"Maybe," Kit said, biting her bottom lip. Then, after a long moment, she frowned. "But only under one condition."

"What?"

Kit pushed into a sitting position and leveled her friend with a hard stare. "I don't want anything with damned wings."

Your knowledge does nothing for me," Grif told Frank now, his whisper harsh enough to scratch his throat. Suddenly he didn't feel sorry for the Pure. He damned well should feel it all.

"I know," Frank whispered, and his eyes were shining with tears, too. It was novel, and it was shocking. It was as unnatural to see a Pure feeling human emotion as it would be to hear a dog meow.

And all Grif could think was, Good.

"Then what do you want?" Because it wasn't just to reminisce about old times.

"I have a message from the Host."

Grif closed his eyes. The entire legion of angels. Every order in the hierarchy of Pures, from Seraphim to Rulers to Guardians.

"Your refusal to carry out the will of God as outlined in the agreement formed as a condition of your return to the Surface has angered them."

"Well. That's a mouthful," Grif said at last, flashing again on Kit's heart-wrenching sorrow. "So what are they taking from me now?"

His wings, he hoped. There was little else left.

The voice struck, clapping like thunder behind him. "We're not taking, Griffin Shaw. This time we're giving."

Whirling, Grif cringed, immediately shielding himself with his arms against the light that flared before him. If Sarge had radiated with light, this being *was* light. The image that burned itself beneath his eyelids had wings of flame, tips dripping with lava, and a burned-out double negative of blackened holes where eyes should be.

A Seraph. The power emanating from it was unfiltered, raw as a lightning bolt and as sharply static on the tongue. Angels, unmasked, were awesome in the original sense of the word, and reverence, like survival instinct, forced Grif to his knees. He felt his next breath, heated from the flame, shaky in his chest.

I am God's child, he thought, over and again, trying not to be overwhelmed.

The Seraph knew he was glorious, created of the first triad and the highest order. His mighty wings arched across half the room, rippling with muscle. Sarge, who was of the Cherubim tribe, shielded his true nature by taking on the aspect deemed most familiar by the mortal souls who viewed him. Yet this angel, and the four flared behind him in an offensive phalanx, didn't bother. That, more than anything, told Grif he was in trouble.

The realization brought forth an abrupt dimming of the blistering light. Grif removed his hand from his eyes and caught sight of a veil being dropped between them as he straightened from his prone position. It was a see-through scrim, likely sewn from starlight and dark matter, and it would keep any of the Seraph's errant rays from attacking Grif. The Seraphim could never truly hide what they really were.

Monsters, Grif thought, lifting his chin.

Though the Seraph had to have heard the thought, he gave

one short nod, and Grif stood. With his glory dimmed, the angel was youthful in appearance, with long, dark hair shining and thick and skin as smooth as a polished opal. Yet he was alien in his perfection. But for mankind, all of God's creatures were.

"What are you giving, then?" Grif said, still blinking.

"More than you deserve, but less than you would like," answered the Seraph, his voice like a rushing river. "Though that always seems to be the case with your kind."

"Donel," Sarge reprimanded. A stone in that river.

"Don't *you* presume to correct me!" Donel's head whipped Sarge's way, rapids roaring in his throat. "One look at the two of us and it's clear exactly where righteousness lies!"

Protectiveness welled inside of Grif, and he shifted to shield the Pure behind him with his own body. He and Sarge weren't always on the same side of the playing field, but he had more history and fondness for this angel than any other.

There was no way to look directly into the faces of angels if they didn't will it, and even with the veil between them, it wasn't easy to face Donel full-on. After only a glance that felt like looking into the full sun, Grif wondered if the Pure wanted him to see the contempt that lived among the burned-out embers of that celestial gaze.

After a long moment, Donel held out an arm to the side, palm upright. The limb extended longer than it should have, with fingers that did the same. One of the Pures behind him handed over a scroll. Grif's heart thumped. An official decree. Holding it straight out before him, Donel unrolled it, then began speaking in tongues.

Grif understood none of it, though he recognized the pattern of jumbled sounds, intonations, and pitches. The heralds

trumpeted it regularly in the Everlast, and he'd once asked
Sarge what it meant.

"It's the angelic anthem. It's a call to arms, a war cry for the
Pure."

"What does it say?" Grif had asked.

"It begins with an introduction to the angelic orders. 'We
are Pure spirit, the mighty who dwell in and of Paradise, we
are the Orders charged with dispensing God's divine Will . . .'"

Grif stopped listening after that. To him it was just postur-
ing and posing and politics. All it meant was that the Host was
throwing its weight around. Again. The Pure could do whatever they wanted in the Everlast. For now, he breathed a little
more deeply and relaxed enough to tuck his hands into his suit
pockets. Next up would be a formality, a recitation similar to
the Miranda rights, and that, too, mattered little to Grif. As
far as he could tell, he was already eternally under arrest. So
he tuned out until he once again recognized the English language.

"Griffin Shaw," Donel said, lifting his voice so the syllables
sluiced. "You have been found guilty of violating the conditions of your unprecedented return to the Surface, and failing
to actively pursue your true purpose on earth. Therefore, it
has been decided after much deliberation that there is no other
recourse but to invoke the sacred act of prophecy . . ."

Donel, eyes like banked coals, paused long enough to look
up and gauge Grif's reaction. Apparently the way Grif's knees
automatically weakened was satisfactory.

". . . hereby ordering you to fulfill additional conditions as
outlined by the Host," he continued. "These shall commence
directly upon utterance."

Hell, Grif thought. That's not prophecy. That was an ultimatum. And it was just like the Host. A bunch of winged monsters with nothing better to do than micromanage God's Chosen.

"That's right," Donel hissed, breath roiling as he made no attempt to pretend he wasn't reading Grif's mind. "And make no mistake, we will strip down every memory you hold dear and dissolve them in the waters of incubation before allowing you to cause any more harm."

Grif froze, and not only out of fear. No way, he thought, swallowing hard. Forgetting himself and his past wasn't an option. He'd come too far. "I don't understand. What did I do?"

"You mean you don't know?" Donel said in a voice that made clear that he both did . . . and relished telling Grif. He glanced at Sarge. Grif did the same, a look that told him nothing and everything at once. Because Sarge's eyes were downcast, his wings dragging on the floor. Grif turned back around, and the Seraph brightened, literally.

"Why, Griffin Shaw," he said, smile beatific. "You killed Katherine Craig."

CHAPTER THREE

N o." Grif jerked his head. It wasn't possible. He may have watched Kit when she didn't know he was there, but he had been very careful to do as instructed and refrained from making contact. For six long months he'd left her alone. Therefore she couldn't be dead. "No, Marin would've called me if something happened to Kit. We've stayed in touch."

He'd told himself it was smart to make an ally of the *Las Vegas Tribune*'s editor, especially one with a Rolodex for a brain. What she couldn't remember off the top of her head, she hunted down like a bloodhound in the countless files she hoarded for herself. No bit of information—or gossip—was too small or insignificant to escape her notice. That's why he'd told her about Evie . . . or at least that he was looking for an old relative named Evelyn Shaw.

And that's why, Grif told himself, his desire to keep in touch with Marin had nothing to do with her being Kit's aunt and only living relative.

"Marin couldn't call you," Donel said shortly. "Because she doesn't know it yet."

Grif almost laughed. If Marin didn't know about it, then it hadn't happened. "It's six P.M. on a Monday. If Kit skipped work today, Marin would've known it before nine A.M."

"Except that Kit did go to work today. She put in a full shift, and stopped for gas on the way home. She prepared an early dinner of salmon for one before she went to a club called Jitterbug to watch her friends dance. She left early and alone, and was assaulted at nine P.M., as soon as she entered her home."

Grif looked at his watch. It wasn't even nine o'clock yet. Though it would be in five more minutes. He whirled.

Sarge just stared back with those sunken eyes. "Her Centurion has already been dispatched."

Grif swayed, and it had nothing to do with the water beneath them. "And we're just talking about it? On a fake pirate ship?"

Donel shrugged. "We do not interfere in human affairs."

Grif did. Growling, he lunged for the hatch leading to the deck. He even anticipated Donel's charge—or maybe he'd been *hoping* for it—because all the pent-up anger and sorrow and guilt of the past six months gathered and coiled in his left fist and he let it fly even before thunder cracked across the room. The blow careened into a jaw as hard and sharp as lava rock, and vibrated through Grif's arm, separating joints. Still, a cry like river rapids tore at the air and flashes of images— Donel, strange and twisting, falling back . . . then bright and burning and whipping forward.

Grif cringed, but the returning strike never came. His

breath rasped hard in his chest. Of course, he thought. The Pure couldn't harm the Chosen.

He couldn't open his eyes, not with Donel's rage burning up the room, but he fell to his hands and knees. He didn't mind begging. Not for this.

"Please," he said. "Please, she's been through enough."

A whoosh of air, the ethereal scrim lowering between them again, and Donel merely glowed. But his words now sizzled. "Yes," Donel said, mouth turned down. "We believe so, too."

Desperate, Grif turned back to Sarge. All the strange new furrows in his face had shifted, and Grif watched a tear carving a new track in his destroyed cheeks. Yet he only shook his head. "Donel is right. That's why we are *here*."

He flared his eyes at Grif, his words weighted oddly, but Grif was too worried, too grief-stricken, to care. He didn't want to play games. Not with this. "I'll do whatever you want."

What he couldn't do was shoot the breeze with a bunch of feathered monsters while Kit was attacked, injured. Murdered.

"We already gave you the opportunity to run down your fate, Shaw, and you chose to stroll." Donel folded his arms inside his robe. "Allowing you the opportunity to solve your own murder was supposed to heal you so that you could move on into God's presence. Had you truly been working toward salvation, Katherine Craig would not be dying now."

Oh, God . . . oh, God . . .

He prayed as he hadn't in years.

Donel sneered. "Instead, you continue to obsess over the past, and things you cannot change."

"Yes," Sarge said again, gesturing around. "That is why we're *here*."

Again, that hard inflection. Grif suddenly realized that only

Sarge was posted on the aft end of the ship. And he was directly across from the other Pures. Trying to slow his breathing, trying to think despite his instinct to run for that hatch again—for Kit—Grif worked to calm himself.

"How did it happen?" he asked, because he couldn't say, "How *is* it happening?"

"The way it was meant to the first time she was destined to die," Donel said. "In her home, in her bedroom."

Grif fought off a wave of nausea by locking eyes with Sarge instead. The Pure narrowed his eyes at Grif. Marble churned.

"There is at least one silver lining for you," Donel continued, voice again flowing evenly, again in control. "Katherine Craig will no longer distract you from your salvation."

A snarl rose in his throat and Grif was about to lunge again when Sarge was suddenly there, standing between him and the arrogant Pure. "Donel is right. You must brook no distractions."

Grif gritted his teeth before catching Sarge's eye. What the hell was he going on about? Then he realized Donel was also looking at Sarge. Looking like he'd never seen him before.

"What are you doing?" Donel asked. The Pures behind him moved for the first time, edging closer, every eye narrowed on Sarge. Grif took the opportunity to scan the room with his celestial vision—softening his gaze so that the meager light blended, the shadows melting into each other, the ions of every surface shimmering as they shifted. "Oh," he said, and that's when everyone turned to him.

He rose to his feet, and stood shoulder-to-shoulder with Sarge. "We're not really on the Surface."

Donel growled.

They were in the Everlast. That's what Sarge had been

trying to tell him. He clearly knew what Donel had planned, and he could feel what Grif and Kit felt, so . . .

"I had Nicole Rockwell bring you back to the Everlast while you were unconscious." Sarge waved at Donel, as if presenting him. "It's easier on the Host that way."

"So why make it look like a real place in Vegas?" Grif asked.

The other Pures remained still and silent. They knew something was going on, but Sarge was standing between them and Grif, blocking them from him both physically and mentally. They were as lost as he was.

"Because I knew that if you realized you were in the Everlast you'd immediately try to return to Kit."

That was it. He could reappear at any time or place he wanted on the Surface, as long as it was the future. He just had to get to Kit before . . .

"Too late," said Donel, not even needing to read Grif's mind. His thoughts were plain on his face. "She is even now being relieved of her mortal coil."

"Then what the hell are we doing here?" Grif yelled, and had the pleasure of watching the Pure cringe at his curse. "Why are you telling me this now?"

Sarge appeared in front of him so suddenly that Grif jumped. He jumped again when one dark hand gripped his shoulder, fingers tense and digging, demanding Grif's attention, his eyes swirling with emotion that threatened to pour in rivulets down his ruined face. "Your time is short, moving forward—"

"Prophecy now bears down on your head like an anvil!" Donel added for good measure.

Sarge glared at him from over one destroyed shoulder before turning back to Grif. "No, prophecy is a gift. It's a message from the Divine."

Grif glanced at Donel. Then why did it feel like a threat? Sarge moved aside.

Donel lifted the scroll once more. "Time to earn your fate, Griffin Shaw."

"Just read it," Grif said, because he didn't care. Kit was dying. Or dead.

Kit . . . God, Kit.

Donel opened his mouth. Teeth like daggers winked as he drew in a deep breath.

"Of course, you should give him his miracle first," Sarge said.

The room froze over. Arctic wind rushed in, numbing Grif's limbs. He looked at Donel and trembled, but not from the cold.

"What?" Sarge said innocently, like nothing had happened. He blinked at Donel. "You're giving him prophecy. The scroll states he's equally entitled to one miracle." When no one moved, he shrugged. "Didn't you read the fine print?"

Donel's eyes narrowed into slits. "That option's only exercised if a Pure is willing to grant one from his personal coffers . . ."

And for the first time, Sarge smiled. Grif smiled, too. He already knew what he . . .

Donel roared, and light rippled from his skin. Grif cringed as it stabbed at him, rays like swords, the sound threatening to rupture his eardrums. It was no use. Donel's anger infused the room with infernal heat. The world was afire. Suddenly, the air twisted and a cooling balm of shadows encased him. Grif blinked the haze from his eyes and saw that the heated rays were still trying to reach him, but he was enshrouded in black feathers and arms—shielded by Sarge's wings, he realized— though Donel continued to roar.

Then the ship's deck disappeared above them, and the heavens surged overhead. Lightning flashed, and Donel's roar cut off with a chagrined yelp. For a moment, the fullness of the silence was deafening, the heavy hand of God's presence stifling. Donel fell to his knees. Shifting, Sarge lowered his head and folded his wings behind him. Grif risked a skyward glance but saw only the deck closing back over them, plank by plank, though the air remained sulfurous and shocked.

"I wash my hands of this, Francis," Donel rasped, when time began moving again. His teeth were bared, and his voice rushed like rapids. "You are playing favorites with these mortals! You are interfering!"

Sarge shrugged one tattered shoulder. "I'm not the one who just got reprimanded."

Donel unfurled his wings with a sharp snap. They spanned one end of the ship to the other. "This is all on you!"

"Yes." Sarge looked at Grif, no longer speaking to the other Pure. "It is."

Donel roared and shot up, directly through the newly built illusion of the ship. The report of the wood splintering was like cold and hot air crashing together. The other Pures followed his storm cloud, and, breathing hard, Grif watched them go until Sarge reached out and gently waved his hand over the breech.

"Jesus," Grif breathed, as silence again loomed.

"No. *That* was His daddy."

Who else, Grif thought, could cow a Seraph?

Sarge answered the thought by quirking one eyebrow. "Donel forgot himself. It's not his place to impart lessons to the Chosen."

That's right. It was Sarge's job.

"You knew what he was going to do."

"What, ambush you with prophecy? Yes. And I couldn't stop him . . . there's nothing anyone can do to stop prophecy, Shaw. Once it's uttered, you are on a one-way street leading directly to your fate. You will either fulfill it or you won't. But I could at least offer a little guidance."

He meant that even one-way streets could be littered with potholes.

Grif nodded to show he understood, then licked his lips. "Okay. Thank you."

"Don't thank me yet. Donel was right. It's time to figure out once and for all who killed Griffin Shaw."

"Fine. Tell me about this prophecy."

"And?" Sarge quirked one eyebrow.

Grif huffed at the Pure's knowing look. "And, yeah. I'll go ahead and take that miracle now as well."

And sharing a dual thought of Kit Craig, Sarge and Grif both smiled.

Grif normally traversed worlds using actual doorways. Windows worked, too, but a recognizable portal of entry into the Everlast was calming for souls who'd been traumatized by sudden death. Grif rather liked it himself, even when returning alone to the Surface. Fifty years of skipping along moon shadows, and the sudden emergence from the silky black cosmos onto the Surface—especially the Las Vegas Strip—was a bit jarring. So he took a moment to compose himself, imagining the time and location he wanted to reappear on the Surface, then reached out and opened the hatch that Donel had been blocking.

As expected, he levered himself up onto the deck of a ship

rocking beneath the weight of a faux pirate battle. The bridge between worlds was that simple for him. Sure, the wooden hatch bent like putty when he touched it, and rippled as if rustling wind lived inside the slivered surface, but for Grif it was like stepping from a dry sauna into a wet one. When you were both human and angelic, the membrane between worlds was rice-paper thin, and crossing from one to the other was as easy as blowing out candles and making a wish.

"Hey!" The shout sounded behind him as he headed toward the gangplank, and he turned to see an actor squinting at him through a dashing black eye patch. The faux pirate rushed to block him, pointing at Grif with a wooden sword. "You shouldn't be here."

"Yeah, I've heard that before," Grif muttered, shoving the sword aside like a turnstile, and leaping to the dock next to some wide-eyed tourists. Germans, if their tube socks were any indication. Ignoring them, he began heading south . . . on a Saturday night that he'd already lived.

That was his miracle. Not a rush to Kit's defense. Not, thankfully, an arrival on the scene to a murder in progress. No, this was a real miracle—a return to the Surface *and* to the past. Not only that, Grif was using his miracle to kill two birds.

"How far back do you want to go?" Sarge had asked, leaving it up to him.

"You mean do I want to go all the way back to 1960?"

The incline of Sarge's head indicated it was an option. "You can't alter your own fate, of course. But . . . there is Evie."

Evie, whom he'd married in 1958, when he was already thought to be a confirmed bachelor at thirty-one, and she still a dewy-eyed twenty-two. Evie, whom he'd loved so much he couldn't imagine living without her.

Evie, who'd also fallen under attack because Grif had neglected to protect her.

But these memories were dusty and light compared to the boulder of grief that'd slammed into Grif when Donel told him Kit was dying. That was a blow that'd stopped the breath in his chest, and made his lungs scream along with the denial in his mind. That was an event that, if true, made him want to simply lie down and die as well.

Again.

"Send me back to the time of Barbara McCoy's death," he told Sarge, with a nod of his head. "I can stop that murder, question her killer, and then she can help me find Evie."

From there, he'd go on to protect Kit and find out who killed him fifty years earlier.

Easy-peasy. Right?

"No," Sarge had said, reading his mind again. Grif huffed in annoyance, but Sarge just crossed his arms, looking more like his old self. "It's anything but easy. If you choose this path, if you go back in time, nothing will happen as it's meant to. You'll be rewriting history, and fate will try to rip the pen from your hand and scribble over your intentions. Do you understand what I'm saying?"

"Yeah. I get a shot at saving Kit's life." And nothing else mattered. "So let's get on with it."

So Sarge agreed, saying he'd allow enough time to get to McCoy's home before she was killed, and now Grif was quick-footing it down the infamous Las Vegas Strip, dodging tourists like a salmon swimming upriver. He ignored the scattershot music blasting from the giant LED screens overhead, the roar of cabs and car horns on the wide, joyous streets, and the river of cascading lights overhead, so bright that they shuttered out the heavens he'd so recently inhabited.

The first time he'd lived this night he was playing cards with a bunch of old-timers in the back of the Italian-American Club, a social circle that'd been surprisingly hard to infiltrate. He'd been hoping they could give him some leads on the boys who'd run this town in 1960 . . . if any of them were left.

No chance of that now. He'd stood them up, and there'd be no second invite, though he might not need it if he reached Barbara McCoy in time. It was almost seven at night. She was slated to die within the hour.

He sidestepped, barely evading a body blow from a woman who was laughing as she looked behind her, swinging a neon drinking cup the length of her arm. A loud couple nudged by in the other direction, the male hitting Grif's shoulder as they passed, but he ignored it, turned down Flamingo, and headed east. He overtook an older couple, both huffing as they dragged luggage down the sidewalk in search of McCarran Airport.

"It's farther than it looks," the woman grumbled, steering wide of a homeless man slumped against the wall. He smelled of alcohol and was arguing with ghosts. Unlike on the main drag, the homeless were more evident here. Another reminder that frivolity existed in the same world as abject cruelty, not that Grif needed it.

He paused before the man and handed him a few bucks. Then he thought about it, and handed over the entire roll. He'd been fresh off the craps tables when he died, plenty flush. Plus, no matter how much money he spent in this lifetime, the full amount would return to his wallet at the exact time of his original death: 4:10 every morning.

"What if I steal your wallet?" Kit had once asked, after learning of—*seeing*—his angelic nature.

"Then I slap your wrist," he said, playfully doing just that as she curled up tight, warm at his side. He linked his fingers in hers. "But it'll be back in my pocket at 4:10. Same as everything I died in."

"So that explains the sweet vintage suit, the wingtips, the shit-hot stingy-brim."

Yes, it explained all of his clothes, along with the photo of Evie he'd carried in his wallet, the snubnose with four remaining rounds secured at his ankle. All that was missing was his wedding ring, his driver's license, and the memory of his death. The latter was why it was so damned hard for him to move on. His thoughts were still caught in 1960. Yet how could he look to the future when so many questions remained?

Strange, but the question no longer felt as important as it had before Nicole Rockwell had knocked him upside the head. Knocked some sense into him, too, it seemed, because Donel had been right about one thing. Grif'd been caught in an emotional limbo, stuck waiting for something, anything, to happen.

And now something had.

Gradually the streets shifted from bright and gaudy to a more muted chaos, and the Panorama Project, where Barbara McCoy lived, loomed before him. The high-rise was famous for its opulence and valley-wide views, which meant it was easy to spot as well. Good. The thought of having to ask for directions made him break out in sweat.

Drawing close, he studied the billboards touting the building's many amenities and, with unit prices close to the seven-figure mark, there were more than a few. It boasted its own grocery "boutique," as well as a dry cleaner, a workout facility and spa, and conference rooms for executives who preferred to take a mere elevator ride to work. There was a secure underground parking garage for residents, and a private guard to assist visitors. Barbara's death in the guarded and stacked high-rise should have been a near impossibility. Grif shook his head. He also wondered how the hell he was going to get in.

He glanced straight up and took in the soaring twenty-floor facade as he approached the main entrance. Yet one look from the building's guard, who gave Grif a good once-over as he circled the short drive, and a second glance at the security cameras dotting the shining glass entryway, and he knew he wouldn't be entering from the front.

"Just gimme a door," he muttered, shoving his hands into his pockets. He headed around the corner, pausing there for a moment.

It was Saturday night, but this neighborhood purposely lacked a thoroughfare, making the depths of it quiet, a stillness enhanced by the evening's chill. Yet the high-rise was in the foreground, and there a steady stream of limousines and taxis were ferrying couples along the complex's circular drive. The men were in tuxes, the women in furs, and all were greeted by the doorman or the security guard before disappearing inside.

Grif glanced down at his classic suit, smiled, and buffed his wingtips on the back of his pant legs. Then he straightened his skinny tie and decided to take a little stroll.

He timed his approach as a powder-blue Bentley rolled into the drive. The sleek, humming ride had the doorman jumping to attention, and Grif waited until the man had his hands full with fur pelts and perfumed wrists, assisting a woman wearing heels so stacked they resembled hooves. The doorman stead-ied her on her pins as she tried to find purchase on the faux cobblestone, and Grif slipped behind him . . . then plowed directly into a most inflexible chest.

"Good evening, sir," rumbled the security guard. "Can I help you."

It wasn't a question.

"No, I'm fine." Grif rubbed his chin and made to move around the guard.

The guard—HOWARD, said the name tag—intercepted like a linebacker. But not before Grif spotted the placard directing guests to the pool house.

"I'm afraid all visitors must check in with me, sir. Which resident may I call for you?"

Grif wasn't about to say Barbara McCoy, not with her pending murder, so he motioned in the direction of the pool house. "I'm here for the Hastings' vow renewals."

He sidestepped the guard again, but Howard countered by widening his stance. Apparently, this was a full-on scrimmage. "Your invitation?"

Grif turned up his hands and motioned down his body. "I'm the entertainment."

Howard's brow remained low for a moment longer. Then a slow smile bloomed across his weathered face. "Of course! The funny hat should have tipped me off—"

Grif crossed his arms. He suddenly felt like scrimmaging.

But Howard motioned him inside, even holding the door wide as he pointed to the left. "Mr. Hasting loves all those old crooner tunes. Go on in. I think your band is already setting up."

He was being so helpful that Grif forgave the hat remark. "Warming up," he said, shooting Howard a wink. "They need more practice than me."

The pool house lay tucked to the rear of the giant property, where a pert hostess in black silk cradled a clipboard, cheerily checking off guests' names while a swing band was indeed setting up behind her. A normal enough scene, except that the band was suspended directly atop the pool. Vegas had to do everything bigger. He bet even the lemonade stands sported strobes and sequins.

Grif strolled over to the twin elevators leading to the residential towers, and bent to tie his shoe. When he rose, he sent a warm pulse of energy into his hand, and flashed his palm over the security card reader. The doors slid open with a soft ding.

Grif caught one last glimpse of the woman wearing furs and glittering hooves before the elevator doors slid shut, and he began his ascent. At least the paper had mentioned that Barbara lived on the fifteenth floor. When he stepped out again, it was into a hallway carpeted in elegant grays. A soft chime seemed to greet his arrival, but no . . . it was just the second set of elevator doors sliding shut, heading down. Good timing.

Moving quickly, Grif waved his hand in front of a smoky, half-domed camera. A sizzling sound slithered through the air before smoke began trailing from beneath the dome. The celestial powers left to him after his return to inhabit flesh didn't extend much beyond this simple magic trick, but sometimes it was enough.

"Okay, Barbara," he muttered, turning to face the long, silent hall. "Let's find out why you think I deserved to die."

CHAPTER FOUR

S uite 1509. The exact number hadn't been in the paper—the one not due to be printed for another two days, he reminded himself—but Grif didn't need it. The plasmic thread snaking down the hall was enough to tell him he had the right place, and that Barbara was home. Sarge hadn't given him much of a lead.

He considered knocking, but decided he'd rather risk frightening Barbara, and saving her life, than alerting her attackers to his presence. So he pulled the snubnose pistol from his ankle holster and placed his other hand on the door, which snicked open with one well-directed thought.

The marble foyer was black and white, and flanked by two grand marble pedestals, each holding fresh flowers destined to live longer than the woman who'd bought them. Unless I have a say in the matter, Grif thought. Pistol up, he edged around the glossy center console.

The arched ceiling thwarted his caution and amplified his footsteps so that his soles squeaked, even as he tiptoed, careful to avoid the crystal urns and ceramic statues clustered nearby. Dust catchers, he thought. Or that's what they called them in his day, and they seemed to serve the same useless purpose now.

A short hallway linked the entrance to the main room, and Grif craned his head to find a creamy pastel living area dotted with soft fabrics, cashmere throws, and velvet settees. It was vast, too. Grif could feel its size as he edged forward, taking note of the bold artwork hanging in ornate gold frames. The vibrant swaths of paint put Grif in mind of bodies intertwined, the whorls and loops somehow erotic despite the lack of function or form. One more step allowed a slivered view of the glittering valley from a floor-to-ceiling window that was currently open at one end and sucking out room spray . . . and the scent of gunpowder with it.

Gun braced before him, Grif swiveled around the corner, and pivoted left, then right, before straightening his knees. He sighed.

"These dames and their white carpeting," he muttered, and stepped into the blood-splattered room. A woman lay splayed on her stomach, facedown, or would've been if she'd still possessed a face.

Softening his vision and allowing his celestial eyesight to rise to its forefront, he searched for signs of the plasma he'd spotted in the hall, but it was gone, as was the murdered soul and her assigned Centurion. Just as well. Victims of violent death could develop an emotional tic if they stared at their mortal remains for long. It made regret and grief harder to work out in the Tube.

So much for saving Barbara McCoy, Grif thought, cursing himself as he ventured closer. His feet sunk into the thick carpeting, though he was careful to skirt the still-widening ring of blood. He thought of the elevator dinging just as he gained the fifteenth floor, and cursed again, knowing he'd missed this murder by minutes. Why the hell had Sarge allowed that? Bending, Grif inspected the body. Barbara had been wearing a white silk pantsuit, as if dressed to match the grand suite. It was probably what they'd call winter white—also an impractical color for death—but at least she'd look sharp for eternity.

Grif slid his gaze up the body to where her head should have been. The shot had come from up close. Personal, he thought, glancing up and around. Despite all the crystal and vases and array of tchotchkes lacking any practical function, there were no frames, no photographs, and no way for Grif to see what the woman had looked like before someone took her head away.

Eyes scanning the floor again, Grif also realized Barbara had already been prone at the time of her death. The blood splatter was wrong for a standing kill. The killer, or killers, had levered themselves low, too, eye-level with the victim just in case the bullet passed through the brain. It would then strike the wall, not go straight down into floor.

But why hadn't any of the neighbors reported a blast? Grif wondered, gaze winging to the hole in the wall. And where were the footprints leading away from the body?

One thing was certain, Grif thought, lowering his gun. The killer was gone—likely out that open window—and so was her Centurion. So why, he wondered, gaze winging up to the dark hallway across from him, was there still plasma snaking down the . . .

Grif's .38 flew from his hand as a thump cracked the back

of his skull. The shards from one of the ceramic figurines scattered around him, and Grif thought, Oh. Not just for catching dust anymore. He pushed to his knees, but the gun was too far away and instinct had him spinning instead. He barely managed to raise an arm to block the faceful of flowers hurtling his way. Then a shot rang out, and glass fragments rained over his head. He shielded himself again, shocked at how close his head had come to looking remarkably similar to the dead woman's.

But the gunshot from the hallway had done the job. Grif's fedora was askew, blocking his vision, but he could sense that his attacker was already gone. He lunged for his .38 anyway. Then he cleared the center of the room, holding himself up against a wall until his vision stopped scattering into geometrical patterns. He didn't know if the person down the hall—the one the plasma had been chasing—had been trying to hit him with that shot or not, but he had to find out.

Ears pricked, Grif stood unblinking, trying to thrust his mortal senses outward. It would be just like Sarge, he thought, to set him up. The story about feeling their pain could be pure baloney. Taking him two days back in time, directing him to a murder scene so new that nobody had even learned of it yet, would be a good way to appease the Host, get his errant charge killed and back into the Tube.

"C'mon, Shaw," he chided himself, even as he thought it. Sarge wouldn't do that.

Would he?

Cocking the hammer back on his snubnose, Grif sidestepped the body and moved farther into the silent condo. The footprint of the home was intuitive, and favored the north side of the building. That's where the money view was, so the guest bath lay on the right, while the stunted hallway broke to the left. More of the strange, sexy artwork swirled up the walls like colored smoke, but Grif put his back to the largest frame, softened his gaze, and stared at the closed door rounding out the home.

He couldn't see through it, his celestial powers didn't extend that far, but he was looking for signs of plasma, an indication that someone was about to die. Unfortunately, he wouldn't be able to see the telltale warning if *he* were the fated victim. You never saw the plasma when it came for you.

But instinct, honed by two lifetimes and fifty years of limbo in between, told Grif that something was moving behind that door. Besides, who the hell went around closing doors behind them in their own house?

Grif planted himself to the side of the door before turning the handle and shoving it open. He didn't enter. Experience had taught him that most people found silence and stillness unbearable when anticipating confrontation.

More pastels and white, he saw, risking a glance inside. Ruffles and lace, silken pillows and more knitted throws, things he knew were expensive though he didn't know why. He had no desire to snooze atop some oversized doily. McCoy had been in the green, no doubt about it, but she was too showy about it. If he had to guess, she hadn't always possessed the funds she did now.

Or used to.

Sidestepping into the room, Grif angled toward the walk-in closet and the attached bath beyond that. He'd just emerged when a muffled voice sounded from beneath the bed. "Grif?"

He damned near shot off his own foot.

Then a slim hand appeared atop the bedspread, red-stained, not with blood but lacquer. The half-moon manicure had a silver base and metallic maroon tip. He only knew what it was called because the woman who edged from beneath the bed had once taken an entire half hour to explain it to him.

Katherine Craig looked exactly the same as the last time Grif had seen her, maybe a little thinner, though still lush where it counted. She wore a pencil skirt in the same crimson color as her nails and a black sweater that echoed the hue of her hair. Her pearl brooch competed with her skin for translucence and even the fear widening her eyes couldn't erase the seductive slant of those lids. Maybe it was her makeup, maybe it was just the lighting, or maybe it was the fact that they hadn't made eye contact like this in six full months, but Grif couldn't remember her ever looking so fragile and beautiful at the same time.

"Wh—" she started breathlessly. "How did you get here?"

"Why—?" He took a breath, but the words tumbling in his mind curled into a knot by the time they reached his throat, so he exhaled and tried again. "Why the hell would you reveal yourself like that when there's an intruder in a home with a dead body?"

"Grif—"

"Jiminy Cricket!" He jerked his hat from his head and slapped it against his leg. "No, it's like you want to get clipped. You might as well just wave a flag. 'Hey, bad guy, next victim right here. Come and get it.'"

Kit's spine seemed to grow another couple of inches. "Are you seriously yelling at me? Right now?"

Grif was about to tell her that someone needed to, but snapped his mouth shut instead. Nerves did strange things to a man.

"I wasn't revealing myself, okay?" She put a hand to her

chest, coming around to his side of the room. "I wouldn't have come out if I wasn't sure it was you, but I was. Besides, I have this."

Grif's eyebrows winged up at the dainty .22. At some point in the past six months, his Kitty-Cat had grown claws. He glanced at the peashooter, looked at her also considering it, and took an involuntary step back. He couldn't be sure yet how sore at him she still was.

"So how'd you know it was me?"

"Eau de angel," she muttered, reaching down and pulling out a vintage doctor's bag from beneath the bed. Grif grimaced as he watched her. Of course she would hide her precious bag, probably some thrift-store find that she cherished more than her damned life. Grif was about to match her sarcasm with a quick rejoinder, but suddenly Kit deflated into herself.

Falling into the wingback in the corner, she blew her thick bangs from her forehead and dropped her face into her hands. Grif would have thought nothing of striding across the room and pulling her into his arms at one time, but now he hesitated, his body wavering with the uncertainty of his thoughts.

Kit didn't give him much time to wonder anyway. She recovered quickly, gazing up at him for a brief moment before gesturing to his shoes. "Vintage Stacey Adams wingtips that look brand-new. Round laces, minimally worn soles, and a faint scuff on the right side. They'd sell for a pretty penny these days." Then she added, almost to herself, "I'd recognize them anywhere."

Sure she would, Grif thought, swallowing hard. She'd seen them every day for six months. Even when he undressed— even after she helped him do it—the shoes would return to his body, along with the rest of the clothes, at 4:10 every morning.

The exact hour of his death. Kit had always laughed good-naturedly and called it magic. Grif called it a pain in the tail.

"Are you here to Take her?" Kit whispered.

Grif shook his head. "No, she's already gone."

She looked up. "Me, then?"

He tried to soften it for her. It would be a shock for anyone to learn they were due to be murdered in two days' time. "Not yet."

A shiver ratcheted up her spine at that. Guess it hadn't come out as gently as he'd intended.

"Of course," she finally said, and sighed. "Why else . . ." Kit gestured at Grif, meaning why else would he be there. He'd have been offended at the insinuation if her life hadn't been threatened so many times since he'd entered it.

"Hey, you're the one sitting in a dead woman's home," he reminded her.

Kit's hand twitched on the .22. They were nipping at each other now, though it was better than having her cry or shake or scream about the body still cooling in the next room.

"Barbara called me," she said, standing. She lifted her chin, knowing that wouldn't sit well with Grif.

It didn't. Grif narrowed his eyes. Had Kit actually become friendly with a woman who thought he deserved to die? *Both Shaws got what was coming to them.*

"She told me she had something to show me," Kit said, joining his side. "But she also said she felt like she was in danger."

Grif tried to feel some sympathy for the dead woman. "Guess she was right about that."

Sympathy wasn't his strong suit.

"I saw the guy. I guess I could pick him out of a police . . . whoa." She swayed, and Grif reached out to steady her. Yet all the strength had gone out of her arms, and it suddenly fled her legs, too. He had to lunge, his palm cradling the back of her skull just before it struck the bedpost. "What's going on? Why do I see stars?"

She meant literal stars . . . because Grif saw them, too. They were tiny and stabbed at her like brilliant needles, swirling around her so quickly that he got dizzy trying to track them. The plasma, Grif realized, too late. It'd been coming for her.

If you choose this path, if you go back in time, nothing will happen as it's meant to. You'll be rewriting history, and fate will try to rip the pen from your hand and scribble over your intentions. Do you understand what I'm saying?

He'd said yes, but he hadn't. Not really. He'd come back intending on saving Kit two days from now . . . and fate had made a run at her early.

Grif tried to focus, but her weight and warmth in his arms was familiar, and all he wanted to do was hold her tight. "It's fate, honey. It's switching up on you, altering directions."

"What does that mean?" she said, managing to lock gazes with him despite the specks of light encasing her like bees surprised from a hive.

"It means this is going to feel a little . . ."

But her head jerked back then, eyes rolling with it as her body arched away from his, leaning hard into a backward dive. The speckled dots of light poured like a shining river into her mouth and her core convulsed, arms and legs jerking in rapid spasms. All Grif could do was hold her, but when he lifted her up to pull her close, her mouth fell open, tongue sparkling like she'd licked glitter. The same sheen of stars pasted over the whites of her eyes.

Kit jerked from side to side, the motion of her body actually ripping her from his arms, and he fumbled to keep her from striking the bed and hurting herself. The movements soon evened out, blurring together until her body just hummed with a single vibration, like the beat of a heart monitor. One line indicating one life, one direction. One fate. She collapsed and fell still, the whole episode lasting less than thirty seconds, and all Grif heard was the rasp of his own rapid breath.

He needed to get her out of there. She was destined to remain alive for now, but anything could change that, a moment when he made the wrong step . . . or one in which he didn't act at all. He just needed to get her out of there, he thought, lifting her deadweight into his arms. Then they could figure out what to do next.

As long as it included him not leaving her side until this thing was over.

Kit wasn't entirely unaware of her surroundings. Although her senses were blunted, numbness coating everything from her fingertips to her tongue to the eyes shaking in her head, she still felt the cold air envelop her as Grif carried her outside. It attacked her skin in sharp contrast to the reassuring warmth of his arms around hers, and his chest felt almost hot against her cheek. She was scared by Barbara's death, and shocked by the changes writhing like snakes inside her own body, but somehow she also felt safe.

Kit had grown up afraid. When your mother falls fatally ill when you are twelve, and your father is murdered four years later, it rather deepens the suspicion that the world is not a safe place. She'd fought the effects of that by deliberately choosing things that, while not safe, were inherently good.

Her job was good. She fought to uncover the wrongs and

ills in the world, and make it a better place through fantastic reportage. She might not be able to change anything on a large scale—nothing globally or cosmically, like Grif—but she could do her part, one story and one person at a time.

She also chose her attitude. The swing skirts and crinoline and Betty bangs were more than just show. When you walk around the world attempting to make it a brighter and better place, sometimes a bit of that shine actually takes hold. So now, she chose to focus on the feeling of safety as if it was a talisman, and after a few more seconds she was able to focus her eyes, her mind, and her other senses outward as well.

"Put me down," she rasped when they were tucked around the back of a nearby steakhouse. Grif obliged wordlessly . . . and Kit doubled over. Her legs buckled and her knees scraped the pavement, but Grif caught her under her arms once more, and again, his contrasting warmth made all the difference in the world. His arms were strong and firm around her shoulders, and the Sen-Sen that always scented his breath wafted over her as he spoke soothing words in her ear.

I'm in shock, Kit realized, as one last shudder numbed her core and reverberated out through her limbs. From the moment the first gunshot had roared through the suite, she'd been wondering when the shakes would start. Yet the subsequent jolts—Barbara's body splayed on the floor, the surefire instinct that the killer was coming for Kit next, and then Grif's almost immediate arrival—had delayed the onset, at least for a bit.

She'd have chided herself for falling apart in front of Grif—of course, *he* was as coolly assessing as ever—but then why would he mind after walking in on such a grisly murder?

He could see death coming and going. He practically held the door open for it every time.

Kit realized her teeth were chattering, and she clenched her jaw shut and tried to right herself again. Grif released her only after he saw that she was stable, and she caught one last whiff of his pomade as he steadied her on her feet. Then it, and the security of his arms, was gone.

"What?" she said, realizing he'd been speaking. She rubbed her nose, hating the way gunpowder clung to the soft lining inside.

"We'll get somewhere safe and work it out . . ." Grif was saying, taking on most of her weight as he pulled her forward. Here he was, after so many months of her wishing it to be so. Absent, and then there. A memory and then her reality, once again. That alone was enough to make her dizzy. It also made her want to laugh and cry at the same time . . . though that could have just been the shock.

"Not going anywhere . . ." he was saying, ". . . stick close to your side . . ."

But hadn't he said that before?

Don't be a fool, Kit. I don't see anyone else helping you up off the ground.

And there was certainly no one else she trusted with her life more than Griffin Shaw. Maybe not her heart, not that ever again, but her life? Yes.

"How did you get here?" she asked.

"How did you?"

"I told you. Barbara invited me over."

"You *knew* her?"

Blowing out a trembling breath, Kit gave Grif a nod, both in answer and to let him know her legs would hold. Yeah, she thought, as they walked more swiftly, this grumpy retro angel had broken her heart. He'd been so obsessed with the past that he couldn't see through it to a future with Kit, but he was never cruel. Besides, if Grif thought she was in trouble, then she believed him.

She halted again suddenly, and saw him brace, ready to catch her if she fell. "I am in way over my head," she said suddenly.

Grif stared at her for so long she wasn't sure he was going to answer. Then he gave his own shaky laugh. "Have you ever uttered those words before in your life?"

And Kit laughed. Or at least she did in her mind. On the outside, where the wind was blasting a chill up her skirt and a woman lay headless in a high-rise suite behind them, she just stood and stared. But the levity helped in a moment when she realized that danger was once again a certainty in her life. It also helped her ignore the way her mind had unclenched for the first time in months. She was suddenly no longer burdened with the task of trying not to think about Griffin Shaw.

Unfortunately, the very first thought that whipped through her head when she saw his sturdy, shit-hot wingtips pointed directly at her, like divining rods, under that guest-room bed was another shock: God. I don't love him even an ounce less than the last time I saw him.

It was also partly why she still shook. For Kit, it was perhaps the most dangerous thing of all.

The hired help came in sweating and shaky, smelling of gunpowder and blood, and huffing even though he'd driven all the way across town and there was no way he should be out of breath. Working beneath the trained glare of a green banker's lamp, the man behind the desk gripped the pencil so tightly that the lead splintered between his strong fingers, and he had to force himself to relax. It's okay, he told himself, as he removed his glasses and rubbed the bridge of his nose. He'd been working for hours, a way to keep his mind off the night's planned events. The numbers in the ledgers were beginning to squiggle before his eyes anyway.

Swiveling in the office chair, he folded his hands over his belly and stared at the man who was supposed to be a cold-blooded killer.

"Justin," he said by way of greeting. He would ask nothing, though he expected those who worked for him to tell all.

Justin fidgeted on his feet, which was rare. "Shit."

And that said it all.

The man sighed and waited.

"My man . . . he screwed up."

The man closed his eyes and waited some more. "First of all, we weren't seen on the way in. You were right. The party was a great distraction. We used the residents' parking garage to go up and back."

"But." Not a question. When someone overexplained, there was always a "but."

"And I offed the old bird, it was as easy as you said. I think she knew what I was going to do, but she laid down on the floor and practically pulled the trigger for me."

Yes. Fifty years of guilt would do that to you.

"But," he said again.

"But then I left Larry to clean up while I readied the car, and the other woman, the Craig girl, got away." Thus the sweating, the fidgeting, the lost breath when every damned thing should be under control.

Clenching his teeth together so hard that one of his crowns began to ache, the man shook his head. Goddamn Justin. He was going to make him ask. "*How* did she get away?"

"Griffin Shaw."

Shaw. "You're sure it was him?"

"Larry said it was the same man who busted up that drug ring six months ago. The same one who stopped the kiddie sex ring before that." There'd been photos in the *Las Vegas Tribune,* and the man had shown them to Justin. He always read the *Tribune,* hard copy only. It was what had alerted him to Shaw's return to the valley in the first place.

"Besides," Justin was saying, voice hollowed like he was in a tunnel. "Who else dresses like that?"

The man stood, pushing from his desk and crossing to the window that overlooked a wide, cool lawn that should never exist in the desert. He couldn't see it in the dark, but he could feel it, cold and vast, like life itself. Dropping his forehead against the icy pane, he decided to break his own rule. He was the one asking questions now.

"And why didn't Larry kill them both?" Because Shaw had dropped off their radar in recent months. They'd tracked the Craig woman, but never once had their surveillance shown Shaw at her side.

"She shot at him."

A chill arrowed through the man's chest. "Barbara did?"

Justin made a face. "No, Craig. Apparently she carries a gun." He gave the man a hard look. "You forgot to put that in your report."

The man didn't apologize. Instead he thought about the revolver in his bottom desk drawer. He thought about shooting Justin, and then finding Larry and finishing what Craig had not. If he wasn't so sure he'd need them later, he might have done it. No one would object. After all, he made up the rules around here.

What he needed to do now was figure out what to do *next*. First Barbara McCoy had returned to the valley. Now Griffin Shaw. And they'd been on a collision course tonight, which couldn't be a coincidence.

No . . . the man had seen too much, and knew too much of this couple's respective pasts, to believe in coincidence. He was willing to bet these two were looking for the same thing he was, though he'd been at it for fifty years.

"Bringing old ghosts to life," he muttered, his breath going white against the cold windowpane.

"What?" Justin asked, not knowing he shouldn't be asking questions anymore. Not aware that he could already be dead.

"I said that those two are bringing the past back with them." And this time *he* was going to take his share of it.

CHAPTER FIVE

So where was the perfect place to be when you weren't sure where to go but knew only that you didn't want to be found?

Vegas, baby.

Part of it was the tourists, yes; the thousands of nameless faces moving and shifting throughout the city made it easy to hide. Sensory overload took care of the rest—flashing lights and LED signs, music and horns and PA systems blasting outdoors—noises normally reserved for airports and hospitals and train stations, all desperate to stimulate ADD in the calmest of souls, at least long enough to separate them from their money.

Ignoring it all, Kit and Grif strolled across the cavernous floor of the Desert Dream, the city's largest casino. It was past midnight, but the foot traffic was as thick as at the Rockefeller Center at Christmas. Kit nervously eyed the smoky-black domes of the ceiling security cams anyway, then ducked her head as they passed the raised stand bearing not one but two security guards. Yet even Kit's and Grif's retro clothing wasn't enough to raise an eyebrow in this environment, and the in-house security was actually a blessing. It meant there was less chance of running into any city police.

In fact, Grif and she could likely spend a whole weekend in the cavernous building and never run into the same employee twice. Slot machines, pit games, bars, lounge entertainment—visits with wild tigers and dolphins—and strange combinations thereof, there was no end to the manufactured entertainment vying for their attention just in the Desert Dream alone. As long as they didn't make a run on the blackjack tables, it was the perfect place for Kit and Grif to hide.

"Where exactly are we going?" Grif asked, eyes darting from face to face from beneath his lowered stingy-brim.

Kit looked at her watch. "It's just as early as it is late. That makes it the perfect time for Temptation."

Grif tripped over his own feet. "What?"

Kit pointed to the glittering, cavernous red mouth of the hotel nightclub. Warm satisfaction momentarily dislodged the remainder of her fading shock when Grif winced. The club's bassline throbbed all the way out onto the casino floor. Before he could come up with an alternative, Kit paid the cover. Grif was out of money for some reason, though he said he'd pay her back later, and she thought, Damned right, and sprung for bottle service as well. She knew that no matter how much he spent, the amount he'd died with in 1960 would return to his pocket at 4:10 sharp every morning. That was only a handful of hours away.

A pretty but dead-eyed hostess led them directly across the dance floor and to an elevated "room" curtained off by black sheers and velvet ropes. By the time they were settled, Grif was grinding his teeth together so hard that Kit could almost hear it over the monotonous rap, though she pretended not to notice. Temptation was dark enough to be private, yet loud enough to prevent intimacy, and Kit needed each of those things for her first meeting with Grif in six months. A stiff drink wouldn't hurt, either.

"They're up-charging by five thousand percent," he grumbled as their personal server sauntered away. If she didn't know better, she'd say he was more upset by that than by the headless body he'd found earlier that evening.

"Tip not included," Kit said, just to see if she could ruffle his feathers. Ha, ha.

Grif slumped in his pleather seat and almost slid to the floor. "She plunked down an ice bucket and walked away. She's not getting a tip."

"She plunked down an ice bucket, showed you her cleavage, and walked away," Kit corrected, lifting her drink as he righted himself.

"Why would you even bring that to my attention?" He shot her a look so jaded—so old and so new—that she blinked in the flashing strobes and wondered for a moment if she was seeing things. How many nights had she dreamed of just that look? She firmed herself against it by downing her entire first glass of overpriced vodka.

"Because no woman actually wants to do that for free, and because it's not her fault that they overcharge here. She's not going to see any of it. She works for *tips*."

Grif grumbled and leaned forward, and Kit reclined farther into the curtained-off alcove and studied him from the shadows. Out of their element, still trying to find their footing in the aftermath of murder, and they were already bantering with ease. Forget the frenetic beat pushing at them from the multitudinous speakers, this was a true call-and-response pattern, one as easy and deliberate as a sexy blues phrase. It calmed her.

And *that* made her down her second overpriced drink in one nervous gulp.

"Tell me what happened tonight," Grif said, light flashing across the angular planes of his face so that he appeared deconstructed. It made him easier to look at, and answer.

"You mean the murder?" The scene flashed again, jumping out at her like it was a part of the choreographed light show. She'd seen a dead body. She'd shot at a killer. Blinking hard, Kit poured herself another drink.

"I mean all of it." How she'd hooked up with Barbara McCoy. How she'd ended up in the suite on the night the woman was murdered. How she could even think of sitting and talking to a woman who hated him and his not-dead wife.

Sipping now, Kit decided she'd tell him enough to assure his help, but she wouldn't reveal all of her actions, her life, herself. Never that again.

"I located Barbara McCoy about four months ago, though didn't approach her immediately."

She let that sit between them, a loaded moment. Barbara had first popped up on Kit's and Grif's radar while they were investigating Grif's murder in 1960. She'd become Barbara DiMartino not long after that by marrying Vegas's most infamous mobster. Sal DiMartino was up there with the greats—Spilotro, Siegel, Lansky, and Berman. Names that were like royalty in Vegas. "I told her straight out that I was press, though she remained suspicious."

"Just suspicious?" Grif asked.

She huffed at his knowing look. "Downright rude. Regarded me like I was a fly to be swatted, and looked more than willing to do it herself."

Kit could usually charm her way into a story with honest gregariousness or genuine interest or effusive charm. She didn't often elicit a death glare from anyone . . . never mind from a woman close to her eighth decade.

"She finally agreed to meet me in person seven weeks ago. Said she'd had time to suss me out."

"How?"

"Given her background? I was afraid to ask."

So they'd met at the Bootlegger Bistro, the successful off-shoot of a downtown restaurant that'd been serving Italian-style family fare since 1947. Those recipes and the bistro had moved to the south end of the Strip since then, but the interior paid homage to Vegas's golden era. "Barbara was seated in the back of the room in a booth all by herself. I knew she was waiting for me, but she watched everyone. The singer crooning Sinatra. The waitstaff, who were wary of her. The bartender. The women."

Especially the women.

In fact, she'd taken one look at Kit, narrowed her eyes and licked her over-dyed lips, drew in a deep breath of smoke from the mother-of-pearl cigarette holder cocked in her right hand. "You're not like the other girls, are you?"

"What do you mean?" Kit asked politely, removing her gloves. She'd been especially careful in dressing for the occasion. After all, this woman had actually lived—had thrived—in the era Kit most revered.

"Because you can't wrap these girls in fur." She waved her hand in the air and sent ash scattering. "Bacon, maybe, but not fur."

Kit clenched her jaw but couldn't risk calling the woman on it and running her off.

"She was bitter," Kit told Grif, because she knew he'd been wondering about Barbara for so long. He knew that she thought he'd deserved to die fifty years earlier, and she hadn't changed her mind in the ensuing years. Not that Kit could tell. "She smoked. Said she was dying of emphysema. Said that her neck was draped in pearls, but what she really needed was a pair of good lungs."

"Why, so she could continue spewing more of her filth?"

That's exactly what Kit had thought, though she didn't say it then or now. "You know, it's not rare to see someone sur-rounded by so many things still so indelibly unhappy, but it felt like it was more than that. Like she had greater regrets. Things that were so far in her past that she knew she'd never be able to touch them again."

Grif nodded briefly, not looking at her. Of course, he'd know about that. He swallowed hard. "Did you ask her any-thing about, you know . . . me?"

Kit wanted to say that it—*he*—wasn't why they'd met, though again, she wasn't ready to share that with Grif. He was just an interloper here, right? A footnote in her past.

"No," she said, and watched Grif's jaw turned to granite. "Not the first time."

His eyes brightened at that, and though braced for it, Kit felt an old emotion break through her shock. One that hard-ened in an instant, giving her purchase and making her feel like flint. He was still obsessed with the past, she thought, shaking her head. Still so consumed with it that he couldn't see her sitting right in front of him.

Maybe it's the lack of light, Kit thought wryly, sipping at her drink.

"So you met more than once." It wasn't a question. How else would she have ended up at Barbara's home?

"Not willingly. She was just so obstinate. One of those people who answered every question with one of her own. I wasn't going to say anything about you but . . ."

"But?" He had the nerve to look hopeful.

"But she was just so damned nasty," she said, and it was true. Kit hadn't done it for him. She didn't owe Griffin Shaw a thing, and something of her anger must have rolled across her face, because he leaned back like he was giving her space. Not wanting to let on that she needed it, Kit just shrugged. "So I decided to give her a jolt. I spit it out, just to see the look on her face."

"Griffin Shaw is still alive," Kit had said then, and watched as Barbara McCoy choked on her martini olive. Kit hid her smile behind her old-fashioned. She was actually matching Barbara drink for drink, a woman's duel, unspoken as all duels between women are. And now she was winning.

When the choking had subsided and Barbara had wiped her chin and fortified herself with another sip, Kit added, "So is his wife, Evie."

"Well, I knew that," Barbara snapped, splashing gin. "But no way is Shaw still alive. No way in hell."

"How do you know?"

"Because I spit on his corpse myself."

And she threw back her head and laughed like it was the funniest thing she'd ever said or heard. Laughed like it fed her soul. The sound sawed through the air, and Kit realized she was wrong. This woman wasn't just bitter. She was vile.

"But now you're digging up really old corpses," Barbara said, flaring her eyes. "And you don't want to do that. Trust me, the boys may not run this town anymore, but they still guard their secrets carefully."

Kit couldn't help herself. She was shaking so badly, and she wanted to shake Barbara, too. "But this was no secret. We already know you hated him."

"We?"

"Grif and me," Kit said, because they were still united in this at least. A broken heart was one thing; darkness and cruelty and obsession that fed on itself for decades was quite another.

Barbara leaned incrementally closer, her gaze running over Kit's face like darting fish. Finally her nostrils flared and she pulled back, giving Kit a brand-new head-to-toe appraisal. She took her time studying Kit's vintage swing coat and scarf. She traced the outline of her cat's-eye glasses with cold regard, upper lip curling as she took in the matching black eyeliner. She tried on another laugh, but this one didn't flow as freely. "Why, you got that sheen in your eyes, my girl."

"What sheen?"

"That hazy-dazy look of love. Don't tell me . . . you and *Shaw*?"

Kit's mouth firmed into a thin line, saying nothing. Barbara was picturing Grif near the same age as her, an octogenarian battling gout and the ability to stand to his full height. Yet Grif was eternally thirty-three, stronger than this woman could ever imagine, and with wings that rose well above any doorframe to boot.

He also wouldn't stop until his murderer and his wife were found, though she didn't tell Barbara that. "He just wants to find Evie Shaw. Truthfully? He wants nothing to do with you."

And neither did Kit. Not anymore. This woman's mind was as toxic as stagnant water. No matter what information might be stewing inside of it, the attached lethal tongue could only spread disease.

"Why?" Barbara finally asked.

"Why what?" Kit replied coolly.

"Why does he want to find Evelyn?"

Because he needed closure, but Kit wasn't going to give Barbara any ammo for that shotgun mouth. So she just shrugged.

"And why do you?" Barbara said, flashing her a knowing look.

Kit flinched before she could stop herself, but it was plain to them both. She wanted to see how she fared against the infamous Evelyn Shaw.

"We just want to know who killed him . . ." She blushed, correcting herself when Barbara's eyes narrowed. "Who *tried* to kill him—them both—fifty years ago."

Barbara huffed and shook her head, so that her hair spread in a cloud. "What does it matter? It was a long time ago."

"It always matters!" Kit slammed her palm on the table, causing her drink to topple, and they both jumped. She rarely lost her temper, not in public, not with informants, but this woman's sewer brain and toxic-waste mouth made *her* feel dirty. "Those two people were driven apart because of what happened that night and there's been a lot of pain as a result. Grif lost . . . years of his memory and life, most of which he'll never get back."

"Most?" Barbara said, voice oily with interest.

"He remembers *her,*" Kit said, because as much as it pained her to say it, Grif and Evie's relationship seemed to affect Barbara even more adversely. Kit couldn't help but rub a little salt into that old wound. "So despite your wishes, your words, and someone's terrible actions long ago, they *are* both alive today, and he means to find her. And I'm going to help."

But Barbara was staring off into the distance. "What words?"

"Huh?" Kit paused as she reached for her bag.

"What *words?*" Impatient, she waved her cigarette holder at Kit. Kit dodged, but Barbara didn't notice that, either. "What wishes are you talking about? What words?"

Kit tilted her head. "You reportedly told one of my sources that you hated Griffin and Evelyn Shaw. You said, and I quote, 'The past doesn't matter, and they mattered even less. Both Shaws got what was coming to them.'"

Barbara stared at Kit for a long moment. "And you're sure it's really him? That he's still alive?"

"Yes."

Barbara huffed. "Then I guess I was wrong about that."

Shocked silence wrapped around Kit, a blanket of burrs and thorns. She shouldn't say anything, it would only put the power back into Barbara's hands, but she couldn't help it. How could *anyone* hate Griffin Shaw that much? "Why do you hate them so much?"

Barbara put on an innocent mien that almost worked, due to her age and sex combined. The sharpened gaze, though, kept the innocence from truly reaching her eyes. "I don't know. I'm old, honey. I can't remember shit."

Disgusted, Kit threw down her business card and enough money for the drinks. "Call me if you ever really want to talk."

But she wouldn't hold her breath.

"Hey. Hey!" Kit didn't stop at first. She didn't want to watch this woman's painted mouth curving up to tell more lies. "You sure it's him? Shaw?"

Hand on hip, Kit turned. "Dead sure."

Barbara tilted her head. "And he's still sweet on Evie?"

Kit forced a shrug. "He's been searching for her for fifty years."

Barbara's whole face seemed to turn inward at that, and she shuddered down to the base of her spine. But then she remembered Kit standing there, and instead of giving an admiring nod, she shook her head. "Some P.I."

Kit couldn't stand it anymore. She whirled and left Barbara there, a small woman in a red velvet booth contemplating a love that was epic and enduring and true . . . and one she'd clearly never known in the entire length and breadth of her mean and bitter life.

You did something to her," Kit told Grif as they sailed from the casino's parking garage back onto Vegas's main drag. Kit had actually allowed Grif to take the wheel of her beloved Duetto, a testament to how much she trusted him . . . and to how much vodka she'd downed due to nervousness and shock. Besides, she was still working through her thoughts on Grif's abrupt return to her life. It seemed like a magic trick to her. There, gone, then back again. *Poof.*

"Hand to God," Grif said, lifting his palms to the sky, and Kit pointed, directing them back to the steering wheel. "I never met any Barbara McCoy."

"Her name used to be Barbara DiMartino."

Grif jerked his head. "Sal was married to a woman named Theresa when I was alive. Barbara came . . . after."

No she hadn't, Kit thought, turning away, watching as the neon glare of the Strip was snuffed out in her rearview mirror. Barbara had married the old mobster only months after Theresa's death, and Kit would bet the car she was sitting in that Barbara had been lurking around before then. "What if she was part of the reason you were killed? After all, *someone* spread the rumor that you hurt"—*raped*—"the twelve-year-old niece of a mobster."

They'd discovered that nugget of information last summer. It was a ludicrous lie . . . but one that'd gotten him killed.

Grif hummed, considering it. "I only worked that one case for the DiMartinos. Beyond returning little Mary Margaret unharmed, and getting dry-gulched for the effort, I had no dealings with that family whatsoever."

Kit said nothing, because she hadn't been there . . . but she did know women. She could read them inside and out, and Barbara had all the markings of one who'd been scorned. A woman didn't hate a man in the way she hated Grif unless he'd all but crushed her.

There was more to consider, more to ask, but it was late, and Kit was exhausted. Grif was, too. She saw it in the slump of his wide shoulders, and the circles stamped beneath his eyes, though she could tell from his frown that he was still stewing over Barbara. That's why she was surprised when he asked, "We going home?"

Silence swelled in the car.

He'd said it without thinking, his tired brain lagging behind his mouth. Kit ignored the slip, knowing that if they were going to work together there were bound to be others— *home* and *honey* and *Kitty-Cat*—all the things that had once marked him as hers, and vice versa. Swallowing hard, she told herself she'd take them as they came. She'd also protect herself this time, and surround herself with people and places that did the same . . . but for Kit that meant home. She nodded, and silence reigned from there on out.

Kit lived in Paradise Palms, a mid-century neighborhood in the middle of Las Vegas, and situated behind the city's oldest existing mall, the Boulevard. Though Paradise Palms had few rivals for its retro-style homes and spacious streets, it was no longer the crown jewel of the Las Vegas Valley. The brick facades were crumbling at the edges, and the once sweeping lawns were dustier as the desert attempted to reclaim its territory. Its central location also made it a favorite of both gang and police patrols.

Yet the function and form of the neighborhood was solid, hearkening back to a simpler time. Butterfly rooftops, sleek lines, and large glass panes—Kit could practically see the mid-century scrawl of the signage that had once flanked the neighborhood's entry. THE FUTURE IS NOW, TOMORROW HAS ARRIVED.

The phone rang just as they pulled into the restored carport.

"Oh, yeah." Grif dug it from his pocket. "I grabbed your phone before leaving Barbara's."

Kit just looked at it. Then she lifted her identical one from the center console. "Mine."

"Then whose—?"

Gasping, Kit lunged for the device but fumbled it, so it fell in the footwell. By the time Grif located it again, the ring had gone silent. "Shit!"

She snatched Barbara's phone from his hands and lifted it so she could see the lighted screen. She pushed a series of buttons, then sighed. "It's password-protected. We'll have to wait until someone—"

And the phone rang again. Kit answered before she could even think what she was doing. There was a moment of silence after she put the phone to her ear, when Grif and she both held their breaths, and Kit was trying to work out how the irascible Barbara McCoy would answer the call. She finally answered with a terse, "What?"

Silence, and Kit's eyes flashed on Grif's. She'd blown it.

"Hello?" came the tentative response. *Male,* Kit mouthed to Grif.

"Yeah?" Kit said immediately, pitching her voice lower than her normal tone. Grif shot her a dead-eyed stare, as if to say, That's *what she sounded like?* Kit just shrugged.

"Is it done?"

Kit just bit her lip. Barbara was dead, though, so something had definitely been "done."

"Barbara, I asked if it was done. It's been crickets over here. I'm going crazy."

"Uh-huh," Kit said, wordlessly trying to draw more out of the caller.

But apparently Barbara hadn't been a reticent woman. A long silence passed, then the man's voice dropped low as well. "Who is this?"

Slapping a hand to her forehead, Kit tried to think fast, but the line went dead before she opened her mouth, and her answer swerved into a growl. Squinting at the phone, she began pushing more buttons.

"What are you doing?" Grif asked.

"Working the home button before the screen times out. She's got it set so you can't get into this thing after you hang up, but once a call is answered you can work the functions." The first thing Kit did was remove the password protection.

Then she clicked over to the contacts. It was growing chilly in the car, but both the cold and her fatigue were well-forgotten. "Still carry your Moleskine with you?"

Grif pulled the notebook from his inner suit pocket.

"Okay, we're going to write down every number in her contacts just in case we can't get into this thing again, starting with our mysterious caller." There was no name displayed on the incoming screen, just an uppercase X, but Kit rattled it off anyway, then did the same with the rest. Grif scribbled fast, but was barely keeping up until she paused. "How the hell did Loony Uncle Al get in Barbara McCoy's address book?"

Grif's pencil fell still. "That's what she named her contact?"

"Nope. But that was his pet name around the paper back when he was chasing bylines." She flashed Grif the screen long enough to show the name, and this time Grif jolted in his seat.

"Al Zicaro," he said, suddenly wide-eyed as well. He circled the name and number after writing them down on his pad. "How does Barbara know that old newshound?"

Zicaro had worked at Kit's paper in the sixties and seventies, even though any mid-century bookie worth his salt would've laid odds on Zicaro getting rubbed out before Grif. The man had covered the crime beat, and was a thorn in the side of the boys, including and *especially* the DiMartinos. Kit had combed through the archives and knew he'd even tried to intimate that Grif was made after he'd brought back Sal DiMartino's niece, but it wasn't anything that would stick. Especially once Grif disappeared shortly after.

"God knows he was around," Kit said now. "And he certainly had his hands in the DiMartinos' affairs."

But why keep up with Barbara after all this time? The boys' time in this valley had long passed.

Kit rubbed her eyes. "Your past is beginning to resemble a thousand-piece puzzle."

Grif snorted. "And we're missing all the corners."

Kit nodded. They'd had few leads on his cold case: first, Mary Margaret, the child he'd once saved, now a recovering addict in her sixties. She'd given them the Barbara lead, now a literal dead end.

But then there'd been Zicaro.

"He's gotta be, what? Seventy-six years old?"

"Around there. He's been at the Sunset Retirement Community for years," she recalled. It was knowledge she'd let slip away after Grif had disappeared from her life. Unfortunately, as they both knew, ignoring wasn't forgetting. "Last I heard he was still scribbling far-fetched pieces about alien abductions and conspiracy theories and pasting them around the old folks' home."

Kit flipped screens on Barbara's phone, leaving the address book to dip into the voice mails. Grif's gaze was steady on her as she scrolled, but he remained silent until she sat up straight. "What?"

"Bingo." Flashing him the screen, Kit then flipped it back around and pushed the speaker button. Seconds later, a shaky, reedy voice sounded in the cold shell of Kit's car.

"Barbara, it's Zicaro. I don't know what the big idea is showing up here like that, but you're going to get me killed. You don't fool no one with that fake name either, so don't give me that bullcrap. Once a DiMartino, always a DiMartino."

Kit locked eyes with Grif.

"I don't know why you're back, but listen good. Stay away from Sunset and stay away from me. I ain't lasted all these years just to get rubbed on your account. Besides, whatever you're into, whatever you want, I ain't got it. You lived the life, remember? I just reported it."

The message cut off, and Kit immediately brought up the address for the Sunset Retirement Community.

"When was that call made?" Grif asked, voice no more than a whisper.

"Friday."

"So Barbara visited Zicaro the day before she died."

"Which is what we'll be doing first thing in the morning," Kit said, and flashed him Zicaro's address. He began writing again without another word, and they emptied out the rest of the phone book as well. When they'd finished, it was with a start that Kit looked up and realized they were still seated in her car. Just like the old days, she thought. Working together, finishing each other's sentences, losing track of place and time. Kit reached for the handle.

Grif didn't move.

She glanced back. "You coming?"

"I'm waiting to be invited."

Invited where? Kit swallowed hard, but Grif was gazing at the front of the home they'd shared . . . briefly but passionately.

"And if not," he said, refocusing on her with the same intensity, "I'll sleep outside."

"You think I'm in danger." She'd already seen it in the way he studied the bushes and pockets of darkness the streetlights didn't reach. He just shrugged, confirming it.

Fine, she thought, narrowing her eyes. You keep your secrets. I'll keep mine.

"Come on," she said, breaking the silence and the stare. She'd allow him in her house because the best chance to get through this individually was by working together. But that was all.

Because even if working together felt right, they'd be doing so for a future they would never share. Kit had walked this world in love with Griffin Shaw for six whole months—and they'd solved two major crimes along the way—but then she'd spent another six trying to forget that he'd ever lived. After all of that, Kit thought, she'd learned to hold a little of herself back. She now knew how to hold *herself* together.

And she knew exactly what she could and could not survive.

CHAPTER SIX

I t turned out the Sunset Retirement Community was aptly
named. Not just a nirvana for those living out their golden
years playing golf and cards, the facility was set up for end-of-
life needs. It provided medication and full-time nursing care,
and for most residents, these were the last walls they'd ever call
home.

Of course, Kit and Grif didn't learn this until Kit'd pulled
her pretty, purring convertible into the front parking lot, and
she used her smart phone to research more while they waited
another twenty-five minutes for visiting hours to begin. The
late-morning hours gave the caregivers a jump start on the daily
grooming and medical needs of the residents before breakfast,
and time to get them settled again after. So even though it was
Sunday for the rest of the world, it was just another day for the
Sunset residents.

"Maybe Zicaro had an abrupt decline in health," said Kit, while they waited. "Maybe Barbara just—"

"What? Stopped in to say good-bye?" Grif scoffed, and they fell silent, watching as a caregiver in all white pushed a wheelchair-bound resident on a path along the building's side. The crisp blue sky did nothing to actually warm the day, and the resident had a blanket over her lap, while her caregiver remained careful to keep to the thin, straining sunlight.

Grif just rubbed his eyes. He might have been tucked into a place like this by now . . . if he hadn't been killed first. It made him realize that no one was Surface-bound for long.

"This may require a new plan," he said, and held out his hand for Kit's smart phone. They had one—after another ten minutes and the use of the device's map application—and when they finally climbed out of the car, Grif headed to the main entrance alone.

The double doors eased open like he was expected. He emerged directly into an open office area decorated with blue and yellow flowers so vibrant they were without parallel in the natural world, their plastic vases filled with clear marbles instead of water. A corkboard was splayed across the wall directly in front of him, community activities and photos displayed atop bright construction paper more suited to an elementary school than a nursing home. A sitting area with two chairs and a settee was anchored with a side table and yet more fake foliage. Two residents sat there but didn't talk, and while one stared expectantly at Grif, the other didn't notice him at all. A faint antiseptic smell permeated the whole place, and if Kit hadn't told him he was in a building offering full-time health care, the scent alone would've done so.

"Good morning!" The cheerful voice rang from behind him

and a woman emerged from a side office, moving smoothly behind the L-shaped desk. "How can I help you?"

Grif shoved his hands into his pockets and cleared his throat. "I'm here to see Mr. Zicaro."

The receptionist's name tag said ERIN, and she sat, giving Grif an ample shot of her full bosoms bursting beneath a low-cut sweater. "Family or friend?"

"Old friend."

Erin gestured to the guest book, which Grif dutifully signed, catching sight of a surveillance camera over Erin's left shoulder. They were everywhere these days; not like his first go-round on this mudflat. Too bad all they could reveal were actions and not motives.

Though in this case that might be a good thing, Grif thought, as Erin picked up the phone to ring Zicaro's room.

"That's okay," Grif said, motioning for her to put the phone down. "I called earlier and he said to go on back. Room 128, right?" He took a few steps, like he was already on his way.

"No, um . . . room 238 actually, but you can't go back yourself. All guests must be accompanied by a staff member." She studied Grif, her bubblegum gloss momentarily fading, but smiled again when he just shrugged and shoved his hands into his pockets.

His view while he waited was that of a common area, obviously where the entire community gathered for their meals—three squares a day, if the notice on the bulletin board was correct. More lumpy chairs and a sofa clustered around a large television on the right, and a bank of curved windows sat beyond that, acting as a sunroom for the tropical plants scattered among dark wood chips along the wall.

Spotting a flash of stocking-clad legs outside the windows,

Grif moved to block them, and looked behind him to see if Erin had noticed Kit, too. The woman just beamed at him, and held up a finger as she spoke into the receiver, mistaking his glance for impatience.

Grif turned back around. The rest of the room held dining tables, each spaced widely enough to allow wheelchair and walker access, while a wall to the left hid what was obviously the kitchen. Breakfast was over, but a lone woman sat at a table, her back rounded and chin down as she stared, unblinking, at the orange tablecloth before her. Grif waited for her to move, but she didn't, and as he glanced around the empty space, despair carved a pit into his stomach.

Could Evie be in a place like this?

He'd once had a dream of her, a vision where she'd lamented being alone and that nobody came to visit. What if it hadn't been a simple dream? The veil between this world and the Everlast was thin. What if she'd been calling out to him in her dreams, begging for help in the only way she could?

The image of Evie—blond and bright and dancing, her head thrown back and her red-tinted lips wide with laughter—blew through Grif's mind. He actually jerked his head, unable to imagine her stripped of all that color, sitting in a home with fake rubber plants and food that likely tasted the same.

Grif gave the lone woman one last look, then returned to the reception area to gaze out the window. Kit's Duetto sat silver and gleaming in the sun, and he used it like a lodestar to anchor his attention and settle his mind.

"Mr. Shaw?" The voice rose directly behind Grif, deep and booming, and he turned to find himself facing the widest chest he'd ever seen. Scanning arms like boulders, and a head that looked to be made of the same, Grif was tempted to scale the man. Unfortunately, he'd left all his climbing equipment back in the Everlast.

"I'm Mr. Allen," the walking outcrop said, holding out his hand. "I'm Mr. Zicaro's Life Enrichment Coordinator. I'll escort you to his room."

It was like shaking hands with a bear, and Grif discreetly flexed his fingers at his side once they were released. Turning, Mr. Allen motioned with his other paw for Grif to follow him across the dining room. Grif did so silently, noting that even as Allen's shadow fell across the two residents, even when he gave a cheerful hello, they didn't acknowledge him. He extended the same greeting to the lone woman in the dining area.

"That's Martha," Allen said softly once they'd passed. "She's in her own little world. Many of the residents here are."

Grif glanced back and was startled to catch Martha's watery blue gaze, but then she shifted and he realized, no, she was looking right through him.

"Ya know, I think I'll go wash my hands first before heading back," Grif said suddenly. The impatience that flashed over Allen's features was erased so quickly that Grif wasn't sure he'd seen it, and he gestured back to the reception area with a smile. Grif accessed the restrooms there—stalling for time, hoping Kit was already with Zicaro—but he also needed the moment to splash water over his face and clear his head. To clear Martha's vacant look from his mind.

Please, God. Don't let Evie be in a place like this.

"I know Al will be happy to have a visitor," Mr. Allen said as soon as Grif returned. If he noted the way Grif had paled, he said nothing as he led him to the residents' hallway. "Not one person has stopped by in the time he's been here."

"I just got back in town," Grif said, and realized he sounded defensive.

Allen just nodded, lips pursed. Lonely tenants were likely nothing new. "Mind if we take the stairs?" he asked. He was obviously a man who valued his exercise.

Their footsteps echoed in the empty stairwell, and Grif wondered how a place teeming with people could feel so empty. When they reached the second-floor landing, they stepped into a hall identical to the one below. "This floor is obviously reserved for our more agile residents. Al has lost a few steps, but don't worry. He's kept his zing."

Remembering what he did of Al Zicaro, Grif wasn't sure if that was a good thing. He just hoped there wasn't anything wrong with Zicaro's ticker. If he recognized Grif as the man he'd reported on fifty years earlier, he might just have a heart attack.

Mr. Allen stopped before a door that barely obscured the sound of a blaring television, and rapped loudly. Room 238. The same one Grif had texted to Kit as soon as Erin had relayed it to him. Head tilted, Allen shot Grif a calm, closed-mouthed smile as he listened at the door for movement. There was nothing beyond the voice of a female news anchor.

Allen rapped again. "Mr. Z? You got a visitor. I'm gonna come on in now, okay?"

He palmed the handle as he whispered to Grif, "We keep all the residents' doors unlocked so the caregivers can respond quickly to emergency calls, with medicines, bath times . . . that sort of stuff."

Grif barely contained his shudder. At least in the Everlast he could pretend he had some semblance of independence and privacy. This sort of care indicated a sort of demoralizing dependency, and the Al Zicaro he'd known—bespectacled and suspicious and high-strung—would absolutely feel the same.

"Well, that's strange," Mr. Allen said, his mask of politeness turning to a frown. "He usually answers immediately."

"He probably can't hear you above the TV," Grif said, as Allen twisted the door handle and poked his head inside. His surprised grunt confirmed Zicaro wasn't in the room, and Grif plastered a look of mild confusion on his face. If there was ever a woman who could draw a man out of his shell, it was Kit.

"Maybe you should check the can," Grif said helpfully as Allen swung the door wide, already heading into the second room of the small suite.

"I don't understand," he called back loudly. "We usually have to beg him to come out. He's always in here watching the news, taking notes, talking to himself."

Grif could see that. A large-screen television took up an entire wall, angled in the corner to face a room that was empty but for one wide lounge chair. That was flanked by a floor lamp and an unimpressive, if sturdy, side table. A command center for one, thought Grif, noting the yellow notepads and sticky notes, dozens of pens in a coffee cup bearing the Sunset Retirement Community's logo: WHERE FRIENDS BECOME FAMILY.

Though not readily apparent, Grif sensed a sort of order to the papers mounded everywhere. A nondescript desk sat beneath the room's only, curtainless window, the slats of the cheap metal blinds cutting across the stacked papers in harsh blades of light. Copies of the *Trib,* Kit's family's paper, and the one Zicaro had worked at for so many years, were stacked beneath the desk and along the wall in tottering stacks.

Curious, Grif reached for the edition lying on top. It was

dated two years back. He didn't know what was going on with Al Zicaro's body, but he clearly still had a very busy mind.

"He's not here," Mr. Allen said, returning to the room. Grif dropped the paper back atop its stack, and gave Allen an amiable smile. He could afford it, since a quick glimpse out the window had revealed another couple making their way along a path with a sign pointing toward the gardens. The woman was pushing the man in a wheelchair, but their heads were bent close together, one with thick, dark hair sporting a bright pink rose, and the other completely bald.

"That's okay." Grif leaned against the desk, blocking Allen's view. "I'm more than happy to wait."

Despite the news broadcast blaring from Al Zicaro's room, the man had responded to Kit's gentle knock with surprising alacrity. The image that popped into her mind when she first saw him was of a plucked chicken, one with a few strands of gray hair sprouting atop a freckled pate, and an assessing dark gaze that pierced his bifocals. He took one look at Kit, leaned his full weight on his walker, and scowled. "If you've come to offer me my old job back, I don't want it."

"You recognize me," Kit said, placing a hand on the door when he moved to shut it.

"Of course I do."

She wasn't surprised. Though they'd never met before, she could see a vast expanse of hard-copy clippings sprawling over the walls of the room behind him. He obviously kept up with the news. Besides, as the heiress to the town's largest newspaper—no longer the jewel it once was but still a respected voice in the community—she'd be recognizable to anyone in the *Trib*'s extended journalistic family.

"But you don't seem surprised to see me, Uncle Al." She used his pet name intentionally, though he was no uncle to her. She was hoping it would calm him.

Zicaro's thin top lip raised in a snarl instead. "I always knew that someday a representative of the Wilson family dynasty would end up crawling to my doorstep on hands and knees."

Kit laughed brightly. "Oh no, honey. Not in this outfit." She whirled, showing off her fit-and-flare skirt. "Besides, these gloves are vintage. They don't touch the floor."

Zicaro just growled. "Wanna hear the spiel I've been practicing for just this day?"

Kit shrugged and crossed her arms. "If you feel you must."

"Go to hell!" he yelled, and tried to slam the door.

Kit's arms shot out, more firmly this time, and her lashes fluttered as Zicaro's wiry eyebrows almost lifted to where his hairline used to be. "I wasn't the one who fired you, Zicaro. I'm a different kind of reporter. And I aim to be a different kind of editor one day, too."

Zicaro refused to be appeased. Eyes bulging, he leaned close, his hot breath washing over Kit's face. "The world doesn't need a different kind of reporter! I was the best that paper had! I brought readers rock-solid reportage and exciting news angles."

"You claimed the Nevada Test Site was building robotic soldiers, financed by the U.S. Treasury."

"And nobody ever proved me wrong!" Zicaro shouted, pumping one fist into the air. He began to topple and righted himself by grabbing at his walker. It didn't slow him down any. "Yet my own paper, the one I'd given thirty-one years of service to, never a deadline missed, gave my beat to some uppity, backstabbing cub and then threw me out like trash!"

Kit bit her lip and mentally recalibrated the situation.

Clearly, she wasn't going to talk Zicaro out of his memories. She didn't have time to argue over whether artificial intelligence really existed, either. So she decided to appeal to his ego instead.

"You obviously haven't been doing your homework," she said, causing his dentures to grind. She hurried on before he could move to slam the door again. "If you had, then you'd know that when I say I'm different, I mean that I'm different like *you*. I'm not afraid to get my hands dirty. I go after the truth, no matter where it might lead. And I've had more brushes with danger than an entire robotic army could dish out . . . not that you'd know anything about it."

She turned to leave, and got just as far as she'd expected. Zicaro's reedy voice chased her into the hall. "Don't tell me what I do and don't know, missy! I was penning bylines before you were ever born. You're Katherine Craig, daughter of the doomed paper-princess, Shirley Wilson Craig, and of the man who was killed as much for the knowledge in his head as the badge on his chest."

Kit whirled, and sharp-eyed Zicaro caught her flinch and laughed. "That's right, I know all about you. From your rocky start at your own paper to the way you shut down a kiddie prostitution ring. I know about the way you got yourself mixed up with those drug cartels last year, too. You *do* have a knack for getting in trouble, Craig . . . and I admire that. Question is, can you get out of it, too?"

She held out her arms, palms up. "I'm here, aren't I?"

She meant that she'd survived both those stories, but Zicaro snorted as he tapped at his freckled scalp. "Yeah, and my Scooby senses tell me you're getting *into* more trouble . . . and aim to take me with you."

He began to shut the door.

"Whatever," Kit said, tossing him the word that summed up her entire generation. It had to irk him. It irked *her*, but then she'd never been one to shrug off anything lightly. "You're so old now you likely couldn't help me if you wanted to."

The door cracked against the wall inside, and, already smiling, Kit turned again, this time catching Al Zicaro in all his aged glory: bony knees sticking out from beneath striped boxers, a ribbed tank revealing more hair on his chest than on his head. He pushed the walker into the hall before him like it was a shield.

"You little pissant! I've got more knowledge stored in my left ass cheek than you do in that entire pretty head of yours! So roll that up and smoke it for a while."

"Really?"

"Hell yeah!"

His face had gone red and mottled, his rib cage heaving as he glared at her, and, wondering if she'd pushed him a little too much, Kit took a placating step forward. "Then why don't you tell me about a woman named Barbara McCoy, who recently returned to the valley after fourteen long years away?"

The question didn't surprise Zicaro the way it should have, and seeing her note it, he colored and turned back around. "No."

"Yes," she retorted, following so that she could stick her foot in the door this time. Her shoes were vintage patent leather, too, but she'd sacrifice them if she had to. "Why did you call Barbara on Friday?"

He fell back a step at that, eyes going wide, and Kit reached out a hand to steady him, but he shook it off. "Who told you that?"

Kit just shook her head. She was asking the questions now. "What did you mean when you told her you weren't going to get rubbed on her account? What was she into that you were so wary of?"

"I don't gotta tell you squat!"

Kit inclined her head. "True, but here's what I already know. Barbara was a user, a nasty woman who liked to mess with people. She had secrets that went all the way back to her time as a kingpin's wife, and an old newshound like you might prove particularly useful to her."

"A DiMartino active in the valley again," he said, almost to himself. He smacked his lips as he leaned forward. "You think she's working with someone? Like a conspiracy?"

"You tell me."

Zicaro made a sucking sound through his teeth, and Kit waited. She didn't insert herself in the doorway, banking instead on his satisfaction that someone was finally listening to him. Finally, he motioned her inside.

But Kit shook her head. "Let's go for a walk."

"I don't walk so well."

"And I don't trust this place." She tilted her head at him. "Do you?"

He said nothing to that, but his averted gaze spoke volumes.

Feeling the momentum swing her way, Kit pushed. After all, Grif could only stall for so long. "Someone is telling you that you're safe here, am I right? That there's security? That Barbara and the DiMartinos and the past can't get to you here? Is that why you stay? Is it why you keep your television volume so high? Or why you probably check for bugs in your room? For drugs in your . . . drugs?"

Kit was reaching now, but Zicaro's expression was blasted

wide like he'd been waiting for someone to confirm all his greatest worries. He shook his head, and it was like erasing a drawing on an Etch A Sketch. Wonder replaced his anger. "You *are* paranoid."

"And you're a legend," she said firmly, holding his sharp gaze.

It was his emotional trifecta. She'd appealed to his reason, his ego, and his pride. He considered her with narrowed eyes, then nodded once. "Let me get my wheelchair."

Kit nodded too . . . then inclined her head. "Don't forget your pants."

How do you know Mr. Z?" Mr. Allen asked, making small talk. He'd used the walkie-talkie at his waist to call Erin at the front desk and report Zicaro missing from his room. Grif had assured Allen that he could go look for the old guy himself, but Allen replied politely, and firmly, that under no circumstances could he leave Grif alone in Zicaro's room.

So Grif spouted the same rap he'd told Erin, saying he was an old friend. Since there was an obvious age difference between his thirty-three years and Zicaro's seventy-six, he added that his grandfather had known Zicaro first.

"They were both beat reporters back then," he said as they waited. "My old man followed in Granddad's footsteps, worked at a paper in Philly, but he lost his job in the recession. The newspaper business isn't what it once was."

"Nothing is," Mr. Allen replied in a soft, bland voice. Grif imagined that working in a place like this, he'd seen that first-hand. "And how about you? You in the family business as well?"

Grif hesitated, but Allen's wide face held nothing more than mere curiosity. "Nah. I don't have the newshound bug in me. All that fact-checking, you know. I'm a man who relies more on gut instinct."

Mr. Allen smiled. "Me, too."

Then the phone rang at his hip. Turning away, Grif feigned interest in the wall clippings, glancing at Allen while trying to appear as though he were not watching. He wanted to go through each and every stack of paper. He had a feeling there were more answers he and Kit were seeking in Al Zicaro's humble room than in the rest of the entire Las Vegas Valley, yet Mr. Allen headed back into the adjoining bedroom just as he put the phone to his ear, and that wouldn't do. Why was a Life Enrichment Coordinator taking personal calls while on duty? Wouldn't Erin have contacted him via the walkie-talkie at his other hip?

Grif followed, peering into the bedroom in time to catch Allen leaning over the nightstand, staring out the single window. It faced the same direction as the one over the desk, so Kit and Zicaro would be easy to spot if they hadn't moved quickly. But what really had Grif holding his breath was the holster attached to the belt at the small of Allen's back. A Life Enrichment Coordinator with a gun? That, along with the flash of white outside the window—two orderlies jogging in the same direction as Kit and Zicaro—brought Grif around the corner.

He kept his feet light and his movements relaxed as he slipped into the room, and just stared when Allen—still squatted low—turned back around. His worry for Kit must have shown. Maybe his shoulders were already drawn in a fighter's hunch, or perhaps Mr. Allen didn't like the way he flexed his fingertips.

Or maybe it was simply uncomfortable for a man used to towering over others to turn and find himself eye-level with Grif's chest.

"What do you mean he's with someone?" Allen said into the receiver, eyes rising to meet Grif's. His gaze was no longer questioning or kind, and he was careful to remain in his half-crouch as if unwilling to scare a sleeping cobra. Good instinct. Because that's exactly what Grif felt like, knowing that two men were after Kit.

Never losing eye contact, Mr. Allen whispered into the phone. "I don't care if it is a woman. Round her up . . . because she's not working alone."

The plan had been for Kit to lead Zicaro away from the building, then circle back around to the Duetto in the front lot. That would keep them out of the eye of the surveillance cameras for as long as possible. However, Kit and Grif had clearly underestimated the staff's interest in Zicaro.

Allen slowly lowered the phone from his ear as he straightened. Grif shifted, catching the slight bend in Allen's knees, the looseness in the elbows. He leaned forward at the waist, a way to keep from telegraphing his lunge, and his left foot was forward, marking him as a righty. He had at least forty pounds on Grif, and from the way he mirrored Grif's readiness, he knew how to use it.

"What an accomplished Life Enrichment Coordinator," Grif said flatly.

"Who are you?" Mr. Allen said.

"The guy with a gun pointed at your chest."

Allen's gaze flicked to Grif's hands, empty and hanging at his sides.

"Oh, yeah." Grif rolled his eyes, pulled the gun from his

pocket, and pointed it at Allen's chest before the other man had even blinked. He'd taken it from his ankle holster and readied it when Allen had slipped into the bedroom. "*Now* I'm the man with a gun pointed at your chest. Question is, who are *you*?"

Because he wasn't merely some assisted-living helpmate.

"Fuck you."

"That seems to be a very common name these days. And how long have you worked here, Fuck You?"

Allen responded by ducking low and stomping on Grif's right foot at the same time. Grif curled forward automatically, and by the time he saw Allen's uppercut, it was too late. Stars danced before his eyes as his jaw cracked. Were he 100 percent mortal, he'd be out. As it was, he managed to pull Allen with him as he went down, then flipped and stilled the struggling man by tucking his gun in his left ear.

Grif bore down on the guy, breathing hard. How the hell had Allen hit him? He'd read the other man's body language. He should've seen the blow coming. Growling, he shook the worry off for later.

"Why are you watching Al Zicaro so closely?"

Mr. Allen didn't move at all, but Grif was a P.I. with two lifetimes' worth of experience in reading people, and he caught the triumphant cast in the other man's gaze.

"And why," Grif said slowly, "don't the other residents have any idea who you are?"

That drew a smile from Allen, though it was far less kind than the one he'd shared with Grif before. "You have no idea who I am, either."

"Sure I do."

"Who am I then, smartass?"

Grif flipped his gun in one quick motion and walloped Allen in the temple twice, once to get the job done and a second time as payback for the blow he'd unexpectedly delivered to Grif. The big man dropped face-first onto the thin carpeting, and a sick crunching sound came from where his nose used to be. Grif left him facedown as he rifled through his pockets.

"You're Justin Allen," he said, reading from the wallet. "A.k.a. Fuck You."

And he dropped the wallet back on the ground so the man would see it when he came around. Then, locking the door behind him, he went in search of Kit.

Kit often said that she was born at least thirty years too late. She'd have preferred to roam the Las Vegas Valley in its heyday, when the Rat Pack was crooning cool at the Copa and when dressing up for a night out meant donning more clothing and not less. Yet despite her love for crinoline and cocktail culture, rockabilly music and the mid-mod sensibility, Kit had to admit that her nostalgia for all things rockabilly was just that. Everything she'd gone through in the past year—starting with the murder of her best friend and culminating with the loss of Grif, a man literally of that era—had forced her to admit that there was no era unmarred by greed or corruption or just plain meanness. Reality was? Those things touched every life and every time.

Sure, Kit would continue thrifting and jiving and swing-dancing, but the cat's-eye glasses she donned were no longer rose-tinted, and it was with clear vision that she spotted trouble coming from the corner of her eye as she pushed Al Zicaro's wheelchair down a thin walkway behind his home at Sunset.

And this time, Kit was ready.

"How badly do you want to get out of here?" she asked Zicaro, picking up the pace.

He caught the direction of her nervous glance and leaned forward in his chair, eyes bulging behind his bifocals as he spotted the two orderlies rushing their way. "You didn't say nothing about getting out of here."

"You're saying you want to stay?" she said dubiously.

"I'm saying . . . I don't know." He pursed his lips, looking sullen.

"Then why did you grab that?" She jerked her head at the unnatural bulge in his pants, and he covered it with his hands like he was ashamed.

"I bring this with me everywhere. It's the most valuable information I own," Zicaro said, patting his pants to reveal the outline of the plastic container he'd shoved in his pocket. "I even sleep with it under my pillow."

"Uh-huh," she said, glancing behind her, then ahead, mentally calibrating how far it was to the parking lot. "I have a feeling your most valued information is held in your head."

"Got that right, missy," he said proudly.

"Good," she said, and left the path to make a beeline across the grass.

The orderlies broke into a loping run. They'd catch up well before she could gain the corner of the building, forget about reaching the car.

"What the hell is he carrying?" she said, more to herself than Al. The larger man held his right arm in front of him, and was careful not to let it swing as he ran. His hand was folded around something that glinted in the thin sunlight. It looked like . . .

"Oh, that's a gun," Al said matter-of-factly, and Kit stumbled. "They all carry them."

"At an end-of-life care facility?" she said incredulously, and picked up her pace.

"They take their jobs very seriously."

Heart revving, Kit searched for signs of Grif, but there was no other soul nearby. She wondered about angels, though. She worried about plasma.

And she knew she was going to have to use the dark experiences of the past year to handle this herself.

"Just follow my lead," she told Zicaro, and while the guards—not orderlies—were still a hundred yards away, she pulled her lady's pistol from her bucket bag. Then she swiveled the wheelchair around, and held the gun to Zicaro's head.

"Hey!" he tried to climb from the chair while it was still moving, scrawny limbs flailing.

"It's not loaded," she muttered, grabbing his shoulder and yanking him back into his seat. "Now take mental notes, my attentive friend. Because if my hunch is right, you're going to be starring in your next feature story."

The old man's mouth opened and closed a few times, which made him look like a fish pulling at air, but curiosity finally won out and he snapped it shut. Shooting her a saucy wink, he turned back around and put his hands in the air.

The two orderlies—the guards—reared back on their heels.

"Don't come any closer," Kit told them, pitching her voice loud and low, hoping she at least sounded sure of herself. This was improvisation; she and Grif had planned for her to be out of reach well before anyone had noticed Zicaro missing. Again, she wondered what had happened to her reluctant angel.

"Just put the gun down, lady," one of the orderlies said. He was so ginger he was almost blond, florid in the face where he wasn't pockmarked, and destined to wear a boy's face on his man's body for long into old age. He held his free hand out before him, the other poised at the small of his back.

"Since when does an assisted-living facility require armed guards?" she asked, backing away. The two men mirrored the movement but angled their footsteps in opposite directions, trying to flank her. She tapped Zicaro on the shoulder. Getting into the spirit of things, Zicaro flapped his arms a little.

"No, I mean, help me."

"Oh." Zicaro reached for his wheels.

"Just put it down," said the second guard. His gun was still out, and it was all Kit could do not to stare solely at him, yet the other man, though smaller, was moving fast, and she had to keep him in her sights as well.

"No," she said. "Why don't you call the cops instead?"

Neither moved to lift the radios at their waists.

"Maybe we already did," the smaller guy said. His name tag said ERIC. The other's? Harry . . . Barry . . . Larry . . .

Zicaro would know, so Kit let it go for now and bared her teeth, an approximation of a smile. "I hope so. I like the police. I have a lot of friends on the force."

For some reason, that made both men chuckle. "Honey, none of your friends can save you from this mistake."

"Maybe, maybe not," Kit answered, "but they are powerful enough to come out here and investigate this facility and everyone working in it."

"You have no idea what you're doing," Eric said, teeth gritted.

"*You* have no idea what I'm doing," she corrected, and leaned forward. "Here."

She handed Zicaro the gun so that she could pull him backward over the grass. He looked at it for a moment, then cocked back the hammer and pointed it at Larry. He'd drawn close enough for Kit to make out his name now, but he fell back at this and froze as he stared at Zicaro.

The reluctant show of respect emboldened the old man. He flicked the barrel of the gun at Larry, shooing him away. "You thinking about rushing us, buddy?"

"No," Larry said, falling back again. "No."

"Good," Kit said, pausing long enough to meet Larry's hard gaze. "Now I just have one question for you. Why'd you kill Barbara McCoy?"

Zicaro sucked in a sharp breath next to her.

"I don't know what you're—"

Kit jerked her head, cutting him off. "You think I don't recognize you? I was there last night! I saw you."

And though the details were hazy—a jumble of ringing blasts and smoky air and stars that realigned themselves and her fate before her eyes—Kit knew she had seen this man dressed in black, looming over Grif in the moments after Barbara's death. He'd killed a woman in cold blood . . . and Kit? Kit had used the gun that Zicaro now held to fire a warning shot back his way when he was about to do the same to Grif.

And now here he was again, alive and watching over Al Zicaro . . . and looking once more like he wanted to kill her.

"We don't know what you're talking about," Larry lied.

"You will," Kit swore, jerking her chin. "The world will."

And that's when she spotted a giant of a man sprinting toward them all, one arm pumping at his side for speed, the other at his head as if trying to keep it from falling off. His furious expression was visible even three hundred yards away.

Shit. Kit's gaze darted back to the building as if she could see through it to whatever may be happening inside. Where was Grif?

Seeing the other man, Larry returned the gun to the small of his back and folded his arms over his chest. Eric held up his hands and even backed a few steps away, though his gaze had gone predatory. Kit swallowed hard as the giant joined them. At least she knew who was in charge.

"Your move," Larry said, mouth curling in a knowing smile. He was right to be smug. Two on one was a chess match. Three on one, even with a gun in play, was plain stupid. Besides, she didn't even have Zicaro to use as a foil anymore. It was pretty evident that she wasn't going to harm him the moment she handed him the gun.

"Here we go," she warned Zicaro in a low voice, and he made a high-pitched sound in the back of his throat. Kit was having a bit of trouble breathing herself. Muscles tensing, she darted around the building, pushing the wheelchair. The chase was on.

The wide front parking lot was just as Grif and she had left it, absent of any other vehicles, which gave the front of the building an aspect of abandonment. The leafless trees and wilting perennials sat forlornly in the arid chill, and even the birds had fled. The wheels of Zicaro's chair rattled across the pavement, as did his breath, and Kit waited for the shouts to rise behind her . . . and even looked for the plasma that Grif was always going on about. Running, she cast about for the effervescent purling of a mist that was supposed to be invisible to the human eye. If she were about to die, she wanted to know it.

The figure stepped forward, emerging from the redbrick building so quickly that they collided. Kit rammed into the back of Zicaro's head, and her gun flew from his hand. They both squealed . . . but Grif steadied her. Hand gripping her arm, he swiveled so that she was behind him, and then flipped Zicaro around.

"Where the hell have you been?" Kit asked, rushing to pick up the gun.

"Had to make a phone call," he said, moving fast with Zicaro.

"Make a—?"

"Hurry. We gotta get him in the car," Grif said, rolling the chair backward, and Kit hurried to open the Duetto's passenger door. Eric and Larry reeled around the corner just as Zicaro finally managed to swivel in his seat and see who had taken the reins. He took one long look at Grif, let out a strangled squeak, and passed out. Grif caught the old man before he could fall from the chair, lifting him like he weighed no more than a feather.

Kit helped him wedge the old man into the passenger's seat, and it took all of her willpower not to turn to see how close the three men were now. Though they were armed, she had to trust Grif to protect them. She even thought she heard the sharp cutting sound of blades slicing air, and imagined his wings snapped wide to shield them. Even so, it would be an automatic reaction to danger, and though it was effective against supernatural foes, here he was bound by the same laws of nature as everyone else who wore flesh.

As evidenced by what came next.

"Duck," he said, just as the first bullet flew. She fell atop Zicaro and he did the same, so that they all lay flat against the seats. That shielded them from the second bullet as well, but the footsteps were growing closer.

Then, suddenly, everything grew too silent. Kit lifted her head. Zicaro groaned beneath her weight, and she shifted as she looked at Grif, now in a squat at the open door. "What—?"

But they both heard the engine by then, and Grif glanced down at his feet as if looking for something.

"Plasma?" Kit asked.

"Not even a bit." He blew out a breath and offered a hand to Kit. "Looks like we'll live to piss these guys off another day."

Trusting him, Kit reached out and they rose together to face off against the three men on the other side of the lot. None of them held a gun now.

Perhaps because of the police vehicle pulling to a stop between them.

CHAPTER SEVEN

The officer climbing from the driver's seat of the patrol car stared at the three men in the parking lot. His back was to Grif and Kit, though his partner certainly gave them a good once-over. Kit read his badge. OFFICER STOKES.

"Let me guess," Kit whispered to Grif once Officer Stokes glanced the other way. "Your phone call?"

"I figured I've perfected the Lone Angel act, so I decided to give Smart Angel a try," Grif said as he casually shoved his hands into his pants pockets.

Kit had deposited her .22 in the pocket of her flared skirt as soon as she'd spotted the patrol car, but she knew its outline could be seen if one were looking close . . . and Larry was glaring at it pointedly. Yet, despite the hatred flashing in his dark eyes, he said nothing.

"We got a call that there was some trouble out here?" The

first officer still hadn't turned their way but he was tall, and his broad shoulders were currently bunched. His arrival had done nothing to dissipate the tension in the parking lot, and he seemed to know it.

"No problem here," replied the giant man, never taking his eyes off Grif.

The first officer turned to see what or who was so engaging, and if his shoulders had been tight before, they practically rose to his ears now.

Kit's heart dropped into her gut. "Hello, Dennis."

Dennis inclined his head at her feeble wave, eyes shifting to Grif and then back to her, and as was the case recently, he shook his head and sighed.

"Why is it," he finally asked, "that I only see the two of you together when there's trouble?"

"There's no trouble," Grif said, jerking his chin at the men on the other side of the car. "Is there, Justin?"

"Nope," the big guy said, crossing his arms over his chest. They looked like giant clubs. "No trouble at all."

But Dennis was still looking at Kit.

"You're on patrol again?" Kit asked, wishing she could alleviate the weight of his look. It was also gratifying to see the men behind him shrink just a bit at they realized how well she knew him.

"Requested a transfer from Homicide after my leave ended." Dennis shrugged, and then, unable to help himself, he added, "Getting shot was getting a bit old."

He hadn't just been shot. He'd thrown himself in front of a bullet meant for Kit, and the rub for him was that Grif could've prevented the shot from being fired at all. Dennis would have died if Kit hadn't bartered with one of the Pures for his life;

however, he didn't know that. All he knew was that after Grif was out of the picture, Kit had chosen to be alone rather than be with him.

"So what's going on?" he asked her, expression shuttered in professionalism.

Kit shrugged. "Just visiting a friend."

"These guys your friends?" He jerked his head at the three men behind him.

"Sure. New friends, anyway," the large man said affably, and Dennis turned full on him. "How you doin'? I'm Justin Allen. I'm the Life Enrichment Coordinator out here."

"Life Enrichment Coordinator," Dennis repeated, staring at the proffered hand so long that Justin finally withdrew it. Only then did Dennis look up. "What happened to your nose?"

Justin's eyes flashed to Grif as he touched his broken nose, and so did Officer Stokes's. Grif's expression remained carefully blank.

"I took a fall helping one of our residents out to the car. This car," he said, and smiled at Kit and Grif despite his crooked nose.

Officer Stokes leaned to peer around Kit and Grif. "Who is it?"

"Oh, that's just Al," she said, giving a little laugh, but her voice sounded unnatural even to her, and Dennis's eyes narrowed. Behind him, Justin broke into a less careful grin.

"Could we meet him?" said Officer Stokes.

"Meet him?" Kit asked.

Grif took her by the arm and pulled her to the side. If he noticed the way Dennis's jaw tightened when he touched Kit, he didn't show it.

"Mind if I approach your car?" Officer Stokes said.

Kit and Grif answered at the same time.

"Of course not—"

"Sure—"

Now Justin chuckled.

Officer Stokes drew near just as a groan sounded from the front seat. "Is this man okay?"

Al Zicaro's head popped up in the front seat so quickly that Officer Stokes took a full step back. "Sir? Are you all right?"

But Zicaro was squinting past him, rubbing his eyes like he couldn't believe what he was seeing. When he rose, Grif nodded and gave him a sheepish shrug. Zicaro broke into a giant grin and hurtled himself forward.

"Why, you old dog!" he shouted, using the car to steady himself before throwing his arms around Grif's shoulders. Zicaro pounded his back with surprising strength before pulling away to regard Grif in closer detail. "Just look at you. Either my eyes are bad or your genes are good, because you haven't changed a bit!"

"Hasn't he?" asked Justin from his post behind Dennis. Kit shot him a dirty look, but that just made his smile widen. Dennis noticed it, and his frown deepened.

"Nope," Zicaro said, oblivious to the tension around him. He removed his bifocals and rubbed them on his shirt. "What's it been? Fifty years or so? Look at you, you look *good*!"

"Not quite that long, I don't think," Grif muttered, then rolled his eyes at Stokes, as if to say, *These old-timers.*

Officer Stokes relaxed enough to lean on the hood of the patrol car. "So if everyone's so friendly here, why did we get a call that there's trouble?"

"Sorry about that," Justin said. "It was likely Mr. Blakely. He's our newest resident. We try to monitor the phone in his room, but sometimes he slips one by us. Guess we'll have to take it out altogether. We encourage our residents to be as independent as possible, but sometimes the elderly can be a harm . . . even to themselves."

Kit filed away the lie, along with the knowledge that these men—no "caregivers"—didn't want the police nosing around. For now, it gave her and Grif the upper hand. At least, until Zicaro spoke again.

"Jiminy Crickets, I thought you were dead!" he exclaimed, still shaking his head as he reached back for his wheelchair. He plopped down, exhaling loudly. "We all did!"

"Why would you think that?" Officer Stokes asked, also likely wondering why the man in their car seemed to be only now recognizing Grif.

"Yeah," said Justin cheerily. "Why?"

"Because Griffin Shaw has a knack for getting himself in sticky situations," Dennis said, out of the blue. Kit froze. All three men behind him *beamed*.

"He does?" Larry asked, earning an elbow in the ribs from Eric.

"You mean ol' Griffin Shaw?" Justin said, drawing out the name. Grif sighed.

"Yup," Dennis said, seemingly oblivious to the way the men were digesting this information. "And everyone around him, too."

"Like who?" Justin asked, before jerking his head at Kit. "Like her?"

"Dennis," Kit said, before he could say her name. "Can I talk to you for a moment, please? Privately?"

"Sorry. I'm on the clock," he huffed, giving her and Grif one last glance before turning his back on them both. He jerked his head at Justin. "We're going to have to make sure there's nobody inside who needs help. It's procedure."

"Of course," Justin said magnanimously, gesturing to the building. He shot a wink at Zicaro, then put a finger to his chin like he'd just remembered something vital. "But I don't think the young lady signed in. If you'll be so kind as to accompany us?"

Kit didn't move.

"That's okay," Dennis said, misreading her hesitancy. She could tell from the way his gaze darkened that he thought it had to do with him. "She looks like she's in a hurry."

Kit almost breathed a sigh of relief.

"I'll sign in for her."

And then she wanted to cry.

Justin clapped his approval, then pointed one of his sausage fingers at Zicaro. "Now, Al, you make sure you get back before curfew. We don't want to worry about you getting into any sticky situations . . . especially considering you're with Griffin Shaw."

"Ol' Griffin Shaw," said Larry, rocking happily on his heels.

"C'mon," Dennis said, and without even looking at Kit, he and Justin turned toward the building. Officer Stokes gave Kit and Grif a polite nod, shut the door of the patrol car, and followed. The two orderlies, though, remained where they were. They watched Grif and Kit pile Zicaro and his wheelchair into her Duetto, memorizing Kit's license plate. Watching them drive off.

Filing it all away for later.

Man, that was close," Al Zicaro said as soon as they cleared the lot. He craned his chicken neck around, making sure they weren't being followed, face bright and eyes shining. Kit and Grif flanked him, shoulders hunched in the tight front seat. Feeling their gazes upon him, Zicaro turned back around. "What? I haven't been that close to being busted by the fuzz in years!"

"Why would they want to bust you?" Grif asked.

"Because they know I'm onto them," Zicaro said, emphasizing each word.

Grif said, "I'm the one who called them."

"And thank you for that," Kit put in, peering around Zicaro to meet Grif's eye.

"Sure," Grif replied, and couldn't help but add, "Gave you a chance to see your old buddy Dennis again."

Kit stared straight ahead, jaw clenched, and Grif sighed. He shouldn't have said that. He could tell from Dennis's reaction that they weren't seeing each other, and it clearly wasn't by the other man's choice. Besides, she wasn't Grif's girl anymore. In fact, it felt like she belonged more to herself than ever before. But it still sent a white-hot pang soaring through his gut to see another man look at her with the same sort of hunger gnawing in his own belly.

"So *why* would the cops be after you?" he asked Zicaro, getting back on track.

Zicaro put his hands down his pants.

"Oh, God," Kit said, gripping the wheel, eyes trained on the road.

But the old man just pulled out a plastic denture case, and shook it. Grif relaxed. He'd been wondering what was going on down there. "Because they've been keeping tabs on me, and they know I've got this."

Kit glanced over, then immediately directed her car into the first strip mall they saw so that Zicaro could relate his whole story to them over three cups of overpriced coffee.

"The Sunset Retirement Community isn't just an end-of-life facility," Zicaro began, once they were settled. Steam rose from their cups in comforting deceit. Nothing was settled; this was only respite. "It began as a retirement community, which is how I got there. But a year ago everything changed."

"What changed?"

"Sunset was taken over by a new company. The workers were summarily fired and replaced by new staff. The caregivers changed overnight. Long-term residents were allowed to stay, because we had contracts, like leases, and I don't think they wanted to draw attention to themselves by turning a bunch of old geezers out on their behinds." He shot them a winning smile. "We're predisposed to complain and have all the time in the world to do it. But they didn't allow any new retirees in after that."

"Is that when Larry and Eric came along?" Kit asked, and was given a quick nod.

"And Justin." Zicaro explained how he was rousted in the middle of the night and taken to the administrative office, where Justin quizzed him about his relationship with one Barbara DiMartino. "That's why I was so surprised when you said she was dead. Is it true? Did they kill her?"

Kit nodded, and reached out to give his hand a quick squeeze. "I know it's hard to hear, Al, and we're going to find out why, but just to be clear . . . they called her DiMartino? Not Barbara McCoy?"

"Yup, and that's when I knew something was fishy." He turned to Grif. "But you know my history with the DiMartino crew. We weren't what you would call friendly."

"You were what I might call downright antagonistic."

Zicaro beamed.

"How long did Justin question you that night?" Kit asked, taking notes, ordering them in her mind.

Zicaro shook his head so that his neck-skin wobbled. "Not sure. But by the time it was over I was thirsty and tired, and would've said anything he wanted if he'd just let me go."

"And what did he want?"

"Your guess is as good as mine! All I know is that they moved my room!"

"What do you mean they moved your room?"

Zicaro's eyes bugged. "Instead of returning me to my old room they took me to one on the second floor. That's where the overnight staff bunks up. And when I walked in? All my stuff was waiting for me. It looked as though I'd lived there for years."

"Anything missing?" Kit asked, lips pursed.

"Hard to tell. All I know is that they trained cameras on me twenty-four/seven after that. Not that they said as much, of course, but I knew it. There was an alarm system on my suite door, my phone was tapped, and I even caught them searching my papers at night." He winked at Kit. "That's when I stopped taking my meds."

Zicaro didn't seem to notice Kit and Grif's shared look.

"I'm watched day and night," he said, shaking his head. "I was essentially kidnapped, and now I'm never, under any circumstances, permitted to leave the grounds. I'm a hostage. A prisoner in my own home!"

"I dunno, Al," Grif said, leaning back, folding his hands around his coffee cup. "Sounds like one of your own conspiracy stories."

"Grif!" Kit said. "Those men had guns!"

Zicaro nodded vigorously, strands of hair wisping atop his head. "They were cops! Or military! That's how they knew how to interrogate me, what questions to ask. That's how they got the technology to bug my room!"

Grif just raised his eyebrows. Equally skeptical, Kit nonetheless tried to keep her tone neutral. "Big Brother watching? The Man holding us down?"

Zicaro's shoulders drew up, his eyes bulged, and he began to visibly shake. "And clearly I was onto something, wasn't I? And then something happened that surprised everyone."

"Barbara came to visit."

"Damn it!" Zicaro pumped his fist at Kit. "You've been spying, too!"

"Relax," Grif said, rolling his eyes. "We heard the message you left on Barbara's phone."

"Oh." Zicaro thought for a moment, clearly considering whether that constituted spying, then shrugged. Apparently he was only bothered when someone was *watching* him. "She left at the end of visiting hours on Friday. Justin and his cronies had gone for the day, but I knew the interrogations would start up again in earnest the next day. And I knew they wanted something from me that I didn't have. So I decided to figure out what."

So Zicaro planned a break-in, from within, just after the med techs' evening rounds.

"It was just like the movies," he said, fingers splaying as he leaned forward in his chair. "Except better. I even borrowed the military uniform from the guy next door just in case I was seen. He's known to wander."

Kit looked at Grif. "Weird."

Grimacing, Grif nodded.

"The administrative offices are located at the exact opposite side of the building from the residences. No security patrol there at all."

"I saw them," Grif said.

"At first all I found were personnel forms and patient charts and the usual admissions data. I tried to access the main desktop, but it was password-protected. Finally, I jimmied open a file cabinet, and that's when I hit pay dirt. These."

He flipped open his denture case and out clattered three small black objects. "Disk drives."

"Flash drives," Kit corrected.

"Whatever." Zicaro rolled them like dice across the table. "I took them back to my room and hid 'em in my dentures box. They never look in here."

"So what's on them?" Kit asked.

"How the hell do I know?" Zicaro shrugged. "I don't own a computer. But it might have something to do with you."

Grif blinked in surprise, realizing Zicaro was looking at him. "Why me?"

"Because Barbara didn't visit out of the blue just because she was concerned for my health," Zicaro said, eyeing Grif carefully. "She was there because she wanted to know about you."

CHAPTER EIGHT

They reached a bit of an impasse after that. Grif asked Zicaro what Barbara had wanted to know about him, but Zicaro only shrugged, saying she'd left as soon as she realized he had nothing to tell. And why would he? Grif had been dead for all but one of the past fifty years.

After that, they all agreed they next needed to find out what was on those flash drives. Yet after the standoff at Sunset, Kit no longer felt safe heading home. If Dennis had signed her name in the Sunset guest book, then Justin and company now knew who she was, and likely where she lived.

"What about the paper?" Zicaro said, eyes glinting as he wheeled himself back out to the car. He was practically salivating at the chance to get back into the newsroom, and his craggy face fell a good inch when Kit shook her head.

"I can't go around Marin. Not on this." Though it was possible. Ever since Marin's life had been threatened the previous summer, she had loosened her grip on her reins at the paper. She no longer overnighted in her office, and even took a full day off each week without going in at all. Most would still consider her a workaholic, but Kit had watched her aunt work a seventy-five-hour workweek for years, and the difference was glaring.

Grif finally spoke, saying what she knew he would, even though it was the last thing she wanted to do. "So maybe she could help."

Of course, she could . . . and she would, too. But it still galled Kit to ask.

Seeing it, Grif put a hand on her shoulder. "Now is not the time for pride."

No . . . and so they headed directly to her aunt's town house, located on a west Vegas golf course with sprawling views of the ninth green. Kit didn't call ahead, and the guard at the gate recognized her, or at least her vintage Duetto, and just waved her in. That's why her breath caught when Marin answered the door in a silk robe, one far too decadent for the late-afternoon hours. Zicaro whistled softly from his wheelchair, and Grif tilted his head like he'd never seen her before. As for Kit, she blushed the same bright hue as Marin before clearing her throat. "We need help."

Six months earlier, she'd have thought nothing of showing up on Marin's doorstep with her former lover and a paranoid senior citizen. They were family, and Marin would know in a glance that Kit was desperate, and that would be enough. Yet an ever-widening wedge had grown between them since Kit discovered that Marin had knowingly withheld information about the murder of Kit's father. They worked in the same office, they saw each other daily, but conversations were short and never personal.

And now Kit was on her doorstep with another case that could bring harm to them all. She bit her lip, wondering if that was immediately apparent. Probably, from the way Marin's eyes narrowed as she spotted Grif. She opened the door wide anyway.

"Hello," said Zicaro, holding out a hand. "I'm—"

"Crazy Uncle Al," Marin finished shortly, earning a scowl from the old man. Grif flared his eyes at Kit, but she only shrugged. Marin ran the paper like a sea captain facing down the perfect storm. The longitudes and latitudes, and indeed all the workings of the bowl-like valley, were seared in her brain. She knew exactly who Al Zicaro was.

And it was that mental cache of information that Kit needed now.

"The Wilson family archives are infamous," Zicaro enthused when Kit told him where they were going. "Is it true that she's ferreted away every story ever brought to her in her whole tenure as editor in chief?"

Not just every story, but every rumor, old wives' tale, eyewitness account, and bedroom gossip . . . whether it could be substantiated or not. It was a habit she'd learned from her own father, and no matter how great or minute the information, if there was even the hint of truth to it, she squirreled it away. "Some people hoard money or collect tchotchkes," Kit told Zicaro. "Marin stockpiles information."

And so focused was Kit on getting that information that it was only after the door had shut behind them, and Kit was leading the way into the familiar living area, that she smelled the vanilla-scented candles burning in the air, accompanied by the remnants of what could only be a late, or very extended, brunch.

"Hello." The sight of the petite blond woman seated in the corner of Marin's slipcovered sofa had Kit pulling up short.

"I'm sorry," she said, turning toward her aunt. "We interrupted your evening. Er, afternoon."

"You're not sorry," Marin replied, sweeping into the room with the wave of her hand, before resecuring the sash at her waist. "Would you like some wine?"

Zicaro, missing the sarcasm in the question, wheeled past Kit to enter the room, heading straight for the dining-room table. "Absolutely."

"No," said Kit, putting one hand on his chair and the other on her forehead. "Oh . . . shit."

Chuckling, the other woman rose from the sofa and offered her hand. "I'm Amelia. It's good to finally meet you."

"Kit Craig," Kit replied, shaking hands.

The lines bracketing Amelia's eyes deepened with her smile. "I know who you are."

A sense of sadness swirled in Kit's gut as she realized she couldn't say the same. Pulling away from Marin didn't just mean they were out of touch at work, it meant she was disconnected from the only living family she had left in this world. Strange how sometimes you didn't notice how much you missed that sort of connection until faced with it again. Blowing out a hard breath, she tried to ward off her sadness by motioning to the others. "This is Griffin Shaw and that's Al Zicaro."

Grif shook Amelia's hand as well, but Zicaro had already made his way to the wine. Apparently they didn't offer sauce with the meds at Sunset.

Marin just smirked. "So what's a reporter, a P.I., and a washed-up newshound—"

"Hey!" That finally drew Zicaro's attention from his wine-glass.

"—doing on my doorstep on a Sunday afternoon?"

The uneasiness fell away as Kit explained about Barbara McCoy's murder, Zicaro's kidnapping, and the beef that'd chased them from Sunset. Marin was silent throughout the telling, just biting her lip while Amelia stood behind her, head tilted attentively. Kit didn't worry about her presence. If Marin trusted her, she was worthy of it.

It made Kit's feud with her aunt, she thought, pointedly ironic.

"Can I see the flash drives?" Marin finally asked.

Zicaro immediately stuck his hands down his pants. When he tried to hand the plastic drives to Marin, she leaned back in her chair and gestured for Amelia to take it.

"Wait a minute . . ." Zicaro drew his arm back.

"Amelia is a computer nut. I can locate information easily enough in the family archives, but if those things are encrypted she'll be able to crack them well before me. Not to mention flag any unusual files."

"And why would she?" Grif asked, earning a glare from Kit, even though she was thinking the same thing herself.

"Because I'm happy to help Marin's beloved niece in any way I can." Amelia smiled, once again holding out her hand. "And I owe Marin for saving my nonprofit with a particularly timely piece on the city council member who was trying to shut it down."

Marin scoffed, a sound that meant Amelia owed her noth-ing. The sound stuttered when her gaze found Kit's.

You owe me, Kit thought, but said nothing as Amelia gave Marin's shoulder an encouraging squeeze.

"What else do you know about the men who chased you today?" Marin asked.

"One of the guys' name is Justin Allen," Grif put in. "Calls himself 'Fuck You,' though."

"The others were Larry and Eric," Kit said. "Surnames— and, uh, nicknames—unknown."

They all looked at Zicaro. The old man shrugged, eyes never leaving his full glass. "I never thought to ask while they were drugging me up to my eyeballs."

Marin, at her writing desk, was already scribbling the names down. "Of course I'm going to want something in return."

"The full story, right?" Kit had been anticipating that.

"Hey!" Zicaro was suddenly sitting up in his seat, eyes bulging like an angry bullfrog perched atop the lily pad of Marin's Persian rug. "I got the disks, it's my story!"

Marin may have been seated in her living room wearing nothing more than a kimono, but as she shifted her gaze his way, she was every bit the editor in chief. "Why should I give you a byline? Because your crazy-ass rants finally got you locked up?"

"Marin—"

But she held up one finger, silencing Grif. Kit, too, would've gone easy on the old guy, but she knew better than to interfere. If Zicaro wanted a byline, he'd have to earn it. Knowing it, he straightened in his seat. "I had to put up with those knuckle-heads questioning me day in and day out. It got on my nerves. And the food was crappy there, too."

Marin just stared.

"It's bad if my blood-sugar levels get low," Zicaro told her.

Picking up her own wineglass, Marin shrugged. "Well, my kitchen is closed."

That was Kit's opening. "You know what? I'm pretty hungry, too. Let's go hunt something down while Amelia goes to work on the files, shall we?"

Zicaro sputtered. "But—"

"Thanks again, Marin," Grif said, moving behind Zicaro, clearly intending to wheel him out forcibly if he had to. Yet all Zicaro did was chug his white wine before warning Amelia not to muck up his damned story.

Zicaro was still ranting as Kit swung onto Sahara Avenue and arrowed past a city block advertised as the world's largest gift shop. Kit made polite noises as Zicaro continued to huff and puff, but Grif tuned him out, coming around only when struck by a bony elbow or a faceful of wheezing breath. If the old-timer was going to roll with them, he thought, they were going to have to get a bigger car.

But then Kit swerved and even Zicaro fell silent at the sight of a giant golden cow.

"The Golden Steer?" Zicaro asked, and pumped his bony fists at Kit's answering nod.

Shooting Grif a smile, Kit shrugged. "I think Loony Uncle Al deserves one of the best steaks on earth after his time of enforced confinement. Besides, if the past is intent on rearing its head, we might as well go in for a touch of nostalgia as well."

"Oh, honey," Zicaro said before Grif could reply. "I'd kiss you if it weren't already dangerous enough with you behind that wheel."

He wiggled, doing a little dance when Grif snorted, though

he stopped when Kit exited the car and slammed the door shut, leaving Zicaro to fend for himself.

"Good job, sport," Grif muttered, and went to wrangle with the wheelchair by himself.

They met up with her again inside the Golden Steer, Las Vegas's first steakhouse. Built in 1958, the iconic gold steer out front was still hard to miss, though now overshadowed by spearing towers, plummeting roller coasters, and flashing signs. Yet back in Grif's day, this was the stomping ground of Sinatra, Monroe, the Duke—John Wayne—and every made mobster ever to set foot in the valley. Longhorn steaks at just five bucks a pop, a private dining room, and a hidden exit door just in case the fuzz busted down the front.

The prices had changed in the ensuing years, but the decor had not, and as Grif stared at the mahogany wainscoting and deep velvet wallpaper dotted with landscapes of the Old West, he felt himself being dragged by the collar right back into the past. The burgundy carpeting muffled even Kit's heels as they sidled into the bar. Tuck-and-roll booths could be seen lining the walls, offering both intimacy and a clear view of the entire dining room. The waitstaff, all male and tuxedoed, looked like they'd been there for almost as long as Grif had been dead.

"My God," Grif said, turning around. "Some things never change."

He glanced at Kit, who was watching him carefully. So the old-school atmosphere wasn't a mistake. It'd get Zicaro talking, yes, but after the events of the past day, and in a world where everything changed too quickly, it was nice to take refuge in a place that had roots.

"Thanks," he said softly.

"Don't thank me," she said, and smiled sweetly. "You're paying for it."

The maître d' approached. "Reservations?"

Grif peeled off a bill that made even this jaded man's eyes go wide. "Table for three."

Kit immediately corrected him. "Four, actually," she said, and gestured back to the entrance. Grif turned just as Dennis Carlisle spotted him, and they both scowled. The intimate dining room no longer seemed as homey.

"What?" Kit said, as Dennis joined them. "You called him when we were out at Sunset."

"I called the cops."

"I'm still a cop in my off-hours," Dennis reminded Grif, his gaze almost shining it was so hard.

"And a friend, remember?" Kit said, voice gone soft. Grif's eyes flashed between the two of them, though he relaxed a bit when he saw Dennis doing the same with Kit and him.

And Dennis *was* off duty, his jeans cuffed high, T-shirt sleeves rolled, hair now slicked with enough grease that the candlelit tables might prove a danger. He, too, looked like he'd just walked out of the fifties, though the maître d' didn't seem to appreciate it as much.

Dennis caught the look. "I brought a jacket," he said before the man could speak, and he shrugged into a sports coat while Kit nudged Grif. He sighed, dug into his wallet for another bill, and handed it over.

"This way." The maître d' led them to a corner booth where Zicaro shunted aside his wheelchair and squeezed in between Dennis and Kit. Oblivious to the tension at the table, he proceeded to pore over the timeless menu, face stretched in glee. "Look at that! Beef and spuds!"

Grif and Dennis, seated across from each other, propped their menus in front of their faces.

"So," Grif finally said, eyes trained on his menu. "Still like the beat?"

"Why wouldn't I?" Dennis replied flatly. Kit swallowed, almost audibly, and bent her head over her menu, too. "Every day is different. You never know if you're going to get a domestic disturbance, a routine traffic stop. An anonymous tip about a dead woman in a high-rise apartment."

Dropping his menu, Grif speared a look at Kit, and this time Dennis's gaze, too, stuck.

"It's *Dennis,*" she said, with a lift of her slight shoulders, causing Grif to sigh and pinch the bridge of his nose.

"So are you going to tell me about it?" Dennis asked, flicking his napkin to his lap.

"We all are," Kit said, but didn't look him in the eye.

Nope, Grif thought, as the waiter poured water and brought bread. They hadn't been seeing each other. He'd have felt good about that except that his relief came at Dennis's expense. And what had the poor sap done, really? He'd fallen for Kit, he'd taken a bullet for her and almost died because of it. Nothing Grif wouldn't have done himself.

Except that he hadn't.

"And how's the head?" Grif asked, more softly, jerking his chin at Dennis's right ear. The hair had grown back in the months since his hospital stay, but a bright red scar still peeked from underneath.

"Pretty good," Dennis admitted, unconsciously touching the scar. "The doc gave me a clean bill of health. Said it was a miracle I didn't die."

Grif nodded. Miracles were commonplace when one was

possessed by the Pure. Even if the angel was only using the body to manipulate his environment, and, he thought, looking at Kit, those in it.

"I'm glad, Dennis," Grif finally said, lowering his menu and nodding once. "Really. You saved Kit's life, you did it square. It was the bravest damned thing I've ever seen."

And just like that, the tension eased from the room. Dennis's hunched shoulders dropped, and the hardness left his gaze so that he looked both younger and more himself. Kit let out an audible sigh next to Grif.

"And now that we've got that settled," Kit said, which was clearly what she'd intended all along, "let's eat."

CHAPTER NINE

Breaking bread with another person went a long way toward smoothing over old hurts. What started out as a tense reunion between Kit and the two men who had most defined her personal life over the past year gradually eased into an amicable evening. Following up that broken bread with seared filets; fat, round wines; and tableside Bananas Foster settled both bellies and old grudges for good, and Kit smiled to herself as she leaned back in the booth, mentally patting herself on the back.

The stop at the Golden Steer had been a spontaneous but inspired bit of theater. However, her gut had told her they all needed it. There were bad things coming in the next few days—Kit could feel it even without Barbara's death or Grif's sudden reappearance in her life—and her gut also whispered that she was going to need both Grif and Dennis working as a team if she was to survive the forces she'd put into motion by visiting Barbara in the first place. There were more balls to juggle now that her unlikely team also included Zicaro and Marin, but she'd acted as ringmaster in this sort of circus before.

And if grilled meat in the belly and burned sugar in the air were needed to keep the lions tame, then so be it.

Otherwise, it was a hell of an almost-last supper.

"Schwear to God," Zicaro was saying, spilling gin over the lip of his martini glass for a half-a-dozenth time, "I saw Monroe sitting right in this very booth. Saw her with my own eyes. She was with DiMaggio, though they were already divorced. And she was throwing her head back, opening her mouth with that wide, beautiful smile. Showing her neck . . ." He threw his head back to demonstrate. Grif and Dennis both cringed. "But when she stopped laughing with him, man, she was looking right at me."

"Bullshit," Grif snorted, looking relaxed for the first time since Kit had seen him. He'd taken off his jacket and hat, and had one arm flung over the back of the red leather booth, his shirtsleeves rolled, candlelight sparkling in his stubble. "You were even a scrawnier sonna bitch then than you are now, and Monroe liked 'em beefy."

"How do you even know that, Shaw?" Dennis asked, while Zicaro scowled into his drink. Fortunately, Dennis was no longer entirely sober, either, and scoffed as he said it.

"I know that because this old stringer was a reckless fabulist. He'd catch scent of a story and run it down like a bloodhound, often to the same effect."

"I told the stories everyone else was afraid to tell!" Zicaro said defensively, then waved his spotted hands in the air with practiced drama. "I brought things that were festering in darkness right into the glare of the neon-splattered night!"

Grif raised one dark eyebrow. Dennis just continued staring at Zicaro as he rolled a toothpick between his fingers before turning to Grif.

"Is that why you're carting him around hours after you were supposed to have returned him to an assisted-care facility where a man the size of a freight train is waiting for him?"

Zicaro, belly full and tongue loose, came to life. Bringing his fist down on the table, and spewing a string of profanity that was nothing short of astonishing, Zicaro alone managed to bring Dennis up to speed. Kit listened, sipping her after-dinner cappuccino.

"Lemme get this straight," Dennis said, throwing his arm over the back of the booth when Zicaro had finished. "You were taken from your room in the middle of the night, questioned to the point of exhaustion, and then relocated and held against your will by the men I met today?"

"Poor guy," Kit said, earning a soulful look from Zicaro.

"And they were questioning you about Barbara? Of the old DiMartino gang?"

Zicaro's thin lips pursed into a solid line at the doubt underscoring Dennis's words. Sure, the criminal element was alive and well in Vegas. But Italian mobsters? Those days had died with Spilotro . . . and Dennis said as much.

"Here's what you greenhorns can't seem to understand," Zicaro said, and hiccupped before he continued. "A made man can't just jump into normal life like the rest of us schleps. They operated outside of normal for so long that living by the law would be akin to living on the moon. And

that goes for the women, too. The woman who died yesterday was Barbara DiMartino long before she was Barbara
McCoy."

"So?"

"You don't know anything about the DiMartinos, do you?"

Dennis shrugged.

"They ran the Marquis, best hotel and casino in town. But
they weren't the only outfit here."

"The Salernos owned Vegas Village," Grif put in.

"And old Nick Salerno was after more," Zicaro said, nodding. "He began running chip hustlers and card counters
through the Marquis, bragged about it, too. That's when
things got nasty."

"What happened?" asked Dennis.

"It was never proven, but rumor was Sal DiMartino retaliated by donning a ski mask, walking into the Vegas Village
at the height of midday, and holding up the cage himself. But
unlike old man Salerno, he didn't flaunt his take. Instead, he
bought his wife, Theresa, a gift with it."

Dennis held up a hand. "Wait, I thought Barbara was his
wife."

"Theresa was his first wife," Grif told him. "Love of his life."

"She died in nineteen sixty-one," confirmed Zicaro. "He
married Barbara in 'sixty-two."

"Fast," commented Kit.

"Can I finish my story here?" Zicaro said, glaring until
the table was silenced. "So Sal spends every stolen dollar on
this necklace he had designed for Theresa. Lemme tell you,
it could rival anything in the Queen Mother's jewels. Three
perfect diamonds, each the size of a silver dollar. He then
parades her around in it at the city's annual Fall Festival.

Really stuck it to the Salernos, right in public. As you can imagine, this doesn't go over well with Nick. So Sal DiMartino gets a phone call. 'You take something precious from me, I'll take something precious from you.'" Eyes gleaming, Zicaro leaned forward. "The call comes at the exact same time DiMartino's twelve-year-old niece, Mary Margaret, is abducted from his front yard. I believe this is where you come in."

Feeling Dennis's frown on him, Grif just shrugged. "Sure, I'll tell the rest of the story, but it's real basic. The Salernos kidnapped little Mary Margaret. The DiMartinos got her back. End of story."

"Except it's not," Zicaro argued. "These families are like the Montagues and the Capulets . . . except for the lost love. There's none of that. But there is a code."

Grif nodded. "You don't mess with a Family's children."

"So the feud hinges on this: The DiMartinos say the Salernos planned the attack, but the Salernos maintain that someone inside the DiMartino home told them there was a way to get their diamonds back. She—and they were clear it was a woman—told them when to be in front of the DiMartino estate. She said 'a little doll' would appear, and to take it. So Mary Margaret showed up, and they did."

"Who did the DiMartinos trust with their children?" Kit asked, wondering about Barbara. If she married Sal DiMartino within a year of Theresa's death, then she'd been around before then.

"Just one person. Gina Alessi, Mary Margaret's longtime nanny. But Gina disappeared right after Mary Margaret's return, and for years everyone thought Sal showed her the back door . . . and not in a good way."

"Ugh." Kit made a face.

"But Barbara didn't think so," Grif muttered, closing his eyes to better see the picture that was beginning to emerge.

"Now you're using your noggin'," Zicaro said, tapping on his own head and poking himself in the ear. "She was on a cold rant the night she came to see me. Going on and on about Gina. Said she was back in town and that she had one of the diamonds all these years."

"And Barbara wanted it."

"No," Zicaro said simply. "Barbara was after the other two."

"So why'd she come to you?" Dennis asked.

"Because of one of my old stories. Of a map that's still out there," Zicaro said, licking his lips and leaning forward. "It supposedly shows the location of the diamonds. A literal buried treasure. Anyone wanna take a guess as to who she thought had that map?"

"Shit," Kit whispered, head whipping to Grif.

"Ol' Griffin Shaw," Dennis said, aping the way Justin and Larry had so knowingly said his name earlier that day.

Zicaro toasted Grif, and then drained the rest of his gin. "Good ol' Griffin Shaw."

Justin called exactly four minutes after the appointed time, and the man—who'd been pacing his room, nearly ready to howl at the full moon—answered immediately.

"The cop's name is Dennis Carlisle," Justin said without being asked. It was a good sign. He still knew how things worked. Despite the events out at Sunset, he was still aligned with the man's greater plans. "He's a longtime friend of Craig's, and was a detective up until a few months ago."

So he had some skills. "Demoted?" the man asked, wondering why a detective would end up pounding the streets again.

Justin made a dissenting sound, and the man could practically see Justin's giant head swiveling on his neck like a big slab of meat. "Voluntary. He was shot six months back, made some sort of miraculous recovery—"

"I remember," the man murmured, squinting out the window at the cold night, trying to pull the details from the vast stores of his mind.

"He was investigating the Baptista-Kolyadenko drug war. Apparently took a bullet for Craig."

"Invested, then."

"Not likely to turn on her," Justin confirmed.

The man stopped pacing and closed his eyes, feeling suddenly old. Life was so much simpler back when the boys were running this town. It was easier to tell who to push and where. Men, even cops, could be as easily bought as killed, and the whole town had been smaller. More controllable. Too bad he'd never had any control back then.

He opened his eyes, realizing that he really did prefer things as they were today.

"Okay, here's what we're going to do. You stay with them. Did you put the tracker on Craig's car?"

"While they were at dinner," Justin confirmed.

"Okay, so lay off. Don't approach them—"

"But—"

"*Don't* fucking approach them." His voice hardened, like he'd been through fire and was changed at the cellular level. He was certainly a different man than he'd been fifty years prior, that was for sure.

"We can't go at them directly," he explained, as he resumed his pacing. Walking, moving around, helped him think.

"They're smart, and there's a bunch of them working on this now."

"And the Sunset operation?" Justin asked hopefully. The long-running scam had earned them both a fine amount of money.

"Blown." And he'd put a lot of time into that one. Those vulnerable trust funds had been ripe pickings for someone who knew how to hide his tracks. And this man did. "It doesn't matter. If we're patient and we stay with them, they'll do all the legwork for us."

Craig and Shaw would lead them directly to the diamonds.

"Got it?" the man asked Justin. He was going to have to go soon. It was late, and he did need some sleep.

"Yeah," Justin answered, but there was a note of uncertainty in his voice.

"What?" the man said coolly.

"It's just that . . ." Justin hesitated, and this time the man could see the dolt scratching the side of that big melon head. "She's not happy."

She. *She?*

"She," the man said through clenched teeth, "is dead!"

The past, he thought, had chased him long enough, but now it was dying all around him. And *she* was a part of that.

"All right, all right," Justin said, and the man fought the urge to put his fist through his bedroom wall. He was not going to let some twenty-first-century meathead make him lose out on his biggest racket yet. Unfortunately he needed Justin's eyes and ears right now.

The man blew out a long breath, pushing out an anger that'd been building for decades, wondering if Justin felt its singe on the other side of the line.

"All right, then," he finally said. "Got a pen? Because I've got a plan."

And with Justin's pen scratching in the background, the man laid out exactly what was going to happen to Kit Craig and Griffin Shaw next.

CHAPTER TEN

After saying good-bye to Dennis, they all returned to Marin's town house. Kit's aunt might be unwilling to play hostess to their ragtag bunch, but she certainly wouldn't turn her niece away when she needed a place to stay. Thus, Kit took the large guest room, which left Grif to bunk up with Zicaro in the study. The old geezer claimed his side of the pullout bed by dropping his drawers and falling into the cacophonous sleep of a well-sated man. Yet even without Zicaro's lusty snores, Grif wouldn't have been able to find sleep. He'd just learned that he'd been murdered for diamonds, for money. Worse, for a *map* that he didn't even possess. Besides, for him slumber meant dreaming of the woman who was only a few steps away in the next room.

He shouldn't go in there—she'd made that clear after he'd left that lone feather on her pillow months earlier—but he also knew he wouldn't rest until he saw her one more time that night. It reassured him that she was safe. His actions thus far had altered her fate enough to have the telling plasma release its lustrous, silvery hold from around her ankles for now, but he couldn't be sure that her original destiny—to die only one day from now—wasn't still true.

Kit was already asleep when he slipped into her room. She had one hand resting upon her forehead, like she'd fallen in a faint, the other arm draped across her middle. Wishing neither to startle her nor to leave, Grif slipped across the room and tucked himself into the corner armchair to watch her sleep. Moonlight slipped through the crack in the drapes, lighting her furrowed brow, and he wished he still had the right to reach over and smooth it. If only there were a way to reassure her, as he couldn't when she was awake, that everything would be okay.

"I'm here, Kit." He risked the whisper. "And this time I'm going to stick."

Because along with the knowledge that he'd likely been murdered over a grab for diamonds, he'd come to realize something else in the past twenty-four hours. He loved this woman with all that was left of him. Enough, he thought, to make a shrine of his blood and bone for her. To dedicate this life to seeing her safe. Even from him.

Grif watched the steady rise and fall of her chest, ears pricked to the evenness of her breath. The movies and books got it all wrong. Virgin brides and dashing suitors. A romance made special just because it was the emotion's initial bloom. First love was a slice of life, yes, but it was more of a soft, wispy petal than the root of the thing. Mature love was what really curled a man's toes. Finding a person you could graft yourself to and be better and stronger for it. That's what allowed you to find purchase on this great mudflat.

The sad truth was that first love rarely lasted, but a union between those who'd pruned away the infatuation of youth allowed stronger emotions to sprout in its place. A good cutting could later result in a love that had no end.

His love for Evie, he now knew, had ended. He didn't think he'd have realized that if it weren't for Kit. In retrospect, Grif could admit that marrying the then-twenty-two-year-old back in 1958 had been impulsive, the folly of a young man. They'd only been married two years. They hadn't even had time to suss out each other's deeper preferences. He'd known her favorite color, red, but not the why of it. It wasn't that he didn't want to know. They just hadn't gotten that far.

And after that, after his death, it was his obsession that became his true love. He was consumed with the way his life was supposed to have been, and devoured by the regret for never seeing it through. He couldn't even say now if he and Evie would have lasted the whole of the last fifty years. Had it been a love to survive decades?

Kit had once been married as well, and he wondered if she'd understand this if he tried to explain it. Did her previous union have the same sinewy greenness to it as his relationship with Evie now seemed to have had? Did she ever feel that her marriage hadn't preceded her relationship with Grif as much as it paved the road for it?

He didn't know. He certainly couldn't ask. However, he did wish—with the same obsessive regret—that he hadn't been so in love with his own heartbreak that he forgot to look ahead. Because what he and Kit had found together—fifty years apart and from beyond the grave—had been beautiful and stabbing at the same time. Like a breath drawn after a long, hard sprint.

And wasn't that when you needed to catch your breath the most?

Grif's shoulders began to shake, but he stilled them as soon as he realized it. He wiped his eyes. Love was fine; a fact, even. But this emotion wouldn't do him or Kit any good. Fact was, Evie was still alive, and Grif was still technically married. If nothing else, there had to be an end to that before there could ever be a new beginning. So he could keep watch over Kit all he wanted, he could long for her in this life or the next, and love her for eternity. But he wasn't going to torture her with it any longer.

And *that* was really why he remained in the corner and simply let her sleep.

Kit's eyes shot open right before her phone rang. It was the dead of night, but she felt watched somehow, as if waking in the jarring brightness of an airport, and pulling her coat from over her head to find that her plane had already boarded. Yet the moonlight trailing through the curtains revealed only the unrelieved right angles of the guest room's furniture and the concave scoop of the empty corner chair. That's when her ringtone blasted the psychobilly chords of the Reverend Horton Heat.

She reached for the phone automatically, her brain still slow to realize that this particular ringtone signaled an unlisted number.

"I believe you have something that's ours," said a low, male voice.

"Maybe." Kit pushed into a sitting position and reached for the light. "What does it look like?"

"It's old and gray and forgot its toothbrush."

"Oh." Tucking the phone between her shoulder and ear, Kit scrambled for a pen and paper. "It's sleeping right now."

"And what about you? Are you having trouble sleeping?" The voice managed to sound concerned. "Because you should be. You really should."

Kit froze with her pen poised over her small notepad.

"You're going to need to keep your eyes open from now on. I mean every second of every day. You're not even gonna want to blink."

Kit clenched her jaw so tight her teeth ached. She was so tired of being bossed around by faceless men with mean ambitions. The past year's events had left her with little bounce-back. Experience was supposed to make a person stronger and give them a foundation from which to bound to new heights, but Kit had taken a series of relentless hits: she'd been kidnapped by men who peddled women's flesh, and threatened by others, who poured drugs into the same. Then there was the issue of patriarchal angels who toyed with mortal lives like they were game pieces, just because they could.

And now this?

Kit pulled the phone away from her ear and stared at it for a long moment. Then she hung up.

Adjusting the pillows behind her, Kit repositioned herself against the headboard. Maybe it was the wine she'd consumed earlier in the evening. Or the muted, late night hours. Or Grif's steadying presence back in her life. Yet, for some reason, the phone call didn't scare her.

Gaze fastened on the bedside clock, she'd counted to twenty before the phone rang again, but waited until the half-minute mark to tuck it to her ear. "What?"

"Have you ever been in love, Ms. Craig?"

Kit thought of Grif in the next room, but didn't answer. Seriously. Screw this guy and his threatening midnight questions.

"Because love," the man continued, "at least, the most passionate love, comes from a deep place. It's born somewhere far inside of us, and once it takes root, it's almost impossible to ferret out."

"Your point, please. It's late."

"Passion *is* my point. There's passion in love, but there's also passion in hate and greed and lust. Those are all my favorites," he said, and Kit thought, I bet. "Yet love is still the strongest passion of all. Oddly, the etymological root of 'passion' is the Latin *passus,* and that means 'to suffer.' That's what we really do when we love. We suffer. We submit."

Kit said nothing at all now.

"Your aunt is the only family you have left, is she not?"

Oh, God.

"I wonder how she'd react if that fancy town house she's letting you stay in suddenly caught fire. I'm not saying it will, but gosh. What if there's a gas leak? Or an electrical cord gone bad? What if—and I know this will sound totally unbelievable—but what if some sort of rocket were to crash through that front living-room window and blow it all to smithereens?"

He let her think about that for a minute.

"I mean, that's the crazy thing about life, isn't it?" he said, his voice calm by contrast. "Anything can happen at any time at all."

Yes, Kit thought, shaking now. Just like with her mother, attacked from within her own body. Just like with her father, assaulted on the street. Was there no safe place? Kit wondered, the thought coming perilously close to a prayer.

"One thing's for sure, though," the man continued. "Something like that occurs, and your dear aunt Marin, your family, your *love*, will know the true meaning of passion. She will suffer. And you? You will submit."

Kit's mouth was dry, head swimming like she'd drank two bottles of wine earlier instead of two glasses, but she managed to speak. "What do you want?"

"We will meet tomorrow at the Paris Hotel. Let's be civilized like the French and arrive say . . . after lunch? I always like to take a restful afternoon siesta."

Kit didn't bother saying that siestas were a Spanish cultural tradition, not French. She had a feeling he already knew.

"Don't forget to bring the old man, our information, and our new friend Griffin Shaw. We're most anxious to have a little chat with him, too."

Kit caught sight of her own gaze in the dresser mirror, and was surprised to find her exact feelings reflected there. Her eyes were narrowed and mouth downturned. She looked just a little demonic.

"Hey, Justin," she suddenly said, and knew she'd named the right man when only silence met her words. "We'll meet you tomorrow, and you'll get your fucking flash drives, but if you hurt my aunt, your knowledge of what it means to suffer isn't going to be some dusty old dictionary definition. Trust me when I tell you . . . there won't be an angel in Paradise who will lift a finger to save you."

She swore it on her soul.

Justin scoffed again, though not as readily.

Kit didn't care if he believed her or not, because the beings she was really swearing this oath to, the angels, did. "The heavens owe me, Justin, and I won't hesitate to call down the wrath of the entire Host on your head."

There was a short hesitation and then a long, drawn-out scoff. "And they say Zicaro is loony."

Kit opened her mouth, snarled reply ready, but the line went dead and reply was no longer an option, and neither was swearing. And neither, she thought, was sleep.

CHAPTER ELEVEN

Recalling how lightly Grif slept, Kit was careful to make little noise as she tiptoed down the hall and then the stairwell, rounding the corner into the cozy living room only to confront a single table lamp glowing in the dark. She made out the figure curled in the armchair, and smiled wryly.

"Somehow I knew you'd be up," she told Marin, taking a seat across from her.

"Funny, I was just going to say the same of you," Marin answered, and motioned to the coffee table where a second glass of wine was already poured and waiting. Kit smiled as she took it, and felt steadied despite Justin's threatening call. Her aunt and she might not be on the best of terms, but there was comfort still in being known.

"Where's Amelia?" she asked, curling her feet up beneath her.

"She went home."

"Because of us?" The apology was in Kit's voice.

"No." Marin smiled. "She has to work tomorrow."

Kit was again struck by how little she knew of her aunt's personal life. It thawed some of the anger she'd built up toward Marin these past many months. Her aunt had just been trying to protect her, and Kit may have done exactly the same thing in her place. Still, it was precisely because Marin did know Kit so well that she should have told her what she'd known.

She shouldn't have had to learn of it from a demon.

Marin Wilson lied to you.

Kit shuddered at the memory. Like their lofty brethren, demons could slip into the mortal world using the bodies of the very young or old, the weak or infirm. Marin had been in a drug-induced coma when this particular member of the Fallen had entered her body and rifled through her memories.

Kit sipped her wine, using the liquid strength to draw herself back to the present. Focusing on the past would do nothing for her. "What does Amelia do?"

"She's an ER doctor."

"So she's a workaholic like you," Kit said, nodding her head.

"She's worse," admitted Marin, but the censure was muted.

"Is that even possible?" Kit teased, pleased that her aunt had found happiness, that she wasn't alone.

Not like Kit.

The realization lanced through her, and Kit took a long pull at her wineglass.

"You might be surprised at what's possible, Kit," Marin said, watching her closely.

Kit snorted as she thought of the angelic human upstairs. "Try me."

Marin looked down, her hands knotting. "For one, I've come to realize lately that there's more to life than just chasing down the next story. Such as creating stories, and a life, of your own."

"I could have told you that," Kit said softly.

"I think you tried," Marin said, looking back up. Her chin wobbled. "I'm sorry, Kit. For hiding things from you, for trying to protect you from the truth. It's just, after your breakdown, after you were institutionalized—"

"I don't want to talk about that." She wasn't that person anymore. She didn't even know who that was, which was comforting. You could actually become someone else in the same lifetime. Maybe it meant she wouldn't always be a silly mortal yearning for a brooding angel she could never have.

Marin held up a hand to let Kit know that wasn't her point, and that she agreed. "I simply didn't feel like I could risk it after you were released."

"But I put myself back together." And she'd do so again. She *was* doing it again. Proof? She wasn't up there banging down Grif's door.

"You did, didn't you?" Marin's gaze went distant as she remembered for herself, and after another moment she shook her head. "I've seen a lot of things in my day, but I swear, that was the gutsiest thing I ever did see. Yet somehow it made me want to protect you all the more. And then you started in with the rockabilly phase—"

"It's not a—"

"I know, it's a *lifestyle*. It's a way of life. And it's your armor."

Kit jerked, but realized it was true. A coat of arms comprising crinoline and cat's-eye glasses. Half-moon manicures to paint over her vulnerabilities. Fears reined in by the discipline required of heels, in the exactness of a pencil skirt. Why hadn't she realized it before?

"I didn't understand that at first," Marin said, talking faster, like she'd opened a spout and now couldn't turn it off. "But honestly, Kit, you're as tough a woman as I've ever seen. Tougher than me." She glanced down again, and swallowed hard. "Tough like your mom."

And the spout turned off. The relationship between Kit's mother—the flighty and aristocratic Shirley Wilson Craig—and Kit's aunt—the plain and steadfast younger sibling, Marin—was a rarely broached subject between them . . . and never initiated by Marin. But the hour was late—or early now—and they were drinking alone in the moonbeams. Besides, Marin seemed different, more open and vulnerable. Perhaps Kit wouldn't have recognized it without the distance of the past few months wedged between them, but she saw it now, like clouds parting to reveal the face of the moon.

"Do you know she used to lock me out of the house?" Marin said suddenly.

Kit knew Marin and her mother hadn't been bosom friends. She was starting to understand that the woman she loved then, and in memory, was not the only Shirley Craig that there was. That her mother, though fiercely loving and always supportive of Kit, had also been a bit of a bully. "No. I didn't know that."

"Yeah, it was in retaliation for always getting As. For being better in track. For, I don't know, breathing." Leaning forward, Marin over-poured another glass of wine, though she didn't drink it. "She stole my first boyfriend just to prove she could. Not that I was really that into him."

They both chuckled, but Marin's smile fell almost immediately. "Sisters are weird that way. They can be each other's biggest champions while still being each other's biggest adversaries." She shuddered, evidently remembering a different slight at the hands of her older sister, then shook her head clear of it. "She loomed over me like a giant shadow. I felt lesser, judged. I was nothing like her, and she let me know it."

"I'm sorry," Kit said. It wasn't at all the way she remembered her mother, but who could ever truly know another person? Last summer she'd actually been inside of Grif's thoughts—again, because of that malevolent demon—and she still didn't know the whole of him.

"I just want you to know that though I never had a child of my own, never intended to—"

"Until I was thrust upon you."

"No." Marin put her hand out, spine straightening. "No, you were a gift. One I never dared dream for myself. I felt this huge responsibility to care for you. You were all I had left, and vice versa, but in addition to grief, there was guilt. Because I had you and I knew she wouldn't have wanted me to. I hadn't earned you. You were hers."

Kit had no idea what to say to that.

"I did what I thought best by you, and have ever since. But I complicated it," Marin said, and Kit knew this was her way of apologizing.

Again, a memory shared by that demon seized her, though this one was Marin's. In it, her aunt was secreting away a file from a room Kit recognized, her father's study as it'd looked fourteen years earlier. And afterward? Marin had gently stroked Kit's forehead as she slept, and said, "It's for your own good."

And that was why her father's murder, always suspicious, was now a cold case.

Kit glanced away. She loved Marin, she missed her, and even understood her . . . but she couldn't quite forgive her. Not yet. So instead of simply accepting the apology, she said, "It's not too late, you know."

"What do you mean?"

"To come clean. To tell me the truth about my dad's death." Kit bit her lip. "And about the folder he sent you the day he died."

Marin froze. "How do you know about that?"

A little demon told me.

"I think the real question is, after everything you just said, why aren't you telling me about it now?"

Marin remained quiet.

"Let me make this a little easier on you," Kit finally said, folding her hands together. "I know that my father sent you something, and I believe that something was the reason he was killed."

It was the secret she'd been keeping from Grif, a nugget of information that she was hoarding for herself until she knew what to do about it . . . if anything at all.

"Now," Kit said. "We can keep going down this path we've been on, with you professing to be sorry about the very thing you continue to do"—*lie*—"or you can tell me right now. What was in that folder?"

"Nothing."

Kit shook her head. "I went back into the family archives and looked, Marin. I knew you wouldn't leave something so important undocumented. You annotated it. You cross-fucking-referenced it. There was something in that folder that made you suspect my dad's murder was more than a routine line-of-duty death."

Marin's chin lifted. "And it looks like I was right to hide it, wasn't I?"

"Did it have anything to do with Barbara DiMartino?"

"You tell me."

Kit stood, amazed. "Why are you stonewalling me on this?"

"Because in addition to putting up with your mother's shit, I swore to her that I'd keep you safe." Marin's softness had disappeared and now she only glared. "And I'm keeping that promise, Kit. Even if it means protecting you from yourself."

"He was murdered right after he left Sal DiMartino's house," Kit said, glaring back. "Did you really think I wasn't going to put it together? That I wouldn't find out?"

Marin just shook her head. "Some things are best left buried."

"Like the DiMartinos? Like their feud with the Salernos?"

Like mysteries that spanned fifty whole years?

Marin just sat on her sofa, looking suddenly small . . . but resolute. She wasn't going to speak.

Kit whirled away so fast she felt dizzy. "Fine. I'll figure it out myself. I'll also be out of your hair"—unspoken was, out of your *life*—"first thing in the morning."

"Leave it alone, Kit," Marin called from behind her.

"Oh, Marin." Kit just shook her head, pausing with one hand on the doorjamb. "It's like you don't even know me at all."

Grif moved in and out of his dreams like a fish swimming from light into shadows. Therefore his sleep was similarly clouded, and he woke late with a dry mouth and a pulsing behind his eyes. Already dressed, he headed downstairs to remedy both, and found Marin and Kit seated across from each other at the long dining-room table. Marin's laptop was open between them, but the wedge of space that separated the women was made greater by their matching postures—stiff and straight, legs crossed so their bodies formed a V. Neither woman looked up as Grif headed to the kitchen, where he found Zicaro nibbling toast and perusing a stack of printouts over the top of his bifocals.

"It feels good to be on the beat again!" Zicaro said, voice too loud.

Grif motioned for Zicaro to turn up his hearing aid, then looked at him as he poured some coffee. "They put you to work?"

Zicaro nodded, and Grif's gut automatically clenched. His inclination was to tuck people away somewhere safe while he pounded the pavement and did the heavy lifting. But Zicaro was nearly shaking with excitement as he showed Grif a printout of the Paris casino floor. Grif began to shake, too, when the old-timer went on to tell him about Kit's midnight call and the threat to Marin's life.

He hid his frown behind his mug. There was a time when Kit wouldn't have hesitated to come to him first with a problem, even in the middle of the night. He knew he no longer had a right to expect it, yet he still wished she had, and not merely out of pride. Grif was already running out of time. It was now Monday, the original day on which Kit was scheduled to die, and though he believed his actions the previous day had altered that fate, he wasn't taking any chances.

Besides, he hadn't forgotten about Donel's prophecy.

Lifting his large mug of coffee, he rejoined the women in the dining room.

"How did you first find out about Sunset?" Marin asked, without preamble and without looking up, as Grif pulled out a chair.

"*I* found it," boasted Zicaro, rolling in, toast balanced on his knees.

Grif helped him to the table and settled his papers before him, but pointed out, "No, you didn't. You just happened to be living there when Justin Allen and company took over." He turned back to Marin. "Why? What'd you find?"

"Wait till you see," Kit said, finally looking up. She was already made up for the day, face powdered, eyes lined, dark hair pinned in front, the back tucked inside a crimson snood. He knew she always kept a change of clothes in the car, so didn't wonder at that, but what had his breath catching in his chest was the excitement that brimmed beneath all that gloss.

Eyes shining, she motioned him over, her mouth curling up at one corner, a nearly forgotten look. It slid into his heart like a splinter, and he tried to forget it again as he sauntered over to stand behind her. She was just excited; the look wasn't meant for him.

"Amelia shot these over a couple of hours ago. It's only the contents of one flash drive so far, but it's enough."

"For what?"

Marin tapped the screen with her pencil. "To suss out the scam. Here's the gist: the caregivers and therapists working at the Sunset Retirement Community are legit, but the management and the administrative staff? Not." She looked up at Zicaro.

He nodded. "No one has been there longer than a year."

"And the resident list has changed as well. Only those with health issues so debilitating that they overwhelm family members are admitted. More than that, most have no immediate family at all."

"No one to advocate for them," said Kit softly.

"The stated goal is to provide every resident with a gentle and dignified end to their life once it's acknowledged that the end is, indeed, near. But there are various levels of 'care' going on at Sunset, with the most intensive care given to the terminal cases."

"Not those with a chance of recovery?"

Marin shook her head. "I've begun a preliminary comparison between Sunset and Blue Diamond Medical, its biggest competitor in town, and the discrepancy in recovery rates is startling."

"So more people are dying at Sunset?"

"No. I mean, that would be a big ol' red flag, wouldn't it? But they're not getting better, either. In fact, they never leave. Instead, their lives are extended."

"And so are their illnesses." Kit reached over and shifted Marin's laptop around so that both Grif and Zicaro could see the screen.

"The residents are given one of three grades upon admission to Sunset."

"Like in school?" Grif said.

Kit inclined her head. "An A means they'll likely regain their independence. B means they're still in control of bodily functions and mobility."

"And a C?"

Kit shook her head. "That's the thing. There is no C. There's only a steep drop to F. End of life. The mission is to get patients in the A group back on their feet, and a handful of those actually do leave full-time care. But look at what happens to the Bs and Fs at Sunset. It's a slow decline into F status, but it happens down to the last person."

Grif crossed his arms. "What about their families?"

"Notified, but look, if a family member was having trouble taking care of their elderly loved one before, they'll naturally find any new complications impossible."

Grif frowned at the screen. "So what happens to the Fs?"

"Here's a report given to the family of a resident just last summer." Marin pushed it his way, and he slid it across the table so Zicaro could see as well. "The chart is marked 'terminal' at the top, yet you can see from the files that efforts to sustain and extend his life go far beyond that expressed on the admission forms."

"So it's an insurance scam," Zicaro guessed.

"No," Marin said, turning the screen back to face her. "The claims are never filed."

Grif shook his head. "I don't understand."

Kit leaned back in her chair and jerked her chin. "Turn the page."

Zicaro did it for him. Shifting the stack around, he flipped it open. After a moment he said, "These numbers. They look like . . . what? Bank accounts?"

"Trust accounts," Kit corrected excitedly. "Trusts that management takes over shortly after each patient arrives. All monies are kept in a single account. They don't ask the families for the numbers directly, but they don't have to when the cost of care is withdrawn automatically each month. Social Security goes through those accounts, military retirement pay, Medicare, Medicaid . . . the wealthier patients even have wills and deeds attached . . . but the most telling are these."

She leaned across the table, sending a rose scent wafting Grif's way. He refocused as she pointed to a row of cells. "Credit card numbers. I don't know if you knew this, but most elderly people have stupendous credit."

"Not me," Zicaro said, and they all looked at him. He shrugged. "I'm really bad at being elderly."

"So's he," Kit quipped, pointing at Grif. "Anyway, we've only begun searching these files but it looks like all of these cards are maxed out, but only after the limits were raised."

"Again and again," Marin added. "Minimum payments are made to the cardholder accounts, though not from the individual's bank account."

No, thought Grif, catching on now. Some eagle-eyed family member might be keeping tabs on that.

"They all come from a central account at Sunset," Kit explained. "Meanwhile, other credit card accounts continue to be opened under the patient's name, which is strange as most people living at an assisted-care facility don't get out much."

"What about TV and telephone pitches?"

"Calls are monitored," Marin said. "I checked. Solicitors don't get through."

"There's online shopping now," Grif pointed out, nodding at Marin's computer.

Kit said, "Not for people who have trouble even seeing the screen."

"Not," clarified Zicaro, "for people whose hands shake too much to navigate the keys."

He cleared his throat, like his toast had suddenly gone dry in his throat.

"And not for people," Marin said, swinging the laptop back around, "who are kept so drugged up that they don't even know their own name."

"Jesus." Grif rubbed his eyes, and thought about all the blinds that could be put in place to hide income and expenses over time. How a family's desperation could be used against them. How someone could be systematically stripped of their material worth without even knowing it.

"No family has ever challenged the creditors?"

"You mean the grief-stricken families? The ones who couldn't even change a bedpan?" Marin looked at Grif. "Tell me this, how much do you know about your financial situation right now?"

"I know I have enough money to get through the day," he said, and Kit snorted.

"I check my statements every month," Zicaro said proudly. "I get yearly credit reports."

Marin lifted her eyebrows. "Really? So you have the contact information for every credit card you've ever opened? Every bank account? The passwords for each of them?"

Marin shook her head when Zicaro said nothing. "And what if you had children? Would they be able to locate them if something happened to you? Because I've dealt with a loved one's personal effects and I can tell you it would take months and months of searching and discarding and fighting through red tape to figure out what's going on here. Most people don't have the resources or time for it. It's hard enough for them to arrange for the casket and pack up the house for Goodwill. Forget proof of wrongdoing on the part of a caregiver."

"But we've got proof," Grif said, nodding at the computer.

Marin's eyes gleamed now. "Oh, we've got enough to bury everyone involved."

"No wonder they want to blow up your house," Zicaro said, returning to his toast.

To her credit, Marin didn't blink. "No wonder they want to meet with you this afternoon."

"I'm not afraid," said Zicaro. "We're meeting at a casino in the middle of the Strip. What could go wrong?"

On what was supposed to be the last day of Kit's life? Grif looked at Kit, who was biting her lip, noticing his concern. What, indeed?

"I'd like to ask you to stay here at Marin's this afternoon," Grif said to Kit. He knew better than to demand it. "Uncle Al and I can see to the business at the casino."

He was praying that they wouldn't have to fight about it for long. He couldn't explain in front of Zicaro and Marin why it was important, but she'd want to know. She always did. So even Grif was surprised when she only nodded. "I think that's best."

"You do?" Marin asked.

"You do?" said Zicaro, also goggling.

"You do?" Grif said.

"Sure," Kit said, blinking back at them all. "Divide and conquer, right? You guys can go compare the size of your flash drives with the bad guys, but there's a ton of information that still needs to be combed through." She glanced at Marin, her look growing pointed. "I can't do it all myself."

Marin's jaw clenched as she shoved back from the table. "I have to get ready for work."

She strode from the room without another word, obviously upset, though Grif didn't know why. He was just relieved that Kit would remain out of danger. "So you'll let me handle this part?"

"Us," Zicaro corrected.

"Happy to," Kit said, and rose as well, heading to the kitchen with her coffee cup, gone before Grif could even frown, much less question why.

CHAPTER TWELVE

Grif worked the North America beat as a Centurion, but it'd only been that way for the past decade. When he'd started ferrying wounded souls to the Everlast—the murders and the suicides, the hit-and-runs, the skydivers with badly packed chutes—Sarge had been worried that Grif wouldn't be able to keep his emotions in check, so he'd confined Grif's Takes to Continental Europe, where speech and cultural relativism were barriers to Grif's understanding. Where the dead couldn't burden him with the details of their demise.

In retrospect, Grif could admit that it'd worked. He'd been so busy using body language to convince some newly dead sap to follow him into oblivion that he didn't have time to consider how their deaths, time and again, made him *feel*.

Most memorable from those first few decades were the Takes he'd been assigned in France, a society that, as a whole, continued to baffle Grif to this day. Broadly speaking, they were resistant to change, and had extreme and unyielding opinions regarding what constituted the joie de vivre, the dual starting points always being family and France. These stubborn traits seemed to double immediately upon death. Try pulling a soul that nationalistic away from his home and family and *terroir,* even after death.

Yet what struck Grif most about the French was each person's heartfelt reluctance to leave not only their bodies and loved ones behind, but to be forced to abandon the raw minutiae of life itself.

"But the *frommage,*" lamented one Frenchman, staring back at the Surface with sad, hangdog eyes, even though he was perched on the cusp of the Universe. He'd been decapitated while riding his motorcycle through the Alps, so Grif didn't understand his complaint. He no longer had a mouth to savor said cheese with anyway.

"But I will not be able to feel the sea breeze upon my face," complained another Take, a woman who had, ironically, drowned. "If there is no Riviera waiting for me in heaven, then I want no part of it!"

Grif had been pressed for time that day—he had another Take within the hour in Corsica—and told her that if that's the way she felt he'd go ahead and let her sink to the bottom of the sea. She stoically said *au revoir.* Sarge had forced him to double back for her anyway.

So it was with those experiences coloring his view that he gazed up at the tricolor atop the Paris Hotel with more than a little trepidation. He tried passing the look off as boredom when he caught Zicaro watching.

"I don't get this place," he grumbled, carefully avoiding eye contact with the doormen as he wheeled Zicaro through the front entrance.

"They're trying to make it feel like Pair-ee," said Zicaro, inhaling the casino air deeply, and gagging on air-freshener instead of smoke.

"Not *this* place," Grif said, though that was exactly what he meant, but he gestured back to the long bank of doors and the Strip behind them. "The whole damned street. Paris is over here, old Rome is over there. Venice is down the block, and a mountain village is spraying water all over the corner of Flamingo Boulevard. They've gone and mashed it all together and none of it looks like it's supposed to. It tries to look like everything but ends up looking like nothing at all."

"Sure it does," Zicaro argued, taking another deep breath and sighing contentedly. "It looks big and shiny and fun."

"It's not fun to me," Grif grumbled as machines clanged on every side of him, making him hunch his shoulders.

"Because you're boring," Zicaro scoffed, as they rolled past the craps tables. "That's your squeaky-clean midwestern upbringing rearing its head."

Grif cut his eyes at Zicaro. "You did do your homework, didn't you?"

"Absolutely. Though one look at you and it's clear you're corn-fed."

"Then why were you always trying to intimate that I was made?" Grif said, tone curt. "If you'd really done your homework, you'd know that I would never cotton to working for the boys."

"Oh, I knew that." Zicaro waved his hand in the air, scoffing as Grif stopped in place. The couple walking behind them cursed, then swerved, nearly hitting Grif with a plastic drinking cup. "But poke enough bears and you're bound to rouse at least one growl."

"You're lucky you didn't rouse more than that," Grif grumbled as he resumed pushing the chair.

The old man shrugged. "Why do you think I threw in the stories about aliens falling through hidden portals?" And this time, when Grif stopped to stare at him, Zicaro's face widened into a grin so large it almost erased the wrinkles.

"Why, Loony Uncle Al," Grif said, tilting his head. "I think you just said something incredibly sane."

"Finally." Zicaro pointed at a sign that read PROMENADE. "Someone who appreciates my genius."

The Promenade of the Paris Hotel was linked to Bally's, its sister property that had held court on the corner of Flamingo Boulevard for more than forty years. While Grif stood by his censure of the themed casinos, they *were* something to see. Everything on the glittering main drag had been produced by minds that believed anything was possible. It was an ode to excess, and since Vegas averaged a hundred thousand new visitors a day, despite any complaint Grif lodged about shopping malls with painted ceilings made to ape the outdoors or neon that strong-armed nighttime skylines into burning like midday, the general public seemed to enjoy it. It was a world meant to turn everything on its head.

So it was fitting that, as they wheeled into the replica of a Parisian street corner, he and Zicaro would do the same.

"Follow my lead, right?" he said, as the Parisian street scene engulfed them.

"I don't know," Zicaro replied, undaunted. "Hard to do when you're pushing me in front of you."

Grif spotted Justin and the two orderlies. They were taking

up the whole of a park bench, lounging beneath a faux ever-green, and sharing, it seemed, what was left of a warm baguette.

A snort rose from Zicaro's wheelchair as he spotted the trio, too. "Yeah, that helps them blend."

Though warm enough indoors to remove his coat, Grif kept it buttoned, and felt Justin's coal-dark gaze on his right pocket as they approached. He was clearly remembering the gun Grif had pulled on him the day before.

The wheelchair bumped over the faux cobblestones, a jarring journey that the three men evidently found amusing. When they came to a stop, Larry, no longer wearing his name tag, flanked Grif's left. The other man, Eric, took up the right.

"Where's Ms. Craig?" Justin asked, squared in front of them all.

"We figured you got well enough acquainted with her on the phone last night," Grif replied drily.

"That we did," Justin said, motioning Grif to the bench. "Sit."

It wasn't a question.

Grif just tucked his hands into his pockets and rocked back on his heels as he glanced around. Spotting a cocktail waitress on her way back to the casino, he beckoned her over.

"Can we get a few of those?" Grif asked, nodding at her full tray.

The cocktail waitress gave them all a bored look. "You can have them all. My 'customers' put in an order and then left without tipping me."

"Well, that ain't right," Larry said, taking a drink from the tray. Justin and Eric followed suit. "Tip the girl, Griffin Shaw."

"Sure." Grif pulled out his wallet. "Might as well make it a party."

"That's what I'm talking about," said Justin, accepting his drink and toasting Grif. "We'll celebrate you returning our flash drives."

Grif nodded at Zicaro, and the old man pulled the flash drives from his sweater pocket. "So now what?" he asked, handing them over.

"Now you walk out of here with us," Justin said, tucking the drives into the pocket of his leather jacket. "And then we take you to an undisclosed location where we can kill you."

"That's an interesting proposition," Grif said, nodding like he was considering it.

"Or we could just play some craps," Zicaro tried, angling his drinking glass up as if in toast.

The large man just looked at it for a moment before slapping it out of Zicaro's hand. It shattered musically across the glossy cobblestone.

Eric and Larry laughed and clinked glasses. Larry downed his drink, while Eric merely sipped. Grif remained still.

"You're with me," Justin said, angling himself behind Zicaro. "You two, get him."

This was not going as planned. Grif looked around, but their backup hadn't arrived yet, and the waitress—a friend of Kit's—was long gone. So he reached out to stop Justin himself . . . exactly what the man was expecting. Justin swung to backhand Grif, who dodged just as Larry stepped between them. Justin immediately whirled away with Zicaro, and Larry grinned as he reached for Grif's arm.

He stopped grinning when he wobbled.

Realization struck Eric's face just as Grif's fist struck Larry's jaw. Eric was so shocked that he, too, dropped his glass, and though he tried to grab Grif's forearm, he swayed as well. "You fucking—"

A voice interrupted, causing him to jolt. "Is there a problem here?"

The police officer stood directly behind Eric.

"Yes," Grif said to Dennis, though his gaze darted in the direction that Justin had disappeared with Zicaro. How could they have vanished so quickly? "These men are inebriated."

"Intoxicated?" asked the officer.

"And assholes," Grif said.

"Intoxicated, inebriated assholes at a casino in Vegas?" Dennis's eyes went wide and he lifted a groaning Larry from the ground. He turned him toward the exit. "We can't have that."

And Dennis couldn't carry Larry and control Eric at the same time. So, despite his worry over Zicaro—despite spotting an empty wheelchair parked at the elevator banks—Grif looped his arm around Eric as if they were buddies.

"Anything happens to him," Grif whispered, steering Eric toward the garage, "and I'm going to take it out on you."

And finally, rightfully, Eric looked scared.

Ray DiMartino was the infamous Sal DiMartino's only son.

Ray DiMartino was the man who, just last year, had told Kit and Grif about Barbara, saying that she hated Griffin Shaw, though he couldn't say why, or where she was now.

Ray DiMartino would also know about the three jumbo diamonds that went missing from his mother's dressing room fifty years earlier.

Which meant that Ray DiMartino hadn't just been holding out on Kit and Grif when they questioned him earlier this year . . . he'd been out-and-out lying.

And that was why Kit was going to question Ray while Grif and Zicaro were busy returning the flash drives. Kit knew she'd surprised Grif when she'd agreed to let them handle the meet, but she just couldn't get the phone call out of her head. The one that'd come through Barbara's phone on the same night of her murder. *Is it done?*

"They were working together," Kit muttered, jaw going tight as she squinted up at the sign of the Masquerade strip club. It was only two in the afternoon, so the rest of the lot was near empty, with only a few cars pocking it like a disease.

Kit wished she had Grif's ability to bypass any alarm system with nothing more than a flick of her wrist. She'd rather have done that than call to make an appointment under a false name, claiming she wished to audition for a job. She'd once asked him what it felt like to be able to enter any secured structure without obstruction, and he tried to explain to her as best he could what it felt like to be angelic.

"The power starts behind my shoulder blades," he said, and she nodded. She knew there were two feathers from a Pure angel buried back there. It had been meant as a form of punishment. Just like his forced return to the Surface. "It spreads to my shoulders from there, then shoots through my veins to whatever part of the body I'm thinking of."

"Does it hurt?"

"It's . . . uncomfortable. Warm and thick and sluggish, like salsa in the blood. But it's also powerful, quick as a solar flare."

But Kit didn't know what that felt like, either . . . and she didn't care. To a woman with relatively little physical power, it sounded . . . well, divine.

Checking her image one final time in the rearview mirror, Kit sighed. She'd just have to use what she had. Unfortunately, she'd curated her retro look so rigorously over the years that she could do little to alter it now. She simply didn't fit the modern standards of female perfection. Her skin was too pale, her hair too dark, her curves too aggressive.

So she'd chosen to go boldly in the opposite direction with her appearance. Instead of trying to camouflage the things that made her different from the other girls, she overstated the pitch-black liner of her feline eyes. Instead of pale pink, she'd chosen the most vibrant red lip color in her palette. She'd thrown on a vintage swing coat that likely made her appear coy, but that was more to hide her vintage clothing than the curves beneath. She'd been inside Masquerade before and knew she already stood out against the throng of rail-thin blondes.

"Well, at least you'll be an original," she muttered to her reflection in the rearview mirror before locking up the car and heading inside.

The hostess said almost the exact same thing before leading Kit to Ray's office, located at the back of the building. The club music pulsed through the walls like some druggie's cranked-up heartbeat, and the strobes and blackout curtains turned day back into night. Some people, and some things, were just meant for the dark.

"Mr. DiMartino will be out in a moment," the hostess said, then offered what might have been an apologetic smile. "He's just showering, but he knows you're coming."

Kit couldn't keep her mouth from falling open as the door shut behind her. *Showering?* She looked at the black leather sofa, then glanced up at the cameras, eyes glowing red and recording everything. Then she indeed picked up the sound of water running from the adjacent room.

"Gross," Kit said, shooting one of the cameras a dirty look as she tossed her handbag on a side table. It didn't matter. Ray would know as soon as he saw her that she wasn't there to dance.

They'd still go a few rounds, though.

Ray's office was not exactly a den of iniquity. The walls were off-white and sterile, with only one picture to break up the monotony, an amateur painting of two women kissing as a man looked on. "Glad to see you're keepin' it classy, Ray," Kit muttered, moving back to the center of the room.

Other than the door leading to the room where Ray could be heard singing in the shower—again, gross—there was one other exit, sporting a bright red sign above announcing the same, and a lockbox that meant business. It likely led to the parking lot, allowing Ray—and whomever he summoned through that back door—a quick and private getaway.

Two long, lacquered desks were pushed together to form an L-shaped command center where paperwork was haphazardly piled and cabinets were shoved underneath. A small bookshelf was tucked beneath the desk's far end, and Kit scanned the titles with raised eyebrows. *Wine for Dummies. Spanish for Dummies. Finance for Dummies.*

Either Ray liked to take shortcuts, or he didn't think very highly of himself.

Outside of the heavy desks and long leather sofa, the rest of the room was aesthetically forgettable but for one thing: the raised platform with a shiny pole spearing from its middle. Giving the makeshift stage a dismissive glance, and listening to Ray struggle to find a tune as he showered, Kit crossed the room to riffle through his mail.

He didn't seem to be living the life of a big mobster, Kit thought, spotting two delinquent notices addressed to another location, likely his home. She wrote the address down for reference. Maybe he was just getting back into the game. A strip club, and the way cash moved through these doors, was certainly a good jumping-off point. And lack of funds meant he might be desperate to lay his hands on a bigger con. Like a half-century search for diamonds.

She thought about the case Grif had gotten involved in back in 1960, the kidnapping that'd had him working for the valley's reigning kingpin of the day. The DiMartinos believed Griffin Shaw had helped the Salernos kidnap little Mary Margaret from her front yard. They were also told by an unidentified source that he sexually assaulted the twelve-year-old before returning her to her uncle. Forget that Grif would never even contemplate such a thing, which Mary Margaret had confirmed last summer; Kit knew he was beyond reproach.

"So who hated you enough to spread a rumor that got you killed?" she murmured, though one person already came to mind: Barbara. "New question, then . . . why?"

The shower snapped off in the adjacent room, stilling Kit as she thumbed through a second stack of papers. Ray would have to dry off. She still had time. She didn't know exactly what his reaction would be upon finding her in his office, though he'd acted friendly enough the few times they'd met. Based on those encounters, there'd be no reason for him to object to speaking with her. He hadn't known she was a reporter the first time, and after that he hadn't seemed to care.

"So then why do you have this on your desk?" Kit pulled a news clipping from the bottom of the stack, yellowed and torn at the edges. Squinting, she scanned the headline, dated fourteen years earlier. OFFICER KILLED IN BOTCHED CONVENIENCE STORE ROBBERY.

It was the article that ran the day after her father's death, too soon to identify him by name.

"'The veteran officer, killed in the line of duty . . .'" she read aloud, just as the adjacent door swung open. She looked up and caught a still-sopping Ray glaring at her. He had a white towel draped low around his hips and a scowl on his face. She spotted a bank of security screens over his left shoulder, and her own image, snooping behind his desk and holding the news clipping of her father's death, sat dead center.

"What the hell is going on?" said Ray, baring teeth.

"Funny," Kit answered, steadied by the weight of the gun in her pocket and the growing fury in her own heart. "I was just going to ask you the same thing."

CHAPTER THIRTEEN

The tiki lounge was Grif's idea. It had bamboo walls that muted sound, an island god guarding the front door, and was dark enough to remain discreet despite all of that. Frankie's Tiki Room was also a sort of home-away-from-home for the rockabilly crowd, marrying South Seas nostalgia with the mid-century aesthetic to create an escape from the brazen glitz of modern Las Vegas. It was the perfect place for two men to come back around from their drugged stupor, yet still remain a little disoriented.

The last time Grif had been here was with Kit. She wore a Hawaiian dress with flowers in her hair, and though his suit and fedora had been remarked upon, the glances he got had been more covetous than wondering. He lost count of the number of times he'd been complimented on his straight-razored pomp. Grif smiled, remembering that they drank rum until sunrise, then went home and made love until sunset.

But now it was a late Monday afternoon and the crowd at
Frankie's was thin, with only three men taking up real estate
at the bar, none speaking and none interested when Grif and
Dennis walked in and settled two groggy men into the far
corner of the room.

"I gotta finish changing," Dennis said, nodding at his uniform. He'd removed the shirt, but the utility belt would eventually attract attention from the bar.

"I'll work on these guys."

"Think they'll talk to you?"

"I got ways to make 'em talk."

"How Perry Mason of you," Dennis said, but there was no
censure in his voice. Dennis, too, was rockabilly to the core.
"You sounded just like Raymond Burr."

Grif rolled his eyes but put a hand on Dennis's arm before
he could leave. "Check the scanners again for word about the
old man, too, will ya?"

Worry clouded Dennis's brow. "I'll work on getting the hotel's surveillance videos, too. We can piece together their exit
from the casino, maybe get a license plate, but it'll take time."
He jerked his head at the two semiconscious men. "This is our
best bet to get Zicaro back quickly."

Grif nodded and turned back around, and a moment later a
giant swath of light cut across the floor as Dennis exited. Then
the darkness settled in again. By that time, the bartender had
arrived with the three tiki mugs they'd asked for when they'd
arrived. Grif had pushed two square tables tight to the two
men's bellies to keep them from falling over. The larger one,
Larry, was propped between the wall and Eric, making a run
at Grif near impossible.

The bartender eyeballed Eric, who had drool pooling at

one corner of his mouth, as he set the drinks in front of them.

"Bachelor party," Grif said, before he could ask.

Straightening, the bartender placed his hands on his hips. "Who's the unlucky man?"

"The little one."

The bartender nodded at Eric and gripped the ends of the towel he'd flung around his neck. "You the DD?"

No one who actually knew Grif and his penchant for getting lost would appoint him designated driver, but he just nodded. "And the best man."

"Well, best man, just make sure they don't puke in here. You have no idea how hard that shit is to get out of bamboo." And he walked away.

Grif had just finished handcuffing each man's right wrist to the table legs—and "blessing" their drinks—when Larry said, "Whas-ha-ma-ha-sha?"

His eyes were watery and fixed on a space between Grif's eyes and hairline, and his breath punctuated his words in all the wrong places. He tried again. "You . . . dead . . . guys."

Grif yawned. Been there, done that. "I got some questions for you."

Eric's head whipped up suddenly, and he laughed so hard that he hit the back of his head against the wall when he snorted.

"We know who you are," Grif continued, tossing their wallets, emptied of IDs, atop the table. "And the police know it by now, too. So I'm going to ask you some questions and . . ."

And Larry—mouth wide, head back—had fallen asleep again. Leaning forward, Grif slapped him once on each cheek. Eric gasped and reached out to stop him, but froze when the table he was cuffed to jerked in front of him. Grif slapped him anyway.

"Now that I have your attention . . . where did Justin take Al Zicaro?"

The two men just stared, but at least Eric had stopped laughing.

"How 'bout this, then . . . who killed Barbara DiMartino?"

Now they both looked away.

Grif sighed and nodded at the tiki mugs in front of them. "Take a sip. Each of you."

They didn't move.

"I'm not asking."

Larry tried to meet Grif's stare at that, but his eyes were still pinballing, and his chin still wobbled. He finally slumped and lifted the dark mug with his free hand. Hesitant at first, he drank deeply once he realized there was only rum inside. Seeing it, Eric followed suit and both men looked more relaxed when they sat their mugs back down.

"Now," Grif said quietly, staring down at Larry's mug. "Who killed Barbara?"

The sound of splintering wood ruptured the air as the tiki mugs stretched. The carved, gaping mouths widened as if giving a great yawn, and then the two mugs began yammering in unison.

"Who cares? She was a bitch of the first degree. I'm just surprised it didn't happen sooner."

"Yeah. Whoever it was, they have my regards."

"Oh, shit," Eric said, using his real voice. And then he passed out.

"You pussy!" Larry jolted as his mug voiced his thoughts, and watched wide-eyed as it swiveled toward Eric's mug, sloshing rum. But Eric's mug had fallen still. With him out cold, it was just a normal tiki mug.

Enjoying himself, Grif winked at Larry. It'd been a while since he'd been able to use this particular celestial trick. "You're very drunk," he said while they waited for Eric to come around. "You probably won't remember a bit of this in the morning."

They wouldn't. This was not a true possession. Angels could take over the bodies of people, but not inanimate objects. The mugs weren't sentient, just animated through an ethereal exchange. The men's thoughts had been emptied out in trade for the divine elixir, which was another reason why Grif had chosen Frankie's. Unless he wanted to gain their knowledge by sharing from the same cup, the vessel needed to have a face. A coffee cup, for example, would never work.

"Let's try this again," Grif said once Eric had recovered, earning a wink from Larry's mug. "This time we'll start with Eric. Do you steal money from the long-term residents at the Sunset Retirement Community?"

"I'm not going to—"

"I've got this one," said his mug, and made a sound like cracking knuckles before angling Grif's way. "We work in tandem with a few planted employees to extend the lives of . . . certain patients."

"Shut up!" Eric blurted, not realizing it was his own consciousness talking.

Larry's mug butted in. "For example, we have a couple of hospice workers who know that we're skimming, and the receptionist takes care of them along with taking her own cut, but they're in the dark about the trusts. For that, all you really need is an accountant and a good recruiter. You want to keep the pool small."

"I'll keep that in mind for the next time I wanna bilk old

folks of their savings," Grif said, glancing up and locking gazes with Larry. "And what do you do?"

"Whatever needs doing," his mug answered, and Larry gritted his teeth so hard that Grif could hear them grind over the video screens blaring behind him.

"He's the recruiter," said Eric's mug, wood stretching as he smiled smugly. Teacher's pet. "Who wouldn't trust that face?"

"And Eric?" Grif asked it.

"The accountant. Eric is a computer genius. He's my brother, so that's why we let him in."

"Goddamn it!" Larry slammed his meaty hand down on the table.

Grif turned his attention back to him. "And have you ever killed anyone in your care, Larry?"

"No." His headshake was exaggerated, but his eyes were clear. "No way."

"What he means to say," his mug elaborated, "is that by the time we're through milking those old-timers dry, they're beyond ready to die. Once the credit cards are maxed out and all revenues of possible income are depleted, the in-house physician returns their medication to normal recommended dosage—"

Eric's mug interrupted. "You mean *reasonable* dosage."

"And they let go pretty quickly after that," Larry's mug said. "Most of the time, as soon as someone gains even an iota of awareness of how badly they've deteriorated, they have no desire to go on."

And now, thought Grif, he had heard it all. There were scams . . . and then there were people who had simply lost every ounce of their humanity.

"Look," said Eric, palm up, catching Grif's wince. "Most of

that cash would end up in government pockets anyway. The families won't ever see it, because they don't know how to look. They have no idea how to exploit the loopholes, and it's not like the IRS is going to point out the missed opportunities. So we file the proper forms on the patient's behalf . . ."

"And keep the difference for yourself."

"Finders keepers," Eric's mug sneered.

"It's stealing," Grif replied, shaking his head at the mug before redirecting his attention toward Eric.

"It's free money," the man tried, and Grif realized that for some reason he liked Eric the least. He was less physically intimidating than Justin and quieter than Larry, but Grif found his watchfulness unnerving. A man who let others make the big plays, then lunged for the opportunities created by that chaos.

Right now, with Grif's heavy gaze upon him, he shrugged and said, "Hey, man. What would you do?"

Grif leaned forward, forcing Eric to look him in the eye. "I would choose not to be a stain on all of mankind."

It was an effort to sit back in his seat, and a bigger one to unclench the fist at his side. He forced himself to turn to Larry. "So you use every means possible to extend a patient's life—"

Larry's mug snorted. "Hell, we drug 'em up to their eyeballs and force them to live past their body's capability. It doesn't matter if they're begging to die, or as lonely as shit. As long as they're breathing, they're paying."

Larry gave an enraged cry and swatted the mug with his free hand. It yelled as it clattered to the floor, and Larry stared at it with a mixture of satisfaction and horror. It was the same way Grif was studying him.

"You guys have no idea what you're really doing," Grif finally said. He had to work to unclench his jaw. His heart was beating too fast in his chest. How the hell was he supposed to talk about this, to explain it, and still keep his cool? He pushed out a hard breath, trying to empty himself of the anger roiling inside of him. It was getting harder and harder to sit across from these guys. "You are keeping souls trapped in their bodies long after they require release. It's a form of torture, understand? And you're doing it *for money.*"

Laughter burst out of Larry, harsh and high, and he looked at Grif like he was a kid, some rug rat in need of schooling. "We're torturing them? What about the people who throw them into that place? It's like they're placing their belongings into storage. And why? Because it's more convenient for them to pay for care instead of give it. If they actually gave a shit about their parents or grandparents, then they'd catch the monetary discrepancies, but you know what? Most of them can't even bear to think about it. Their guilt over abandoning the people who raised them keeps them from looking at anything too closely. So if you ask me, they don't deserve to profit from the old."

"But you do?" Grif said coolly.

Eric's slim jaw just flexed at that. Grif thought again about putting a fist through it, but the bar door opened just then, letting in light cut by a large shadow.

"Let's nail these bastards," Grif growled, as Dennis reached his side.

Kit retreated from the desk as Ray DiMartino advanced into the room. His sculpted nose and dark eyes were pronounced beneath his still-wet hair, and dimples flashed in his stubble as he clenched his jaw. Although there was no place to hide a weapon beneath his towel, she perched on the armrest of the long leather sofa, a good place from which to access either exit, but kept her gaze trained on Ray as he padded, barefoot, forward.

"What the hell are you doing here?" Ray said, gaze darting over his desk, cataloging its contents, trying to see if anything was missing.

Kit slipped one hand into the right pocket of her skirt and slid her fingers around the .22 weighted there, but didn't pull it out. Her instructor had told her that pointing it at a human being wasn't the same thing as leveling it at a paper target, and he was right. Even contemplating shooting at someone again made her light-headed. Still, seeing the dark look in Ray's eyes, and the way they narrowed while assessing her, she was glad she had the gun with her.

"I have some questions about your dear deceased step-mother, Barbara. And Ray? Don't lie to me this time."

Ray's expression shifted at Barbara's name, morphing from one of surprise to hatred, with a brief pit stop at anger in between. Kit swallowed hard, unable to hold back her shudder. She had seen the look before—both on the face of a man who'd tried to kill her and in the gaze of a fallen angel. It was pure evil, and it made her uneasy, even though it was meant for a woman who was already dead.

Seeing her shake, Ray smiled and leaned on the edge of his desk, towel gaping. "She's dead. What else is there to say?"

Kit lifted the article about her father, holding it at eye-level in order to study Ray as he studied it. "This was my father, Ray. He was murdered the same day he took a call at your dad's house, fourteen years ago. Pretty amazing coincidence, huh?"

"They happen," he said unconvincingly.

Except that Ray had this article sitting in his office now, fourteen years later.

Ray looked at her for a long while, and finally said, "I know, okay? I was there."

Kit's heart thumped. "Was Barbara?"

"Yup. Me, dear ol' dad, his bitch wife, and her cousin." He scoffed. "One big happy family."

"Back up." Kit shook her head. "Cousin?"

"Yeah, you didn't know about her, did you?" He shrugged one shoulder, caught her looking, then rolled them both. Flexing. "Granted, she was quieter than Barbara. Plus she disappeared after the hullabaloo in 1960."

"Mary Margaret's kidnapping," Kit murmured. And *that* was the tie to Grif.

Ray nodded absently, but frowned as he cast his mind back in the past. "They were cut from the same cloth, though. Cousins, grifters, chip hustlers, whores. Those two trick-rolled so many men they probably lost count. It's why they came to Vegas in the fifties, you know. At least if my mother was to be believed."

"Theresa knew them?"

"Knew 'em, and saw right through 'em." And another puzzle piece snapped into place. Ray shook his head, and for a moment his gaze grew faraway. "My old man shoulda listened to her."

"Did you know them, Ray? I mean, back in the fifties?" He was only seven at the time, but there was a chance . . .

He looked at her and then stood, amusement brightening his face. "Of course. Barbara's cousin was Gina Alessi. She was Mary Margaret's nanny."

Kit opened her mouth, but nothing came out. She tried

again, but managed only a head shake. Ray, enjoying himself now, chuckled as he circled the desk and took a seat. He leaned back in his chair and waited for her to recover. Fortunately, the third time was a charm. "I . . . I'm at a loss."

"Because you're a reporter. That's your problem, see? You have to stick to the facts, cold and hard, black and white, right?" He waited for her nod. "But this is a story of emotion, and emotions make a bigger mess of things than facts. So the unsubstantiated fact is, those girls were after money and power, and in those days that meant the Family."

And in those days *that* meant the DiMartinos.

"So Gina gets a job as the family nanny, and she was actually all right, you know? I think she woulda gone straight, or at least tried, if she wasn't unduly influenced, if you know what I mean."

"By Barbara."

He inclined his head, mouth turning down. "She was a summer visitor at first. Just a girlfriend to keep Gina company while she watched over all of us kids. It was 'fifty-two that first time, Barbara was only sixteen. Fresh-faced, wide-eyed. It's amazing how much deviousness a pretty face can hide."

He looked at Kit, drawing out his pause, and she lifted one slim eyebrow. "Insinuating something, Ray?"

"Not at all," he lied, but the cunning smile slipped away as he continued. "Anyway, over the next three years, Barbara keeps visiting, and she gets a taste for the life, you know? The power and money that come along with being a part of the DiMartino dynasty. We used to catch her trying on my mother's things—her furs, her costume jewelry."

Her husband, Kit decided, watching the way Ray's eyes clouded over. Because Barbara had eventually married Sal . . .

and Gina—the longtime nanny and Barbara's *cousin*—was the link.

It was the smoking gun that Grif and she had been searching for. She couldn't wait to tell him.

"So what happened?"

Huffing, Ray rocked in his seat. "You think they're going to tell a seven-year-old anything? I don't see Barbara again after 'fifty-five or so. Then Mary Margaret gets kidnapped a few years later in revenge for stolen jewels. Old man Shaw rescues her, then he gets knocked off. That's when Gina disappears. Barbara comes back, though. After my mother died."

Back in 'sixty-one, then, Kit thought. Back for the one thing she really wanted. Sal DiMartino.

"So fast-forward thirty-seven years," Kit prodded.

Ray nodded. "And Gina shows up at my dad's place out of the blue. Whatever she says has Barbara both hopping mad and running scared. And if you didn't notice, Barbara doesn't scare easily. The police get called because some do-gooder heard a 'domestic disturbance' and that's when your dad shows up. His partner takes on Barbara. Your dad gets Gina."

Kit's instinct kicked in again, and she wrapped her fingers more tightly around the .22, trying to both work out what Ray was hiding and keep him talking. "What did Gina say to my father that was worth killing him for, Ray?"

"She tells him that Barbara isn't who she seems. That she took on the name of an infant who'd died back in 'forty, one named Barbara McCoy."

Kit blinked. "You mean . . ."

"Barbara didn't get remarried again after my father died, she hadn't gone from DiMartino to McCoy, she went *back* to being Barbara McCoy."

The truth hit Kit hard enough to make her gasp. And hope, too. *Now* she and Grif had a name to work with. Barbara *had* been around when Grif was killed in 1960.

It wasn't everything Kit had come here for, but it was a start. She blinked at Ray, who was still watching her closely.

"So why'd you tell Grif that you never spoke to Barbara anymore?"

"Hand to God, I hadn't spoken to her since the day my father died."

"Yet you called her after Grif and I came to see you." She wasn't sure of it, but how else would Barbara know? Why else would she return?

"Some reporter comes poking around, asking to see my dad's files? Why wouldn't I?" Ray scowled. "Didn't matter, though. All she cared about was Griffin Shaw. Wanted to know when he'd gotten back in town, what he wanted, who he was with." He jerked his head at Kit. "She went crazy when I told her about you. That you two were a couple. I tried to tell her that it was a different Griffin Shaw, younger, the grandson, but she didn't believe me. She Googled you, pulled up all your articles. Your photos. She became . . . obsessed."

You're not like the other girls, are you . . .

But Barbara had already known all about Kit when they first met.

"I asked her why she cared so much," Ray said, shrugging one naked shoulder, "but she just said not to talk to you. That Griffin Shaw had some sort of sway over women, a magnetism that made them do what he wanted. Whatever the hell that means."

Kit knew exactly what that meant. But how did Barbara?

"What else?"

"Nothing else. I gave Barbara your contact information," Ray said. "She took it from there."

The only sound in the office was the hum of the heater and Kit's own thoughts, screaming, Liar.

"Then why'd you call her last Saturday, Ray? You asked if 'it was done.'"

It was another gut instinct, but her gut was rarely wrong. "Were you asking about me? Was I the one who was supposed to die up in that suite?"

Ray leaned forward, staring intently like he was about to tell her something that would change her life. He waited until Kit leaned forward, too.

"Honey," he finally said, dark gaze unblinking. "You're *still* the one who is supposed to die."

And he rose with a sawed-off shotgun primed in his hands.

CHAPTER FOURTEEN

Tossing three IDs onto the table, Dennis grinned down at Grif. "You gotta love free Wi-Fi," he said, pulling up a chair. It meant he hadn't needed to use his police contacts.

"Eric and Larry Ritter, twins, ages twenty-eight, though Larry is the elder by two minutes. Their friend, Justin Allen, is thirty-six and a Gemini."

"You're showing off," Grif said admiringly. He couldn't help liking Dennis. He would have even liked him for Kit . . . if he didn't still want her for himself.

Dennis wiggled his eyebrows like an actor in some old silent flicker. "You ain't seen nothing yet."

"Impress us." Grif folded his arms and grinned at Larry and Eric. They remained unsmiling, though Larry did give a perfunctory jerk on his cuff. The table jolted. Grif's smile widened.

"Turns out Larry here used to be Metro. Ditto Justin. This one was suspended and eventually fired due to disciplinary problems. Do you know how hard it is to get fired from the force for minor infractions?"

"You guys are so dead," Larry said again.

Grif just nodded. "What else?"

"Files are sealed," Dennis said, eliciting a smile from Larry. "But I did find out that he used to work gang crimes, intelligence unit. I got a contact there. It's only a matter of time before I know more."

Grif took up smiling as Larry's smile fell. "And Eric?"

"Ah yes. Quite the IT guy before joining Sunset. Got scholarship offers to MIT and Carnegie Mellon. Made a pretty penny in the private sector until he all but disappeared off the tech radar a few years back. Climbed to the top of his field and just . . . poof. Quit."

"You must have had a very compelling reason," Grif said to Eric, who only glared.

"So two disgraced cops and a rogue tech nerd working at Sunset." Grif tapped a finger on the table. They hadn't been lying. They did keep it tight.

But they'd have to, especially with the possibility of family and guardians checking in on their charges' accounts and trusts. Still, Grif was surprised that they hadn't been caught before now. More often than not, greed and pride would loosen the stays on such a long-term scam. *Look what I bought . . . look how much I have . . . look, look, look at me.*

"There had to be someone in charge," he muttered, rubbing his chin.

"What's that?" said Dennis.

"There's someone else," Grif said louder, and leaned forward, propping his elbows on the table. "Someone bigger than Justin, smarter than Eric. Meaner than Larry."

Someone who could hold a whole group of criminals to a vow of silence for months on end.

"So who's running you guys?" Dennis asked, crossing his arms. The mugs, of course, were quiet and still in his presence, but the animation had been a one-trick pony, and not one Grif needed now that Larry and Eric were rattled. They knew Grif and Dennis had enough information to nail them all. Larry was trying not to show it, but Grif recognized panic disguised by steely silence.

"We don't know him," Eric finally blurted, and his brother turned and glared.

"What?" Eric asked, knocking into Larry's shoulder. "You think he's going to stick his neck out for us? Fuck that. They already know our names."

"Justin has the flash drives," Larry countered. "And the old man."

"And we have copies," Grif said, and kept his shrug easy. It wouldn't do Zicaro any good to let these guys know how worried Grif was about him. "Of the flash drives, not the old man. But we'll get back to him shortly. Tell us more about this other guy."

"I've never seen him. Justin has, though. They're thick as thieves."

The men were unraveling, and turning on each other as they did.

Larry was now nodding. "I've talked to him on the phone, but that's all."

"No idea at all what he looks like?" Grif asked.

"Sure," Larry said, then smiled coolly as he leaned back.

"He looks like you. He looks like me. He looks like anyone you've ever seen walking down the street. He just blends, and you never see him coming."

"Sounds like a ghost," Dennis said.

"Which is what you'll be if you cross him. He'll turn on you in an instant, and I *have* seen that before."

"Trevor." Eric nodded, a movement Larry took up as they recalled some shared memory.

"I don't want that shit bearing down on me," Larry said, shaking his head. "And believe me, as soon as he finds out what's going on, he's gonna come looking for you. Both of you."

"I hope he does," Grif said evenly. "I'd like to see this ghost in person."

"You'll get that chance. Guaranteed."

Larry's confidence was real enough, but there was also something off about it. Grif couldn't put his finger on it, and Larry's mug was silent, its contents now splashed over the floor. Still, something nagged at Grif, like a needle poking at the base of his spine. He felt suddenly like he'd been asking the wrong questions and now it was too late.

"Don't go nowhere," he told Larry and Eric, then looked over at Dennis and jerked his head.

They congregated by the front door, using the center tiki god to block them from the bartender's view but still keep the two men in sight.

"What the hell have you guys gotten into?" Dennis muttered. He ran a hand over his head, causing his tight pomp to flare. "First Barbara DiMartino's death. Now this. Some unnamed criminal mastermind?"

"And it's all related somehow." Grif could feel it. Zicaro had been questioned about Barbara right before she'd visited him, right before her death. "Has anyone notified Barbara's next of kin yet?"

Dennis inclined his head. "There's a stepson. Ray DiMartino."

"Yeah, I know him," Grif muttered darkly.

"Why am I not surprised?" Dennis said.

Ignoring that, Grif dug out the digital recorder Kit had let them borrow, turned it off, and handed it to Dennis.

"None of this is admissible in court," Dennis said, but took the device anyway. "Sounds like Justin's the one we need. If we can get an admission on record, we can set a formal inquiry into motion."

But that wasn't going to be easy at all.

"I hope the old man's okay," Dennis finally said, expression shifting into one of worry.

"They didn't hurt him in all the time he was out at Sunset," Grif said. "I get the feeling they want something from him, too. That old newshound probably knows things he doesn't even know he knows."

"Old ghosts," Dennis said, nodding.

Grif tilted his head. "What's that?"

"What Zicaro was saying at the steakhouse last night. About old ghosts rearing their heads. New ones, too . . . like Barbara DiMartino."

"You think this has something to do with some fifty-year-old mobster turf war?"

"I think it has to do with the diamonds he was talking about. I looked it up when I got home, Shaw. These things were the size of silver dollars. Three of them. Perfect cuts."

Grif didn't remember. When he took on the job of locating

little Mary Margaret, he was very clear with Sal DiMartino that he didn't want to know anything about their business or lifestyle. He was there to help find the little girl, and that was all. He thought if he kept his nose clean, he could keep his hide safe, and Sal—though amused—had agreed.

A lot of good it'd done him. A cache of diamonds had disappeared, and now these pikers thought Grif had the map to locate them.

So then why had Justin just taken off with Zicaro? Why not make a play for Grif?

"Hostage," Dennis guessed, when he asked him the same thing. "Watch. They'll want to trade Zicaro for the map."

The map he didn't have. The map that probably didn't even exist.

"Sure you don't know anything about it?" Dennis prodded, holding up his hands when Grif glared.

"Get bent, Carlisle. You should know better than to ask that of me. I'm a good man."

"Yeah? So am I, Shaw," Dennis said, leaning too close. "And I don't like working this way. It straddles the line, and I'm a good cop, too."

He was. The aura around him glowed in a healthy ring. He was fully recovered, and it looked like he was destined to stay that way. Grif realized he was glad. So he put a hand on the man's shoulder, and nodded once. "I appreciate it."

"I didn't do it for you," Dennis snapped, still hot.

And there it was, finally out between them. Grif tucked his hands in his pockets. "I know that, too."

Turning away, Dennis stared with clenched jaw at the video screens behind the bar. Whatever he was seeing, it wasn't topless hula girls, swinging hips.

"You broke her, you know," he finally said, causing Grif to jolt. He hadn't been expecting that . . . or the quiver in Dennis's voice. He shook his head, still not looking at Grif. "I don't know how she's walking by your side, and talking to you now—she couldn't even move at all a couple of months ago. *She* was a ghost."

Grif found he was unable to defend himself. "She's very strong," he said instead.

"She's more than that, Shaw," Dennis shot back, and now he did look at him, his honed gaze finding Grif's. "She's honest and good. She's beautiful and pure and you don't often find that in this world. Not all in one person. And you . . . you just broke her."

"Can you please stop saying that?"

"No," Dennis said sharply, nostrils flaring. "Because you need to know. This obsession you have with the past? This Evelyn Shaw you keep mentioning? It's costing you the kindest person I've ever known. Like I said, I don't like to work this way, but I'd damned well cross the line for her. She's worth it, and you're an idiot if you don't know it."

"I do know she's worth it." Grif swallowed hard. "I just don't know what to do about it."

"Then you're an even bigger idiot than I thought," Dennis said immediately, then shook his head before Grif could answer. "Forget it. I'm gonna pull the car 'round. Bring those assholes back through the kitchen. I'll tell the bartender that we need some discretion."

Then he was gone. Grif took a minute to breathe. He rubbed his jaw and realized his hand was shaking. He stopped it with effort, but couldn't halt the sense that despite trying, he was doing nothing right.

Taking a deep breath, he headed back to the two men wait-ing on tenterhooks in the corner, determined to change that.

Kit dropped behind the leather sofa, falling more than dodg-ing the shot that rang across the room. She couldn't find air; there suddenly seemed to be so little of it, and none within reach of her lungs. And while she was also shaking, she instinctively knew that she had to move. So she fought through the scent of gunpowder shocking the air to remember how to work her legs.

The door leading to the club banged open, and Kit's head swung around. The woman who'd led her into the room took one look at her trembling on the ground, then at Ray, still on the other side of the room and still, apparently, holding a shotgun in lieu of his towel. The hostess then swallowed hard, backed out of the room, and closed the door behind her.

Ray's footsteps resumed and Kit tried to inch back, but her skirt kept hampering her. She was climbing up into it, getting caught in the voluminous folds, and while one part of her was screaming to make her shaking hands work, to reach for the gun in her skirt pocket, another part was already anticipating a second shotgun blast through her head. *At least I'll spend eternity in fabulous clothes.*

Jesus.

"I liked you, Craig," Ray said, voice closer. Kit knew he could shoot her right through the sofa, but he didn't. Not yet. "But Barbara was right. You're just as dangerous as Shaw is, in your own way. All those questions bubbling up behind that pretty little face."

Kit didn't answer. She was too focused on those footsteps, which were a metronome of aggression, and frighteningly calm compared to the calamitous beat of her heart.

"But right now what I want from you is an answer. Where's the map?"

The map. The mystery. The diamonds.

"I don't—"

"I know Gina gave it to your father. I saw her. So where is it?"

Kit would give it to him if she knew. She realized in that moment that she would give him anything if it meant she would live. Then, suddenly, the answer was there, like it suddenly crystallized in the shocked air. "Marin has it."

That was what she was withholding from Kit. The information her father had died for . . . that Grif had died for . . . and that Kit was going to die for, too.

"Does Barbara know that?" Ray asked, and appeared around the sofa's edge, naked as the day he was born, if heavier and hairier and holding a shotgun in front of him. Kit kept her eyes on his face, because when he decided to shoot her, she'd see it there first.

Barbara's dead, Kit was about to say, but Ray knew that. He was just on a rant.

"Because Barbara has no right to those diamonds. That necklace was made for my mother, by my father. Barbara took everything else from my family. Those diamonds are mine."

Kit needed to buy time to find something with which to distract him. Struggling not to move, to *scream*—fighting just to think—she managed, "I— I thought you were working with her."

"I thought you were," he answered immediately. He sounded calm, but too calm. Like a receded shoreline right before a tsunami. "It would be just like her to enlist someone else. She never got her hands dirty. She liked to say she had people for that."

For some reason, that made him sneer and pump the slide on the shotgun.

"We— We're not," Kit said quickly, and she was unable to help herself now. She shoved herself backward on her palms, but got caught up in her skirt again. Reaching down, she pulled the folds free. Ray's eyes flickered, lighting on her legs.

"I knew that as soon as I saw her reaction to the news that you and Shaw were a couple, but honestly? I don't care. I just want you all out of my way."

Kit needed more time. Drawing her legs in tight, she went with her gut. "Barbara killed your father, didn't she?"

Ray's expression darkened at that, and his mouth slowly altered, some sort of mute misery drawing it down at the sides. "Her story was that Gina rolled back into town and killed him, which is possible, given that Gina disappeared again, too." Ray sighed heavily. "But I don't think so. Gina was genuinely spooked. I know, because I followed her that day."

Kit froze, trying to wrap her head around that. "So you . . ."

"I left the house."

He had left.

"You . . . you followed . . ."

Ray's mouth re-formed into its hard line as he waited for her to catch up, watching her struggle for words with a look that was almost hungry. When she finally figured it out, jolting as she stared at him, his lips shifted again, this time turning upward.

"Life can be so ironic," he finally said, almost to himself. "I mean, who'da thought I'd be using the same gun on you fourteen whole years after I killed your father?"

Silence flooded in so quickly that Kit had the sense of dropping into it, as if submerged. Yet it was also the loudest thing she'd ever heard in her life. Both out of breath and unable to take another, she couldn't even feel her ribs in her chest. Instead, she floated up, up, and up as Ray aimed the shotgun at her, and from within the folds of her skirt, her arm rose as well.

The bullet that tore through Ray's naked body was muted, too. All Kit heard was its sizzle as it left the gun, and the only thing that brought her back around was the recoil of the .22 in her palm.

Ray's body jerked first left, then right—she must have shot him twice, she thought dreamily—and even after he toppled behind the sofa, his surprised expression was burned into the air where he'd stood.

Gunpowder fogged the room. It had tears springing up in her eyes and felt thick in her buzzing ears. It worked to clog her throat, and seeped into her pores as well. It weighed her down. Violence now lived inside of her. She breathed death.

A sound, half sigh, half moan, filled the air like keening as she wiped at her face. Was that her? Then she began to shake, the shudders so great that her breath sawed through the loaded silence. She felt like toppling to her side, curling into herself, and never getting up. She should move. She should run out the back door and never look back, but all she wanted to do was squeeze her eyes shut—like so—and . . .

"He was going to kill you, you know."

Kit's eyes flew wide as she gasped, and she froze, surprised into stillness. She knew she was going into shock . . . but she also knew that voice.

Gaining her knees, jerking up that damned skirt—now with two holes blasted through its pocket—she pulled herself up by the back of the sofa and peered over the edge. When she saw the half-transparent form there, blond and beaming, she felt herself sway. "Nic?"

"Hiya, girly-friend," Nicole said, perching on the arm of the leather sofa, downy wings folded as she shot her a sweet smile. Kit wobbled and fell back to the floor.

And Nicole Rockwell, her best friend in the world, dead an entire year, called out to her from the other side of the room. "Go ahead and take a moment there. No one is coming in for a bit, and this guy certainly isn't going anywhere."

Kit's mouth moved, but no sound emerged and she had to blink furiously to keep her eyes from rolling back in her head. It wasn't enough. She slapped her own face, then did it again when she realized that made her feel more present, more solidly there.

Nic snorted from the other side of the sofa.

When she was finally able to take in a real breath, Kit managed to pull herself to her feet—though she still needed the sofa to steady her shaky weight.

Nic, whose grave Kit had sobbed over, was wearing gold-tipped wings that rose in beautiful ivory arches. Her hair was somewhat mussed, giving an indication of its state when she died, but she otherwise looked whole and perfect, and would have even appeared serene were it not for the psychedelic swirling of stardust winking in her otherworldly gaze. Kit took a shaky step in her direction, and Nic smiled encouragingly.

"How am I able to see you?" Kit managed to ask.

And when, she wondered, had she become so comfortable talking with angels?

Nicole frowned, as if the question disappointed her. She snapped her fingers like that would suddenly make Kit understand, yet the movement produced the sound of bells, which only had Kit jerking her head in disbelief. "C'mon, honey. After all you've seen and done this past year? After *that*?" She pointed down at what Kit presumed was Ray's body. "Don't be dramatic."

"Are you a—"

"If you're going to say ghost, I'm leaving now."

The sarcasm was pure Nicole, and that's what really, finally calmed Kit. She hadn't been about to say ghost. She didn't believe in ghosts, she believed in angels . . . specifically in Centurions.

"How long have you been listening?"

"I got here when you did. It's my punishment for disobeying heavenly orders." Seeing Kit's dropped jaw, she shrugged. "I take it Grif didn't tell you about my new gig."

Kit shook her head. It came out as more of an uncontrolled jerk.

"I'm not surprised. He probably didn't want to upset you, and he really just learned of it himself. My Take is usually some sob story." She cut her eyes back at Ray. "But I get the occasional riffraff as well."

Which meant Nic's soul was tortured. She'd be stuck with a Centurion's responsibilities until her soul healed enough to forgive and let go of her earthly regrets. Kit's heart sank, and she placed her hand over her chest as tears filled her eyes.

"Don't." Nicole held up a hand and softly added, "Don't cry for me, Kit."

The understanding in her gentle tone ripped a sob from Kit anyway.

Nicole sighed. "Okay, it was hard at first. I mean, letting go of your dreams about a life not lived is like a death all in itself. But I've seen some awesome things since then. I get to go to amazing places, and I don't have to pay some crappy airline to do it."

That surprised a laugh from Kit. She immediately covered her mouth. There was nothing funny about this situation.

"And before you can say it," Nicole went on, "I know you're sorry. I'm sorry, too, but the only way to move on is to let go, and . . . I think I'm almost there." She nodded at Kit, an acknowledging bow. "You guys have helped, you know."

"Us . . . ?" Kit asked, inching around the sofa. They were only feet apart now. Two more steps and she could reach out and touch her old friend . . . if she were still alive. She had an almost uncontrollable urge to try, but refrained, just to maintain the illusion.

"You and Grif," Nicole clarified. "I've been watching you. Especially you, Kit. Every time I'm assigned a Take I pop back to the Surface a little early and find you. As a Centurion, I can always spot others like me, and your man Grif is like a beacon to me. So I find him"—she shrugged—"and I find you."

"You've got it wrong. He's not my man, Nic." Kit shook her head, not bothering to hide the sadness in the movement. Nic would see it even if she weren't a Centurion.

"We haven't been together for months."

"Honey, didn't you hear me?" Leaning forward, Nicole quirked an eyebrow, causing the stardust in her gaze to shift and swirl in a different direction. "I've been *watching*. I saw you together. I saw you apart. I even saw you following him when he didn't know you were there."

"Grif has a terrible sense of direction," Kit said defensively, and felt the heat rush back into her cheeks. "Someone had to look out for him."

"But it cost you to do so," Nicole said softly.

It'd cost her more to be away from him. Kit looked away. Unfortunately, her eyes landed on Ray, prone where she'd felled him, and she shuddered.

Nicole followed the direction of her gaze. "He would have done it, you know. Killed you just like he killed your father."

Yes. Kit had seen that . . . and she told herself that's why she'd fired. Not out of revenge for her dad, or for the havoc the deed had wreaked on the remainder of Kit's mind and life, but in self-defense. Right?

Swallowing hard, she inched forward and then propped herself on the coffee table before Nicole. Dead or not, Take or not, Ray could damn well wait while she talked with her best friend.

"You're still helping Shaw find his wife," Nicole stated.

Kit frowned. Maybe it *was* time for them to go. "I want what's best for him" was all she said.

"Is that all?"

Kit sniffed. "I forgot what a pain in the ass you could be."

"I mean, have you asked him lately?" Nicole went on, ignoring her. "Because like I said, I've been watching."

"He's the one who's still looking for her," Kit pointed out.

"Yes, but he's looking *over* you." Nicole gave her a meaningful look, then feigned looking at a wristwatch before stepping behind the sofa and giving Ray a little kick. "Hey. Get up! We gotta go."

Kit stood, too. "Nice bedside manner."

"Learned it from Shaw," Nic admitted, and surprised she was capable of it, Kit actually smiled. Nicole glanced back down at Ray. "The bastard's hiding in there. Even newly harvested souls know when they have to answer for their crimes."

Kit's heart resumed an unnatural thud. She put a hand to her forehead. "I can't believe this is happening."

Nicole just shrugged the magnificent wings at her back, causing the gold tips to flare as if lit. "What do you expect? That big lug gave you awareness. He handed you an apple of knowledge and you took a big ol' bite of it. Now you can't unknow it. That would require someone more prone to fantasy, and the Kit I knew and loved valued the truth above all else."

"Still do," Kit admitted, because it was what her father had taught her, what he'd died for, and what she had lived for ever since.

Don't just find the easy answer, Kitty-Cat! Find the truth!

"And *that's* why you can see me," Nicole said, crossing her arms. "It's why you can see Grif for who he really is, too. The Pure actually love that about you, by the way."

"You mean Grif's angelic asshole of a boss?" Scoffing, Kit shook her head. "He hates me."

"He didn't understand you," Nicole corrected, "but now he does. He's had to feel what it's like to be one of us. He's actually felt every ounce of your pain and sorrow. It's excruciating for a Pure."

Kit was not going to feel sorry for that bombastic, judgmental, blackmailing Pure angel. "I don't care."

"Is that why you won't allow yourself to feel good things anymore? You just don't care?"

Kit crossed her arms now. "You calling me on my shit, Nic?"

Nicole smiled and pointed at herself. "Bestie, remember?"

Yes, they were besties . . . and Kit wasn't just happy to see her, she was relieved to be with someone with whom she didn't have to feign strength.

"It's hard," she finally said, chin wobbling.

Nic smiled. "Because it's worth it."

"It hurts."

"Because it's passion."

"I'm afraid," Kit finally admitted in the smallest voice yet.

"But feeling love, even losing it, is better than simply existing," Nicole said, and shook her head as she frowned. "Take it from someone who doesn't have to worry about anything anymore, taking a risk is a gift. It means you still have a chance to build something great and new. You should throw yourself at that."

Kit just stood there.

"I said throw yourself," Nicole said wryly, and Kit laughed self-consciously. Nicole laughed, too, then straightened and took a step toward Ray. "I really do have to go. This ass-nozzle is starting the Fade, and it's my wings if he gets Lost."

But Kit just stared at Nicole, and there was no room for thoughts of Ray or, momentarily, even Grif. This was it, she somehow knew. She wouldn't see Nicole again, not on this side of the life/death divide, and that reopened the wound that she thought time had healed. A million little memories and moments raced through Kit's mind: Nicole's love for potluck cookouts and swing-dancing, the way tears streamed down the apples of her cheeks when she really got to laughing, how their sides would hurt afterward, sometimes for hours.

Kit bit her lip, feeling tears well up, and wished she could hug her friend one last time, or that they could at least link arms as they had so often after a long night out, gazes turned toward the rising sun, making wishes upon the new day.

"Careful," Nicole said, her star-speckled gaze now surging. She was remembering, too. "Father Francis is going to blame me if he feels all of *that*."

Kit still didn't care. Her sorrow at Nic's violent, needless death struck her all over again, and as her heart swelled in her chest, she realized that was why God never let people see the loved ones who'd passed on after death. You'd never heal if the scab was continually ripped from the wound.

"I'm glad we get to say good-bye," she choked out. "We didn't get to . . . the first time."

"Yeah, sudden death due to multiple stab wounds and strangulation tends to interfere with the more heartfelt farewells." Nicole laughed darkly at Kit's responding wince. "Don't worry about me, Kit, just . . . don't shut down. I know it's not easy, but I think I can deal with facing eternity on this side of things as long as I know that you still have your face turned toward the sun."

Kit blew out a shaky breath and finally gave a matching nod, though she wasn't sure that would ever be the case again. She'd always valued knowledge and truth, but now it felt like she knew too much to ever be that blithely, or blindly, happy again.

"Go out the back," Nicole told her, jerking her head at the far door. "I've messed with the cameras, so they'll never see you leave."

Kit nodded, and Nicole just smiled and gave her a slow blink when she hesitated. Kit drank in the sight of her, committing this new-yet-old girlfriend to memory, then finally turned away. She'd just touched the handle when Nicole called out to her.

"Do you still love him?"

"I do," Kit answered, and as soon as she said it, a weight seemed to lift from her chest. Her head felt lighter, too, almost dizzy, but she couldn't be sure that wasn't just shock settling in. Still, it felt good to admit. She turned, and they locked eyes one final time, and Kit grew momentarily lost in the stardust swirling in her friend's pupils. It was still startling, but somehow it made Nicole more beautiful than ever. "It's the truest thing I know," she admitted.

Nicole smiled and her stardust gaze glinted. "Then throw yourself at that."

Biting her lower lip, Kit tilted her head. "I love you, Nic. Always."

"Of course you do. I'm your forever friend." Nicole tossed her mussed hair, jerking her head at the door. "Now hurry. You have a life to get on with."

And so Kit got on with it, leaving quickly and closing the door behind her on stardust and wings and a smile she would never forget.

CHAPTER FIFTEEN

After Dennis left to get the car, Grif retraced his steps back to the tables where Larry and Eric waited. He thought about drugging them again, but decided against it when he looked into their gazes and saw the resignation there. They were defeated and knew it. All that was left was to bundle them up and roll them out.

Grif uncuffed the smaller Eric first, and then kept hold of Larry's arm as he straightened and jerked his head to the door. That's when he stumbled and swayed. It was a tossup as to who was more surprised, the men hemmed in by the tables or Grif, suddenly braced against them. He tried to shake his head of it, this fugue that hadn't so much crept up on him as it had sprung in an unexpected attack.

The two men needed no more encouragement than that.

Grif had time to turn his head, though it was in the wrong

direction and all he caught was a glimpse of Eric's teeth—
straight as railroad ties—before catching Larry's knuckles as
well. The blow caught him square, he didn't even have time
to back away, though his legs had already quit working in any
case. They were ensnared in plasmic chains that only he could
see, banded silver coils pulling tight, as if meant to tie him to
the tracks. Two of the three tables toppled, pinning Grif to the
ground, and then a chair thrown from overhead crashed into
his skull.

A spear of light tore through his vision, either from the blow
or the front door as Larry and Eric fled. All Grif saw after
that were twilight grays rushing him as the blood in his borrowed flesh tingled, zinging through his limbs and pooling
in his toes. The bar shimmered and lost its shape. Movement
undulated from the corner of his eye, and Grif gasped as more
plasma rushed him, a flood now.

Grif lost all control of his body then, his limbs shorting out
like faulty electrical wires. His eyes were open, he was sure,
yet they were also rolled far back into his battered skull. A
thrumming reverberated around him, which he registered as
his heartbeat, but even that knowledge couldn't touch him.
Plasma soaked into his pores, sizzled in his brain, and burrowed between the folds of his mind to separate past from
present like playing cards divided into two different piles.

Then it began to burn. Flames roared to life in his skull
with a searing crackle, a crescendo that whipped down to fill
his chest. It was as if he were centered in a fire, burning like
a dry log, and just when he thought he would die of the anguish, his body temperature plummeted, and his veins hardened in an arctic freeze. The abruptness stole his breath . . . and
whisked him away where plasma could no longer reach him.

And then he was *there*. Feet planted firmly on the Surface, he glanced around and saw that he was no longer in the bar but on a garden path, standing in a night that was quiet but for the soft chirping of crickets and a woman's tipsy laughter. He turned without willing it, as if a giant hand were swiveling him around on a platform.

When he stopped, Evie was beckoning to him and smiling as she reached for his hand. "Come on, Griffin."

She pulled him forward. *Into the past.*

The horseshoe-shaped courtyard of the Marquis Hotel and Casino was exactly the same, and so were they; young and comfortably entwined as they headed to their bungalow. The room had been comped by Sal DiMartino, he remembered. A thank-you for saving his niece. This time, however, Grif was also burdened with the knowledge that he was about to die.

Though Grif had recovered this particular memory before, he'd never experienced it with such remarkable clarity. The surrounding foliage shimmered with the green of a storm-laden rain forest, while the path before him was bone-white, sparking beneath the full moon, but both fell flat compared to the blinding white-blond hair of the woman in front of him— the one he'd loved and lost and sought for the whole of the last fifty years.

"Evie," he said breathlessly.

She turned to face him fully this time. She had rose-petal lips and a dress that matched, and the lacquer on her fingers glinted in the cold light. With the hindsight of a Centurion, Grif tried to stop himself from continuing his death march, but for all his angelic powers, he couldn't change the past. Evie laughed and pulled him toward her, bumping his hip with hers and murmuring into his ear. He laughed just as he had the first time, though inside he was sobered with the dark knowledge that he would be dead within minutes.

Evie's heels click-clacked over the bright path, each step a rocket going off in his mind. "I have plans for you, Griffin, my dear." Her eyes glinted with promise, and their wedding bands tapped gently together. He remembered this, too, because it'd been the last time he'd felt this band on his finger. It would disappear before he took his final breath.

"This is our night, Griffin," she said, just as she had the first time. "All your attention of late has been on the DiMartino case, but now it's over. We won."

"I think the real winners are the DiMartinos," Grif said, yet he still glowed with her praise. He was pleased to have solved the case, and proud to have delivered Mary Margaret DiMartino into her mother's waiting arms.

"Oh, sure," Evie said, as the intricate brick face of their bungalow came into view. "The Salernos won't be bothering them for some time . . . but I don't want to talk about the Salernos or the DiMartinos anymore. Tonight belongs to us."

"You smell like lilacs," Grif murmured, when she tucked her head beneath his chin, cuddling in tight as he shoved the key into the lock.

"And soon I'm going to smell like you." She tilted her head up to kiss him as the door swung open, and they pushed into the room blindly. All over again—despite the passing of fifty years—he was hungry for her mouth, her tapered neck, those limbs, which twined and tangled with his own. They wrapped around his body, and he drove her up against the wall. He was thinking of taking her here, like this, hard like she sometimes liked it, and he didn't think she'd mind. Not given the way her hands were pulling him tightly against her sweet, smooth curves.

He was just wondering if he'd had too much to drink, and worrying that he might somehow be a disappointment to her, when a footstep fell behind him. He turned in time to catch a shadowed movement, a sliding darkness in the shape of a man; fast, certain . . . not a shadow at all.

Evie was yanked from him, and suddenly it was his back against the wall. He pushed off, instinctively trying to create space between him and their attacker, but made a sound he didn't recognize when white heat pierced the center of his body. Glancing down, he spotted the handle of a butcher's knife protruding from his belly. He wondered briefly how it got there, and then looked up into dark eyes that were too wide, and a face that was too young, with cheeks still carrying the whisper of baby fat.

"Tommy?" Grif said, and then glanced back down at the knife, trying to put two and two together.

"You hurt my baby sister, you son of a bitch," Tommy DiMartino said, and for the first time Grif saw what he was holding, waving, in his other hand. A child's doll with strangely sparkling eyes.

I want Cissy. Please, Mr. Shaw. I need my Cissy. My doll.
We'll get your doll, baby. But for now, you have to be quiet.

"You can't do what you did and expect to get away with it," Tommy said, and Grif found himself thinking, You're right. I should have found Mary Margaret's doll for her.

Too late now. He looked over to find Evie standing just out of arm's reach, arms up in surrender, mouth open as she stared not at Grif's face but at his belly. Wincing, Grif looked down again as his stomach began to burn. The blade wobbled as he stumbled back, which he found disturbing. It looked all wrong just protruding there.

"This isn't mine," he slurred dumbly, feeling something rising inside of him, like a tidal wave shoving upward through his body, and catching in his throat. He had the fleeting thought that he might just drown in his own body, and, panicking, pulled the blade from his belly so that all that choking warmth immediately fell, pooling over his wrists.

It's not blood, he thought, head going light. It couldn't be blood. It was just more of those moving shadows.

Grif looked up again to find that Tommy's face had gone white. He stuttered this time, but still waved the doll at Grif, like it was some sort of talisman, fending him off. Its odd eyes sparkled, winking at Grif, even in the dark. "You fucking deserve it, you kiddie-molester. You—"

I need to get that doll for Mary Margaret, Grif thought, lunging for it. After all, he'd promised. But Tommy jerked back, holding on to it tight, and suddenly Grif's wrists *were* covered in blood. Evie screamed, and Tommy roared, and it reminded Grif of his army days—stepping into the ring in the summer heat, the men chanting his name as he faced some other pugilist, hand-to-hand, as men should. *One-two, one-two-three-four.*

The flurry of jabs and hooks automatically came back to him, and with a final mean uppercut Grif snapped back to find a Tommy-shaped outline lying stark against the white marble floor. His black driving gloves were still wrapped around Mary Margaret's Cissy doll.

A doll, Grif realized, blinking, with diamonds for eyes.

Then Evie screamed again, and Grif felt his skull pop open like a can. He dropped and suddenly found himself face-to-face with Tommy's unblinking gaze. Evie fell between them with a grunt and a thud, her cheek landing in a puddle of blood. Grif realized it was where he had been standing when he'd pulled the blade from his gut. And now she was lying in it, eyes fastened on his, shock forcing those chocolate irises wide with horror and tears. "Damn it. Griffin, no . . ."

She reached for him and he tried to do the same, and he finally felt her fingertips curl again around his left hand. Squeezing tight, she tried to pull him close. "Griffin," she said, and his name echoed in his brain like a train rattling on its tracks.

"Griffin." The rattling intensified, pushing apart the sides of his skull. Keep your head together, he thought, then convulsed with the black humor.

Grif's life poured out over the floor.

"Griffin, dear," she repeated, one last time, clinging fast to his numbing fingertips. "Why do you . . . ?"

But another voice filled his head just then, overwhelming the rattling and Evie and the past. "Dude. Dude!"

Hold on, he thought, reaching for Evie. Yet the voice ripped through him, clean as a butcher's blade through the belly, cleaving the past from the present. His eyes rolled back around and he found himself nose-to-nose with the bartender, who was peering into his face with too-wide eyes. He ignored the man and pushed to his knees, and though he already knew it was futile, his gaze shifted to the ring finger of his left hand. There was nothing there.

"Where?" he rasped to the bartender.

The man didn't have to be asked twice. "Out the front," he replied, offering Grif a hand.

Grif accepted the help up, and when he was steadied, said, "Go tell Dennis they're gone."

The bartender just nodded—knowing questions could wait—and Grif staggered to the front door. He whipped it open and had to shield his eyes from the burn of the harsh daylight. When they'd finally acclimated, he realized he was leaning against the bar's unlikely guard—a tiki god the circumference of a redwood, with a carved mouth large enough to swallow Grif whole. He pushed away from it to scan the lot at the same time that the telltale creak of wood sounded over his shoulder.

"Shit," he muttered, rubbing his pounding head.

"What's wrong, Shaw?" The sound, wood straining against its own grain, slivered through the late-afternoon air. "Can't take a dose of your own medicine?"

Sighing, Grif turned to face the twelve-foot tiki god. The surface of the whittled face had already shifted to take on Sarge's features, though the wood was carved in the wrecked mien of his most recent visage, the face ruined by emotion. Grif briefly wondered if Sarge's old face was gone for good.

"How much do you know?" Grif asked, rocking back on his heels.

"When it comes to those in my charge, I know all."

"Know, but don't tell," Grif scoffed, and put his hand on the door. He'd had enough of this creature's games. "I'm going back inside."

"But don't you want to ask your question first?"

Grif glanced back at the hunk of wood.

"The one that's worrying you beneath that sore knot on your head."

He meant how did Larry, a mere human, manage to hit him? Why had he grown dizzy? How could he have not seen it coming?

Because Grif *had* been looking for the man to strike. Looking . . . and yet unable to stop it.

"How you been feeling lately, Shaw?"

"Fine." But other than the flash of heat that then swerved into a biting cold—the agony of the newly returned memory—he was hardly feeling a thing at all. Yeah, he was trying to keep his feelings for Kit at bay, but it was more than that. He actually felt drained. Numbness had been pressing at his skull from the moment he'd awoken today.

A creaking sound, as Sarge gave the tiki equivalent of a shrug. "That'll change soon. In another day you'll start having problems with your five senses, one at a time at first, but they'll all worsen."

"Why?"

"The prophecy, Shaw."

The prophecy.

Reunite with your true love before the anniversary of your death . . . or all is Lost.

That was it. Reunite with the woman he loved. Do it before the anniversary of his death . . . or be whisked back to the Everlast for his mind to be stripped down so he wouldn't even know himself.

"You can't keep ignoring it." And the carved holes where Sarge's eyes should have been pulsed with pity. "You're weakening, Shaw. Your celestial strength is fleeing you. Nobody in the Everlast expected you to still be here a full year after your return."

"So they were wrong."

"But you're not a stone, Shaw. You're not meant to last on the Surface forever. Like all living things, you have an expiration date. Yours happens to be the fifty-first anniversary of the day you died. That's why the date was referenced in your prophecy. As soon as you've reached the exact date and time of your return . . . you'll start the Fade."

"Even though I'm wearing flesh?" Grif's heart thudded so hard in his chest that he heard it in his ears. The Fade only occurred after death. So . . . "I'm dying?"

"As soon as you're born," Sarge said, as annoyingly cryptic as ever. Then the giant head tilted. "However, in your case it's not the flesh that's deteriorating. It's your angelic side. After all, you know as well as I do, Pures were never meant for this world."

Grif focused, did a mental countdown. "But that's only one more day."

Sarge shrugged again. The wood groaned. "If you haven't satisfied the prophecy by that time, you never will."

So he'd just Fade away instead. His body would weaken until he caught back up to Zicaro and everyone else from his first life. Only he wouldn't take fifty years to get there. He'd manage it in a single day.

"And then back to the Everlast," Grif muttered. "A full Centurion once again."

Sarge barked out a laugh, and it sounded like bushes rattling. "After all the trouble you've caused? No. The Host won't allow that. What would keep you from just repeating your mistakes?"

"So another wash through the forgetful chamber," Grif muttered.

"That's right. Back to incubation." The tiki mouth reformed into a wide grin, but Grif had a feeling Sarge was watching him carefully. "And this time they're going to recycle your soul."

Grif froze. "No."

No way. He didn't want to come back to this blasted mud-flat as another person entirely. He wasn't perfect, and not re-motely a good angel, he knew that. But at least the memories in his head were his own, as were his thoughts and feelings. This was *his* life.

"Your time left on the Surface can now be counted in hours" was all Sarge said. "I'd use it wisely if I were you."

But to do what? Help Kit find out who killed her father fourteen years earlier? Find out who killed Barbara? Or try to find Evie?

But then he thought of leaving Kit again, forever this time, and closed his eyes as everything else dropped away. These were all epic questions, and the last had consumed him for half a century, yet what would it matter if he ever solved them or not?

Without Kit, he wondered, what the hell was the point?

"Now you're asking the right question," Sarge said approv-ingly, but when Grif opened his eyes, the great wooden gaze had gone flat again, and the tiki god was once more a mere statue.

Kit drove blindly, hands shaking on the slim mahogany steer-ing wheel, eyes too wide in the rearview mirror. She didn't know where Grif was, and had no way to get a hold of him, so she veered toward Marin's town house and the only family she had left. Panic was growing inside of her, pushing at the edges of her psyche and threatening to attack. She had to get somewhere where she felt protected and safe.

She was still shaking as she knocked on Marin's door, one arm clutched about her middle. When Marin answered, she took one look at Kit and pulled her inside her home, into her arms. Amelia strode into view behind her, and there might as well have been an audible click as the woman's professional mask slid over her face. She took hold of Kit's arm and led her into the kitchen. She must, Kit decided, look worse than she'd thought.

"Sit here," Amelia ordered, already pushing Kit onto a high-backed stool. "I'll get my bag."

She left soundlessly and returned the same way. She must have kept her doctor's bag close, and Kit thought about how nice it must be to always be ready for an emergency. The thought surprised a laugh from her, and she smothered the sound with one hand. Marin looked panicked.

So Amelia was the one who asked, "What happened?" as she pulled Kit's hand away to treat it first. Kit stared down in surprise. Where had the blood come from? She didn't remember cutting it.

"Katherine!" Her aunt's voice, strong and familiar, snapped her back to the present, and she was suddenly directly in front of Kit, blocking Amelia's ministrations and cupping Kit's cheeks. "Tell us what happened."

Pretend you're pitching a story, Kit thought, closing her eyes. Like you're angling for a lead at the paper. Make it good.

So, leaving out the part about seeing her best friend outfitted in wings and stardust, Kit told them about going to see Ray at the club, emphasizing that it was a public space, open at the time, and that she'd felt relatively safe given their previous encounters.

"You were obviously mistaken about that," Marin snapped, the bite back in her tone, criticism crowding out her worry. She was recovering more quickly than Kit, and that pissed Kit off.

She wouldn't have had to go to Ray, or ask about the past, if Marin had been straight with her last night. "Why would you want to meet with him at all?"

"Because of you," Kit answered coolly, and was pleased when Marin gaped. "I asked you about the old feud between the DiMartinos and the Salernos last night. You told me that some things were better left buried. That's how I knew exactly where to look."

Marin's lips thinned as she ran a hand over her head, causing her hair to stick up in spikes.

"He killed my father, Marin," Kit said, before her aunt could speak. Holding out her left palm so that Amelia could clean it, she studied her aunt's reaction. Had she known that all along and not told Kit? "Ray DiMartino said that the police were called to his father's house fourteen years ago on a day that a woman named Gina Alessi showed up. There was talk of a map leading to stolen jewels. Jewels that had been missing since 1960. When one of those officers, my father, left with Gina, Ray followed."

Marin had stilled in place, and now only her mouth moved. "He said that?"

Who'da thought I'd be using the same gun on you fourteen whole years after I killed your father?

Kit shuddered. "Right before he tried to kill me with the exact same gun."

And Kit didn't feel any different, or better, for having solved the mystery. Maybe it was still the shock, but she had no sense of peace to replace the wonder that'd always driven her. "Did you know?" she asked Marin, her voice low as she wondered something new. "Did you know that Dad was killed by the son of Vegas's most notorious mobster?"

"No."

"But you know why he died. You know what was in those papers he gave you." Kit angled her head, giving her aunt time to do the right thing, but after just staring back at her, silence stretching for so long that even Amelia's practiced hands took on a tentative touch, Marin only gritted her teeth.

"I don't want to lose you, too."

"But, Marin," Kit said coldly. "That's exactly what's going to happen next."

And she leaped from the barstool, snatching her keys from the counter as she yanked away from Amelia. She only paused at the kitchen's threshold long enough to spare Marin one hard backward glance, and was gratified to see that it was now her aunt who was white-faced and too-still. "The truth, Marin. That's all I've ever wanted."

"And are you willing to die for it?"

"I'm willing to *live* for it," Kit retorted, swinging back around and down the entryway. Her point was already made, but she slammed the door behind her anyway, and hurried down the trio of steps that led to the drive. She was so focused, so furious, that she hadn't realized Amelia had followed until a hand touched her shoulder.

"It's just me," the woman said, holding up her palms and taking a step back. She didn't know Kit, and maybe Marin hadn't yet told her that Kit wouldn't hurt a fly.

No, she thought, heart collapsing in on itself. Not a fly . . . just the mob-rat that had killed her father.

"She loves you so much," Amelia tried, tucking a soft wisp of blond hair behind one ear. "She's only trying to protect you."

Kit knew that. She huffed and climbed behind the wheel of her car anyway.

"I'll try to talk to her for you," Amelia said.

That surprised Kit so much that she almost flooded her engine. "You will?"

Amelia nodded. "I understand why you're upset . . . and she does, too. No promises, though."

No, they both knew Marin was too stubborn for promises. Kit nodded once. "Thanks. And for the medical care, too."

"The blood on your face was just . . . spatter." Amelia blew out a breath. "I didn't get to the scrapes on your knees, though. You'll need to take care of them when you get home."

Kit drove by rote, looking neither left nor right, and not glancing down until she hit the first stoplight. It was only then that she felt the burn in her skinned knees, as if viewing the injuries was what made them exist. There was one cut that was more than a mere scrape, though she could butterfly it easily enough with only a Band-Aid.

But maybe she'd leave it. She had escaped near-death, after all. There should be a reminder of it. Fleur had made her get a tattoo to announce her return to the world after heartache, but maybe surviving near-death required more. Maybe blood and scars were what cemented your refusal to leave it at all. Glancing away from her injuries, Kit drove on.

CHAPTER SIXTEEN

The night had softened at the edges by the time Kit pulled into her drive, smoothing out the age and decay of her mid-century neighborhood, cutting back on the crumbling concrete walls and cracked walks that sat exposed in the raw daylight. Grif had never told Kit, but he'd been to this neighborhood before, back in *his* day. It was at some party that Evie had dragged him to, either on or near Kit's block, and he could still hear Slim Whitman blaring from the record player as voices and laughter sailed up into the air and the arid desert night.

Back then the biggest headliners on the Strip had all wanted to buy these lavish ranch homes . . . for pennies on the dollar, too. Though it was long gone, he remembered the spot where signage had once flanked the wide community entrance, no backdrop, just that giant cursive scrawl that had been so popular back then: THE FUTURE IS NOW, TOMORROW HAS ARRIVED.

He wanted to share the memory with Kit. He wanted to take her hand and lead her to the community entrance, where she would glance at the crumbling wall posts and smile as he wrapped his arms around her from behind, as taken by the minutiae of the past as she was by him. It wasn't just her car and hair and clothes that were faithfully retro, it was her mind and her thoughts, too . . . at least the dreamy ones. They ever lingered in the past.

"If tomorrow has already arrived," she'd likely point out, "we wouldn't be worried about tonight."

"Or the future," he'd say.

"Or even the past."

But that's where it all started, Grif knew now. Back in 1960, with Tommy DiMartino, who'd held a doll with diamonds for eyes in one hand and a butcher's knife in the other. Despite his best efforts, Grif had gotten in someone's way back then, whether it was old Sal DiMartino; his nemesis, Nick Salerno; or Barbara—who could have been at that long-ago party, lurking in the shadows, wishing him dead. Whatever he'd done, Evie had suffered an attack because of it fifty years ago, and now Kit was paying for it, too.

Grif waited in the corner of her home, in a classic womb chair that put his back to the wall and gave him a view of the living area and the expansive front yard. He watched Kit approach the house. Her movement seemed rote, exhaustion weighing down her limbs, though it was too dark to make out the nuances of her features. Closing his eyes, he sighed deeply and felt, for the first time, the weight of the last fifty years as if he'd truly lived them. He was tired, too, but more than that? He was old.

And with that thought, a trembling voice, one he'd never heard before, sawed through his mind. *It's time for you to go.*

"Where did you go?"

Kit was a shadow in the foyer, facing him so that she stood like an hourglass, skirt flared in silhouette. She'd somehow known he was there, and exactly where to look. He wished he could just stay in this corner for the next fifty years, coiled in the womb chair, pretending he was safe.

It's time for you to go.

Grif could now see her face, and watched the emotions shift over her features in waves as she looked at him. His second death was a train in a tunnel, oblivion bearing down in relentless approach. He would be dead within twenty-four hours. He could accept that now.

But he had to fix this first, he thought, and stood. It wasn't Kit's time to leave this blasted mudflat, the beloved Surface. This was her lifetime, and she had a right to live it in its entirety, both in safety and in peace.

And in love.

"You're exhausted," Kit said, shrugging off her coat and throwing it onto the sofa, as he reached her side.

I'm dying.

He put a hand to her cheek, a move that caused her to jump.

"What are you doing?" she whispered. Her face was almost bone-white in the shadowed room. He drew her close and placed a resolute kiss on her forehead. "Grif, please . . ."

I'm giving you your life back, don't you see? I'm letting you go properly this time.

"You can't touch me like this," she said, and covered his hands with hers, fingers bent to wrench his away. "If you don't love me, you have no right—"

"Don't love you?" He drew back, palms cupped firmly around her jaw, almost too tight. "I will love you beyond my very last breath."

Whatever had happened to her tonight, whatever had put the wooden expression on her face and in her step, dropped away. "Throw yourself at it," she murmured, as if to herself, and then slipped her hand up to pull at the nape of his neck, drawing him closer, down so that this time his lips met her own.

"No." He paused, though her mouth was right there. He could feel its heat on his own. "That's not what I'm—"

Like Larry had, earlier that day, she surprised him by moving too fast for him to stop it. In one instant he was trying to say good-bye, and in the next his back was against the wall. He was immediately grateful. It was the only thing that held him upright as her mouth crushed his, and the room began to spin. He wrapped himself around her, all that warmth and woman filling his arms and his mouth and his mind with the one thing he'd been trying to forget for six long months. The only thing, he realized, left to live for at all. Gasping, he reared back for air and then shifted, reversing their positions. Suddenly, he wasn't feeling so old or tired anymore.

"Hurry," she said, her whisper harsh in his ear, as if she knew time was short.

Grif lifted her from the floor. She grunted softly when they hit the entry wall again, but didn't complain, locking her mouth on his instead. Her hands were quick and busy, relieving him of his suspenders, raking the buttons from his shirt with her nails. They hit the floor like rolling dice, and neither of them looked to see how they fell. Grif just dropped her to her feet so she could free his arms of his shirtsleeves and kick off her shoes at the same time. He peeled his undershirt from his body in one smooth move, and her mouth was on him immediately again, delicate palms warm on his chest, cupping his beating heart.

He was more careful with the stays on her dress. It was vintage, and she might catalog the injury to it. He'd do nothing to distract her from him. Not now. It finally slipped to the floor, the lining hitting the floor with a sigh that Grif echoed as he bit one sweet bare shoulder.

Kit grabbed his hand then and led him down the long hallway, which they navigated slowly, leaving a trail of clothing behind. As they broached her bedroom doorway, Grif recalled the first time he'd been there. He was hiding behind the dressing screen in the corner, watching Kit towel off after a steaming shower. Watching, too, the two men who were sneaking along this very hallway, ready to pounce as soon as she appeared.

But Grif had pounced instead, and that's why Kit still lived. Now he was finally here again, living out his last fated hours as well. He looked around, wanting to remember this room. Wishing he could hold its contents inside of him for another lifetime. "Did you know that I've slept better in this room than I ever have in any place in my entire . . ."

"Lives?" she provided for him, one side of her mouth quirking in a smile.

"Yes."

"Well," she said, drawing him near again. "You won't be sleeping tonight."

No. Because he'd already wasted too much time. He was going to take a good deal more care of the little of it that he had left.

Don't close yourself off.

Nicole had practically begged it of her, but it was only after spotting Grif in that corner, anguish carving furrows into his features, that Kit really understood what that meant. If she closed herself off to him—to the knowledge that she loved him like she had never loved another—then she'd regret it until her dying day.

And that was no way to live.

So Kit kissed him with all the passion that'd dammed up inside her in the long months past, her nerves smoothing out at his very touch, her heart soaring when his mouth immediately moved against hers.

There was time enough to talk later, and always more mysteries and violence to face off against, bulls against capes. Instead of intruding on the moment, all of that only underscored the importance of it. They could draw swords and fight later, but after six long months of dreaming of just this, it felt like the victory was already hers.

Grif obviously agreed. His mouth was firm over hers, and his furrowed brow had eased so that his expression was one almost of pleading. So Kit gave in for them both, expanding the kiss and pressing her mouth to his so that their tongues twined tentatively. She pressed harder. She knew what she was doing for the first time tonight. Perhaps for the first time in her life.

Grif returned her touch, his both forceful and giving, stoking her need so that it shuddered through them both. Kit slid her hand along his firm jaw, skimming stubble, before cupping the back of his neck. She pressed and pulled, and deepened the kiss she'd dreamed of for half a year.

Shifting, Kit aligned her body with Grif's, dips meeting

contours like a key sliding home in a lock. *Click.* She knew Grif was afraid that this was going to cause her more pain, she could taste the worry on his breath, and she was worried, too.

Yet what greater pain was there than regret?

So she put aside the past and future, and focused on the warmth of his neck beneath her lips, the curve of his wide, strong shoulders under her fingertips as she pushed him to the bed, and the length of his torso as he tilted upward to her. She slid the heel of her palms across the scattering of hair on his chest, causing him to tremble beneath her, though his gaze remained steadfast on hers.

He was fighting to memorize it all. Kit just gave herself over completely to her senses, inhaling deeply the dark licorice scent of his warm breath, letting the light coconut of his pomade coat her fingertips, even dabbing it behind her ears. The hair at the nape of his neck tickled her cheek, and, sliding upward, she allowed the same of her neck. She loved the softness of the flesh encasing his hard body. She craved the moan that rose from his mouth to hers, and felt it jostle in her breastbone, shaking her soul.

Placing her palms on the bed, one on each side of his head, Kit rose atop him and stroked his sides with her calves, her thighs, caressing him as she pressed into his groin. Grif thrust his pelvis upward, attempting to flip, but she palmed his hip and eased him back down.

This was hers, she thought, eyes narrowing. Not Evelyn Shaw's or anyone else's. This man in this time and place was hers alone. And this, she thought, throwing back her head, was living.

Slowly, deliberately, Kit settled, Grif palming her hips as she began to glide. Rhythmically, he pushed with the heel of his palms and pulled again with his fingertips, but ultimately he allowed her to set the pace. He tilted upward beneath her, increasing the pressure of him inside of her, a movement that made her moan and slide more insistently. She had a need for him to brand her there, a tattoo on the inside, a craftsman leaving his mark. She wanted to feel him deep within her even after he was no longer there.

Grif bent his knees and Kit leaned back against them, curling her legs tightly beneath and around him. Every moment that passed and that they remained joined was a chance to slip further away from the confines of time and space, leaving behind who they were alone. It would all still be waiting for them when they returned. Even now Kit could feel the force of time pressing its oiled fingertips against the windowpanes.

For now they disappeared together in this bedroom, in these walls, fused together by long-banked desire, and stoked by the greed they felt for each other's flesh. Tongue and breasts and lips and cock all melded into pure sensation.

"No matter what," Grif rasped, devouring her neck, "I'll never forget this."

His words were the first thing, and the only, to give her pause, but then he raised her up and found her breast with his mouth. So, arched forward, Kit swore the same silent vow. She hoped the heavens were listening. She hoped they watched. This was love, and it could not be confined to lifetimes or breaths. The soul was eternal, and the simple eternal truth was that Grif's place inside of Kit's body and mind—inside of her *life*—was, very simply, the truest thing she'd ever known.

CHAPTER SEVENTEEN

Kit wasn't sure what woke her, and for a moment she couldn't even care. She was in her favorite spot in the world, head burrowed into the dip of Grif's left shoulder, his arm draped over her naked back like a protective shield. Their legs were entwined, heavy with heat, and her inner thighs were satisfyingly sore. She wished she could stay here forever.

Instead she went to the bathroom to fill her now-empty tumbler with water, and leaned over the basin to touch her head to the mirror, letting the cold water run over her wrists. The chill shocked the sleep from her, but that was what she wanted. Grif was back in her bed. She could sleep when she was dead.

Yet for some reason tears began to well. She should be happy. She and Grif were together, he'd lived again in her body, but something was wrong. There'd been desperation to their lovemaking, a longing to his touch even though she was right there, and it felt too much like he expected her to disappear.

And, of course, he had sat in the corner of her living room, intending to say good-bye.

Don't worry about that now, she told herself again. He'd had his reasons, and even might try to do so again, but if she were to think about that, to anticipate his absence, she'd miss his very presence.

Living in the future like that, Kit thought, putting the water glass to her lips, was just as bad as living ever in the past.

She caught her reflection at the exact moment that she took a sip. Stiffening, she gasped, and the glass shattered on the marble countertop, yet she didn't look away. Her image was an opaque outline at best, the mirror steamed like when she took a too-hot shower, yet obscured and glowing with gray-blue pearlescent fog. It roiled on the other side, trapped there like a silent storm, but then thinned enough to reveal another head exactly where her own reflection was supposed to be.

Kit did not scream or growl or rant; she recognized that unworldly, churning gaze.

"Am I dreaming?" she asked Sarge.

"Technically? You're sleepwalking," Sarge answered, his features growing sharper, forming like clay, then hardening like he was standing in a kiln. He waited for her to finish studying him, and Kit took her time.

He looked nothing like what she expected. Grif had described him as being large and dark and intimidating, and while this being did have the wings of a Pure, the soaring arches were bald in spots, black feathers clinging to sinew as if for dear life. He had long troughs carved from his eyes to nose, and again to his mouth, and they slipped down his jaw and disappeared beneath his chin. His skin was ashy—though it could just be the mist—and the outline of his collarbones protruded in slashes from beneath the white robe. Though clearly otherworldly, he looked beaten down and diminished, at least to her untutored gaze.

"And what are you doing?" she asked him, because she knew the Pure hated visiting the Surface in any form.

"Something even God Himself would find shocking," he admitted. He inclined his head. "I am apologizing."

Kit was shocked, too, but she didn't ask what he was apologizing for. A better question would've been where he intended to start. This being had manipulated her with almost cruel indifference. Nicole had said that Sarge knew Kit had suffered, but he couldn't possibly know the extent of it . . . or the fear that his appearance in her home, coinciding with that of Grif in her bed, struck through her now.

She wouldn't say it though, she thought, crossing her arms and leaning against the wall. She wouldn't give him any more ammunition to use against her.

"I harmed you. I didn't mean to," he said, then stopped himself with a slow shake of his head. "No, that's not right. I didn't even care that I was harming you, because I knew that what I was doing was right. God's will was, and remains, for Griffin Shaw to heal enough to move safely into His presence, forever wrapped in His glory and light."

"Yeah, I wish those things for Grif as well." She narrowed her eyes and had to force her jaw to unclench. "But I would have gone about it differently."

"I thought you were what was keeping him from returning to the Everlast," the angel explained, his ruined face moving in strange directions, stretching so that he grimaced in pain. "I was wrong and I was punished for it."

"How?"

"I was forced to feel every pang in your heart. Every tear that you shed. Every emotion normally denied a Pure. I know your sorrow, Katherine Craig."

Good. The thought came before Kit could stop it.

"I felt that, too." A corner of Sarge's mouth lifted wryly, and Kit felt shamed, but Sarge held up a hand in the mirror. His overly long fingers were white-tipped where they pressed against the glass. Leaving them there, he looked at her, and after another moment, Kit placed her hand against the glass so that they were palm-to-palm.

"You gave me new knowledge. You made me see that mankind's love for one another is the same as your love for Him. That no matter what form it takes, love is the very essence of God. It is what makes you so very like Him."

He heaved a sigh, then dropped his head and hand. Kit's fingertips tingled where they'd been touching the glass, and she pulled away, holding it with the other, close to her chest.

"I didn't know that before, not in any way that mattered." He shook his head, and Kit winced at the sound of cutting glass. "Outside of worshipping God, I could not fathom any sort of emotion that could make you aware of both everything and nothing at the same time."

The Pure's voice cracked then, and a tear appeared at the corner of one eye. He winced when he saw that Kit had noticed, but didn't try to hide it or blink it away. Instead he stared at her with an almost blazing defiance. And vulnerability, Kit saw. She knew what that felt like, but his was so raw it was almost perverse.

Kit stared back, some old warning about looking directly into the faces of angels chiming through her head, yet she couldn't look away. Tears rose and swam against his opaque irises, then shimmered there, like a heat wave against the road. The liquid pooled to take on a hard edge, sliding to the corners of his eyes. Then his tears began to glow green as they fell, and Kit watched with growing horror as malachite carved an even deeper furrow into those dark, lined cheeks. The grooves were already well established, and a scraping sound cut through the room as sorrow etched his face. A milky-white foam was left in the wake of the tears, some universal matter similar to blood, though Kit didn't know what it was.

"Tears are filled with emotion," Sarge explained, watching her watch him. "Emotion is your link with His power, but for a Pure? A being that was created, not birthed? Emotion is poison."

And one of the sharp stone tears tipped off Sarge's dented chin, fell to the floor, and shattered with the sound of breaking glass.

"I didn't know how much pain I caused you," he said, emeralds now forming in his eyes.

But he knew now.

"Please," Kit whispered, as her own eyes filled with tears. She could taste *his* pain now, because it was shared. Because it was her own. "Please stop."

"But this is my punishment for the sorrow I have caused, and for the sorrow yet to come." Kit froze, fear flooding her in one great rush. She knew it. There was more to come. That's why he was here. A Pure wouldn't deign to appear on the Surface unless there was something in it for him, after all. And Grif's previous hesitancy still nagged at her mind.

Kit surprised herself by sounding so calm. "Just tell me."

And, without preamble, he did. "Griffin Shaw is dying."

Kit just stared before shaking her head. "No. No, he—"

"It is fated, and has been since the beginning of time." This time, crystalline tears shattered against the floor, and the Pure shuddered like he was trying to escape his own body. Kit couldn't blame him. Three more edged teardrops ripped through his face in quick succession, the white blood welling to flood the crevices of his face. "In just over twenty-four hours, he will be dead."

"So stop it." Stop the tears, stop the pain. Stop the very wheels of fate.

"I can't. I—"

"You owe me," she finished for him, voice rasping harshly.

"In a fair world, I would owe you."

Kit closed her eyes. But life wasn't fair, everyone knew that. Life was a place where angels stood by and watched people use free will to destroy each other. Kit shook her head side to side now, almost violently. "No—"

"You'll have to be strong, Katherine," he said softly.

"No!" She screamed it now, pounding the counter. "Don't you just tell me this and then leave. You fix it!"

"I cannot involve myself . . ."

In human affairs, he was going to say. In their lives. In fate's plan. Yeah, she knew that. And she didn't care.

"Fix it!" she screamed, and she punched the mirror so hard that a web splintered from its center. Her hand exploded in pain, knuckles ripped apart, wrist jarred.

Sarge reached out, through the mirror, which rippled like water, to try to touch her. Kit jerked away.

"Let me heal it," he pleaded, and attempted to wrap his overly long fingers around her knuckles.

"I'm fine," Kit said through gritted teeth. "It's only a dream, right? I'm sleepwalking?"

"Please," Sarge said, and this time she only stared. "Let me at least do what I can."

He held out his hand, unnaturally long fingers splayed palm-up. Breath harsh, Kit finally reached out as well, and while she saw the instant their fingertips connected, she couldn't feel it. And suddenly the mirror separated them again, and she was healed.

She flexed her fingers, then looked up at him. She didn't thank him. "Fine, if you're not going to help Grif, I will."

"What can you do?"

"I can close it all down. Bring his past to an end and ensure his future. If we solve the real mystery that brought him back to the Surface, if we find Evie Shaw, then his heart will finally have relief."

"He'll still have to move on."

"Then at least he'll do it in peace." And, shooting Sarge one last hard look in the mirror, she whirled and headed back to the bed, where Grif still slumbered. She would face whatever the next twenty-four hours had to offer, because if her fate could be altered—if stars could attack her flesh like stinging bees and realign her destiny with their luminous sting—then so could Grif's. Knowing that was possible was how she'd get to the other side of it, and Grif would, too. Even if she had to mow down angels. Even if she had to drag him there herself.

Grif woke expecting to feel different, maybe even *be* different, like an element—water shifting to vapor, there but gone.

For a moment, warmed by Kit's arms, he had felt normal and thought he'd done it. He'd fulfilled the prophecy.

Reunite with your true love before the anniversary of your death . . . or all is Lost.

Then he shifted and caught it purling out of the corner of his eye . . . tiny, just a wisp of silver, and one perceptible only to a Centurion. Yet Grif was hardly that anymore. If he were at full power, the winnowing thread of plasma would be shot through with light. Instead it was dull against the moonlit room, and Grif knew Sarge had been telling the truth at the tiki bar. He was losing his angelic nature. The prophecy was coming true.

Reunite with your true love before the anniversary of your death . . . or all is Lost.

Liars, Grif thought bitterly.

Shifting in bed, Grif reached over and realized Kit was no longer beside him. Shooting straight up, he was about to throw off the covers when he caught sight of her sitting bedside in her Barcelona chair, draped in a flowing white robe. The scent of coffee reached out, teasing him, and she stared at him from above the mug's rim. She sipped without blinking. It made her look more otherworldly than him.

She tilted her head toward the door. "Is that plasma?"

"Yeah. It's—" He stopped himself and did a double-take. Perhaps he was still dreaming. "Wait. You can see it?"

Kit cut her eyes left, where the plasma could still be seen spinning along the floor, low and sparking with silver. "Is it a mist that looks like it's funneled into shape? As if it's sentient and has somewhere to go?"

"Yes."

"Then I can see it."

But how? He was awake enough to know that something had happened in the hours since they made love, but too sleep-addled to know what. And Kit didn't give him a chance to figure it out.

"Were you going to tell me, Grif?" she asked, mug cupped in both hands. "Or were you just going to disappear again?"

His heart sunk. So she knew. He saw the certainty in her dust-dry eyes. "Who was it? Sarge?"

She inclined her head.

"How? Did he come through me while I was sleeping?"

"He used my dreams," she said, shaking her head. "Sleep-walking."

Grif frowned and glanced back toward the doorway. And he'd reached her physically somehow, imbuing her with Divine Touch. That explained how she could see the plasma. Yet that meant he'd have ventured to the Surface, and the Pure angel, the Sarge that he knew, would never do that.

"I'm sorry. It's because of me. This." He rubbed a hand over his face. "I didn't mean for this to happen. I was trying to say good-bye. It was incredible, you're incredible, but this was—"

"Perfect. Overdue. And don't you dare say a mistake."

"I wasn't going to. I was going to say that this"—he motioned around the bedroom—"was me trying to leave you."

"Good job."

He blinked at her sarcasm. "Thank you."

Rolling her eyes, she rose, coffee mug in hand. "Hold on."

She swept from the room, and a moment later Grif heard her moving around in the kitchen. He glanced at the clock. Five A.M. That's why he was fully dressed again, from scuffed wingtips to the fedora he'd left lying on the pillow. As always.

And the next time 4:10 in the morning rolled around? He'd be dead.

Kit swept back into the bedroom then, her long robe flaring around her ankles in a silken swirl. She looked like a movie siren as she dropped down on the bed next to him and handed him his own steaming mug of joe. Her warmth, her nearness, the faint scent of her skin made his heart gave a giant thwack, but he refocused, accepting the cup.

"Now," she said, when he'd taken that first steadying sip. "Tell me everything."

"I'm dying, Kit."

"I know." Her voice was even, but even in the gray shadows of predawn, Grif saw her blanch. He reached out a hand to steady her, but it was Kit who gave him a reassuring squeeze instead, and then a short nod. "What else?"

Shifting, he sighed and laid it all out for her. "Basically, the Host has decided that my time is up. They gave me a prophecy, a timeline in which to complete a task, but it's really an ultimatum. If I fail to fulfill its conditions, then I'll die on the fifty-first anniversary of my death, and they'll send me directly back to the Tube. But this time? They're going to recycle my soul."

She knew what that meant. He saw it in the way her gaze fell flat before she closed her eyes. His soul would have to forget this life—that he'd ever visited the Surface as a man named Griffin Shaw—and take on a new life entirely, from birth to death. She wavered slightly, shaking her head. "I hate them."

"Don't," Grif said, scoffing. "It's wasted on them."

"So what's the prophecy?"

Grif closed his eyes, and recited it by heart. He would tell her the truth—she both deserved and required it—but he didn't want to look at her as he said it.

Reunite with your true love before the anniversary of your death . . . or all is Lost.

"So you need to find Evie," she said after a long silence, and then looked away. Because if she were his true love, the plasma wouldn't be lurking around the doorjamb. He wouldn't be dying, headed back to incubation, or destined to leave her at all. *All* wouldn't be lost.

Grif reached out again to take her hand, but this time she pulled away. Still not looking at him, she said, "I hate her sometimes, too, you know."

Grif found he could say nothing to that.

Kit laughed without humor, and shook her head as she ran her fingertip along the edge of her coffee mug. "I'm jealous of a seventy-five-year-old woman whom I've never even met. Isn't that awful?"

"There's no reason for that, either," Grif said softly. "I don't belong with her anymore. Finding Evie or not . . . it's not going to change that prophecy, because the Pures are right. My stint on this mudflat has come and gone. I feel it in my bones. It's time for me to go."

She shook her head. "Don't say that."

Lifting one hand, warmed from the mug, he cupped the side of her face and felt the wetness trailing there. "You have your own life to live, and it doesn't include some wistful, broken old fogey like me hanging from your skirt hem. This . . . whatever it is, whatever happens next, it's fated."

"No." She shook her head so hard that her curls whipped out at his face. "No, this is not fated. Because you *are* here! Right now! And that is not a mistake."

"I'm here as a punishment, Kit. As a lesson."

"Aren't we all?"

"No." He reached for her when she only huffed. "No, you're here to experience love. God's love made manifest in this world."

Kit blinked at him, but said nothing, staring so long that she looked like a black-and-white movie still. He studied the smooth line of her cheek, allowing his gaze to fall to her shoulder before rising again to memorize the full moon of her face. He knew he was eventually going to have to forget all of this, but he'd try to hang on to this memory until the very last second.

"You're right. You're right about all of it except for one thing," Kit finally said, nodding to herself. Then she reversed so that her hand was on his arm instead. "You and I were what was fated. You gave me my very best moments on this big, round mudflat, and it's because of you that I believe in miracles. I mean, isn't that what this is? You and me?"

"Yes, but—"

"And free will. We've got that, too, remember?" She was leaning in close now, imploring. "And love. The kind that makes angels weep."

Grif just stared.

"So I believe we can still fulfill that prophecy. We'll find Evie, and we'll close down that old life. That will free you up to start a new one, in the present, with me. But, Grif, you have to believe it, too." She squeezed his arm. "Will you do that? For me?"

Staring at her, pressed to his side like she would never leave, Grif realized he'd never believed in anything as much as he believed in her. In *them*. He also wondered how he could have ever thought that he still loved Evie.

And he wondered what his fate would have been if only he'd released the past sooner.

But there was nothing he could do about that now.

"Okay." He finally nodded, then stood and held out his hand. "Okay, then . . . let's go shut down the past."

Kit blinked up at him in surprise. "What? Right now?"

"I'm already dressed," Grif pointed out, then had to grin. "Besides, there's no time like the present."

CHAPTER EIGHTEEN

Grif and Kit had met Dr. Charles Ott the previous summer while working on a case involving a particularly brutal drug that caused the user's skin to fall off—while they were still alive. Those were the first instances of the drug spotted in the United States, and solving the case had revived Dr. Ott's flagging career. So he owed Kit and Grif, and told them as much, though Grif doubted the man had foreseen a five A.M. phone call in his future when he said it.

Still, a half hour later he met them outside the coroner's office, giving them a sleepy wave hello, and a big yawn to the security guard inside. He scratched his head as he led them along the long, linoleum-lined hallway, which caused his bright red hair to sit up in spiky flames as they approached his lab.

"Yeah, I remember Barbara McCoy," he said, turning to

push into his office while facing them. "Still waiting to hear what her next of kin wants to do with her remains."

Grif made an acknowledging sound in the back of his throat, which encouraged Ott to turn away, and Grif used the moment to glance at Kit. She'd told him what happened with Ray DiMartino, an accounting that had them both shaking again by the end of it. So Barbara's next of kin might take up space on the slab next to her, but he wasn't going to be calling Ott back anytime soon.

They followed Ott into the autopsy room, and to the wall of refrigeration units behind him. He studied the accompanying paperwork, then yanked open one of the doors without ceremony. Pulling out a long stainless-steel tray, he made sure the toe tag matched the paperwork, and then looked up at Kit. "You sure you're ready for this?"

She was sheet-white and already trembling. Still, she just gritted her teeth and jerked her head at Grif. "He's the one you need to worry about."

Ott grinned. "Okay, then."

And in a flourish befitting a world-class magician, he whisked the sheet from the body in one fell swoop.

It actually wasn't as bad this time around. After all, they'd both seen Barbara's body before, on the floor of her high-rise apartment, and this time there wasn't the sight and smell of blood pooling around her, or the assault of gunpowder shocking the air. Still, there was very little left of the woman's face, her skull a blasted crater of bone cutting into the remaining gray matter. Grif looked at Kit.

"Geez," she said, putting a hand to her head. "I don't feel so well."

Though Grif was closer, Ott reached Kit's side first. "Can I get you something? Do you want to sit down? Get some fresh air?"

"No, no. I'm sure I'll be fine. It's just that it's so early and I'm not used to this." She paused dramatically. "But . . ."

"Yes?" Eager, Ott leaned in too close to her face. Grif fought the urge to pull the man away by the scruff of his neck. He got a pass, Grif figured, because he probably didn't have a whole lot of contact with the living.

"Maybe a soda would settle my stomach?" Kit pitched the statement high, ending it in a question.

As expected, Ott rushed to her rescue. "There's a vending machine in the hall. I'll be right back."

Grif watched him scramble away, red hair bouncing behind him like a troll doll's. "You gonna scratch him behind the ears when he gets back?"

"Think I should?" Kit smiled as she went to lock the door behind Ott, though they were both serious again by the time she returned to Grif's side. "He's not going to let us in again after this."

"I don't think we're going to need him to in the next twenty-four hours," Grif muttered, because after that he'd be gone, never to roam the Surface again. At least, not as Griffin Shaw.

"Grif—" Kit chided.

"I know. Don't worry, I know." He blew out a breath and refocused on the corpse.

"Just hurry up and do what you need to before he calls that guard."

"No problem. I'm an ace with the newly dead."

And he was thankful for whatever Sarge had done to Kit. If Sarge had gifted her with Divine Touch, then he didn't have to worry about breaking one of the Pures' ridiculous rules about what she was supposed to see. He also hadn't forgotten about Zicaro, stuck somewhere out there with a known killer. They needed to move quickly.

So, bracing himself, he filled his lungs with a deep, rib-splitting breath, felt his angelic nature fire up—originating in the twin feathers tucked beneath his shoulder blades—and then blew all that power out at the corpse.

He had to admit, he enjoyed the way Kit jumped at the same time Barbara's corpse did, or maybe it was just the way Kit clung to him when she did it, and though the white-hot flash of heat and light might have been too fast for her mortal eyes to detect, he knew she scented the smoke when she covered her mouth and nose with her hand.

"What is—?"

"Just sulfur," Grif said, not taking his attention from the coalescing funnel. "Better known 'round these parts as brimstone."

"But brimstone is bad, right? It's hellfire, damnation, stuff like that?"

Grif shook his head. "Sulfur is an essential element for all living things. It acts as both fuel and a respiratory compound. And right now we need both. Watch."

Much like plasma, the yellowish sulfur swirled as if searching for a target, and found it in the phantom shape of Barbara's missing features. It coalesced there, twining about itself before drawing in more tightly, squeezing out the air molecules.

"Why, that's—" Kit began to speak but faltered, now truly looking peaked. Grif took her by the elbow to steady her, and hoped the authority in his voice did the same.

"It's bonding with the proteins left in her body, the amino acids, the keratin."

Kit swallowed audibly beside him. "And keratin is present in skin. And hair."

"Yes, and more importantly, Barbara's face."

Which meant Grif was finally going to be face-to-face—in a manner of speaking—with that face, and the woman who had hated him and Evie for more than fifty long years. The one who thought that Grif deserved to die horribly . . . and who'd probably had a hand in it as well.

Gritting his teeth, he watched the smoke continue to mold itself to the woman's remains, the basic facial features forming first and lightening into an ashy tinge actually befitting death. Even the curls along the hairline popped in stylish relief, and those darkened slightly into a hue similar to Kit's own deep shade. The visage that appeared would be the self-image that the woman saw in her mind's eye, not the one she'd watched age over the years in the mirror. Therefore the smoky face solidifying before them was not settled into her seventies but looked like it could be anywhere from mid-twenties to mid-forties. Whenever, Grif thought, Barbara had felt most like herself.

The eyes were the last part of the face to settle, wispy lashes the finishing touch before the corpse gave an enormous twitch, fell still again . . . and then rose at the waist.

By this time, Kit was huddling behind Grif, a mewling sound slipping from her throat, which she choked off. She was shaking, squeezing his arm—and he was flexing—when she fell suddenly still, before shooting up to full attention behind him.

"That's not Barbara McCoy."

"It's not?" Grif asked as the corpse turned its head to regard them, wisps of smoke trailing the movement.

"Oh, my God," Grif said, feeling the blood drain from his face and likely turning just as white as the corpse they were facing. "It's Gina Alessi."

Mary Margaret's nanny back in 1960, when Grif had been killed. The woman who'd sent the young girl out to play in the front yard the day she was abducted. The woman who'd come to see Sal DiMartino fourteen years ago, on the day Kit's father was killed.

Kit's fingers tightened around his arm. "But if this is Gina, then that means—"

"Barbara DiMartino is still alive."

And, at that, the corpse in front of them hissed.

Doesn't seem to be any love lost there," Kit murmured against Grif's left shoulder as Gina's gritty form continued to glare. Kit was trying to be cool about the whole thing, but talking to the dead—*animating* them—was new to her. She was seeing things no human should, and now she knew why. She'd have nightmares about this for weeks.

However, Grif just shoved his hands in his pockets and took a step forward. "Are you Gina Alessi? Is Barbara McCoy your cousin?"

The corpse gave a slow nod, which would have been fine except that the sulfuric head undulated on her neck, causing Kit's stomach to do the same. She swallowed hard as it rolled back into place . . . and she stayed tucked behind Grif.

There are times when one must be brave, she thought. And this isn't one of them.

"Did she have something to do with your death?" Grif continued.

That rolling nod again.

"Why isn't she talking?" Kit finally asked.

Grif shrugged. "No tongue."

And the stench of rotten eggs hit Kit square in the face as the corpse opened its maw to reveal a gaping darkness. Now she *knew* she'd have nightmares. Kit closed her eyes, but opened them again when she felt the reverberation of Grif's tapping foot through the sleeve she held clutched in her fist.

"What is it?" she asked.

"Where is memory located? I mean, what part of the brain?"

"Frontal lobe," Kit said, and both of their gazes flew to the smoky mass that had been blasted away. "Why?"

"The sulfur can only approximate her visage, not replace it. That's why she can't talk. But if her memory were intact . . ." And it wasn't.

"Episodic," Kit interrupted.

"What?"

"Episodic memory. The stuff brimming with autobiography and emotion, which she still clearly feels." Kit motioned to the angry corpse. "That's stored in the temporal lobe, and that's farther back."

"Really?" Grif tilted his head at the sulfuric Gina, and said, "So, Gina. Do you think you can *show* us what happened?"

The smoky eyes narrowed.

Kit's right eye took on a twitch, too. "What do you mean 'show'?"

But Grif stayed focused on sulfuric Gina. "What if it means helping us capture Barbara . . . once and for all?"

And another blast of gaseous breath hit them as the corpse grinned.

"Hold on to me," Grif told Kit as Gina's head shifted, dust particles expanding when it took a deep breath.

"Are you kidding?" Kit breathed, and wrapped both arms around him, twining their fingers together. He was lucky she didn't demand a piggyback.

"Don't let go," he warned, and she squeezed tighter.

The last thing Kit saw was the smoky section of Gina's head splitting apart. It was as if a firecracker had gone off beneath a mound of sand, yet only a moment after the blast each dusty particle reversed and was funneled through the still-formed lips. Then the corpse blew all the sulfur—the protein and keratin and *life* that Grif had given her—back in their direction. The entire morgue instantly disappeared in a gritty, yellowed haze.

Kit wanted to cough, but there was no air to take in. Her lungs tightened, choking on matter never made for that soft pink tissue, and relief didn't come. She felt entombed, unable to breathe, move, or even blink, and the heaviness of unconsciousness had already begun to settle over her when she felt a tingling in her flesh. Her body went white-hot as sulfur pricked at every pore, but then it dissolved atop her skin, sinking in and settling deep.

Then Kit blinked, and the smoke was gone.

In its place was a sprawling green lawn, a skid mark on an otherwise wide, pristine street before them . . . and the remnants of a scream curling through the air.

"Whose—" But Kit's mouth wouldn't work. The perspective shifted, a dash down the sloping lawn and view of the empty street dizzying Kit so that she realized it wasn't her mouth at all.

We're in Gina's memory, remember? You're seeing everything from her viewpoint.

Grif's voice, connected through touch and massaging her

brain, calmed Kit considerably. So she sent back a mental *Okay,* and settled in to watch.

The street spun, Gina turning around, and suddenly they were back on the lawn, lifting an old Cissy doll from the ground.

Mary Margaret's kidnapping, Kit thought. And, panting hard, Gina began running for the house.

She burst through the giant, paneled oak doors, and the flash of a dark-haired woman was reflected in the hall mirror—late twenties, wide-eyed and gasping and with a heartbeat that shook in Kit's own breast. Gina stared at herself in the mirror. "What have I done?"

The next flash of memory, a moment later, a second episode: Gina hitting her knees on a plush cream carpet at the feet of an elegant, sickly woman. The woman had been lounging in front of a large, crackling fire.

"Forgive me, Theresa . . ." Gina caught herself, the sob cutting off, as she clutched the hem of the woman's nightgown. "I mean, Mrs. DiMartino. It's my fault . . . they took her. They took . . . it was the wrong doll."

A little doll will be waiting in the front yard . . .

Though obviously fatigued, with deep creases beneath each eye, hair graying at the temples, Theresa DiMartino straightened, took the doll Gina held out . . . and ran a forefinger over each diamond eye. Her gaze flew again to Gina; her eyes sparked with fire as well. "Where's my third diamond?"

She may have looked weak, but her voice was strong, as if hardened in the fire next to her. Kit's own throat constricted at the tone, and Gina was too frightened to respond at all. Instead, she pointed to the doll's plastic belly. Theresa DiMartino lifted the gingham dress and, without hesitation, yanked one of the attached legs. Out tumbled the third precious gem, once a part of the necklace Sal had made for her using money stolen from his enemies.

The men who'd just retaliated by abducting her niece, Mary Margaret.

Without moving another muscle, Theresa turned her gaze, like an arrow, back up and through Gina Alessi. Kit felt it pierce her, too, as if Theresa could see all the way into the future and to Kit and Grif listening fifty years later.

"*She's* behind this, isn't she?"

Barbara. Gina shared the thought with Kit and Grif before mutely nodding.

Theresa looked at the doll, her long, thin fingers smoothing the dress down before her gaze slipped back up to the pink porcelain cheeks, rosy beneath the gleaming eyes. "My husband is going to kill you. You know that, right?"

Yes, Gina knew. Fear forked in her belly, spearing them all. "Oh, please, miss."

Theresa roared. "You brought that viper into our home! She tried to seduce my husband—*mine!*—and you were lucky I didn't send you into exile with her! And now"—Theresa was panting, chest heaving with her fury—"now you let her back in?"

"She saw the necklace in the paper."

"And saw that I was sick, too," Theresa spat, mouth drawn down, bitter.

"I— I thought that she was over . . ."

"Say it."

Gina swallowed hard, swallowed bile. "I thought she was over Sal."

Theresa closed her eyes, and then slumped with a heavy

sigh. She turned away from Gina, the doll gone limp in her lap, and faced the roaring flames.

Gina begged, "She changed her name, she altered her appearance. I thought she was starting over—"

"You mean a new grift."

"Yes." Gina cast her gaze down, so that Kit and Grif watched her hands, white-knuckled, twining in her lap. "I thought she forgot all about you."

"Women like her," Theresa said without turning her head, "do not forget. And they certainly don't forgive. I know because I *am* a woman like her."

She did look at Gina now, her face awash in bitterness. "How do you think I knew that she was after my Sal five years ago? Nineteen years old, fresh-faced, peach-pretty. Yet that couldn't hide the greed already lurking beneath. Some people are born with rotten cores and your cousin is one of them." Theresa shook her head, slowly now, mouth curling into a sneer. "She could change her appearance a thousand times, and I'd always know exactly who she is."

Theresa dropped back her head and stared at the ceiling. Gina tried to speak again, but was silenced with only the lift of Theresa's hand. Her other hand fluttered atop her heart, but didn't rest, as if she was afraid it'd break at the touch. Finally, she lifted her head. "Do you want to live, Gina?"

"Yes."

"Then you're going to do exactly as I say. Your cousin thinks five years is a long time to hold a grudge, she thinks she has the patience to exact a thoughtful revenge, but I'm dying, darling. I have nothing to lose." She held up the Cissy doll, and made its eyes blink, open and shut. Open and shut. Thousands of dollars of jewels winking in and out of sight. "And she hasn't seen anything yet . . ."

And then the sulfur closed in again. Somewhere, where Kit and Grif were still standing in a twenty-first-century morgue, she tightened her hold around his arm. *Don't let go . . .*

But when the smoke cleared, they were standing on another street corner, this one more modern, and facing a house that was even grander than the first. They watched through Gina's gaze as a sleek black Mercedes backed from the drive, the platinum-white curls of an older woman sprouting above the driver's seat as it sped away. The car was a late model, something that still sailed the streets today, so as Gina approached and knocked on the front door, Kit knew that a significant amount of time had passed.

It was confirmed when the door whipped open to reveal a man in his mid-forties, relatively handsome and obviously related to Sal DiMartino.

Oh, my God. It's . . .

"Hello, Ray." There was no mirror to reflect the passage of time on Gina, but her voice had grown creaky with age, and Ray's responding scowl was mirror enough.

"Gina fucking Alessi." Of course Ray would know exactly who she was. He was seven years old when her charge, his cousin, had been kidnapped from his front yard. Even a young child remembered an event like that.

"Can I come in?" She hurried on before he could slam the door. "I have a message for Sal."

Ray, curious despite himself, tilted his head. "Who sent you?"

"Your mother."

Ray scoffed and began to swing the door shut. "That bitch isn't my mother."

Gina stopped him cold without moving at all. "I mean your real mother. Theresa."

And for just one moment, Ray DiMartino looked like the young boy Grif had once described. It was hope; it flared, odd and uncomfortable on the set face, and he erased it as quickly as possible. Kit would've cried for him if she could. Even knowing what he'd become, that he would one day try to kill her, she still felt sorry for the boy who'd ever feel hope for his mother. Then his expression hardened again, and he led Gina in to see his father.

Sal DiMartino was dying, no doubt about it. His arms and legs were scrawny, loose skin pooled around his chin, a testament to too much weight lost too fast, and the wingspan of his once-great shoulders had shrunk, making a physical mockery of his former strength. In contrast, it made Theresa's illness look tame.

"Why are you here?" Sal asked Gina.

"I was supposed to stay away from you. Theresa made me swear to never go near you again. She said it was the price of my freedom and life. But it's been thirty-seven years, Sal, and I can't run anymore. I'm tired of hiding." Gina steeled her spine and lifted her chin. "I want you to make her leave me alone."

"Who?" Ray butted in, knowing he was missing something important, that there was subtext at play that he didn't understand, but Gina and Sal only continued to stare at each other.

"And why would Barbara be after you?" Sal finally asked, voice souring over his wife's name.

So he *knew,* thought Kit. He had at least some idea that the woman he'd married had her own dark secrets.

Huffing at that, Gina just threw something down on the table before him. Nobody moved. Sal stared at the lone diamond for almost a full minute before reaching out to pick it up. He leaned back, holding the diamond so close to his face that he almost looked like he was going to kiss it. Then he closed his eyes. "She still wants it all."

"And only Theresa saw it," Gina said.

"Wants what?" Ray asked, inching forward. "What did my mother see?"

"Stop talking, you damned fool!" Sal demanded, his voice suddenly rounding out with his old authority. Ray cringed.

"You knew all along," Gina said to Sal.

"That Barbara set up Mary Margaret's kidnapping? That she led my nephew, Tommy, to his death? That she pinned it all on that sap of a P.I., Griffin Shaw?"

Yes. He knew.

"And you still married her? You lived with her? All these years?"

"I was alive, but that's different from living, isn't it? And I can't say that I did that, not really. Not after Theresa died. When she was gone . . . living was just another job." He shook his head, deflating again. "But maybe I didn't want to see what Barbara was all about. She stayed so long. She mourned the end of the good days with me. She stayed throughout my prison sentence. She stayed after I came home, crowded *her* space. *Her* house."

"Because she still wants the other two," Gina said without emotion.

Ray couldn't hold his tongue anymore. He reached for the gem. "Wait, there are two more of these?"

"Don't touch it, you idiot!" Sal's voice thundered through

the room, and for a moment Kit glimpsed the feared mafia don beneath the sagging meat suit, the criminal patriarch who had run this city like it was his own. He glared at Ray until the younger man backed away, and then turned that fierce gaze back on Gina. "I swear, he's more *her* son than he is Theresa's."

Ray's face fell slack in stricken surprise. Sal pushed into a seated position and turned away before Gina did, so he missed the way his son's face hardened in hatred.

"Help me up," Sal told Gina, and she did. When Kit and Grif next blinked, they were standing before a safe, which Sal opened with shaking fingers. A bank of security cameras displayed different parts of the house in black and white, and tilted angles. Ray was nowhere to be seen.

"I found this when I got back from the pen," Sal said, handing Gina a slim, folded slip of paper. "It's the birth certificate she used to change her name when Theresa ran her out of Vegas the first time. Tuck it away," he said, before she could open it. "Use it as insurance."

Then he reached in for something else. "And this . . . this is mine."

Very carefully, he unfolded a thin, delicate slip of paper, then held it up to reveal a series of nonsensical lines. Tracing paper, Kit saw. Did they even make that anymore? Reaching down, he laid it atop the safe's only other item, a map of the city and the surrounding terrain.

"Your drop zones," Gina whispered, and her accompanying thought hurtled through Kit's and Grif's minds. *Where all the bodies are buried.* Sal smiled bitterly, then pointed to the largest circle, the darkest mark. "This is—"

A loud blast sounded, and Sal jerked back. His gaze narrowed as he caught sight of movement on the cameras above. Barbara was back. And she'd brought two cops with her.

Dad, Kit thought, seeing the fuzzy black-and-white images through Gina's gaze. *Oh, my God. Grif, it's my dad.* But then, in the past, Gina looked away. "She knows I'm here."

Sal's mouth thinned, his bushy brows drawing low. "Stay here in the safe box. I'll take care of this."

"What are you going to do?"

"Fulfill Theresa's last wish," he said, nodding down at the map, then back at the cameras. "Barbara will never see those diamonds."

And he left. But Gina didn't stay put. Instead, she grabbed the gem, the map, and the birth certificate—and ran, like she always had. Out of the safe box, through the kitchen, and out the back door. She glanced back only once, when she heard her name shouted from behind. Ray DiMartino was pointing her way, and one of the officers was squinting at her quizzically, then rushing to follow . . .

No, Kit implored her father, though the memory was already fading, sulfur again crowding in to obscure the past, but not before Kit saw the plasma swirling around her father's ankles. *Please don't follow.*

They came to in the morgue with the sound of pounding at the door. Sucking in a deep breath of air, Kit gasped, and then turned into Grif's shoulder. The sulfur was gone, and Gina Alessi's face had disappeared again, along with her memories.

Along with Kit's father, who had died that same day.

CHAPTER NINETEEN

Obviously, Charles Ott kicked them out of the morgue. As the door shut behind them, and the security guard trailed them to make sure they got into their car and left, Grif and Kit remained silent, heads reeling from the experience of being in Gina Alessi's memories, though likely for different reasons.

Grif cleared his throat as Kit sped from the parking lot. She ignored him, so he simply stared out the window and waited for her to come around. It was only fair that she needed more time to process what they'd just seen. He was used to the supernatural. The experience had obviously shaken her, but he had to trust that Sarge wouldn't have given her Divine Sight if she wasn't ready for it.

"Do you want me to break it down for you?" he finally asked, placing his hand atop the gearshift, where hers was tightly clenched.

"If you wouldn't mind," she said stiffly.

"Barbara knew that Gina was going to go to Sal fourteen years ago. She must have been following her, just like Gina suspected. She probably set Gina up for something, which was why she brought the police along."

"You mean my father," Kit said in a small voice, and then cleared it, speaking louder. "Can you believe it? How unlucky to be on duty that day. That woman destroyed everything she touched."

"Ray killed your father, Kit."

"She had a hand in it."

Yes, thought Grif. Barbara had her hand in all of it.

"You know," he finally said, "men are tough, but women have a ruthlessness to them that I don't think I'll ever understand."

"I don't," Kit said quickly, jaw set defensively.

"You could," he said immediately, and held up a hand to stave off her anger. "Don't take it the wrong way, but I've seen it in you, honey. There's nothing you wouldn't do to protect the ones you love."

Kit finally just nodded. "Theresa knew all the way back in 1960 that she couldn't stop Barbara from going after her husband after she was dead. Not if that's what Barbara really wanted, and she was right. But damn if she didn't keep her from getting those diamonds."

And Barbara, who had learned long ago how to circle back around and hide in plain sight, who they now knew was still alive, was still searching for them.

So where the hell was she right now?

"You know, the past," Kit said, shaking her head. "It's not at all what I expected."

"Not enough rockabilly music for your liking?"

She cut her eyes at him but didn't smile. "No, I mean it didn't feel any different from now. For some reason I thought it'd be . . . simpler. Then again, the future is never what I think it's going to be, either. I'm misjudging both. I have no idea what it all means."

"I think," Grif began, but faltered because he'd struggled with the same . . . and because what he was about to say was a new thought to him as well. "I think that the meaning is in the moment."

He couldn't tell if Kit agreed. She was still reeling from seeing her father, a woman's sulfuric face, and someone else's memory in her own mind. But she finally reached out and took his hand, squeezing like she wanted to hold on to this moment forever. So Grif didn't ask where they were going. He just settled back and watched the streets go by, holding her fingers lightly in his palm, squeezing back.

Kit had composed herself by the time she arrived at the newspaper, and she strode into Marin's office ready to do battle.

Which Marin seemed to be expecting. Sitting behind her desk—usually piled with tottering stacks of paper but now loaded down with a giant cardboard file box—she merely leaned back in her chair and sighted Kit over the top of her reading glasses.

"Amelia said you might be by." Her aunt attempted a smile, a flicker of hope mixed with uncertainty. Kit nearly deflated with gratitude and had to fight the urge to run and pull Marin into a hug. She wasn't going to have to fight her on this. Kit would finally know exactly what her father had given Marin on the day he died.

"You know," Grif said, clearing his throat, "I think I'm

gonna go look for a stale doughnut or something. Some subpar coffee. A magazine to read."

"What?" Kit turned, blinking.

"He means he's going to give us privacy to talk."

Grif just shrugged one shoulder. "Estrogen makes me dizzy." Then he turned to Marin before Kit could snarl. "Hey, do you have an envelope I can borrow?"

She searched around, then held one out to him.

"And a stamp?"

"Jesus, Shaw."

"Here," he said, matching her grumble with his own as he threw down a wad of bills. "That should cover it."

And he strode from the room without another word. Kit stared at the money, blinking because she realized it meant he wouldn't need it. Like everything else on his body, the money replenished itself at 4:10 A.M. . . . but he was supposed to be dead the next time that hour rolled around.

"As chipper as ever," Marin remarked wryly, drawing Kit out of her trance. "Any news of Zicaro?"

"Dennis is working on it, but there's nothing yet." And if Kit was going to change that—if she was going to help both Zicaro and Grif—then she had to keep moving forward. So she refocused and gestured to the box.

"Your father's personal effects. Mostly detritus from his office," Marin confirmed, though she didn't move to open it. Kit realized she was going to let her do the honors. "The department brought it by after his funeral, and I put it aside. We had enough to deal with, and then . . ."

And then Kit had broken down.

Marin shrugged. "I stored it once you came home. Never thought I'd see it again."

Kit moved to place one hand atop the box. "Is it all here?"

"Including what he sent me?" Marin nodded and stood. "I know Amelia already said it, but I was only trying to keep you safe."

"My dad died for this information," Kit said. Because of something in this box.

Crossing her arms, Marin looked toward the door. "It seems right that you're working with Shaw on this. They're cut from exactly the same cloth, you know."

Kit looked at her like she was crazy. "My father was a sweetheart."

And Grif was a lot of things . . . but she wasn't sure anyone would ever call him sweet.

Marin's laughter bounded throughout the room. "Dear, dear Katherine. Your father loved you like you were the breath in his chest, he loved your mother with a single-mindedness that verged on madness. His love was brutal . . . but it was never *sweet*."

Kit had never heard this about her father, or her parents, before. It felt like listening in on a forbidden conversation.

She loved it.

"Really?" she asked, forgetting the box before her, and its mysteries, for a moment.

"Absolutely. He took one look at your mom, and made it his mission in life to sweep her off her feet." Marin huffed and rolled her eyes. "Treated her like the princess she thought she was, though he was smart about it. Didn't try to buy her favor with baubles or flowers or anything like that. No, he knew she wouldn't value anything she could gain for herself. Instead, he gave her something infinitely more valuable."

"What?"

"Himself," Marin said, and even she looked a little awed by it. "His whole life. Like a trench coat laid across a water puddle, he just put it out there for her to walk on. No ulterior motives, no expectations except that she love him the same way in return. It was the craziest, most wholehearted display of love I've ever seen."

Kit closed her eyes so that Marin wouldn't see the tears warming them. After the silence had gone on for a time, Marin finally said, "Do you know why I keep the family archives so meticulous and so intact even after all these years? Even though they don't contain any usable reportage?"

"Because you're nosy?" Kit said, sniffing.

"Yes," Marin admitted with a small laugh. "And because knowing the minutiae of people's lives makes *me* feel alive. Even the obits are comforting."

"That's . . ." Kit thought about that for a moment. "Really disturbing, Auntie."

"Why? Laying it down in black and white strips a story of its emotion so that anybody can face it. That's why newshounds like you and me and loony Al Zicaro try to capture it so precisely. It's why people read the news, even if it's bad."

Especially if it's bad, thought Kit.

"We attempt to tame life on the page so that we can understand it, learn from it, and try not to repeat others' mistakes. Story is memory and memory is story, do you see?"

"Sure." A story was a transcript of a memory. What you remembered of an event or a person became true for you . . . whether it was true or not. That's why Kit had trouble remembering a father who loved brutally. And it was why Grif had trouble forgetting Evie at all.

"And so that's why I never told you about your father's

letter," Marin finally said. "I thought I could keep you safe if you just forgot."

But you never really forgot love. No matter how it left you.

"So." Marin sighed, then, with a shrug, gestured to the box. "Open it."

Layered with dust and weakened by time, the masking tape gave easily. An image flashed through Kit's mind: a doll lying there, blinking up at her with precious, winking eyes.

But there was no doll . . . and no diamonds, either. Just half-used notepads and a handful of pens, along with a photo of Kit and her mother, and another of the three of them together. Kit gingerly set those aside for herself before lifting a yellowed envelope from atop what remained. She read it, then gaped in surprise.

"Do you remember this?" Kit asked, holding up the un-sealed envelope stamped with Albert Zicaro's return address.

"I must have just tossed it in there." Marin shook her head. "I told you. I just wanted to forget."

But Kit needed her to remember. Opening it, she began to read aloud:

> *Dear Ms. Wilson,*
>
> *My name is Al Zicaro. You may recognize it because I was one of the most prolific and illustrious reporters to ever grace the pages of your family newspaper. I remember you from the newsroom (though you likely can't say the same) working like a grunt in the pen and chasing down stories like you were really hungry, even though everyone knew you were heir to the throne.*

"Bitter much?" Marin retorted now. Kit kept reading.

If you're anything like your old man, you're running
that ship like the Titanic—thinking it's both grand and
unsinkable. If you treat your present employees anything
like Dean Wilson II treated me, then you're also a jerk.

As for me, I did good work for the Trib from the
years of 1957–1988, and I'm doing it still. The enclosed
map was sent to me by your brother-in-law, who was
instructed to mail this to me by a woman named Gina
Alessi. His note, which I'll show to you if you deign to
respond, gives further instruction that both Gina and this
map need to be kept safe. He was supposed to take care of
Gina, I got the map. Apparently, you received something
as well.

So why'd he send this to me? Because I'm the finest
damned reporter this side of the Mississippi, that's why.
But why not send it all directly to you, or wait and hand
it to you over Sunday dinner? That is a mystery. All
I know is his name popped up today in the obits, and
something smells fishy.

Of course, I have my own theories, which is why I'll
be coming in next week to discuss the matter further with
you. But I'm gonna want something in return, namely
to return to the Trib with full benefits, and exonerated
of all charges levied against me when I left. (The protest
out at the Test Site wasn't my fault, I don't care what
the military says.) I do hope that at that time you will
remember this great favor.

Most sincerely,

Albert Edward Zicaro

Kit looked back up at Marin, who was nodding slowly. "Yeah, it's vague, but I remember now. I figured he just wanted his old job back."

Kit pulled out the map that Zicaro's letter had referenced. There was no way to date the map, it only held a cartographer's code in the lower left corner, but it was obviously old. Kit could tell from the way the streets she knew either ended in abrupt corners or lacked representation altogether. She was willing to bet the streets listed were a good match for those in existence in 1960.

Frowning, Kit worked back and forth between that timeline and the day this map had been sent, fourteen years ago. Her dad had obviously seen Gina Alessi someplace safe, then mailed this to Zicaro right before he was killed.

"So what's Zicaro talking about?" Kit said, looking up. "What did Dad send you?"

And, heaving a great sigh, Marin finally pointed to the far wall. "That."

Kit glanced at her aunt's bulletin board, a giant swath of cork that was so crowded with papers and note cards and sticky notes that many had dropped to the floor beneath it. But Marin was pointing to the top right corner, where one sole slip of tracing paper was pinned . . . and had been for as long as Kit could remember. So long that I stopped seeing it, she thought, drawing nearer. She guessed that after fourteen years, Marin had stopped seeing it as well.

"I didn't know what it was," Marin said, reaching up to carefully unpin it. "But it was the last thing your father ever did . . . that was clear. It arrived in my mailbox the day after he died. A total mystery, and one that died with him. I thought that if I pinned it up here, I would never forget. But time goes on, and well . . . sometimes it's better to just forget the past."

She handed the paper to Kit. Age had added to its fragility, and lightened the lines scribbled randomly along the middle. Some had end points that were joined in sharp circles, but most were scattered and lacking any sort of pattern.

Kit lifted the tracing paper to peer through it at eye-level, and caught sight of Marin on the other side. Then she let her aunt's concerned face fade into the background, and keyed in on the darkest, largest circle. "Give me the map," she whispered to her aunt.

Marin grabbed the map that Zicaro had sent her fourteen years earlier, and Kit lined the tracing paper atop it, just as she'd seen Sal DiMartino do in Gina Alessi's smoky memory.

"What is it?" Marin said, closing in.

"A treasure map," Kit said, as the Las Vegas Valley took on new meaning and form.

One leading to a buried doll with diamond eyes.

CHAPTER TWENTY

The center mark on the newly recovered treasure map was the DiMartino family home, the exact place where Gina Alessi sent a little girl with a doll out to be abducted in 1960. Located in the Las Vegas Country Club at the height of kingpin Sal DiMartino's power, it'd also been the safest neighborhood in town. And it made sense that the boys would keep some sort of record of where they'd buried the bodies . . . DiMartino could use the knowledge as leverage with his victims' loved ones and enemies alike.

Of course, the city had grown exponentially since the drawing was made, and was now dense with tract homes in places that were once no more than a giant litter box. But some things couldn't be moved or changed, and by tracing ever-widening circles from the axis of Sal DiMartino's home, they tried to guesstimate where exactly the farthest end point now lay.

"The city is a bowl, hemmed in on all sides by mountain ranges. There's no direction key on this thing, but my guess is that this is the Red Rock mountain range," Marin said, pointing at the uppermost corner. "Blue Diamond veers east of that."

"Which would make this the Sheep Mountains," Grif said, pointing west. He'd returned minutes before, carting burned coffee and stale doughnuts for them all.

Gnawing thoughtfully, Kit stared without blinking. Sunrise Mountain wasn't on the map at all, and neither was the valley's sister city, Henderson. Back then it'd been a scattering of trailers on a two-lane road leading out to Boulder City and the ever-impressive Hoover Dam. Her father used to call it Hicksville. However, that wasn't represented on the map, either.

"The scope is tight," Marin said, seeing it, too.

"These are the Black Mountains," Kit said, pointing southeast of the DiMartino home, and pulled out her smart phone to take a picture of it. If the map was lost again, she thought, at least she'd have a permanent record of it. "There's a luxury community there now, but it had to be damned near inaccessible back in 'sixty."

And that's where the most prominently marked end point was. Marin shrugged. "Well, there's only one way to find—"

Kit's phone trilled in her hand, causing them all to jump. It was not a jaunty rockabilly tune that had them all staring at the phone. No Elvis or Wanda Jackson or Johnny Cash to lighten the mood. Instead, this was the canned music of a tinny calypso that she'd assigned to the man who'd last threatened her in the middle of the night.

She answered it by not answering . . . just holding the phone to her ear.

"Let's try this again, shall we?" Justin Allen's voice rang with triumph.

"We already gave the files to the cops," Kit said immediately, because he had to know this. She just hoped poor Zicaro hadn't had to pay for it.

"We want the map," Justin said, and Kit's gaze shot to the yellowing paper that had been missing, and not, all these years. The one that only Zicaro knew about. She didn't even want to think of what they'd put him through to extract that information.

"I suppose we should thank you in a way," Justin went on. "After all, you've made us very desperate men. That's why if there's even the hint of bacon on you when we meet, we'll put a bullet through old man Zicaro's eyes. Right in front of you."

Kit glanced over at Grif, knowing he could hear everything and expecting to see his jaw clenched, fury riding his brow like a storm cloud. But that was the old Grif, the one who'd been granted a second lifetime. This one had only a prophecy and— Kit looked at her watch—sixteen hours left to fulfill it. Their eyes met, and he nodded.

"When and where?" Kit finally asked, and had to wait to take down the directions until after Justin had a good, long chuckle.

The diner that Justin named had anchored the corner of Charleston and Valley View for as long as Kit could remember. It was a simple line drawing of a building, an amalgamation of every diner ever built, every diner ever filmed, every diner that ever served runny eggs and soggy bacon. A long Formica counter stretched along the right-hand side, complete with red pleather stools bolted in place and the kitchen, bright and somewhat smoky, bustling behind it. The booths lay on the left side, closest to the large picture windows, and that's where Zicaro waited as Kit and Grif walked in.

Grif eyed Zicaro as they approached, taking the lead just slightly as Kit lagged behind, then glanced furtively over each shoulder and back again when he still didn't see Justin or his cronies. He *did* see that they'd somehow managed to find Zicaro another wheelchair, and that there were no visible marks on the old man. Overall it looked as though they'd treated him well, though if the grumpy expression on his face was any indication, they'd neglected to order him breakfast after depositing him there.

"Where are your captors?" Grif asked him, nodding that Kit should go ahead and sit across from him. Grif would remain standing guard.

"I don't know," Zicaro admitted, and jerked his chin at the front door where they'd just entered. "They just dropped me off there, then told me to go inside and wait in the last booth."

"Wait for what?"

One bony shoulder lifted up and down. "For you, I guess."

That couldn't be all, so Grif just shoved his hands into his pockets and squinted around the place, waiting for something to happen. Kit's phone buzzed in her bag, and Grif recognized the ringtone she'd assigned to Marin, but they both ignored it in deference to the situation, and Kit pulled out the map instead.

"Is that it?" Zicaro croaked, throat obviously dry. Grif caught the attention of the waitress and motioned for her to bring water. It wouldn't do for the old guy to get dehydrated.

He could use the moisture, too. He felt dry in the pores as well as the throat. Like his body was already readying to turn back to dust. "Is that what everyone has been fighting over?"

"Do you remember my father sending you this map fourteen years ago?" Kit asked, removing the tracing paper and pushing the old cartographer's drawing of Vegas in front of Zicaro. His eyes lit like kerosene.

"So I was right? My old story about the DiMartino and Salerno feud? My hunch about the map?"

Kit slipped the tracing paper atop the map, displayed the whole of the valley—and Sal DiMartino's drop zones—before him. "It seems so."

Almost reverently, Zicaro used one thick-knuckled finger to trace each drawn line, his mouth moving silently as he recited the old locations in his mind. Finally, he looked up. "Holy God. Every body buried, every dupe and stooge, is on this map."

"And," Kit said, pointing out the mark nearest the Black Mountains, "a little doll with two very expensive eyes."

"Jee-zus." Zicaro seemed to be having trouble catching his breath. "No wonder everyone wants this."

"Yeah?" Grif said, looking around. "So then where the hell are they?"

The waitress arrived just then, carrying three waters. "You mean your friends?" she asked, having overheard the question.

She set the clear plastic glasses down on the table, then straightened and wiped her hands on her apron. "What? You've been standing here looking around for almost five minutes. I'd have told you sooner but they gave me a twenty and said to wait until you called me over to let you know that they left." She raised one dark eyebrow. "Y'all need menus?"

"No," Grif said. The waitress rolled her eyes and left.

"So, that's it?" Kit asked, gazing up at Grif. "We're all free to go?"

"Don't have to ask me twice," Zicaro said, and reached for the map. Kit shooed him away, and tucked it into her purse instead. Zicaro scowled, but it didn't matter to Grif who had it. He'd memorized the lines leading to the Black Mountains the second he saw it. It was as if the Cissy doll spoke to him from within the confines of her desert grave, and why not? He'd died because of that doll. Because of diamonds he didn't even value.

Zicaro led the way back out of the diner. It was immediately clear to Grif, even though he still looked around cautiously, that no one waited for them in the battered parking lot, either.

"Why do you think they just left the map?" Kit said, shivering against a gusting wind. Though it was early afternoon, the winter sun was thin in the sky and offered no warmth.

"I don't even care," Grif admitted, surprising them both, but he felt lighter somehow for saying it. "If someone wants to go digging around in the desert for treasure that doesn't belong to them, then they can have at it."

Because what good were jewels to a man laboring under the weight of celestial prophecy? Would they buy him more time with Kit? Would they grant him another life? He certainly couldn't take them with him to the Everlast.

And if he did have them, he thought, staring at Kit, he'd trade them for just a few more hours with the woman he loved.

"Hey," Kit said, leaning close to peer up into his face. "We're still going to solve this thing, okay? You have to believe. Please, don't give up before—"

She cut off as her phone began to ring in her hand.

She'd been about to say, *Before your time is up.* Yet she let it go, because neither of them needed the reminder of that.

"It's Marin," she said instead, flashing him the screen. "She's been calling almost since we left her."

"She must be worried about me," Zicaro piped up, sitting tall.

Yet before Kit could connect, a squad car came peeling around the corner, cutting directly through the lot to screech to a stop before them. Grif pulled Kit close, placing one protective arm around her waist as both patrol doors flew open.

"Hands up!" said the officer on the passenger's side, and he had one hand on his holstered gun, the other pointing, oddly, at Kit.

"Stokes, please," the other man said wearily, and only then did Grif recognize Dennis. It was the expression on his face rather than the uniform that had kept Grif from doing so at first. The man usually looked at Kit with admiration, or barely disguised longing, but now his face was marred with a deep frown. "Kit. You need to come with us."

"I don't understand," she said, the hand with her phone— ringing again—falling to her side.

Marin's been calling almost since we left her.

Shit, thought Grif, looking up again.

"What's going on here?" Zicaro asked, pushing his wheelchair toward Stokes.

"Sir, we need you to step . . . er, roll back."

Instead, Zicaro ran over the man's foot. "I'm not going nowhere! What the hell do you want with Ms. Craig?"

Dennis held up a hand. "We just want to—"

"Ms. Craig," Stokes said, raising his voice to be heard over Dennis as he glared at Zicaro and moved behind Kit to take her hands. She automatically handed her phone to Grif. "You're

wanted for questioning in the murder of Gina Alessi. You have
the right to refuse."

"What?" Kit and Grif exploded at the same time that Zicaro
nearly leaped from his chair.

Stokes grinned. It was the response he'd been looking for,
and he put his hand on the weapon at his hip. "Or we could
arrest you. Then you have the right to remain silent."

"That's absurd!" Zicaro went nuts, chicken neck lengthening as he yelled from left to right. "Police brutality!"

The officer shot Zicaro a warning look, but his eyes shifted
to the crowd beginning to gather in the lot and then back at
Zicaro. It was clear he didn't want to be seen roughing up an
old man. "Sir, back off and don't make me tell you again. You
want to come downtown, too, we can take it up there."

Zicaro stared for a long moment, then cursed and fumbled
in his sweater pocket for his own phone, grumbling about calling the *real* authorities.

Grif turned back to Dennis. "What the hell's going on?"

"I'm sorry, Kit." Dennis met her gaze, but shook his head.
"But your prints were all over the place."

"Oh, come on!" Kit whirled side to side as Stokes pulled
her toward the car. "I'm the one who tipped you off about the
place! And you know me! I'd never kill an old woman!"

"Yeah?" said Stokes, unmoved. "Then what about Ray
DiMartino?"

"Shit." Grif rubbed a hand over his face, and Zicaro slowly
lowered his phone.

"Kit," Dennis warned. "Don't say any more."

"Let's go," Stokes said, nudging her forward. Kit stumbled and Grif reached for her, but Dennis angled between
them.

"You're not helping her, Shaw," Dennis said, hand on Grif's chest. "Let her go. I'll take care of her."

Stokes was propelling Kit forward, even though she was gazing at Grif over her shoulder. Her eyes were wide, her face bewildered. "Call Marin back. Tell her to call our lawyer."

A lawyer? "Kit—"

"She's right," Dennis said, as Stokes lowered Kit into the back of the squad car. "I've seen the crime scenes, both of them. She's going to need one."

Grif finally managed to find his voice. "I can't believe you're doing this to her."

"I'm doing it *for* her," Dennis growled, pushing Grif away. "I'm not the enemy here, Shaw."

And treating him like one wasn't going to help Kit. Grif finally nodded as Zicaro, who'd listened to the whole exchange, and wheeled up to his side, saying, "Go ahead and call Marin. I'll head back inside and make some phone calls from there. I still have friends downtown. I'll cash in some chips, see what I can learn."

"Okay." But Grif couldn't move. Even after the squad car disappeared, he stood in the whipping wind of the old parking lot, the sky bright and wide above him. Somewhere behind that sharp baby-blue cover were stars and comets, universes expanding and dying. Beyond that, the Everlast, where winged beasts awaited his return. Beyond that, the Gates and Paradise, a place Grif was no longer sure he'd ever see.

Glancing down, Grif squinted at his watch. Speaking of seeing, he was suddenly having trouble differentiating the large hand from the small.

You'll start having problems with your five senses, one at a time at first, but they'll all worsen.

Blinking hard, he finally made out the time. Two in the afternoon. Only fourteen hours left until the anniversary of his death. He dizzied at the thought, but not because he was growing weaker. The thought of spending his last hours on this mudflat without Kit by his side exhausted him, but he clenched his jaw and forced himself to dial the last known caller on Kit's phone.

"Marin," he said when she answered, though he had to stop to clear his throat. He should have drank the water the waitress had brought. His mouth had gone completely dry.

"Where's Kit?" was all she said, and he could tell that she already knew. Out of courtesy, Dennis had probably called her first.

"She's being set up," he told her.

"I know," Marin said, and for once he was glad for her curt disposition. "Dennis already called me. I'm headed down to the station now, but you need to go to the Sunset Retirement Community. Now."

"Why?" He could see no reason, but that didn't keep nerves from tunneling through his stomach.

"Because the authorities have spent the last couple of days interviewing the residents. It's taken some time. It's . . . hard. There's dementia to deal with, and the elderly don't like up-heaval, as a rule."

"So?" Grif asked. He didn't see what any of it had to do with him anymore. They'd uncovered the trust-fund fraud. They knew why the staff had questioned Zicaro and held him against his will, as well as why Barbara had visited him.

Barbara, he thought, mind shooting off in that direction. She was behind this. First him and Evie, now Kit . . .

"Grif!"

He realized it was the fourth time Marin had said his name. He shook his head. "What?"

"I got a hold of the county official in charge of the fraud investigation this morning and convinced him to let me speak to the new health services director. Grif, I asked her about Gina Alessi. She's been living at Sunset the whole time. Years. Room 330. Suffers from Alzheimer's. No family. They say that the staffing change has been especially hard on her these past few days."

"But Gina Alessi is dead," he began, but in the back of his mind he heard, *She wants it all.*

She . . . a woman who had a knack for hiding in plain sight. "Barbara," he whispered.

"What?" Marin said, before an exasperated sigh came over the line. "No. Grif, that's what I'm trying to say. The woman in room 330 isn't Gina Alessi or Barbara McCoy." She hesitated, and Grif felt himself go dizzy in the wide silence. "She says that her name is Evelyn Shaw."

CHAPTER TWENTY-ONE

It was late by the time Kit was through being questioned, and it wasn't until she was led back into the bull pen that she saw a wall clock that read nine P.M.—which made her heart jolt in her chest. However, to her relief, Dennis was leaning against the wall beneath it. His brow cleared when he saw her, though aware that he was still in his professional environment, he merely placed one hand on her shoulder and asked, "You okay?"

For a moment, just one, she allowed herself to lean against him. Then she thought of Grif and reminded herself that there were only seven more hours in which to stop him from dying again. Dennis's jaw tightened as she pulled away, but he let his hand drop.

"Where's Marin?" she asked, as he led her to the admitting window where they'd made her check her .22. She knew her aunt had been there. She'd heard her yelling even with the interview room door shut.

"Probably still raising hell," Dennis said, jerking his head at the stony-faced officer on the other side. "She was here for about an hour, but between you and me she was doing more harm than help. I finally told her I could get further with the department than she could. Her tongue is as sharp as barbed wire."

"She's not the most diplomatic when she's upset," Kit admitted, causing the officer on the other side of the window to snort as he shoved a clipboard her way.

Kit signed where instructed, and only then did he return the plastic bin containing her gun.

"You're lucky you got a permit for that," the officer said, nodding at her .22.

"I don't break the law," Kit replied, tucking the gun back into its holster and then her bag. She'd been accused of no crime, so they had to return it. That was the law, too.

"Come on," Dennis said, cupping Kit's elbow as he pulled her away from the window.

"Marin agreed to let me handle things on this end while she went to the paper to write up a story about the relationship between Barbara DiMartino and Gina Alessi," he said as he led the way down the hall. "And the diamonds they've both been after for fifty years. Hold up."

Dennis pulled her back before she could push through the double doors where they'd entered the station. "You don't want to go that way. Reporters."

"Friends," Kit said, reminding him that she was a reporter as well.

Dennis shook his head. "Not this time."

He was right. If some string reporter pieced together the story about two con-women searching for diamonds—and that Kit was somehow involved—they'd start speculating about her as well. That's why Marin was using the newspaper to get their side of the story out first and fast. When it came to the news, a good offense was the best defense.

Besides, if anyone was going to tell this story, Kit thought, following Dennis, it was her. But first she needed to get back to Grif. "Thanks for helping to get me out so quickly," she told Dennis as they pushed against the steel bar of the back door and swung out into the cold night. "I think you set some kind of record there."

"Well, we got a witness who says Ray DiMartino had you cowered and cornered just after a gunshot was fired. We also caught Larry and Eric Ritter downtown, trying to catch a bus to Sheboygan, Wisconsin."

"Where?"

"You gave us the drop on them, so that was in your favor as well." He motioned to his car at the far end of the lot, but stopped her just after she'd cleared the steps. "I vouched for you, too."

"Of course you did. You're my friend."

"Yes. And . . . I remember."

Tilting her head, Kit found that Dennis's eyes had gone surprisingly dark, yet they still shined in the filtered glow of the streetlamp. "What?"

"You. I remember you sitting at my deathbed, Kit." He chuckled wryly when she returned to his side. "It's been six months, but I still dream of it. I knew I was dying. My body knew it. I could feel my mind cramping up against the idea."

It was the first time they'd spoken of it. In six months,

they hadn't once recounted the events leading to Grif leaving her . . . and her ultimate decision to be alone if she couldn't have him. She had wanted to explain the choice to Dennis . . . but how could she explain to *anyone* about Griffin Shaw? Even the Pure couldn't understand him. He wasn't just her partner or lover, or some ideal she'd dreamed up from the rockabilly era she loved so much. And discovering that Grif's and her father's deaths were linked only confirmed that there was more than simple love between them. There was fate.

That was what had propelled him from the shadows the night they met. Fate was what had him defying heavenly orders to save her life. And it was *fate* that had them snapping back to each other like a rubber band, when the tension of being apart grew to be more than either of them could bear.

So Kit now believed that fate would come through once again if only they fought together in these last few hours. If only they both believed.

Yet right now Dennis's eyes were drinking her in. It was the first time he'd allowed his true feelings to show, and Grif was right. This man cared for her. He'd be so good for her.

"I was so afraid you would die." She told him now.

He touched the side of his head, where the bullet had grazed him, in what had become an unconscious gesture. "You know when you're underwater, and sounds are distorted, yet you can still differentiate between noises?"

"Yes."

"Your voice was like that. I couldn't hear what you were saying, but I recognized it and knew you were there. I even think I tried to respond . . . at least that's what I dream about now." He looked at her, gaze gone liquid from the memory.

"Even now I wake with the same thought rolling through my mind. 'She's gonna stick to the very end.'"

He laughed at that, but there was no humor in his laugh, because he had woken up . . . and she left him still. Kit looked down, shamed. She knew how it felt to be left behind. Yet she also knew it was something she'd do again if given the choice.

"Dennis, I—"

"Shh." He silenced her with a finger to her lips, and let it linger for a moment before dropping it to cup her chin. "You can't force the heart in a direction it doesn't want to go. And it's okay. I wanted you then, and a part of me always will, but do you know what I really want? More than anything else?"

She shook her head, throat too full to talk.

"I just want to see you dance again, Kit."

"Dance?" Kit repeated, blinking back tears.

"You don't anymore," he said, and his flashing smile was wistful. "And you used to love to dance."

"Yeah, I did." And so many of the things she'd loved had fallen away, all lost because she thought Grif had been lost to her as well. One thing was certain: no matter what happened tonight, that was going to have to change. It was no way to live.

"Come on," Dennis finally said, holding out his hand. There was nothing romantic in the gesture, just Kit's friend offering to put the past behind them and continue helping her into the future. So Kit took his hand and allowed him to lead her to his waiting car.

"I'll take you to your aunt," he said, keys jangling as he broke free and rounded to the driver's side. "Maybe she—"

The figure that rose behind him looked like it was made from the shadows themselves, and the only thing that saved Dennis from a square hit with the two-by-four was Kit's widening eyes as her gaze darted over his shoulder. Instinct allowed him to manage a half-block as he turned, but it wasn't enough. Dennis went down with a heavy thud.

Then Justin Allen lifted his other hand and pointed his gun directly into Kit's face.

"Honey," he said, eyes glittering in the cold night. "Don't even think of trying to run in those shoes."

It took Grif twice as long as it should have to reach the Sunset Retirement Community. He lost his way twice on Hacienda, despite knowing the road well, and it wasn't out of shock or even nervous anticipation. Not entirely. His sense of direction, never good, was also deteriorating. He hadn't noticed it at first, but it seemed like someone had gradually been lowering a dimmer switch on his eyesight so that every outline blurred. The bones in his fingers ached as well. His knuckles threatened to lock even when he turned the steering wheel, like the marrow and cartilage and joints were beginning to fuse together so that mobility would soon be impossible.

So when he did finally arrive at Sunset, he grunted like the old man he was supposed to be as he climbed from Kit's car and straightened to face the building.

"They'll be expecting you," Marin had said, voice soft because even though she didn't know who Evelyn Shaw really was to him, she knew he'd been searching for her long enough that the moment mattered. The moment, he thought, was *all* that mattered. After spending one lifetime looking only forward to the future, and a second gazing longingly at the past, as least he'd finally learned that.

So he took a step into the next moment, and then into the one after that. And they were indeed expecting him. The interim health services director held out a hand and smiled as if welcoming *him* home, like she'd been waiting for him all along. She led Grif to room 330, then turned to regard him as she placed her hand on the door.

"I normally accompany guests into our residents' rooms, but as I'm new here and she no more knows me than she does you . . ." She trailed off and Grif glanced at her to see why. That was when he spotted the speck of stardust caught at the corner of one of her eyelashes, winking at him as if from the wings.

How 'bout that, Grif thought, impressed despite the gravity of the moment. A Pure taking human form . . . just for me.

"Steel yourself, Shaw. She's not the same woman as the last time you saw her."

And with a murmured blessing in the jumbled language of tongues, she was gone.

Grif turned back to the closed door. Alone.

She was seated in a wheelchair, facing the window, when Grif entered the room, a heavy tartan blanket draped across her lap. The light from the nearby table lamp illuminated her thin, freckled neck, and she was so slight that there was room in the seat for another small person. Evie had always been a slim woman, but he'd never thought of her as frail before. Nerves moved sickeningly in his stomach.

The Pure who'd led Grif in was right. This woman resembled nothing of the Evie he'd loved and adored and married. He'd watched a woman with platinum curls fall to the floor beside him when he died. Now she was sitting up again, those curls gone gray and brittle, that other woman a mere memory to them both. For a moment Grif was unable to take another step. He'd hardly changed at all—not on the outside—but if her mind was as frail as her body, would she recognize him?

He must have sighed or made some other identifying sound, because Evie tilted her head without turning it, a move that put him in mind of a baby swallow. "Is that you, Mr. Justin?"

Justin. Grif burned inside. Justin Allen had known his wife. He had never so dearly wished a man dead.

Yet he couldn't let his anger show, not to Evie. She was fragile, and Marin had said that her charts and meds indicated a heart problem. So, slipping the fedora from his head, Grif took a careful step forward. His knuckles were white around the brim of his hat, his heart beating like mad. Evie's softened profile shifted and rounded out as he approached, and he steeled himself as he slipped in front of her.

Though the room was warm, Evie wore a sweater that swam over her shoulders, in addition to the blanket folded across her knees. Her entire body trembled with the effort to lift her gaze, and her thin, dry lips pursed hard in concentration as she worked to focus on his face. Grif had a flashback: those lips stained red, full and stretching into a playful smile, meeting his with the ardor of . . . well, someone fifty years younger. He blinked, the image replaced by the trembling woman in front of him, and something in his heart cracked.

"No, Evie. It's not Mr. Justin," he said, as quietly, as gently as he could. "It's me."

The woman just stared, the corners of her eyes milky with age. This was not his wife, Grif suddenly thought. Evie would never wear her hair swept so carelessly to the side . . . she did *not* have a face as soft as sagging velvet. This woman wasn't even made up, he thought, swallowing hard, and his girl always pulled out her pancake tin and sponge the moment she awoke.

But then the dark irises found focus, and that vibrant, long-ago girl flashed into view.

Evie's mouth fell lax without uttering a sound, yet those piercing eyes remained on his, and after what felt like a full minute, she rasped, "Griffin? I— Is that you?"

He hadn't even known he'd been holding his breath, but it escaped him now in a dizzying sob and he fell to his knees before her. He'd found her. No matter what else occurred in the next few hours, in this life or any other, he had finally found his wife. When he felt her hand, tentative and shaking, on the back of his neck, Grif lifted his head.

"But you were . . . but I saw—" She jerked her head, eyes going wide.

"Shh . . ." Grif lifted his hand and gently touched the back of her palm. It was cold. "No, I'm alive."

But his words didn't soothe her. She began shaking her head more violently. "No. No, I saw it. You were struck down. Your blood was everywhere."

"Yes . . . and no," he said, hating that of all her memories of him, this was the one she still carried. "It's complicated. But what matters is that I'm here now, and Evie, you need to know. I've dreamed of this for so long. I've dreamed of you."

Suddenly, the already glassy eyes filled with tears, and Evie lifted her hand so that it wavered in front of her mouth. "Oh, Griffin. Oh, my God, it's really you."

And when he bent forward this time, she folded herself around him. They clung to each other for long minutes without speaking. Evie shook above him, and Grif responded in kind below.

"I was so scared," she finally said, her voice muffled in his hair. "I've been so alone. I closed my eyes that night, I couldn't help it, and when I opened them again, you were gone. And then, eventually, I was gone, too."

Grif sat back on his heels and studied her face. He didn't know what that meant, and from the way Evie's gaze began to wander again, he wasn't sure she did, either. His voice, too, shook when he spoke. "Do you think . . . you can tell me what happened?"

Evie seemed to look right through him. It was as if he'd been a ghost to her for so long that she couldn't hold on to him, even when he was right there. But then her mouth moved in a stutter-start, her eyes shifted, and her mind began searching the past.

Then she started to talk. Full sentences. A story that, Grif could tell, she'd told many times over the years. No, she hadn't died back in 1960, but the events of that long-ago night had chased her as relentlessly as they had him. And despite the age rubbing her vocal cords into reedy strands, she laid out the story so clearly that Grif could see it even when he closed his eyes.

She had been dizzy with drink that night, she said, the roar of the casino crowd round in her ears, a rush of approval that felt like a big hug as she kept the craps table alive, throwing seven after seven. The night was cold when they finally left the casino, yes, but she had a large, warm man at her side, and the juice zinging through her veins. Their bungalow had been hidden, as if in a secret garden, a dark pocket of solitude sweetened by the scent of honeysuckle and rose.

"I was blinded by all of that darkness." She'd opened their bungalow door and pushed inside before she ever saw the shadow move. And she stared for so long, wondering with dumb displacement what Tommy DiMartino was doing in their private space, that she hadn't even realized what he'd done until Grif cried out.

"I felt that knife like it'd entered my own gut. Worse, my heart cleaved right in two. I even thought of my little sewing kit on the bathroom sink, and I thought maybe I could just stitch up your belly with red-colored thread so that everything would be as it was meant to . . . as it'd been just one minute before. Then I saw the doll."

It was the strange juxtaposition of a young girl's toy in their attacker's bloodied hands that shocked her into realization, and she screamed as Griffin and Tommy fought. However, nobody could hear her through the isolation of their lush garden. Nobody was there to see Tommy fall, still grasping his sister's doll. Nobody saw Grif blindsided by a clay vase after that, more shadows moving, until they were all facedown in a puddle of blood.

"Do you remember, Griffin? Do you remember how I tried to reach you?"

He remembered the same deep brown eyes that stared at him now, filled with tears as she cried out, *Damn it, Griffin, no . . .*

Her fingertips suddenly found his, and Grif realized Evie had been saying his name over and over again, just as she had then. *Griffin, Griffin, Griffin . . .*

It was all she ever called him. It was what she called him still.

Why do you . . . she had said.

"Why would you dredge all this up again?" she said now.

The question was abrupt, and rocked Grif back on his heels. He blew out a hard breath before reaching into his jacket's inner pocket, and pulled out Kit's phone and the image she'd taken of the newly discovered map. Pointing, he said, "Because I think you're in trouble, Evie. And this is why."

The doll. The diamonds. The dueling families. He explained it to her quickly, simply, then told her the map showed where Sal DiMartino disposed of all the lives he'd ended in his notorious run of the city . . . and where he'd buried one doll with diamonds for eyes.

Evie stared at the image for so long that the screen timed out and the phone went blank. Then she shook her head, placed her hands over her face, and began to sob. Horrified, Grif watched as her little shoulders sank forward and caved in on themselves, and her broken voice lifted and fell like a brittle leaf on a swirling wind.

"Please don't cry," he begged, inching forward and taking her hands in his. She pulled him close, and still kneeling, he put his head in her lap.

"But the world," Evie moaned, hands running over his head just as they used to. "The world is such a dangerous place."

Grif just kept his head bowed, because yes, it was. And even an angel, even a Pure, could do nothing about that.

CHAPTER TWENTY-TWO

Kit rode in the passenger's seat of Dennis's car, with a known criminal at the wheel and a gun pointed at her middle. Yes, she was scared out of her mind; she was shaking, gaze darting from the locked doors to the streets and people just beyond them and back to Justin, who was sitting cool but smelled like old sweat and stale breath, too. He'd been cooling his heels for a long time, and was obviously pleased to be taking action.

Yet Kit had also just spent seven hours in jail, ordering her mind, parsing out possible fates for herself. None of them had included watching Dennis dumped in a dark corner of the jail's side lot, being kidnapped in a police car, or being ferried into the deep heart of the cold Mojave. So she latched on to the thought that she was going to get out of this alive, that there was still time to find Grif and fulfill the prophecy and make some meaning of all this together.

And then Justin Allen spoke.

"You still have no idea what's going on, do you?" He looked at her with a secretive smile plastered across his face for at least the fifth time. It was getting tiresome.

"Sure I do." Kit blew out a shaking but resolute breath. "You're working with Barbara DiMartino, who calls herself Barbara McCoy, to find diamonds that she's coveted for fifty long years."

She had the satisfaction of watching Justin's face fall, and his hard swallow of that stale breath made her realize she'd hit some sort of nerve.

"Why would you say that?" he asked.

"I told you. I saw you leave Barbara's high-rise that night." After fetching Gina Alessi from Sunset, dressing her like a doll, making it look like Barbara had died. They'd been buying time . . . but why?

"You also shot at my partner," he reminded her, knuckles going tight on the gun at his side.

Kit refocused on his face. His eyes glittered in each street-light they passed. He was anticipating something. And she was a part of it. "I also know that Barbara is still alive, and here you are again, a man who should be running scared just like Eric and Larry. So why aren't you?"

"I'm made of sterner stuff," he said.

"No doubt," Kit replied, because it couldn't hurt to appeal to his ego. "But that's not it. You know something they didn't, don't you? Something worth sticking around for. Is it something you found out at Sunset? Larry was just muscle, Eric a computer grunt, but you were the Life Enrichment Coordinator. You didn't just have access to financial information, you had access to the residents."

Their memories. Their stories.

His only answer was silence, and Kit finally smiled. "Tell me, how long did it take you to contact Barbara after learning of the diamonds and the map from Gina?"

Justin's mouth thinned into a tight line, and he made a sharp left on Sinatra. They were headed to the south end of the Strip, angled in the direction of the Black Mountains.

"Let me guess," Kit went on, encouraged by his silence, forming that clue. "You snuck Gina out of Sunset and drove her to Barbara's home on Saturday night. You then dressed her up in Barbara's clothes, and waited for me to arrive. Barbara was setting me up."

She went crazy when I told her about you . . . she became obsessed.

"Like I said," Justin Allen huffed, shaking his head again. "You don't have a clue what's really going on."

Then she was close. Nobody had been reported missing at Sunset, so Barbara must have taken Gina's place. Hiding in plain sight, as usual. And who there would know? The place was in upheaval right now, so who'd really look?

Abruptly, they swung into an empty lot where a long industrial building stretched in the night like a frozen yawn. Kit's heart leaped into her throat. Maybe he wasn't taking her to the mountain at all. Maybe he was going to get rid of her here first, steal the map and dump her body inside one of these bays. Or a Dumpster. Nobody came here at night. There was no one for miles to hear her scream.

Swallowing hard, Kit searched the car's cabin for the plasma she'd seen earlier. She saw nothing, but what did that really mean? Maybe she didn't have the ability to see the ethereal warning sign anymore. Or maybe, as Grif said, you just didn't see it when death was coming for you.

Carelessly, and, Kit noted, without looking for cross traffic, Justin whipped across two dark alleys in the industrial lot before he swerved one last time and his headlights speared the roll-up bay of an automotive store. For a moment, Kit just stared at the lone figure spotlighted there. What she saw was so unexpected, and so out of place, that her mind couldn't make sense of the stark sight.

What was Al Zicaro doing seated in his wheelchair in total darkness, alone in the night?

The old man turned his head and squinted against the headlights. Bound and tied in place, Kit thought, shivering in the winter night with only a thin sweater to keep him warm.

But then he lifted his hand to shield his eyes.

And then he pushed from his wheelchair and strode to the passenger's side of the car without even a hint of weakness or old age.

Yanking the door open, Zicaro hemmed Kit in, and all the blood in her head fled to her toes. Justin chuckled beside her, his voice a razor in her ears. "Hiya, boss."

The world is such a dangerous place," Evie repeated, her fingertips tightening in Grif's hair. He was still on his knees, bowed over as if for absolution, and he was suddenly so damned tired. He wanted to shut his eyes and curl up right here until . . . well, until it was time to die. Because Evie was right. He would leave this dangerous place now via his own wings . . . if only it weren't for Kit.

Evie's fingers moved down to his neck, her palms on either side of his cheeks. How many times had she held his face like this before? Too many to count. It was the way she had held him when he grumbled about a long day, or when she wanted him to listen to what she really had to say. The familiarity must have struck her, too, because when he finally looked up, she was no longer soft-gazed or staring at him with furrowed brow; no longer looking right through him, but studying him with sincere appraisal.

Evie leaned forward and continued to caress Grif's cheeks with her thumbs. Her eyes darted as her fingertips played over his stubble, taking in his features like a sponge, and Grif did the same. He truly saw her then, he *knew* her beneath this new flesh, and for that, if nothing else, he sent up a prayer of thanksgiving before his gaze finally fell to the thin gold chain swinging lightly around her neck. It took him another moment to recognize the charm hanging from it. It kept disappearing into the shadows as it swung, glinting and falling back, leaving and returning again.

A ring. One that was inscribed with both of their initials, the slanting font also marking the date they were married. Grif reached up, needing to see it, and stilled it with his fingertips. This time, though, when the table lamp caught its edge, a memory sliced through his mind like a hot blade, the back of his head throbbing, then the sound of a vase crashing to the floor. He shook his head and refocused. Ignoring the chain, he slipped the ring over the fourth finger of his left hand. So that's what happened to his wedding ring. He hadn't seen it since . . .

The ring notched into place with a finality that spiraled up his arm and swerved back down to drop into his belly. A wave of nausea rose to his throat, and the throbbing of his skull again clouded his mind. The sound of Evie's long-ago scream whipped through him, acting as a battering ram against his brain.

He saw again the moment Evie fell to the floor. He even felt the blood splash on his cheek as she landed, saw it dotting his forearm like end points on a map.

A map . . .

But no, he was still stuck in the past.

Evie's dark eyes were again pinned to his, but in a face taut with youth and filled with tears, and once more he heard her say, "Damn it, Griffin. No . . ."

Blood pooled in the cupping shell of his ear, obscuring her words. Still insistent, *desperate* to be heard, she reached out and curled her fingertips around his left hand.

"Griffin . . ." she said, squeezing tight. He remembered feeling that.

And this time he also remembered her using her bloody fingertips to slip that cherished ring off his hand.

Grif's eyes followed Evie as she pushed to her palms and then her knees, fingers glinting with glittering polish and his blood. She was talking again, but Grif was having a hard time making out what else she said beyond his name, and she paused abruptly as if she knew it. Then, leaning close to his blood-filled ear, she pinned that hard gaze on his, and enunciated her words so that there could be no mistake. "Griffin, dear . . . why do you have to make everything so goddamned hard?"

Grif could only shift his eyes as she reached for the doll with the diamonds tucked neatly into its face. She stared at it for a moment, greed curling the corners of her lips, then pressed it tightly to her chest, like a little girl. She caught him watching.

"What?" she said, giving him the sly smile he thought he loved so much. "You're good at hard, I'll give you that. But *hard* isn't the life I'm looking for."

Pocketing his ring, she began to rise just as a voice rang over the cold courtyard outside. "Tommy!"

Fear swept over Evie's face, blanching it, but she bit her lip, stilling it again as she made a quick calculation. Glancing from Tommy's lifeless body back to Grif's, she cursed beneath her breath, placed the doll back on the floor, facedown, then reached behind him. What the hell was she doing, he thought, feeling her fumble at his pant leg. She was going for his ankle, he thought. She was going for his . . .

He must have whimpered.

"Shhh," she said, and they locked gazes as she wrestled with the gun at his ankle. "Don't talk anymore, Griffin. Just die already."

And she pulled the piece from its holster, pointed it at his chest, and screamed, "Help! Oh, my God! Help me!"

Then she fired.

And then he was dead, wrapped in the wings of his Centurion.

"Why?" Evie rasped now, as he blinked himself back to the present, thinking the same thing. Gasping, he dropped the ring like it burned. "Why do you always have to make everything so goddamned hard?"

And just as she had fifty years earlier, she blindsided him with something else that was harder and denser than his skull, and rapped him soundly over the head with it.

CHAPTER TWENTY-THREE

Though her mind had once again been set reeling by Zicaro's appearance—his health and vigor—Kit was already figuring it out. After all, if anyone could piece together a fifty-year-old mystery, it was the old stringer sitting next to her. A man who'd always been obsessed with the made and the powerful in the Las Vegas Valley.

"My dear, you look so confused." He smiled, running his tongue over yellowed teeth. Kit wasn't sure she'd ever seen anyone looking so healthy in her life. "And you call yourself an investigative reporter."

His snort, and Justin's answering one, had her clenching her teeth. "When did you start working with Barbara DiMartino?"

"With her?" Zicaro's barked laughter was like a slap in the small confines of the car. "I'm not working with her. She shows up out of the blue last year with questions about a story I first broke decades ago. A fairy tale about diamonds in the desert." His eyes twinkled just as brightly while he explained how those questions got him to thinking again about the last time she'd lived in town, and about the letter he'd sent Marin regarding Kit's father.

He was supposed to take care of Gina, I got the map. Apparently, you received something as well.

So when Barbara showed back up in the valley this year, the cagey old newshound went on point.

"But what about the scam at Sunset? The insurance fraud? The trust-fund thefts?"

"Just a grift I've been running." He shrugged and grinned. Even his smile was stronger. "One of many. Isn't that right, Justin?"

Justin just nodded, and kept his eyes straight ahead. He was more relaxed and more reserved now that his boss was with them.

"I'm actually sorry to see this one end. The Sunset scam was almost beautiful in its simplicity. All I needed was one person in sales and another in accounting to oversee things." Larry and Eric, who were *not* headed to Sheboygan. "Justin here is the only one who ever knew who I was, and that I was watching over everything from the inside."

"I've been with Al for six years now," Justin said tightly.

"Yep, and this was our best con yet. Still, if tonight goes well, I'll never have to work another."

Zicaro chuckled, but broke off when he caught the disgust flashing across Kit's face. He sobered immediately, his eyes going rock-hard in the sculpted crags of his face. "Hey! *You're* the one to blame for my inability to make an honest living in this town!"

Instinct had Kit treading lightly. His eyes were wild and wide, his voice too loud and deep. "Me?"

"You . . . your family. Same thing," he said, spittle flying from his mouth. "Do you know that the honorable Dean S. Wilson refused to grant me a letter of recommendation after giving me the boot? Thirty-one years of chasing down leads for your paper and not even a handshake on my way out the door.

"Meanwhile, all that time, I had to sit by and watch—no, *document*—the escapades of the notorious and the immoral in this town. Forced to write about the DiMartinos and the Salernos while they literally got away with murder." He sneered again. "Making money for the Craigs and their newspaper while they laughed at my stories and my methods. Yet they took credit for all my work, right before throwing me out on the street."

Was this what it was like to grow old? Kit wondered, drawing back in her seat as she looked at him. Did everyone harbor such great regret or obsession over the past?

"But I'm not sitting on the sidelines anymore, am I? Let some other sucker chase down bylines. The disappearance of the mob created a void, the whole town was thrown into disarray. But where there's chaos, there's opportunity." He ran his tongue across his teeth again. "First time out, I ran a scam right out of the DiMartino playbook. A shakedown of one of his own men, no less. Dug out some of my old stories and did the same with his buddies once DiMartino was no longer around to protect them. Made more money in a year than I did in five years writing for your grandfather."

Yet he'd still lived at Sunset, humbly, for years. "But you don't spend it."

"Because spending isn't the point. *Possession* is the point.

Besides, you gotta stay inconspicuous if you want to keep your ear to the ground. If I hadn't, I would've missed the biggest opportunity of my lifetime."

"Gina Alessi," Justin said, clearly having heard this story before. Kit looked back and forth between the two men, pressed between evil and more evil.

"That's right. She moved into Sunset fifteen years back, right after I did. Said her name was Angelica, but I know faces. My mind is like a pitbull's mouth. Once it seizes on to something it wants, it doesn't let go."

So he went back through his files, every story he'd written from the time he started at the *Trib* in 1957, and finally struck gold with the story about a little girl's kidnapping and a photo of the nanny who'd allowed it.

"Gina was on the run, but I never let on that I knew it. I just played rummy with her, asked her to sit with me at lunch. Only later, after I had her trust, did I mention I used to be a reporter."

But he never mentioned the DiMartinos or the kidnapping that took place more than thirty years before. He didn't want to spook her.

"That's why she asked my father to send you the map fourteen years ago. She thought you were a friend, she knew you could figure it out, but she fled after my father's murder. She knew that Barbara and Ray would be searching for her."

Zicaro inclined his head. "Ray came by that very night. I heard him ransacking her room. The next day everything in it was gone. I stayed put, hoping Gina would come back or try to contact me again, but she never did." Zicaro nodded, then abruptly stopped. "It would all be over by now if your father had just sent me both parts of that map."

But he'd sent it to Marin instead.

"You're a good reporter, Craig. I'll give you that much," Zicaro said, but his voice was cold, and it didn't sound like a compliment. "You almost figured it out on your own."

"So you joined Grif and me. To see what we knew."

"And because I needed someone to do the legwork. People work for me now, understand? Not the other way around." He settled back as they raced forward on a road that felt like it was lengthening, as if retreating into the past. "Now. Let's go beat Barbara to those diamonds."

The Centurion charged with ferrying Grif's soul to heaven on that cold night back in 1960 had been an old cowboy named Deacon. A farmhand who'd frozen to death in a Montana blizzard, he was hard to rattle and didn't understand why everyone else wasn't the same way, which was why he'd allowed Grif to watch the events that played out immediately after his death, saying it was like sitting in a theater, "watching an old flicker."

So Grif had watched Sal DiMartino burst into his hotel's most exclusive bungalow, somehow alerted that his nephew was there. He made a strangled sound when he saw Tommy, an echo of his cracking heart, and immediately began mourning his nephew with large tears and cursing Grif with the same.

Of course, Deacon had been reprimanded upon his arrival back in the Everlast, with traumatized Grif in tow like a roped calf. A hushed meeting took place the very next instant, when Sarge and another Pure from the Host discussed what best to do with Grif's illicit knowledge. He hadn't known this was unusual at the time—he'd only been dead for a few minutes—but he forgot it soon enough anyway. Incubation took care of that, along with all his earthly memories.

Problem was, emotion imprinted on a soul. So when Grif emerged from the Tube, his past whitewashed into nonexistence, his soul should have been relieved of its heavy burden. But Deacon's actions had stamped horror and sorrow on Grif's spirit, so while Grif's memory was gone, the emotional fallout remained.

That was why, now that the truth had been laid bare, he could recall the way Evie had groveled before Sal DiMartino, spinning up a lie so intricate right there on the spot that Grif had trouble not believing it now.

"Thank God you're here! The lies this man has told!" she wailed, pointing at Grif's body. "The things he has done!"

Of course, Sal believed her. The evidence was right there. Two men dead, each slain by the other, and Evie, just a woman, delicate in a red wiggle dress, unable to lift a glittering hand to stop either of them.

Yet she'd been strong enough to heft a clay vase over her head and bring it crashing down on Grif's head.

"You been betrayed, son," Deacon said, spitting tobacco from the side of his mouth as he patted Grif on the shoulder. "I'm sorry to be the one to show you this . . . but you'll forget it soon enough, anyway."

But Deacon didn't remember how painful it was to be alive, and the Pure had never known. Therefore, watching Sal and Evie plotting what to do with Grif's mortal body, the same way they might discuss burying the family dog, was really what had driven him for the past fifty years.

Who killed Griffin Shaw?

Well, he had that answer now . . . and it chased him back into consciousness.

Tucked into the passenger's seat of Kit's beloved car, ankles and wrists cuffed, Grif could only stare as the woman he'd sought for more than fifty years, the one he thought he'd known so well, drove out of the city and into the dark heart of the desert.

"Oh, stop looking at me that way," Evie suddenly snapped, without even glancing over. "I hate it when you get that lost puppy-dog look on your face."

Just like burying the family dog.

"How'd you do it?" Evie finally asked, and he didn't have to ask what she meant. She had watched him take his last breath. She'd watched him bleed out on that cold marble floor. Grif had a memory—also courtesy of Deacon—of Sal ordering his men around. They'd carried Tommy out of the bungalow with excruciating care. Grif was wrapped in the oriental rug, and at the last minute Sal threw in the doll that Tommy had shoved in Grif's face.

"Leave it!" Sal had ordered, when Evie tried to reach for it.

If there was any moment that Evie's smooth, lying facade had faltered, that was it. "But—"

"I said leave it. Let the kiddie molester be buried with his toys."

And with the city's most powerful don's eyes on her, Evie had no choice but to leave the doll with Grif.

Remembering it all, Grif laughed lightly now. "You came so close . . . those diamonds in the doll, that doll in your grasp. You could have had it all . . . but you were just so damned greedy."

"That's right, Griffin. I wanted it *all* . . . but who was going to give it to me? *You?*" Her laugh was a bark of incredulity, a slap in the face. "You with your big plans and your fancy words and your empty promises."

"I never lied to you," Grif said.

"You promised me treasure, and all I got was fool's gold!"

Her words stole the breath from his body. Grif fought not to cringe, but he couldn't help the way his eyes dropped to the ring, his wedding band, still hanging from her neck. At least he knew now why he had never worn it in the Everlast. Evie had slipped it from his finger before his final breath.

"Oh, did you want this back?" Evie asked, catching the direction of his stare. She lifted his ring with her free hand, and yanked the chain from her neck. Then she threw it across the car so that it clattered into the footwell at his feet. "I was going to hock it along with mine, but I figured I should at least get something from that fucking marriage."

"I *loved* you," Grif said, unable to help himself.

For some reason, that infuriated Evie. She shivered, though she couldn't be cold. Her anger scorched. "Love doesn't pay the bills, Griffin!" she yelled back. "Love doesn't give you any of the things that make this life comfortable or worth living, but you fucking got me, didn't you?"

"Got you?" He blinked.

"You had style and that mystery about you. Big P.I. about town. Shit-hot in your fedora, gazing at me with those big blues. All the girls wanted you, and I deserved what everyone else wanted. Well . . . I sure got it that time. And it almost cost me my future."

Cost her *her* future?

Evie shrugged, oblivious to the irony. "Still, you were useful. You taught me the lengths people would go to for someone they loved. It wasn't until I met you that I truly understood Sal and Theresa."

The DiMartinos.

Evie's mouth thinned, her gaze gone distant as she recalled the first man she'd lost. "Theresa knew she was dying even in 'fifty-five but she was determined to hang on to her love with Sal. Still hell-bent on protecting him, even from beyond the grave. I mean . . . can you imagine loving someone that much?"

Grif just thought, Fifty years.

"She declared social war on me, and Vegas was a small town back then. You remember." She huffed, still indignant. "When the wife of the most notorious don in Vegas shows you the door, you go, but I swore the day I wiped the desert's dust from my feet that I would circle back 'round. And next time? She'd never see me coming."

"Barbara." It was the name of the woman whose photo he'd never seen. Whom he thought he'd never met.

Barbara McCoy back in 1955 . . . Barbara DiMartino later, when she had the man and the power she'd always coveted. But for two short years in between?

Evelyn Shaw. His wife. His Evie.

"Sal didn't recognize you when you were . . . when we were . . ."

"Married to you?" she finally finished for him, then scoffed. "Of course, he did. I wanted him to. While his wife lay useless in her sickbed, he needed to see what another man had, and what he was missing."

Evie—*Barbara*—needed to lurk in the front of his mind so that he would want her—and only her—when Theresa was finally gone.

And when Grif was gone, too.

"Wait . . . are you only now getting all this?" She looked astounded, eyes flaring before she blinked. Then, heedless of the road before her, she threw back her head and roared. Driving one-handed, she clutched her belly and wiped her eyes. Finally, when the laughter had died in all but Grif's head, she scoffed. "And you call yourself a P.I."

Not anymore he didn't, Grif thought, and turned away.

A coyote.

Kit heard its howl on the cold night wind as soon as Justin silenced the engine, and she leaned forward to glance past the windshield and up at the sky. A full moon, too.

"It's an omen," Kit whispered, and her voice sounded displaced in the dark, so that even she felt shivers race up her spine. Zicaro and Justin ignored her, but she was trapped and weaponless. Talking was the only defense she had.

"The Paiutes who originally settled this territory called coyotes the 'trickster gods.' They told stories of their playfulness and humor, but also their mischievousness. It was said that they represented the earth, its need for balance, and that coyotes could sense it when someone had laid a trap. Basically, if the coyote howls, it bodes ill for those intent on mischief or injury."

"Would you shut up?" Justin finally snapped. His jaw had been getting tighter and tighter as he tried to ignore her, staring at some app on his smart phone instead. "We're not interested in your fairy tales. No one believes that shit anymore, anyway."

But if he weren't interested, Kit reasoned with a stiff shrug, then he wouldn't be reacting so poorly.

"Maybe not," she sniffed, "but even the sound of them should worry you. It's winter and they're desperate."

"Coyotes don't attack people," Justin said.

"But they've been edging closer to town lately. Reports have them toppling garbage cans and snatching domesticated pets from backyards. We just did a story on it."

"So they're hungry?" Justin asked, finally glancing up from the phone.

"Very," answered Kit confidently.

"Then we'll let you lead the way," Justin said with a smile, causing Zicaro to chuckle. Yet, despite his words, neither man made an effort to move from the car.

Kit looked back and forth from one to the other, then barked out her own short laugh when neither of them would meet her eye. "You have no idea where it is, do you?"

They'd found access to the Black Mountains from the southeast side, but had stopped the car only halfway to the top. They should have been up there digging, but something had them stumped.

"Sal DiMartino left markers," Zicaro finally admitted, "but only his closest lieutenants knew what they looked like."

Kit thought about that for a moment, then scoffed as realization dawned. "You need Barbara. That's why we're waiting here in the dark."

They'd let Barbara find the exact site, and then they'd ambush her, taking the contents of the grave for themselves.

"How do you even know she's coming?" Kit asked.

"Because I've studied Barbara DiMartino for years. I know her better than anyone else. I know what she'll do probably before she even does."

"We also put a tracer on that pretty little car of yours," Justin said, and smiled as he held up his smart phone. It revealed a moving red dot along with their green one. The red was growing closer by the second.

"How did she get my—" But Kit's question stuttered off and curled into the darkness.

Grif. He'd finally found Barbara . . . and just like Al Zicaro, she'd been ready for him.

"Close now," Justin interrupted, watching his screen.

"How close?" Zicaro asked, leaning over Kit.

"No more than five." Justin clicked his phone off. "We should go up."

"Five minutes in this cold? That's plenty of time for the coyotes to get to us," Kit tried, but Justin was already out of the car, and Kit heard the trunk open just as Zicaro leaned close to her face.

"You mean your trickster gods?" He grinned as he grabbed hold of Kit's arm with one hand and pulled out a zip tie with the other. "Don't worry. We'll be careful of the earth's balance. We're still going to pull those diamonds from this desert floor, of course, but we brought along another little doll to replace it."

CHAPTER TWENTY-FOUR

Try as he might, Grif still couldn't bring himself to think of the woman he'd married as anyone other than Evelyn Shaw. Maybe it was because he'd spent so many years revering Evie and vilifying Barbara. The difference between the two women in his mind was insurmountable. Evie Shaw was a blossom, a woman who gave to the world simply by being in it. Barbara DiMartino was a taker, a black hole that absorbed and annihilated anything that got too close.

And Grif was an utter, pathetic fool.

Name aside, though, Grif had to admit that this woman certainly conducted herself like Evie. Forget the age that'd put spots on her hands and wrinkles on her face and neck. Her posture, when not feigning illness, was straight, but with an anticipatory forward bend. Evie had always leaned into life. Her brown eyes, wiped of moisture, were dark glittering orbs that missed nothing, and Grif had to admit that'd always been the case. He'd thought her clever. Turned out she was cagey as well.

There was also no arguing that despite their disparate appearances, Evie was more energetic and agile than he was right now. Because, for his part, Grif suddenly understood the meaning of "bone-tired." It meant the world grew colder than you'd ever known it, starting from within. It meant mere instants of physical relief, and those only between breaths. It meant being forsaken by your own marrow. He could literally feel the muscles in his legs shrinking, atrophying, causing him to wobble as he tried to rise from his side of the car once they arrived at the mountain. He braced against it, and he knew.

The Fade was coming. His angelic side was dying, just as Sarge said it would, and Grif would be gone from the Surface before the night was through. He had accepted this at some point in their journey up the mountain, and now all there was left to do was climb.

"What time is it?" he asked, as Evie poked him in the back with the barrel of his own snubnose, forcing him around to the trunk of the car. Once again, it seemed he was doomed to die by a bullet from his own gun. At least now he knew why there'd only ever been four bullets in it. That's how many were left when it'd been shoved back into its holster at his cooling ankle.

"What does it matter?" Evie retorted, fumbling with the trunk lock, because it didn't to her. She had no knowledge of the celestial timetable he was on. She had never even given him a chance to explain about his Centurion status, or that he hadn't lived the last half century as she had, but died and spent that time mourning *her*.

No, the only thing she'd openly wondered about was his appearance, how he'd managed to stay so young-looking and whether he'd give her the name of his plastic surgeon before he died.

Dying again, he finally decided as Evie rummaged in the trunk, would be a relief.

As she donned a long fur coat, Grif thought about goading Evie into shooting him, and speeding along the process, but knew that wasn't what the Pures had in mind. Of course, they'd want there to be a cosmic lesson for him in all this. Besides, he knew from the time he'd spent carting traumatized souls into the Everlast that the best way to come to terms with the demise of your life was by facing it square on.

So he took the flashlight and shovel that Evie handed him, resigned to his role in fate's plan, and they began picking their way up this slope of the Black Mountains. The bleak chill of the night was matched only by the brilliance of the stars in the sky. This far out from the obscuring neon of the city, they were diamonds piercing black velvet. It made Grif wonder why, if one sought treasure, they couldn't just look up.

It also made him wonder whether Donel was up there, watching. Gloating. Maybe Sarge was already readying a place for him in incubation. Maybe now that he'd found Evie—now that the yearnings of his heart had proven a total farce—God would deign to see him this time around.

Dropping his head, Grif continued the uphill slog, prodded in the back by his own gun every time his feet lost purchase atop bramble and the porous black rock that gave the range its name. Another scuffle sounded off to the right as they climbed, causing Evie to jolt and stumble. She apparently saw no irony in clinging to Grif's arm to right herself as she took aim into the darkness, before quickly swinging the barrel of his gun back up and into his side.

"Coyotes," he muttered, the last of his celestial eyesight pulsing as he spotted a four-legged creature. Evie shivered and shoved him forward, in front of her. He could have shoved back, it wouldn't take much, but forward was exactly where he wanted to be. He was so tired of living in the past.

He was suddenly so very tired of it all.

Finally, the bobbing beam of light found the hillside's first crest. Darkness still lay on three sides, lousy with coyotes and treasure, but the entire Las Vegas Valley blazed on the fourth, the city lights knifing up into the sky. However, that wasn't what caused Evie to halt, or to draw in a sharp breath, or to take one uncertain step back.

No, most remarkable were the two figures waiting for them beneath a natural black outcropping. Justin Allen, as massive as ever, looking much like one of the craggy formations around them . . . and Albert Zicaro at his side, standing of his own volition, a shovel propped in front of him like he was a developer breaking ground.

For the second time in an hour, the world shifted around Grif. Another trick, he realized, blinking hard. The world was chock-full of them.

But then Grif caught the uneasy smile on Evie's face and recognized it as the one she wore when trying to work out anything, from a crossword puzzle to the handling of a nosy neighbor. She was plotting a course of action, taking inventory of her options. Whatever her thoughts as she studied Zicaro, Grif didn't think she looked nearly as frightened as she should have. Then again, she was using him as a shield.

"Where?" was all Zicaro said.

Instead of answering, Evie just pulled her fur more closely around her shoulders. "You know, Sal always said there were only two durable things in this godforsaken valley. Bills and boulders. He spent the bills, or at least I spent them for him, and marked the graves of his enemies with headstones carved from the valley's mountain ranges."

Grif thought she was stalling again. Zicaro clearly did, too, because his face was shifting into a snarl, but Evie just reached out—gun still steady at Grif's back—and guided his hand, forcing him to scan the hillside with the flashlight. She dismissed the foreground, the jutting outcropping, but jerked the beam back suddenly, a smile in her voice. "There."

"Watch her," Zicaro told Justin as he turned to scour the mountainside, and Justin—eyes trained on Evie like dual moons in the night—began edging toward her as Zicaro stumbled around behind him. Knowing she was outnumbered, Evie didn't move. She couldn't keep her gun trained at Grif's back and on Justin—or Zicaro—at the same time. He had to hand it to the old girl, though. Instead of panicking, she fell even stiller, that strange expression fixed to her face.

"Here!" Zicaro finally called, a note of triumph causing his voice to tremble. Justin waved them forward with his gun. Despite his failing eyesight, Grif then spotted it, too, the giant slab of pink sandstone that was indigenous to this valley . . . but not to the Black Mountains.

"Red rock?" Zicaro guessed, looking over his shoulder, and Evie made an assenting noise in the back of her throat. And there was no way the giant slab of rock could have gotten all the way out to the Black Mountain range unless it'd been deliberately moved. Still native to the area, it would never bleach beneath the onslaught of the relentless summer sun, or erode beyond recognition from the violent spring winds or summer monsoons. It would ever sit there, unnoticed, the perfect way to mark drop zones . . . or buried treasure.

"Thank you for your cooperation," Zicaro said, and was so giddy he bowed to Evie with an exaggerated flourish. Then he straightened and nodded at Justin. "Now shoot that bitch."

Swallowing hard, Justin glanced from Zicaro to Evie and back again. "I don't think that's a good idea."

"You're right." Sighing, Zicaro pulled a gun from behind his back. "I'll do it."

And clearly not caring whom he struck, Zicaro fired three times in quick succession.

Click, click, click.

He looked down at his gun like it'd grown two heads. The confusion on his face was almost comical in the steady beam of Grif's flashlight. Evie chuckled lightly behind Grif while Justin pivoted to flank Grif's other side.

"See, Griffin?" Evie said, fur brushing his shoulder. "You're not the only one who's slow on the uptake."

"Are you fucking kidding me?" Zicaro roared, tossing the gun aside. He glared at Justin with raw fury but still shivered in the small beam of light. "You're throwing me over for that old broad?"

Evie lifted her chin. "I think the line is, 'Et tu, Brutus?'"

"I don't speak French," Zicaro snarled. "Except for 'fuck you.'"

"No, fuck you," Evie said, and fired a shot between his legs.

Despite his waning powers, Grif did see the plasma then. It rolled in like a cosmic wave, a silvery supernatural tide, and there was enough of the luminous warning to mark them all for dead.

"You'd better be real clear on what you're doing here, son," Zicaro warned Justin, who bent to lift something off the desert floor.

"I'm not your son," Justin muttered, and then threw the item at Zicaro's feet. It was a pickax, one they'd obviously brought up with them. "And she promised me half."

"*I* could give you half!" Zicaro screamed, voice threading with plasma to spiral and spark in the icy night.

Justin screamed back. "After six years of watching your back, running con after con, always being promised a next time, and being told that the big one is still to come? That we're going to make out, we're going to be rich?"

Evie, still and imperturbable on Grif's other side, only chuckled. "I just hate a man who can't live up to his promises."

"You think I believe that you're gonna make good on all that now?" Justin's laugh sawed harshly and he picked up a second pickax. He was about to hand it to Grif when a shadow moved along the perimeter. Plasma coiled around both the ax handle and one fleeting brown paw.

But Evie didn't see the coyote or Justin's hesitation. She was still focused on Zicaro, intent on opening that wound more, and rubbing in salt. "You gotta be generous with your people, Zicaro. Sal taught me that. Fear and greed are useful tools to curry loyalty, but nothing makes a man more steadfast than guaranteed green."

Zicaro snarled. "Yeah, you were real generous with Gina, weren't you?"

"Gina had it coming."

"And what about Kit's father?" Grif said, out of the blue. "What about me?"

Evie blinked, and for a moment she appeared genuinely

surprised that he was still there. "Did I say you could speak?"

"No, Evie," Grif said, equally coolly. "I believe what you said was, 'Till death do us part.'"

"Well, then let's get to it." She kicked him in the heels, the barrel of the gun pressing into his back. "Start digging. You, too, Zicaro."

"Fuck you," Zicaro said again, and this time Evie didn't even sigh, she just shot him in the leg. Zicaro hit the ground before the report had cleared from the air. His screams were cutting, but Grif could barely hear them through the buzzing in his ears. The cries were futile, in any case. No one would hear him up here. Besides, what Zicaro couldn't see as he writhed in pain was the plasma purling around his legs, rising along his back, linking smooth silvery tendrils gently around his neck. "You fucking shot me!"

"Actually, I missed. I was going for the gut." Evie turned her back on him and regarded Grif with narrowed eyes. Darkness made a puzzle out of her gaze, obscuring her features, wiping away the lines of age, and revealing only those parts of her face caught in the flashlight's indirect beam. It made her look like she needed to be fitted back together. "As for you, Griffin, dear. Tell me something before you start digging. Before you die."

"What do you want to know?" he asked flatly. Zicaro continued to writhe and moan. The stars kept their icy watch. The coyotes, two this time, moved in closer again.

"How'd you do it the first time?" she said, and narrowed her eyes when he only stared. "Was it a shovel? Bare hands? Did you have an ally? Did the *coyotes* help you?"

"I don't know . . ." But Grif looked down at the pickax in Justin's hands, and he *did* know. The buzzing grew loud in his ears again, but this time it had nothing to do with gunfire. Because the plasma was sliding from Zicaro to him in concentric circles, and it was forming a third link with the pink boulder and the treasure that lay beneath it. The treasure and the grave.

His grave.

"I mean, how the hell does a man survive being stabbed, having his skull caved in, and then getting buried in one of Sal's graves?"

"You forgot being shot and betrayed by his wife," he said, but Evie just shook her head. She didn't care about that. She never had.

"It defies reason." Her upper lip curled in disdain. "It stinks of a miracle."

Grif felt something bubble up inside of him at that, and a snort escaped him before he could stop it. That, too, struck him as funny and he turned his head up to the night sky, as if howling at the moon. "Hear that?" he called out to the heavens, the Pure. "She thinks *this* is a miracle."

Still laughing, he dropped his gaze and studied the bumpy landscape again. Shouldn't he have some sort of recognition of the spot? Shouldn't he be able to recognize the place where he'd been buried for more than fifty years?

But then Evie was directly in front of him. Something moved behind her, but it was gone from Grif's periphery almost instantly, silent and swift. Whatever it was, it was of the earthly plane and of no concern to him anymore. However, Justin was watching the two of them closely, instinctively knowing there was something between them that he didn't understand. Even Zicaro had stopped flailing on the ground long enough to observe their closeness, their marital intimacy.

"I don't think I love you anymore," Grif said flatly.

Evie just jerked the pickax from Justin's hands and forced it into Grif's. "Go dig up my fucking diamonds."

What did it matter? Plasma was already winding up the ax's handle, interweaving with his grip. He lifted his other hand, wondering if he could touch it, but just as his fingertip disappeared into the phosphorescent mist, his celestial eyesight snapped out, and the plasma disappeared with it.

So this is it, Grif thought, and realized that this was how it was supposed to end all along. A full circle back to the grave that held his old bones, now gone as gritty and porous as the rock that marked them. He decided that he'd go ahead and dig out Evie's treasure for her. Then he'd climb back inside his grave and curl up into a past he should have never left. Dust to dust.

Grif trudged over to the grave. Zicaro had ceased writhing atop it and had picked up the pickax Justin had thrown him as well. Zicaro was injured, and Grif was starting the Fade, but they'd do what they could to live a little longer. Survival, it seemed, was the strongest instinct of all.

For a time, the only sound was that of their pickaxes striking the black earth. The volcanic rock was harder than the sandstone that burst from the desert floor farther north, but softer than the caliche plaguing most of the valley. Grif had to admit, Sal had picked a great place to bury him.

After the top layer was dislodged, the digging became easier. His wound and age caused Zicaro to flag, but he pressed on, clearly intent on seeing the diamonds he was likely to die for. Eighteen inches straight down now. It wouldn't be long.

"Go wide," Zicaro suddenly said, grunting as he cut away more of the dense earth. "They're going to want us to make room for three."

Evie heard him and cocked her weapon. "No talking!"

"Unless Justin here has changed his mind about that as well."

"You heard the woman, Zicaro," Grif grunted, sweating and focused. "No talking."

"Fine. Just thought you'd want to know what's gonna happen to *your* dearest treasure."

The vicious heat in Zicaro's words couldn't keep Grif from freezing. He swiveled slowly to look at the old man and, locating him, still saw only darkness.

"She's in the car," Zicaro sneered. "Hog-tied . . . or at least zip-tied."

Justin was suddenly there, squatting next to the hole, his gun level with Grif's gaze. "Shut up and dig, Al."

Zicaro thought about it for a moment before throwing down his pickax. He looked resolute, like he knew he wasn't going to be able to figure a way out of this one. No sense in making it easy on his killers. "Make me," he said, crossing his arms.

A howl rose on the wind as if in response, ripping the silence of the night. Zicaro jumped, and whirled in time to catch the moving silhouette of a lone coyote trotting along the ridge above them. Backlit, it lay opaque and flat against the far-off wink of the city lights.

Cursing, Evie shot at it.

Grif's ears rang again with the report and he dropped his ax, clutching his skull with both hands. The throb in his head pulsed from the center of his brain now, sending concentric ripples of pain to batter his skull. His stomach began to ache in the left side, too, and he realized he'd felt both of these injuries before. They were the ones that'd killed him the first time around.

A blow across his face—Justin's way of getting his attention—brought him back to the present. It wasn't much more than a slap, but it knocked his fedora from his head and gave the throb an extra kick. "Pick up your ax and—"

And Evie screamed behind him. Justin began to turn, but the dark shape that'd sprung from the desert floor was already in flight. Evie hit the volcanic floor on her back, the gun going off as she grunted under her attacker's weight. Meanwhile, Grif did as Justin said. He picked up his ax and, using every ounce of strength left to him, lit up the left side of the crouching man's face.

Yet he'd also lost his equilibrium, and momentum sent him headlong into his own old grave.

The move saved him. Justin recovered quickly, and shot at the first thing that moved. Zicaro grunted once, fell atop Grif, and didn't move again. Justin then trained the gun between Grif's eyes, but behind him was a figure haloed in moonlight. Her hands were bound by zip ties . . . but there was still enough room to grip a shovel. With one solid thwack, she sent Justin sailing into the grave as well. Grif's body was now trapped beneath two still men, and a third—his own aged bones—lay beneath him.

For a moment, there was only his labored breath to break the silence. The wind settled. The coyotes fell still. The city was just a far-off glittering thing.

"Grif?" Kit finally said, voice thick with worry that he wouldn't answer.

Exhausted, in pain from injuries both old and new, Grif closed his eyes . . . and smiled into the cold night sky. "Hey, doll. Think you can give me a hand?"

He heard a click. Grif's eyes shot open and he saw that two

women suddenly loomed above him, and the second one had a gun planted at Kit's temple.

"My husband," Evie told Kit. "Always loved his five-shooter best."

And she had already fired four times.

Neither Grif nor Kit spoke, causing Evie to laugh, a harsh ring of satisfaction in the cold night. "In fact, I'd say he was downright passionate about this gun. Same as with his lousy job as a P.I. Same with me. Every damned thing Griffin has ever done, he's done with great passion."

"That's not a bad thing," Kit said. Her voice was stiff, but with a gun pressed against her skull, it was brave of her to speak at all.

"I agree. Passion can be the most powerful emotion in the world when properly directed. I tried to explain this to Justin once, when we first agreed to work together. I even explained the etymological root of the word, *passus*. It's Latin. It means . . ."

"To suffer," Kit finished for her. Evie blinked at Kit, who looked back, effectively turning her face directly into the gun. "Justin already explained all this to me, so you can save your fucking breath."

Evie's jigsaw expression reordered itself into a cold, firm mask. "Fine. No point in wasting time speaking to the dead, anyway. Though I do need to thank you. I still hadn't figured out a way to get rid of Justin after the three of you were buried."

"So that's how you've lived the whole of your life?" Kit asked disdainfully. "Using men up, then burying them when you're done?"

"It's worked wonderfully."

"I think the men might disagree."

Grif was still too stunned at seeing these two women together, engaging, to speak at all. Weakness, too, turned him
into a mere bystander, gaping as Evie turned fully to Kit,
straightening in her fur.

"Yes, well, if it were left to the men in my life, I'd have spent
the whole of it scrubbing other people's toilets as my mother
did, or thrusting snot-nosed brats from my body, having to
reshape myself, my life, into whatever form they chose. This is
a world led by men, dear. Problem is, if you follow them you'll
always be led into some form of destitution."

"Yet you had a man who would've followed you anywhere,"
Kit said.

Evie bristled, a shiver moving through her, ruffling her fur.
"Fine. In retrospect, I can admit that Grif was different." She
didn't look at him. "A true gentleman. Astonishingly loyal, a
first for me. A man for whom the word 'lover' was created. I
always thought of him as some sort of love savant. Capable of
more of it than most, though that didn't mean he still wasn't
stupid."

"That kind of love isn't stupid," Kit fumed. "It's fucking
regal."

Evie shook her head. "Trust me, girl. Time and again I've
seen a woman grow mightier with age, strengthened by the
hours she's spent forced to her knees by a man. Wash his floor,
bear his children, suck his cock. Meanwhile, those same men
depend on their physical strength to get by. They think it'll
always be there, and when it finally begins to weaken, when
they finally realize how dependent they've become on the
women who run their worlds, they're actually surprised . . .
and as needy as suckling newborns."

"You preyed on that," Kit said.

"I learned early on that a man will give you everything if only you know what *he* values. You become that thing, an ingénue, a victim, a savior, but always hold a little back. It's the small dignity you keep for yourself that will let you rise up and, in time, take it all. As I have."

"And yet," Kit said mildly, "what would your life be like if instead of just taking you'd even once attempted to *give*?"

The night went silent. For a moment, it was so still that it seemed they'd all turned to stone, as immutable and timeless as the surrounding terrain. Then Evie just tucked the gun inside Kit's ear, and squeezed the trigger.

Click.

Grif chuckled darkly. "Four rounds, Evie. You used the fifth on me fifty years ago, remember?"

Kit made a sound then, one that the coyotes surrounding them would recognize and appreciate. Before Evie could even blink, Kit sent a dual-fisted hammer punch right through the center of her startled face. Evie hit the black ground, and this time she didn't move again. Kit, breathing hard, her hair whipping in the cold wind, turned back to Grif, who was still lying in his own grave.

"I can't believe you married that bitch."

CHAPTER TWENTY-FIVE

Grif and Zicaro had done the majority of the digging, so it only took another ten minutes to finish the job. Yet Kit and Grif did not pull a doll with diamond eyes from that grave. It was wrapped inside a rug that bulged in irregular places while a remnant of material—structured cotton and felt—lay decayed on top. It was still recognizable as a once-fine fedora, and Kit lay her hand over Grif's as they both gazed down upon it.

The visual steeled them for what they did next. Propping Evie inside the grave, they refilled the hole so that she was facing the city where she'd plotted and schemed and caused so much destruction. When they were finished, Kit and Grif sat down on the blackened earth, side by side, wrapped in Evie's warm fur as they waited for her to come back around.

"Justin and Zicaro forced me up the hillside," Kit explained, huddling close. "But when they saw that there was no place to hide me, they returned me to the car. They didn't want the sight of me to give you any hope."

They hadn't wanted Grif to fight.

"Fifteen minutes. That's how long it took to get my feet free of the zip ties. I'd done it before, there was a tutorial on the Internet and I thought, you never know. It might come in handy one day. I hadn't anticipated how nerves could counteract your efforts, though, so while I got my feet free there was no time to work the hands. You and Barbara . . . Evie, had already arrived."

She'd followed three criminals up a dark hillside because of Grif. "You never stop fighting, do you?"

She lifted her head and looked at him square. "Not when it comes to a regal love."

Grif kissed her forehead, leaving his lips there for a moment, finding it warm. "I wouldn't have known about her, or this," he finally said, and nodded at his grave, "if it weren't for you."

She inclined her head modestly. "Well, like you said. I'm a fighter."

But he didn't laugh. "And don't ever stop, Kit. The way you're looking at me now, keep that. Keep the fire in your gut, too. Keep asking all those blasted questions . . ."

Chirp, chirp, chirp. That's what his girl sounded like, cheerful and enthusiastic, trilling her way through life.

"Hey," she said, suddenly taking his face in her hands. "I know what you're saying, but I don't want to do any of that without you. Got it?"

He nodded yes. And thought, But do it anyway.

A moan from in front of them disrupted the moment.

"Good news," Kit said, a false note of cheer lifting her voice. "We found your doll."

Evie groaned, head rolling to the side, eyes fighting to focus now that she was the one spotlighted in the night. She likely had a concussion . . . not that they cared.

"The bad news is . . . we buried it again."

Grif shrugged when his wife's unfocused gaze finally snagged on his. There was nothing of the woman he'd loved in that look . . . but it wasn't because she'd changed in the last fifty years. Grif had been the one to project the love he felt, the *passion,* onto her. Even knowing she'd played Sal DiMartino the same way, he still felt stupid. Yet he also knew that, if given the chance to live again, he'd love the very same way. He'd lay it out there and simply hope that the same great and aching passion would return to him if he just gave enough.

But for a woman like Evie? It was never enough.

"What are you planning?" she finally asked.

"Well, we know how long and hard you've been searching for those diamonds," Kit said, huddled close to him. "How many lives they've cost, how many lies you've told. So we decided they really should be yours."

Evie's eyes actually burned. Buried to her shoulders in a grave of her making, and she still had the audacity to hope.

Maybe Kit had hit her harder than he'd thought.

"That's why we buried you with them," Kit finished, extinguishing that greedy light.

"Stretch out fully," Grif added, sickened by the hate that sprung up in Evie's face. "You might even be able to touch them with your toes."

Evie just lifted her head from its sandstone pillow and wriggled her shoulders, managing to loosen a couple of rocks. Kit's hands fisted themselves at her side, and Grif knew she wanted to reach down and firm them back in place. Reaching over, he took her hand in his instead, and had the greater satisfaction of seeing Evie's eyes narrow.

"Griffin—" Evie began.

"Don't talk," he said in a low voice, and somewhere on the jagged sweep of the Black Mountains, a lone coyote howled. As chilling as that was, it was still preferable to this woman's voice. Grif had heard enough of her lies to last two lifetimes.

Standing, Kit made a show of dusting herself off. "We packed the gravel loosely, so you can get out if you want. You can run and hide like you've been doing the whole of your fraudulent life."

"But you won't have time to dig out the diamonds as well," Grif said, pushing to his feet. The sky spun overhead.

Kit linked her arm in his, righting him in place, back on the Surface. "That's right. An anonymous call citing some serious tomfoolery on this mountainside will be placed to Metro as soon as we get down that hill. Of course, you could just sit there and wait for the authorities to find you surrounded by the bodies of two criminals."

They had, in fact, already recovered Kit's cell phone and put in a call to Metro. Any minute now and they'd see blue and red strobes flashing up the mountainside. They'd find Evie . . . along with Zicaro and Justin and the diamonds . . . and everything else that'd been long buried in that warped carpeting.

Grif held the flashlight beam steady on Evie while Kit gathered the weapons Justin and Zicaro had carried up the mountainside. Evie was already fighting her way out of that hole.

"Ready?" Kit returned to Grif's side, and together they turned away.

The cry came after only a few steps. "Griffin! Baby, you're not going to just leave me here like this, are you?"

Kit's hand tightened on his when she felt him pause, but he just squeezed it as he half turned, facing his past one last time. The outline of Evie's skull was all that was visible beneath the moon, and for a moment he was able to project her youthful visage upon that frame, but then he realized that no, this was what had always been there. This blank slate of darkness, an emptiness living inside of her that couldn't be filled, even with the entirety of a good man's heart.

"Hold on," he told Kit.

"But—"

He cupped her warm cheek, pressed his lips to hers. Then he turned and walked slowly back to Evie. Bending low, he leaned so close that all he could see were those deep chocolate eyes he'd once so loved. Then he whispered so that Kit wouldn't hear. "You'd better hurry, Evie. It'll be here soon."

"It'll—?" But she heard it then. The scrabbling of paws slipping over loose rock. The pant of a desert animal's hot breath.

"They don't usually attack humans, but these guys are hungry." Neither of them blinked. "You know what it is to be hungry, don't you?"

Grif returned to Kit then, who only glanced at him quizzically. Then they headed directly back down the hillside, clinging to each other to keep from falling. Even though Evie, buried up to her shoulders, was the only other person on that mountainside, Grif still felt eyes trained upon them. It was a feral night. Even the breeze felt hostile. Then a yelp punctuated the frigid wind, and Kit jolted, but it quickly became a disconnected sound. It could have even been imagined. Grif pulled her forward.

They'd just reached level ground when a scream finally did arch high on the air, spinning into the wild night. Kit stopped

Grif, gripping his biceps. Her head whipped back up the hillside, where a coyote could be heard calling to others, and she gasped in understanding. "You knew."

"She reeked of plasma" was all Grif said, and turned his back on the hillside and headed to Kit's car.

Kit helped Grif into the passenger's seat, and then immediately started the car, cranking the heat high and angling the vents toward Grif. His teeth were chattering even though she'd draped Evie's fur atop him, and his fingers were stiff with cold. Maybe it was just the pale aspect of the moon, but he also seemed unnaturally white. Eyes shut, his mouth was slightly ajar as his head lolled against the headrest.

In just over twenty-four hours, he will be dead.

Kit shoved Sarge's voice from her mind and the car into reverse. "I'm going to get you to the hospital, Grif. I think you're . . ." She didn't say "dying." "Seriously injured."

But his hand stopped her from shifting into gear, his touch weak but insistent. "What time is it?"

Tears sprung to her eyes. "Do not ask me that!"

"After four, then." Grif nodded to himself. "Please, put the top down."

Kit protested again, but he silenced her by pressing his index finger firmly against her lips. "I just want to see the stars."

She couldn't keep the strangled sound from escaping her throat, but she shifted back into park, and worked to lower the soft top on the Duetto. The cold, greedy fingers of the mountain air shifted over her, but Grif was huddled low in his seat, the heater shoving them back out again. Kit killed the headlights, and the black void above them married with the mountain to erase the entire world. It felt like being cupped in a giant onyx palm.

"There they are," Grif said, his voice gone reedy and thin. Kit looked in the same direction that he was staring, but saw nothing.

"They?"

"Her Centurion. He's just there . . ." Grif pointed off into the distance, but his arm fell after only a moment. Then his head swiveled and he smiled at something—some*one*—on the other side of Kit.

They.

"No!" Kit shouted it in the direction he was staring, then shifted so that she was on her knees in her seat and leaning over Grif. Grabbing his face, she forced him to look at her. "No," she told him, too.

"I'm dying, Kit."

"No," she said, slipping his fedora off his head, and pulling him into her arms. He needed comfort right now, that was all, and she could give it. She could. "It just feels that way."

He whispered his next words, one per breath. "You sound so certain."

"I am," Kit said, and fiercely kissed his forehead. She was shocked to find it ice-cold. "Sarge owes me a miracle. He told me so himself."

It wasn't exactly true. What the Pure had said was that he would owe her. In a perfect world.

"And you think I'm your miracle?" Grif tilted his head up and gazed into her eyes. The light from the dash glinted off the severe angles of his face, making him look like he'd just stepped from the screen of an old black-and-white movie. Like he belonged somewhere in the past.

"Of course you are." They both ignored the way her voice cracked. "I knew it the minute I saw you. You appeared in my bedroom, fedora drawn low and fists raised high, and even while you were in the midst of saving my life I said to myself, that's the guy for me. I want him, and no other. And it's been that way ever since. We were fated, don't you see, Grif? Bound together long before we knew it."

She cut off with a shake of her head, realizing she'd begun speaking in the past tense. *No.*

"Maybe you're right." He made an effort to shrug. "Only time will tell."

That's when Kit began to pray. "No, Grif. No. You tell whoever is standing on the other side of this car that we're not done!"

She choked back a sob, and glanced at her watch over his shoulder. Four-oh-eight. He turned his head into her neck, his breath warm, yet somehow cold, on her skin. "Just hold me."

"Hold me back," she hissed in return, and, to her surprise, he did. As her hot tears streaked over his too-cold face, he clung to her like he was rallying.

His whisper, tinged faintly with licorice, sent icy chills up her spine. "We really are a great team, aren't we?"

"The best," she whispered back, and, bending her head, wrapped herself around him and held on tight. The coconut of his pomade tickled her nose. The muscles beneath his suit bunched up, squeezing her back before slowly going lax.

And at precisely 4:10 in the morning, fifty-one years to the day of his first death, Griffin Shaw—Kit's partner and lover and Centurion—died in her arms.

CHAPTER TWENTY-SIX

K it found the note one week later.

She didn't know what it was at first. She hadn't checked her mailbox since before Grif's death, but Marin had gathered all the mail in a neat pile for later. Though she didn't feel up to dealing with the bills, throwing the supermarket advertisements and magazines in the recycling bin made her at least feel like she was accomplishing something. Yet the sight of the slanted cursive had her dropping the rest of the mail heedlessly to the floor. She knew that handwriting, and seeing it now felt like Grif had reached out and touched her, once again, from beyond the grave. It began:

Today I die.

She remembered then, Marin's office. She thought he'd left the room so that she could reconcile privately with her aunt—

and they had; Marin had been steadfast by Kit's side ever since Grif's death—but he'd really been off mailing this. And he'd planned it, she saw, recognizing the stationery as part of the monogrammed set she kept at home.

This morning has more weight to it than others. I can actually feel it, the heaviness of the day. I think I felt it the first time I died, too, but couldn't recognize it then for what it was: the relentless gears of fate picking up speed while my mortal clock began to slow. That's why I'm writing this letter at two in the morning on scented paper in a shockingly pink kitchen while you sleep off our lovemaking as if you're the one about to be thrown into oblivion.

(I love that about you, by the way. Men are supposed to be the ones who lose themselves after sex, but by the time my head clears of your scent and I've finally caught my breath again, you're usually out cold beside me or on top of me or below, limbs like lead, breathing deep. I absolutely love it. I don't think I've ever loved anything more.)

I don't want you to think that just because I'm fated to die today, or because I'm writing this good-bye, that I've given up. I've cheated death before, even from beyond the grave, and went on to live an amazing second life, and who else can say that? But the Host is on my heels now, the heavens are working against me, and someone on this blasted mudflat still wants me dead. It's a pretty full plate, but I'll dig on into it, because I believe that we have a shot at changing all that. More than that, whatever happens will affect your fate, too, and honey, that's really why I continue to fight.

Ten minutes. Kit thought she was all cried out, that there wasn't enough moisture left in her marrow to spare for tears, but that's how long it took before she could continue reading. The note was slightly crumpled now, the ink smudged with her tears, but she could still make out the words of Grif's steady, careful script.

Yeah, I still want to know who set me up for the DiMartinos. Who told them I hurt their little Mary Margaret after I brought her safely home. Who lied about me working with the Salernos to steal those diamonds.

Who the hell took my life away from me while I still had so much living to do?

But all of those questions feel brittle and old under the weight of this heavy, newborn day. They feel like this slip of paper will in another fifty years, filled with thoughts that've been rendered irrelevant with the passage of time. Besides, a more important question thrums in my chest now, and this one is so alive that it drew me away from your flesh and your scent and your bed to ask:

What the hell is going to happen to my girl? My doll? My love?

My Katherine Craig?

I can't answer that. And I don't think I'll be able to before day's end, either. And then I find myself wondering what will your sunrises look like if I'm gone? How will your days stretch out before you, and what will you do to fill in all of those years, all that time? It scares me that after all the things I've done, the lives and the Takes and the joints I've seen . . . I can't even imagine it.

Who will you be without me?

*But I do know what I imagine for you, and it's very
simply more of what's already there:*

*The way you throw your head back when you laugh,
like you're ready to swallow the entire world. The way
your arms stretch wide as if you're opening up your very
chest for a hug. The dizzying chatter that speeds from
your mouth when you and your hens really get going—
laughing and dancing and doing that strange nattering
that women do when they're together. The way your
eyebrows turn down as you work out a story, finding
answers and meaning and truth in your work. And your
day. And your life.*

*I know how important truth is to you, and I want to
give you mine before I go:*

*I love you, Katherine Craig. I love you like God loves
His Chosen. And if fate decrees that this day not go in
our favor, then I will tell the heralds to sing your praises,
and the Guardians to watch over your dark head. I will
threaten the archangels if anything is to befall you, and
I will do everything in my power to see you safe and
protected and duly blessed from my place in the Everlast.*

And, Kit, listen to me: You must live. *I may be the
Centurion, but you're the one with the real wings. You
hold more love for what God has created than anyone I
know. The Host may have thrust the breath back into my
chest as a form of punishment just over a year ago, but it
was you who really taught me how to live.*

*I'm going back to bed now. I'm going to claim you as
mine again before this fated day really gets going, and I'm
going to watch your limbs fall, weighted and limp, across
my chest. Your breathing will be like the ocean's roar in*

my ear, and for a moment, at least, I am going to wipe
your mind of any worry. But no matter what happens,
you must not grieve for me. I have learned something in
this second lifetime that I didn't in my first go-round. You
have taught me the most important truth of all:
   Love isn't just worth remembering and saving. True
love is what saves us all.

It was that letter that finally got Kit up and out of her house. It
propelled her past the bathroom mirror that she'd shattered in
her anger over the heartlessness of a Pure, and into the shower
to wash off the grief that felt like it was caking her soul. She
stayed under the spray until the hot water ran out and her fingertips were wrinkle-tipped, and when she returned to gaze
into that broken mirror, she told herself she felt a little lighter,
a little better. Perhaps in time she'd even believe it.

Her gaze dropped to the cracked webbing of the glass, and
for a moment she saw the dust of stars swirling behind the
aluminum coating on the other side. But, no. It was just steam
from the shower. Kit was utterly alone.

And Grif wouldn't want her to stay that way.

"Live until you die, right?" she said to her reflection. Again,
there was no reply and she hurried to her closet to dress. Afraid,
Kit realized, to answer the question herself.

When she showed up an hour and a half later at the nightclub, she was given a welcome most often reserved for a soldier
returned home from war, which almost felt true. Enveloped
in the arms and chatter of her closest friends and the jumping three-chord change of classic rockabilly, she was happy to
simply listen as Fleur prattled on about a new competing hair

salon offering a blow-dry bar and a makeup menu. As Charis proudly told of her baby, now sitting up, soon walking. Still, it all felt like an out-of-body experience, like she'd been dropped into a fishbowl, told to sink or swim.

She was just sipping at her old-fashioned, thinking she had nothing to add to the environment and that she might as well leave, when she felt a presence at her side. Looking up, she smiled. "Dennis."

He had dodged fate one more time. The blow that Justin had landed on his head had merely gained him a concussion and a healthy interest in watching his back. For now, though, he was looking at Kit with a gentle smile on his face, one that didn't even require she smile back. Just like a true friend. "Please tell me that you've come to dance."

Aware that all chatter at the table had ceased, and that she was currently being studied by a half-dozen curious gazes, Kit set down her tumbler and held out her hand. "This *is* one of my favorite songs."

She ignored the lift of Fleur's painted-on eyebrows, and let herself be led to the center of the dance floor. The band had switched it up a bit, and were giving the crowd a breather with the Eddie Cochran ballad "Yesterday's Heartbreak."

"I'm glad to see you here," Dennis said, palming her right hand with his left.

Kit bit her lower lip. "I wouldn't have come but . . . I had a little nudge."

"Brave," he said, drawing her closer, breath moving her hair. "If there's anything I can do . . ."

She smiled up at him. "You're doing it."

Dennis smiled back and, keeping his touch light, uncomplicated, and chaste, he rocked her through the notes of the song.

Kit closed her eyes, happy to be led. Her eyes opened, though, when Dennis unexpectedly jolted.

"May I?" a voice said from behind him.

A man stood there, tall and thin and dark, dressed in a cuffed suit with a pocket square, and an era-appropriate skinny tie. He looked like a detective from some fifties television show, and Dennis's eyes pinched at the corners as he stared at him, mouth firmed and ready to say no, but then Kit nodded. "It's okay. I know him."

"As long as you're still dancing," he finally whispered, then bussed her cheek, "I'm happy to watch from afar."

Kit bit her lip to keep from tearing up, and dipped her head in a grateful nod. When she'd finally gathered herself, she was in the other man's arms, and she looked up and met his gaze dry-eyed.

"Hello . . . Saint Francis of the Cherubim tribe." The steadiness of her voice surprised her as she locked her gaze with that of the Pure. The Universe swirled where his irises were supposed to be, rich and dark and mysterious, punctuated by stars. Galaxies rose and fell, and stars were birthed and died before her.

"Hello, Katherine Craig."

He was different from when she'd last seen him, fully restored, she assumed, to his former glory.

"Inebriated?" she asked him.

"What do you mean?"

She tipped her head at his body. "You appear on the Surface using the bodies of the very young, old, sick, or drunk. As there's no shortage of alcohol here, I'm guessing you chose the latter."

"Actually," he said, taking a deep breath before dipping her expertly, "I've come to the Surface of my own accord. I'm using flesh granted to me by God to access the Surface. Much like your dear Mr. Shaw."

Though a pang still shot through her heart at Grif's name, it was a relief to be able to talk openly about him with someone. "But Grif said that the Pure find molding their divine nature into human form extremely uncomfortable."

"It's like detonating a nuclear bomb in your chest," Sarge confirmed. "But I still owe you."

"No," Kit scoffed. "You said that in a *perfect* world you would owe me."

"Ah, yes. But who can wait around for that?" The left side of his mouth lifted, and they adjusted their rhythm as Elvis's "Blue Moon" began to play. "Besides, you forgave me the night we last spoke, remember?"

"So?"

"So your forgiveness healed me. I really do owe you now. Even God Himself said it was a miracle, and after feeling all that you felt, experiencing every emotion as you did, I have to agree."

Kit smiled but remained silent, waiting to hear why he was really here. Knowing her thoughts, of course, gave Sarge an advantage, and he inclined his head. "You know, there was a time when I didn't understand why the Chosen wasted their time on love. Even the most ardent affection is ultimately destroyed by death, so why bother?"

Kit thought for a moment. "It's hard to explain to a Pure. You guys are, by nature, fatalists."

He gave a small laugh at that. "When I was first put in charge of the Centurions, all those lost and broken souls, I found myself sympathizing with the suicides the most."

"Why?"

"I thought that because death was inevitable, it meant life

was empty and hollow by nature. Why bother with any of it? It's all meaningless in light of . . . well, the Light. How much better would it be to just shut it down early, avoid the needless emotion, and come directly to God?"

Kit just shook her head. Trying to explain life, or love, to a Pure would be harder than explaining the sun to the blind.

"And now I see," he said, reading her mind again. "Thank you."

"You're welcome," Kit said after a moment, and realized she really meant it. Yes, she was in mourning, but wasn't that life? She was lucky to have it.

"It's good to see you out," he said tentatively.

"Yes, well . . ." She motioned around the dance floor at the other people, at the *life*. "There's still living yet to do."

"And work?"

"There's always work."

He tilted his head, and almost made it look natural. "So are you still a truth-seeker, Katherine? Still value that above all else, no matter how hard or at what cost?"

"Absolutely."

"Good," he said, pulling back. "Then I have another truth for you, though it's not one you can share."

"No?"

"Look around. Who here would believe you if you spoke to them of Centurions and of the Pure and the Everlast?"

No one.

"Who," he continued, and released her to wave one hand gracefully through the air, "would ever believe that a man named Griffin Shaw lived and died two lifetimes?"

Nobody. Sometimes she had trouble believing it herself.

"Who," he finally asked, lifting both hands high, "would believe that miracles happen every day? We just don't see them."

And an ombré gray mist rose around them, causing the room to still as if captured in concrete, a pseudo-Pompeii.

"Are they okay?" Kit asked, whirling about herself, noting that the music had gone mute. She was the only one who moved.

"You looked like you needed a little breather," Sarge said, smiling. She did. Too many eyes had been on her all night, Fleur looking but not wanting to be caught doing so; Dennis doing the same, his longing caged. Sarge looked at her now, too, with the debris of the Everlast glossing his gaze and her own sadness reflected in his eyes. "I'm truly sorry for your loss."

Everybody was. Kit closed her eyes, and an image of Grif flashed through her mind. And everyone could be as sorry as they wanted, but it wouldn't bring him back.

"You couldn't have done anything different, you know," Sarge said, as she swallowed hard. He put a hand back on her shoulder. "Every step you took was the right one at the time."

Yes. Fated. "So . . . how is he?"

Sarge just stared at her with that eternal gaze. It was hard to look him in the face, but Kit didn't even blink. After all she'd been through, she had the right to know.

"These things take time," Sarge finally said. His voice was the gentlest thing she'd ever heard. Somehow that made it worse. "You know, just because something doesn't come in the way you want or expect it to, doesn't mean it isn't a miracle."

"I imagine that's very easy for you to say from that side of Paradise," she said, allowing her bitterness to break through for one moment, but Sarge just nodded. He'd known it was there, lying dormant, anyway.

"I'm causing you yet more pain. I didn't mean to, so I'll go. Just . . . do me a favor," Sarge said, walking backward through the thickened haze. "Don't talk to anybody until I've gone. At least, not until you figure out what's weighing down your left-hand pocket."

"My left—" Her hand immediately went there, and her eyes went wide as she felt the outline of something long and sharp, but Sarge was shaking his head.

"You keep on living, Katherine Craig. The world may not be perfect but . . . it has its moments."

Kit frowned at that, watching him turn around, the plasmic clouds swirling and closing rank behind him. She gazed after him, trying to see the moment he disappeared, but it happened so slowly that she didn't even have to blink. He just dissolved before her eyes. Then the music rose to full speed again, Elvis in a throaty croon, and the dance floor came alive around her.

Kit backed away to keep from being trampled, and then reached into her pocket, feeling for the long shape now poking her in the thigh. Edging into a corner, she lifted the object and peered closely at it in the light. It wasn't one item, but two—both soft, downy feathers, pure white and flashing with quicksilver as Kit twisted them around and back.

"They said I wouldn't need them anymore," said a voice from behind her. "Not where I'm going."

Kit whirled. He wore a five-o'clock stubble that would, she knew, tickle her palm, if only she could move. His fedora was pristine, as was his suit, though his tie had a sideways slant to it, like he'd been yanking at it, trying to get free. His usual half-lidded gaze had gone wide, and he was looking at her as if afraid *she* might disappear.

Griffin Shaw held out his hand. "Care to dance?"

The room still felt like it was moving at half speed, and Kit swayed.

I really do owe you now.

One last dance, Kit thought, and smiled for the first time in a week. She sent up a quick prayer of thanks and accepted Grif's hand.

"I feel like I'm dreaming," she said, ignoring the finer points of the dance to nestle close to his chest. It was the warmest place she knew, and she closed her eyes, breathing him in. Sen-Sen on the breath, coconut in his pomade. Grif—God, it was Grif—again in her arms.

"That's how you know it's a blessed moment."

And not one she'd ever forget. For now, though, she meant to live it. She held up the feathers that Sarge had given her, that she somehow suspected were binding her to him. "I take it you're not currently on duty?"

"Actually, I'm no longer a Centurion." He shook his head at her surprised look and pulled her back close. "No more Pure than you."

She frowned, and then, because she knew she'd kick herself if she didn't ask, said, "And the past?"

"I let it go." He smiled against her hairline, lips sliding back and forth as he inhaled. "I'm moving on. Next time I die, it's straight through the Gates for me. No stopping at incubation. No wings or Takes or prophecies for me."

She was so very glad, she was. But the song, already too short, was almost over. "So how long do we have?"

Grif shook his head, causing her heart to sink. "Not long. Just the one . . ."

He trailed off, leaving her imagining the worst. Tune? Hour? Night? What?

"The one?"

"Life," he finally said, one corner of his mouth turning up in a grin. "It really isn't long, but I bet we can make some memorable moments. That is, if you're still game to ride out your years with an old bull like me?"

She wasn't breathing. She only realized it once she grew light-headed. Then, breathing too hard, threatening to pass out in a totally different way, she began searching the room.

After a moment, Grif asked, "What are you doing?"

Kit didn't answer. Instead, she reached out and poked him in the chest. Finding it solid, she then grasped his wrist. Warm. Bending, she felt at his ankle. No holster. No gun.

"Done frisking me?" he asked wryly.

Straightening, Kit just stared for a moment before poking him again.

"Flesh and bone, Kit. So . . . you know." He grabbed her wrist. "Stop it."

"Oh, my God," she heard herself saying, and then the buzzing overtook her. Kit's knees buckled as her head grew light, but somewhere beyond her consciousness she realized that Grif's arms were still there, strong and tight around her, and he lifted her up again, holding her on her feet until she could manage it herself.

"Go ahead and take a minute," he said, drawing her close. "I'll be here."

They swayed, and then the music slid away from them, bouncing into Buddy Holly, sending the room into a subdued frenzy. Yet Kit and Grif only continued touching each other, treating each other's skin like talismans, reassuring themselves that the other was still there. When she found her voice again, she spoke close to his ear. "So . . . flesh?"

"And hopefully some brains thrown in this time, too."

Couples swung past them like orbiting galaxies. Kit and Grif remained in a world of their own.

"So not Pure?" she said again, making sure. The feathers were bent, clutched in her fist.

"Not Pure," Grif confirmed, then smiled at her like never before. "Just Chosen."

The whole room brightened. She didn't know how long they remained like that, staring at each other, tucked into the corner of their newly born lives, but when the song ended, he was still, miraculously, there. Same as the song after that. And after that. Finally, Grif touched his lips lightly to hers, fusing them both in time and place, in the moment. Together. "I've got a proposition for you, Craig."

"Do you?" she breathed, her head gone light all over again.

"How about you and I go make some memories?"

"How about an entire lifetime full of them?" she replied, finally able to breathe, to smile. To *live*.

She hoped Sarge could feel this. He needed to know that it wasn't the pain and sorrow, but the joy in fleeting moments that told a person they were alive. Sure, Kit thought, death always loomed somewhere in the future, but there were worse things to fear than that. Like going through life and never really living at all.

"I think it's only fair to warn you," she told Grif, as they sauntered from the club. "I've been told that I can be a bit chatty at times."

"And I can be a bit gruff, or so I hear," he said, draping his arm over her shoulders. "But one thing's for sure . . ."

Kit smiled, and finished the thought for him. "We make a damned good team."

And even the angels in heaven couldn't argue with that.